MIDNIGHT MAN

A JAKE MONTOYA FBI CRIME THRILLER

All things are poison, and nothing is not poison: the dose alone makes a thing not poison. — Paracelsus, 500 Years Ago

Breathe deep the gathering gloom. — The Moody Blues, 1974

SAM CADE

MIDNIGHT MAN
Copyright © 2023 by Sam Cade

All rights reserved under the International and Pan-American Copyright Conventions. No part of this book may be reproduced or transmitted in any form or by any means, electronic or mechanical, including photocopying, recording, or by any information storage and retrieval system, without permission in writing from the publisher.

This is a work of fiction. Names, places, characters and incidents are either the product of the author's imagination or are used fictitiously, and any resemblance to any actual persons, living or dead, organizations, events or locales is entirely coincidental.

Warning: the unauthorized reproduction or distribution of this copyrighted work is illegal. Criminal copyright infringement, including infringement without monetary gain, is investigated by the FBI and is punishable by up to 5 years in prison and a fine of $250,000.

Print ISBN:
Published by: Black Point Press
Edited by: Cathy Dee
Contact at Cathy.Dee@gmail.com
Interior formatting by: Rising Sign Books

ACKNOWLEDGMENTS

There are some that can put a book together A to Z all by themselves. I'm not one of them. Thank you World Wide Web! Here are some wonderful folks I've met there.

Katie Salidas (Las Vegas). Katie is an author as well as a freelancer on all aspects of indie book publishing. She lives neck-deep in that world. She took my artwork and turned it into a nice cover as well as formatted the manuscript for this book. Check her out on katiesalidas.com. Find her book *Go Publish Yourself!* on Amazon.

Edited by Cathy Dee Contact at Cathy.Dee@gmail.com

BOOKS BY SAM CADE

Black Point

The Scheme

The Midnight Man

2010
FRANCEVILLE, GABON,
WEST COAST OF AFRICA

DR. EZRA CAIN peered through the plastic faceplate watching his fingers meticulously punch in seven digits on the freezer's digital lock. He heard two clicks, then saw a light change from vivid red to green. A quick shiver raced through his body.

He was hyperaware of the insidious demon hiding in the dark.

Cain heard nothing but the swoosh of air flowing through his suit. His large, six-foot-three, ebony body was covered head to toe in a plastic suit impervious to tiny viral particles. Red, rubber, rain boots covered and protected the suit's booties. Viruses, those treacherous little buggers, are a thousand times smaller than bacteria and are only able to be viewed by electron microscopy.

Normally a natty dresser, Cain wore a utilitarian biosafety suit that would cause someone to think he was about to take a moonwalk. The air infused his suit from a hose connected to a valve at his waist. If by accident the suit was punctured, the positive pressure would force air out of the suit, preventing virus particles from entering.

The very same suit was used at the United States Army Medical Research Institute of Infectious Diseases, known as USAMRIID, at Fort Detrick, Maryland, which was the Department of Defense's lead lab for medical biological defense in America, as well as at Russia's bioweapon research laboratory in Irkutsk.

Two military labs dealing with the deadliest life forms on earth.

After opening the door to the freezer, Dr. Cain gingerly slid his triple-gloved hands inside and removed a clear, rectangular Lexan container holding two small test tubes that were two inches long. They were the thickness of a number two pencil.

Written on the plastic container was one word.

Marburg.

ELEVEN WEEKS EARLIER, Dr. Cain, a brilliant man with an MD degree from Stanford, had arrived in Gabon, a country on the west coast of Africa that straddles the equator. The tropical heat blitzed him as he deplaned. Far different from the temperate weather of Palo Alto, California. But Cain quickly adjusted. Before enrolling at Stanford, he'd spent his first eighteen years in America's Deep South. He knew heat. And he was genetically attuned to humidity. Cain was the son of an African father.

The doctor was at the International Centre for Medical Research, or CIRMF, in Franceville, a biologic research center in Africa that had the appearance of a prison camp. The center was founded in the 1970s and funded with income from the country's oil exports.

CIRMF was only one of two locations on the huge continent of Africa to have a Biosafety Level 4 Lab, the safest and most secure environment to study bacteria and viruses. Scientists liked to joke Level 4 was a bank vault locked inside a submarine.

The campus, encircled by electric fences, was a group of humble, low-slung buildings built far from the town center. Security cameras abounded. A small force of able men lived at the facility, each adept in the use of automatic weapons. Generators were installed for emergency power if the electricity blinked off.

Nobody wanted the power to go off.

Cain had one more week in Africa. He knew he had to hustle to finish his on-site research and get back to New Haven, Connecticut, and edit his Ph.D. thesis. In twenty days he'd submit his document in hopes of completing his doctorate in molecular virology at Yale University.

Dr. Ezra Cain wasn't just a physician. He was also a scientist.

The Marburg virus astounded and frightened him. He often mulled how blissfully unaware Americans were about the potential for agony and death from a living creature in nature that was as small as 0.02 microns in size.

The filoviruses Ebola and Marburg, as well as the Crimean-Congo hemorrhagic fever virus, were housed at CIRMF. So were the Lassa and Rift Valley Fever viruses. Cain thought they were beautiful to look at but, God knows, they were deadly to man in the worst ways imaginable.

Toward the end of his time at CIRMF, Cain became distracted from his goal. There was something else housed at CIRMF. A greater mystery. Something rarely mentioned.

The X viruses.

He'd spotted a couple of containers in the freezer with a name that included the "X" designation. He'd asked one of the lead scientists about them, a tall, lean Frenchman, in his mid-fifties, with an angular face. Dr. Girbaux was known to be focused and brusque, neither a conversationalist nor companionable.

In crystal clear English, when asked Girbaux had responded, "Leave them alone, Cain. They popped up once or twice, years ago. Haven't been seen since." He marched off. Cain watched the man's back leave the room. *Rude Frenchman*, he thought.

Virologists have long hypothesized that hundreds if not thousands of viruses exist that are unknown to man. They hide stealth-like in nature and may emerge rarely. They may cause devastating disease and death to livestock. These mysterious life forms also may possess the capability to annihilate the defense mechanisms of the most highly developed biological system.

Man.

They strike from who knows where, then retreat just as quickly as they burst on the scene, back into a black unknown.

The following morning, after a quick breakfast of banana muffins and strong black coffee, Dr. Cain walked the half mile to reach the segregated BSL-4 building, suited up in the staging area, and entered the most secure lab. He attached his air hose to the suit valve upon entering. Cool, dry air blew over his face, feeling good. He proceeded to a room that held three desks and multiple shelves crowded with lab notebooks. Rapidly, he scanned the shelves and finally located decades-old notes on the X viruses.

He picked up a spiral notebook with **Red X 81** handwritten on the front cover. He'd noticed a single container in the freezer with this designation. He removed the notebook from the shelf, proceeded to a seat at a desk, and riffled through it.

The paper was yellowing, fading with the years. The cursive penmanship was elegant, almost surely the writings of a fastidious woman. It was written with a fountain pen, he mused, a virtual antiquity these days.

The information was sparse, words covering only six pages.

He moved to another desk, sat down, and booted up a laptop computer. He unfurled the cord around a microphone, plugged it into the computer. He popped up a blank Word document, utilized the dictation application, and began reading the six pages into the microphone. He saved the document and emailed it to himself.

Every single written word was recorded.

TEN HOURS LATER, after a full day of research chores and a dinner of salted cod stew, Dr. Cain retreated to his spartan dorm room. He'd printed a hard copy of his dictation just after lunch.

The first section of the document revealed the origin of the name Red X-81. "Red" was a reference that the virus had originated from the Old World African monkey known as the red colobus. Accompanying notes indicated this was a threatened species of monkey, meaning their rarity alone could bring research to a halt. The "X" referred to a virus that had received little research and had no official name in the literature. The number "81" referred to the first time this virus hit the radar of scientists. 1981.

The focus of the notes was the witnessed death of Victoria Ngoy, a thirty-four-year-old Gabonese woman whose home was in a village 276 miles away, in Gabon's Congo basin, a rainforest teeming with lifeforms. Her husband, Joseph, had died a rapid, mysterious death eighteen hours before her arrival at

CIRMF. Fearful villagers placed the woman, who was showing no effects of any disease, in the back of a truck and drove her as fast as they could to the research facility. They described to the center's physicians what was known about Joseph's death.

Although distraught and stunned over the unexpected passing of her husband, Victoria Ngoy said, "I feel fine. Just fine." And she reportedly looked healthy.

Nevertheless, she was ushered to accommodations in the facility's isolation unit. It held ten hospital beds plus a conglomeration of IV poles and medicine cabinets. Five ventilators were stacked in a corner, covered with a clear plastic drape.

Vital signs were taken. They were perfect. She was provided a nice meal, although sadness left her unable to eat more than a few nibbles.

"A waste of time," muttered one of the nurses. "Why drive a healthy woman seven hours across rutted mountain roads?"

But Ngoy was observed. Closely observed. From another room with a large window, one physician and two nurses watched. And saw nothing more than a sad woman.

At first.

Cain recalled the pages he'd dictated in the lab. He found it interesting that the author had increased accuracy by placing actual quotes from the patient and medical personnel in the notebook. He'd inserted the same punctuation in his dictation.

Ninety-two minutes after arrival, Victoria Ngoy had approached the window. Apprehension covered her face. Her hands squeezed against the sides of her head, in the temporal region. "My head hurts," she said.

The staff noticed clear drainage oozing from her nose. Victoria sniffed, then a small, dry cough followed. Mucus reappeared. Victoria swiped the goo away with her wrists, wiping it onto her cotton gown.

Her lower jaw began to quiver. The staff could hear the chatter of her teeth as she spoke.

They looked closely at the woman. *Were her eyes reddening?*

The physician and nurses suited up immediately to attend to the woman. They helped her back into bed in the isolation suite,. She was provided with the dual antipyretic/pain agents acetaminophen and ibuprofen for her headache. Next, another set of vital signs was taken.

In only moments she went from having no fever to one of 104.1 degrees. Her heart rate rose to 139. Blood pressure was dropping. The staff side-eyed each other with deepening concern. A storm looming.

A nurse bathed the patient with cool water. Sweat poured from Victoria, and her whole body shook like it wanted to dance off the bed.

"We need blood samples. Start two large bore IVs. Stat!" said a female doctor.

Two nurses approached the patient. One to start the IVs, the other to hold the woman's trembling arm. A guttural howl emanated from Victoria. She again grabbed her head. The whites of her eyes were now the color of fresh blood.

The petite doctor also helped steady Victoria. "Four milligrams of morphine when you get the line in," she said, fighting to remain calm. Her body was covered with sweat inside her Tyvek coverall. The doctor wasn't just concerned—she was scared. Illness had attacked Victoria like a rocket as they watched.

The IV needle hit a large vein in the crook of Victoria's elbow. Antecubital. But something wasn't right. Blood gushed profusely from the site, covering her forearm.

But the line was in. Six tubes of blood were extracted. Normal saline was started. Four milligrams of morphine were pushed.

After fifteen minutes of Victoria's screaming, the staff was pallid with fear. The morphine seemed worthless. The doctor intervened. "Six more milligrams of morphine plus ten milligrams of diazepam. Dammit, we've got to get her comfortable."

At three hours, blood blisters arrived. Spots formed on Victoria's arms and legs. Then on her belly and back. Finally, her face and inside her mouth. By this time Victoria had been covered with bags of ice around her neck and wrists, in her axillae, and between her legs.

The fever wouldn't budge.

At four hours and fifteen minutes, the patient began to slither on the bed. The doctor explained the situation. "This is called basal writhing. It comes from insult to the midbrain. She is suffering intense intracranial pressure."

A nurse pointed to Victoria's eyes. "Look, doctor." Blood ran freely through the woman's tear ducts. The nurse wiped it with a white towel. It continued to drain.

Thirteen minutes later, Victoria Ngoy fired a river of bloody projectile vomit across the suit of one of the nurses. The African nurse shrieked and ran to the decontamination shower to wash.

The putrid stench of vomitus filled the room. The air also carried the odor of copper, possibly iron. Smells from the blood. Moments later the stench worsened as diarrhea lathered with blood was released from Victoria's rectum. Quickly, it soaked through the towels she lay on. It coated the white sheet.

Vomit, blood, and feces.

"Oh, God," said the doctor, queasy from the ghastly odor.

Victoria Ngoy began to tremble. Trembling escalated into violent shaking. Her writhing launched blood splatters across the room.

The nurses and doctor lurched backward, deathly frightened of the flying blood.

And then it was over. Victoria's body instantly stilled. Vomiting and diarrhea stopped as if a valve had turned off.

Two nurses cried. The doctor's face was etched with horror and awe. She had never seen anything like this.

The chart entry was signed by Gert Haughton, M.D., Ph.D.

Later entries in the notebook indicated there were no other known victims. It was originally thought this was possibly Ebola or Marburg. Genetic testing indicated it wasn't. It wasn't Rift Valley Fever, either. Or Lassa.

The woman's autopsy showed a brain that had disintegrated into a gel. Hepatitis and acute kidney failure were revealed. A helical CT scan of the lungs showed massive inflammation, likely the result of an immune cytokine storm from viral pneumonia.

This was the handiwork of an unstudied, unknown X virus.

Dr. Haughton named it Red X-81.

A highly experienced, superiorly trained doctor watched a patient go from no symptoms to a horrifying death in five hours.

How could all of this happen so fast? Haughton wrote. *What was the incubation period?*

After all, tests indicated this was an undocumented virus, Gert Haughton finished with a final statement.

"With a ghastly magnificence, a sub-microscopic lifeform decimated a 142-pound human being with unfathomable speed. I could not peel my eyes away from the garish savagery."

It was dated December 25, 1981. Christmas day.

Cain's eyes squinted after reading Dr. Haughton's final entry. The words rippled his imagination. He read it again. His lips lined into a malicious smile.

Dr. Ezra Cain took particular note of one thing. There appeared to be no further presentations or research on Red X-81. He checked the shelves again, for another day. Nothing else mentioned Red X-81.

And no medical personnel became ill treating Victoria Ngoy. *Transmission must be difficult,* he concluded. Four hours after death, an attempt to reveal virus particles in her body fluids revealed no live virus.

The virus was *gone.*

How could that be? Where in the world did you come from, Red X-81?

And where did you go?

A WEEK LATER, Dr. Ezra Cain had his hand on an open door to a taxi. It was ninety-six degrees, not a sniff of wind, and the humidity scrubbed him like a sponge. His large duffle was in the trunk. A military-style, canvas messenger bag was in his hand, holding a laptop and various notebooks. He'd finished his research. Two of the physicians he had become close to were there to say goodbye.

"My time here has been amazing, just incredible. Thank you so much for everything you've taught me," said Cain.

They shook hands. "Come back and join us, Dr. Cain. We could use your help." Their smiles were genuine.

Cain slid into the back seat of the cab. The window was down. Cain spoke through it.

"I'll take that under advisement. Oh, hey, one question. Do you know how I could reach Gert Haughton? A virologist that used to be here."

A look of melancholy crossed the men's faces. The man who spoke averted his eyes and slowly shook his head. "Gert's gone. It was in the middle eighties when she died, eighty-four or eighty-five, I think. She was working eighteen hours a day on HIV and AIDS. It got her ..."

Both men shuffled away from the cab, wanting to speak no more about a fate they knew could come their way.

EZRA CAIN FASTENED his seatbelt. Three hours after he'd left CIRMF, he was sitting in an A320 operated by Air France. It would fly him nonstop to JFK in New York.

Any empathy he felt for Gert Haughton left as fast as it arrived. Cain was not prone to emotion about death.

Glancing out the window, he spotted planes from at least six different nations. Clouds grayed miles out in the background but were unlikely to bring rain.

Mainly he carried the immense satisfaction of the work he'd accomplished at the research facility.

A smile crossed his face as he felt the jerk of the plane backing away from the terminal. He carried one other thing with him. An African souvenir.

A two-inch-long, pencil-thin tube packed in Lexan and dry ice.

Red X-81.

1

MAGNOLIA HOTEL
Point Clear, Alabama
1995
Fifteen Years Earlier

MIDNIGHT WATCHED. And thought. And felt. And fought. Fought *The Urge*.

But he was weak. *Why won't somebody stop me?*

It was late spring, a sultry Saturday night. Breeze drifting off the bay.

A sweet sixteen birthday party for Sunshine Gage.

The bash was at Point Clear's Magnolia Hotel pool, one of the largest in the South. The iconic hotel began life as a Civil War hospital, a place formerly suffocated with cries of anguish. Not a single bikini or poolside margarita at the place in 1864.

Sunshine had a trainload of friends. Freaks, nerds, rednecks, rich kids, preppies, jocks, whites, Blacks, and anxious gays, who only chanced a peek through a crack in the closet door.

One special car was in attendance. Sunshine's birthday present. A vintage 1968 cream-colored VW Beetle with a high-amp sound system befitting a rapper's Bentley. The vehicle had been restored in secret by her father, Dr. John David Gage, and her brother, Kimbo.

An earthy, pungent drift of weed streamed on a bay breeze across Dr. Gage's head as he struggled to keep up with burgers and dogs on a rectangular steel grill. Gage had completed his surgical residency at San Francisco General in the sixties, an eighteen-minute ride from the homes of the Dead, Joplin, and Manson, who lived in Haight Ashbury. With weed, he knew the drill.

MIDNIGHT MEANDERED OVER to the table of food. The smoky meat momentarily overcame his lust for the cook's daughter. He placed a hamburger on a bun, slapped on mustard and ketchup, a few pickles, grabbed a handful of chips, filled a cup with ice and tea, and avoided the eyes of Sunshine's daddy.

Midnight dressed the part. Flip-flops under walking shorts and an untucked Panama shirt. An Auburn ball cap sat on his head. He stepped away, sat, watched, and ate. The band was rocking "Your Mama Don't Dance," sounding every bit as good as the original.

If they only knew, he thought. *Her last night.* He felt a quick shiver at the thought.

He caught remnants of a conversation between Dr. Gage and a ripped Black kid, Ezekiel Washington, the top prep tailback in the country, and one of the stars of Black Point's recent state champion football team. "I'll take three of those monsters, Doc. Smells outrageous," said Zeke.

"You bet. You ready for California?"

Midnight disconnected from the dude's jabber, talking about his football scholarship to USC, let his eyes roll toward Sunshine. She was rubbing up against her boyfriend, a big kid,

Jake Montoya, a hotshot ballplayer himself. Six-two, easily 200, still growing, and headed to play for Alabama. Still seventeen, but broad shoulders, big hands, sculpted with lean muscle. Already a man.

Midnight knew Montoya was a nut for mixed martial arts. Fought in tournaments around the South. Tough as a stump. Liked to hurt people. But screw him.

Midnight knew he could bring the heat when he needed it.

SUNSHINE TOOK TWO hits of weed on the bayfront beach. "Whoa! Thanks, Zip, that's some crazy good shit." She giggled. "And I don't even know what I'm talking about." She giggled again.

Zip Streetman, the Weedster, wore round, old-school tea-shade sunglasses like John Lennon. He was the short, wiry, geeky son of a well-to-do seafood wholesaler, and a thoughtful, sensitive young man, always gracious enough to bring a supply of herb for all comers. Grew it himself out in the woods by the Magnolia River.

Sunshine wasn't a doper, not by any means but — *Heck*, she thought, *you only get one sixteenth birthday.* And she had a little performance anxiety. The hired band, three guys and a heavy-set chick who called themselves Baby and the White Trash Farm Boys, was about to take a break. Sunshine was going to sing a few acoustic tunes with Kimbo, her brother, two years older, who could have been her twin. He was tall and lean, with blond hair almost to his shoulders, a high-A student, and had the facial bones of a model, just like Sunshine.

Feeling mellow, she walked back to the stage set up next to the pool. Kimbo, wearing boardshorts and a tee advertising Inner Light Surf Shop, pulled up a tall stool, placing it at the side of the lead singer's mic. He eased up his own mic to catch his guitar and voice.

Grabbed his sister's eye. She nodded.

He ambled to the lead mic, waved her over with his hand. "Happy birthday, girl." Hugged her and went to his stool.

"Wow! You guys are awesome," she said with a loose smile that said, *I'm feeling just right.* "Thank you so much for coming." A wisp of blond hair teased across her face as a light gust blew over the pool. She pushed the strands behind her ear.

"Kimbo and I are gonna play a couple of oldie James Taylor and Bonnie Raitt tunes for y'all. Can't go wrong with "Angel From Montgomery." Whistles heard in the crowd.

"But I've got the song closest to my heart to play first. Where are you, Mom?"

She spotted some kids waving their arms and pointing. Marin Gage, an author and illustrator of bestselling children's books, was sitting in a fold-up camp chair thirty feet from the bandstand, looking breezy, natural, and boho in a mixed-print peasant blouse, faded cut-off jeans, and bare feet.

"There you are ... hey, Mom." She stalled a moment. Her lower lip quivered. "Met you sixteen years ago, today." The back of her hand dabbed at a tear. Her voice broke as she said, "How could a baby get so lucky?" Another dab.

Marin's face scrunched tight, doing everything possible to not start blubbering.

"Mom, this song lives right here." She thumped her chest over her heart. "You sang it to me thousands of times, and it was amazing every single time. And, oh wow, you made me feel sooo safe, and so, so loved ..." She sniffled, found the strength to break it for another smile. "Hey, remember when I was six and I wrote a letter to Kenny Loggins saying you sang it better than he did?"

Marin smiled and nodded, put her hand to her mouth. A

mother never happier.

"Tonight, this song is for you. I love you, Mom." She blew a kiss, glanced back at Kimbo.

"Ready? Two ... three ... four."

Christopher Robin and I walked along
Under branches lit up by the moon ...

2

11:10 P.M. MIDNIGHT HOVERED in the shadows, leaning on the craggy hull of a 200-year-old live oak, watching the party dissipate. The air carried the musky scent from a boggy salt marsh across the street. No traffic.

Fifteen minutes ago, the White Trash Farm Boys had eased off the property in an old F-250 crew-cab farm truck with the bed loaded with music gear. A Confederate flag draped the rear window. *Good riddance, you redneck mothers. Take that fat bitch with you.*

Cricket and cicadas serenaded the still night. Point Clear, Alabama, was asleep.

Midnight's heart boomed in his chest. His spit thickened. But mostly he felt it between his legs. Power. *I'm so damn ready.*

He'd watched Sunshine blossom since the first grade. Only sixteen today but looking every bit a woman. Inside, he laughed. *Hormones in chicken, some said.*

Sunshine wasn't some Alabama peckerwood girl. She was bred from beautiful, intelligent, wealthy people. A doctor daddy who'd bought an estate on the bay. A stunning, bohemian mother who made gobs of money selling children's books about Rufus and Cheeto, a donkey and a monkey traveling around to national parks in a VW van.

Before I'm done, I'll take the mother, too. A warm feeling soaked through him at the thought.

Time for caution. Sure, he had a plan. But he was wary ... and intelligent. And part of his plan employed a ripcord. Abort, if necessary. *Talk my way out of any misunderstanding.*

The girl was smart, he knew that. And strong. She had small breasts on a five-foot-ten-inch frame, perfect for an athletic girl. He'd seen her in the weight room, knocking out bench presses and bicep curls, gleaming with sweat. *She'll gleam tonight, that she will.* All-Star volleyballer in only the tenth grade. Power in her tan legs, which he loved.

Midnight's eyes were dilated, trying to soak in light, as he scanned through the darkness toward the pool deck. He spotted her, could almost feel the smoothness of her teenage skin. He rubbed his hand over his pants pocket, felt it, the steel of a folding fillet knife, new, just out of the box.

A chilling smile crossed his face, thinking about her little titties ... effortless carving.

Sunshine stood next to the trinity, the three to avoid. Dr. Gage, a six-foot-four man with enough blond hair to make him look like a white god. And Kimbo, tall and thin, but carrying wiry muscle. And the boyfriend, Jake Montoya. Avoid him at all costs.

Wait. She said something, maybe "goodbye" or "see you in a few" or whatever the hell and started ambling toward her restored Bug. True enough, the car was a beauty. Didn't see them around anymore.

They were the last ones at the party, everybody else gone.

Montoya picked up a hose and started washing down the grill.

Good. Cleanup time. They'll be a few minutes. Game on!

He watched the interior light pop on as Sunshine opened the car door. The light blinked off. The ringy-zingy sound of a fired-up old Volkswagen reached his ear. Next, the tunes ... *Damn, speakers 'bout to blow out the windows,* so loud he couldn't make out the song ... but a woman singing ... and Sunshine starting to sing along.

Midnight tweaked his ball cap down, walked out of the shadows to the entrance of the Magnolia Hotel driveway, stood next to a decorative column fashioned out of reclaimed warehouse brick. A rustic gas lamp dumped mellow light on the ground.

The Bug was forty feet away when he recognized the song. Whitney Houston ripping through "I'm Every Woman."

Sunshine braked to a stop at the road, saw Midnight, turned down the radio. "Hey, thought that was you at the party. You didn't say hi."

Midnight strolled up to the Bug, leaned down to the open window. *Oh, you smell good.* "Yeah, sorry. Happy birthday, Sunshine. Night started out bad for me."

Facing south, motion caught Midnight's eye, fifty yards away. A Ford sedan, pulling out of the employee parking lot. It turned north, headlights slashing him from a distance, rolling his way. The driver punched down on the gas, heading home after a long night running the kitchen. Midnight dropped his head further, looking at Sunshine's eyes.

The car reached Sunshine's Beetle. Midnight peeked up. Fifteen feet from him, a Black man eyed the VW, red glow sparking on the end of a cigarette.

A man he knew.

"What happened?" she asked.

"My car broke down about a mile back, toward Black Point. Walked here. Now I'm walking home, but ain't no big deal. Hey, tell your dad great burgers."

"Sure. Don't you live somewhere over around Battles Road?"

"Yeah, on Colony, just down from Battles. About two and a half miles from here. An easy walk."

She hissed. "Forget that. Hop in, man, this badass Bug will have you there in five minutes."

Dropping into the passenger seat, his weight caused the small car to dip on the right side. After closing the door he had to ask. "What's that perfume?"

"Peach blossom and jasmine. My mom wears it. You like it?"

"More than you know."

Her eyes briefly cut his way at that response. She clutched the Bug into first, pulled onto Scenic 98, gunned it, upshifted to second.

Ringy zingy into the black night.

Evil arrived in Paradise.

3

SUNSHINE EASED THE twenty-nine-year-old Bug behind the house like he suggested, both of them singing along to Petty on "Mary Jane's Last Dance."

It was only nine minutes from leaving the birthday party, a trace of weed flowing through her blood. Mellow. Happy. Singing like nobody's listening.

"Really appreciate the ride, Sunshine. Never rode in an old punch Buggy, super cool." Midnight opened the door, stuck one leg out, turned back to her. "Hey, come on in, just for a second to say a quick hello to grandaddy and you can hit the road. He'd love that."

"Sure." She killed the engine, hopped out. He pointed to the door with the bug light. "After you, birthday girl."

The night was cooling down. A breath of breeze tousled the waxy leaves on a heritage magnolia. Drifting scent of spring flowers from the yard.

A fine night to be a sixteen-year-old, southern girl.

The house was a one-story rambler, brick-clad, two decades old, 1,700 square feet at the most. The homestead sat on 196 acres, mostly woods, thick with growth. Nearest neighbor was four football fields away.

Eerily quiet. Private.

He followed behind her. Every muscle tight from his shoulders down. Eyed her with the feral eyes of a starving wolf, feeling pride in his plan. But she was smart, tough. Since the third grade, he knew she was cagey in her way, hard to deceive.

Beachy blond hair clipped at the top of her shoulders, liquid blue eyes. Stunning, he thought, as he followed. Wearing short shorts and a tank top. Her shapely muscles were on display.

Waited, waited, waited. Wanted this for so long.

He was a force of nature, a dark beast. Six-three, 230 pounds, all organic muscle. No gym iron, no workouts.

Reaching the door, he felt the weight of the night. But no nerves. He was an intricate planner. Everything had been rehearsed. His precise blueprint demonstrated his intelligence. And he *was* sharp, popping a thirty-five on the ACT exam last year, flooded with academic scholarship offers. He chose the West Coast, Stanford, to pursue medicine and music.

"It's unlocked, go on in. You know he's retiring this year. Only a few weeks left." *He* was the high school principal, the beast's grandfather, a beloved gentleman in Black Point, Alabama.

She took two steps up onto the stoop, twisted the doorknob, and stepped into the house. The door opened directly into the kitchen. Remnant of fried bacon and cinnamon in the air.

Strange, she thought, looking down. She was standing on a white painter's tarp that covered the floor. The kitchen table was moved up against the far wall. She cocked her head, looked to the side, like a dog, listening, pondering.

Cold silence.

She saw yellowing, varnished pine cabinets, dated appliances, and a toaster next to a breadbox. *Looks lived in,* she thought, *the heart of the home.*

... Except for the tarp.

Midnight Man

Her eyes locked onto four strands of thin, white rope tied to eye screws tightened into the floor. The silence began to sound like a scream. *Not right.* Her eyelids closed into a squint of suspicion.

Hair raised on her neck. *Get this over with.*

"Mr. Washington." Almost a shout. Waited for an answer, eyes darting. Nothing. "Mr. Washington, it's Sunshine Gage. Wanna say a quick hello, it's my birthday, I turned sixteen today." Voice louder, words spilling out on clouds of worry.

Too still. Sunshine's feet felt bolted to the floor. *Something isn't right.*

Sensation of movement. A whiff of a man's night sweat.

Hot breath twinkled across her neck, racking her with a shiver.

A slap. A large hand, hard as river rock, cracked across Sunshine's face, knocking her off-balance. Sounded like a gunshot in a house as silent as a cave.

Her nails raked his forearms as she fell to the floor.

A dull thud as her head hit. Bone on wood.

Woozy, her skull full of confusion, blazing white dots flickering in space.

The monster huffed like a locomotive, heart hammering, lips forming a straight-line smile. Totally content.

Midnight sang, *Last dance for Mary Jane ...*

His eyes twisted over to a wall clock made to look like a rooster. His grandmother had bought it at a flea market years ago. The beauty of it. Pure symmetry. Both hands pointing straight up to the heavens.

Midnight.

Sunshine Gage was dying.

But she didn't know that yet.

4

MIDNIGHT GRIPPED HER sports bra through her tank top and ripped them both over her head. Before she could act, a powerful hand cinched around each ankle and lifted.

Walking backward, he speedily dragged her across the rough canvas, the skin on her back feeling on fire.

"What the hell are you doing!" Hands pushing against the floor, trying to brake. Worthless effort. Tried to kick. Midnight barked out a laugh.

He dropped her by the rope. She saw the strong, thin, nylon parachute cord. It was knotted tightly to eyebolts. "No! Nooo!"

He slung a leg across her chest. Had to secure her wrists. Her arms windmilling. Hands knotted into fists, hitting him everywhere she could. Tried to thrust her hips. She was anchored.

"Stop it! Stop! No!" She started spitting through the scream.

"Be still, bitch!" Right hand blazing through the air. Another smack to her face. Harder than the first one. Red blinking dots spiraled like electrons in her vision. Her arms dropped to her side.

Midnight grabbed her right wrist, spooled three swirls of paracord around it, nimbly tied two half-hitch knots. Same for the left.

He stood over her, bent, unsnapped her shorts. About to

pull when a powerful blow smashed between his legs. Sunshine's bony knee. Midnight grunted, felt like his balls were coming out his throat. He rolled onto his side, squeezed into the fetal position, moaned. She gave him everything she had.

Wrist skin ripping with her frantic jerks on the paracord. Going nowhere. She twisted, kicked him in the back of his head with her heel. Kicked again. Like kicking a concrete block. It did little. Kicked his back, over and over.

He turned over, drew back his hand, slammed his fist into her gut.

A gust of air shot from her mouth. Couldn't breathe. Tried to suck in wind. Nothing. Face in a panic. Paralyzed. Air wouldn't come. Mouth open, guttural moans.

He reached over, grabbed the waistline of her shorts and panties, stood, pulling everything off.

Sunshine was naked in front of a monster.

Still fighting to catch her breath when Midnight dropped onto her lower legs. Wanted to fight. No leverage. She had nothing against his weight.

Tears flooded as she felt the rope secure her ankles. A hundred horrible thoughts blurred her mind

"You're dead ... dead, you prick. Jake'll kill you, swear to God he will." The words blubbered out.

Midnight stood, looked down at her, hand running over his crotch. "Why, Sunshine, why? Why'd you have to be this way?"

There was a disconnect in his eyes.

"What way? What the hell are you talking about?" Her face going purple as she strained against the cord. Blood dripped to the canvas from her wrists.

"A controller. You're beautiful ... and evil. Everyone in town knows it." Midnight's eyes glassed over. "You're a queen. A queen bee."

"What the shit are you talking about? Just let me go, okay?

Let's forget about this. Let me go home." Her voice calmed, steadied. Her brain instructed her to take another tact. Politeness.

She knew she'd claw his eye out if he untied her. Both of them.

"Come on, I've known you forever. Let's just forget about this. You don't want my daddy calling the police."

Midnight smirked. "The cops. Good one." He stepped to the counter, looked into a plastic cleaning caddy. It contained his instruments of evil. He lifted out a 32-ounce plastic container, studied the label.

He stepped back to Sunshine, bent, and placed the container on the floor with the label facing her.

She lifted her head, eyed it. "Acid. What the hell! You crazy bastard!" She renewed her struggle, words flying, dog-cussing him.

"That's some salty language, girl." He chuckled, towering over her, looking down. "Look at those little baby titties, just dancing away."

Watching his eyes, she stiffened. Every nerve in her body pulsed with electricity.

He slid a slim, seven-inch-long item from his pocket. Sunshine eyed his hand. In a flash, Midnight flicked his wrist. A blade snapped into place, narrow at the handle and growing even thinner toward the point. The stainless steel shimmered with a titanium coating.

It was hellishly sharp.

"But you know, girl, those nipples sure are pretty, that they are." He swished the knife through the air, wristing it. Blew out swooshing sounds. *Ssshhh, ssshhh, ssshhh.* "I won't have any problem collecting those souvenirs."

Sunshine's red eyes bulged. Panic. Tears covered her cheeks. "Wha—" she said. Voice weak.

The fighter returned. "Nooo, pleeeaaassseee no!" Head twisting side to side. Arms and wrists raging once again, driving the cord deeper into her skin.

Midnight stepped to the counter, lifted out a five-ounce, leakproof container of odorless white powder. He also pulled out a 10-cc syringe with an 18-gauge needle. The syringe was 50 percent preloaded with tap water. For diluting the powder.

He kneeled next to her, held the small container in front of her face.

The label read: **0.5% Strychnine Milo for Hand Baiting Pocket Gophers.** There was a single word on the label written in a far larger font than everything else.

POISON

Sunshine's eyes widened as she read the label. A puddle of urine formed as it emptied from her bladder.

The room stank of pee and sweat. Midnight slung off his shirt, leaving him in shorts and tennis shoes. He popped up off his knees into a squatting position.

Reached to his side, picked up a bottle of hydrochloric acid. Unscrewed the top.

His eyes sunk back into his head. He began talking in another dimension. "Have to, mama. Have to. You're evil, you bitch. Gotta kill the demons." His voice became ragged around the edges. Sounded like another person. Unhinged, dissociated with reality.

He leveled the acid six inches above Sunshine's vagina. Slowly, he turned the container upside down.

The liquid blowtorch flowed.

Sweat soaked her as the acid ate through her tissue. Muscles jerked with spasms, uncontrollable. Arms and legs slammed against the floor.

Midnight jumped to his feet, face twisted. He tossed the

empty bottle across the floor, put his hands to his ears, blocking the screams.

He leaned over her head, eyes blazing. He began to holler, his face contorting in pleasured rage.

Hollering became roaring. Low-pitched, deep, and powerful, like a lion.

"Killing the demons, you evil bitch ... killing them, mama. Killing them, killing them, killing them ..."

5

COTTONMOUTH CREEK
Point Clear, Alabama

BILLY STARR KNEW shit when he saw it. And he was damn well seeing it.

Rolling to a stop, Billy dropped his mountain bike on its side at the edge of two-lane Scenic 98 so he could take a looksee into the creek. Billy and Jase had some damn big plans—trespass fishing off old man Garney's pier today, while that cranky old jackleg was at work.

Air was dead still, oven hot, August heat on a May afternoon. Every breath drawn through a suffocating wet gauze of humidity. *Hot as shit,* he thought.

Billy, ten years old, with sweat stains seeping through a Bama tee over baggy swim trunks, looked down from the short bridge crossing Cottonmouth Creek, a brackish, murky tributary that snaked inland from Mobile Bay. The creek was a narrow squiggle of water surrounded by tall, green cutgrass, barely wide enough for two skinny kayaks. He was two miles south of the landmark Magnolia Hotel. Million-dollar homes with gray, storm-beaten docks lined the bay as far as the eye could see.

"Jase, c'mere, look at this shit."

Jase was shirtless and grimy in red trunks, high-topped sneakers, and wore a Little League ball cap over a summer flat-top. He hustled over to Billy, looked straight down toward the water.

Torrents of stench filled his nose, rising from rotting meat and marsh muck.

Then he saw it.

"Awww, *shit!* What the hell?"

A naked body lying on its side in the black ooze. Gray human flesh with divots of meat carved from the back. Head cocked backward. Back locked into an arch, like the letter C. Blond hair matted into rigid strands on the skull, dried from the intense coastal sun. Platoons of blowflies smothered the body. Spider crabs crawled through the wounds, carving deep into the meat.

But it was the face. Eyebrows arched. Brow wrinkled. The girl's cheeks were pulled back as if someone was ripping the skin from the skull, backward, exposing teeth back to the molars.

A mask of horror.

Jase's face creased. "Is that a smile?"

"Shit no, you dumbass," said Billy. "That's voodoo shit. This witch doctor shit here is from N'awlins, the scariest kind of shit."

"Just call your daddy, Billy," said Jase, face pale with fear. "That girl's deader 'n hell."

The boys bolted in a sprint toward the house abutting the north side of the creek, raced down the long Bahamian rock drive. The place was two stories, covered with white shiplap siding and a tin roof. Window flower boxes overflowed with a rainbow of spring flowers.

A scene far happier than forty yards away.

Their fists banged the door like drunk husbands.

6

THICK NEEDLE IN the butt. Five minutes. Nothing. Seven. Apprehension. Nine minutes. Agitation gripped her.

Neck muscles stiffened, slowly at first, then the abdomen. Muscle fibers pulled taut, wrenched into tight strands. Neck wouldn't move. She fought it, hard. Pain intensifying. Brain screamed at the muscles to relax. Nothing. Ratcheted tighter.

Vomited once. Twice.

Lips ripped backward from her teeth. Tried, tried, tried ... couldn't stop it.

Her legs jerked. Quad muscles on fire. Arms next. Vibrating. Twitching madly. Fibers coiled in agony. Biceps and triceps popped, fighting under the skin.

Moans became groans. Vomited once more. Eyelids pulled taut, open, exposing the vast whites of her eyes. Couldn't close them. Fought to blink. Nothing. Globes ready to launch from the sockets.

"Heeelll meee." Tongue stiff. Pronunciation futile.

The spasms eased off. They were cyclical. Sound-sensitive.

Rope sliced loose. Free. She looked him in the eye, facial muscles drawn into a mask. Couldn't move. CD player next to ear. Finger to a button.

Room exploded in devil music. "Sabotage" raged into her ears. Beastie Boys. Fire on gas.

Neurons electrified. Head slashed backward. Bellows from the gut. Back arching. Toes pointed. Every muscle screwed tight. Anguish.

Body jackknifing with convulsions, back and forth, back and forth, then locked into place. Back hyperextended into a C. Only head and heels touched the floor.

Raging pain.

Rigid as plate steel. Hands fisted. Jaw locked. No voice. Couldn't swallow. Fighting to suck in air. Nothing. Respiratory muscles paralyzed.

I'm just a little girl.

Please ... Make me die.

7

ORANGE BEACH, ALABAMA
27 Years Later

GOOD GOD, SHE'S *beautiful,* he thought. Just like the others. Tall, thin, young, and blond.

But how? How, how, how? How to grab her? That thought has filled his thoughts over the last three days.

The need has been strong for months. *Get on the hunt.*

Midnight was lying by the pool watching Lea Lea Sloane, an early twenties woman in a black bikini, her body gleaming with sunscreen, smelling like a tropical vacation.

Seventy-five feet from his seat, a blanket of sugary sand walked right into the Gulf of Mexico. They were at the Turquoise Place Resort, one of the most upscale condominium complexes on the upper Gulf Coast.

Watching her for hours, he knew ... *She was one of them.* A controller. Sexy lips and tongue teasing the thin straw in her margarita. Knowing eyes hidden behind dark sunglasses. Letting all the men know—*She's the queen.*

The blond had a dude with her. Looked like a bootlicking creep to Midnight. A sycophant. Skinny. Arms like a sixth-grade clarinetist. Never met any iron. Three days of patchy scruff on his face. Shit looked like cat mange. But it was the tattoos. One arm sleeved. Some kind of Asian symbols on his upper back. *You some kind of Zen freak?* Midnight despised tattoos. Desecrating God's creation.

One more pussy boy under the control of a domineering woman.

Now she was *chosen*.

8

FOR THE LAST four hours Lea Lea and Gregg had been drinking and dancing at the Flora-Bama, one of the rowdiest beachfront roadhouses on the Gulf Coast. The bawdy place was its own universe of people, alcohol, and music.

Leaving the bar, they were hit in the back by the trailing words of Buffett's song "Why Don't We Get Drunk and Screw."

Lea Lea fell onto Gregg as she slurred, "Yeah, why don't we ..."

The couple leaned on each other, drifting wobbly toward the car. It was 11:50 p.m., the bloodshot sun crashed for the night three hours ago. The coastal humidity felt intimate, like tropical sex. Party lights tinkled giddily at the restaurant on the Ole River, across the street from the Bama.

Hell, yeah, it was one fine beach night.

Lea Lea's Lexus was parked over a hundred yards from the bar, the closest spot they could find. Cars covered the area like a rash. The SUV was wedged into an unlit area, next to a construction dumpster for a home being built.

Lea Lea had her keys out when Gregg said, "Swear to God, baby, if you can't get laid at the Bama, you can't get laid."

Lea Lea giggled out a soused reply. "Well, I didn't come to the beach to get laid. I came to get ridiculously blitzed and impressively fucked." Smile brighter than a full moon. They both

doubled over laughing, deep, air-sucking belly laughs.
  "You're halfway there, girl."
  Felt so damn good, beyond carefree.
  Those were the last words they'd speak to each other.

9

"HOLLER AND I'LL KILL YOU." Midnight gutted out the words in a growl.

He was stone still, nothing more than a tall shadow, a dangerous creature of the night. Senses on alert. Adrenaline roaring through his vessels, energized like ancient barbarians coming home to ravage their women.

Aware of *everything*. Sounds. Movements. Scents. Pupils blown open in the darkness.

Oh, yes. He closed his eyes, inhaled deeply. Her soft, feminine perfume drifting toward him on the beach air. Could feel his testicles roll in his scrotum.

Any fool would know his words meant business.

Lea Lea Sloan and her boyfriend Gregg Gibson, five feet away from Midnight, were staring down the barrel of a flat black .40 automatic. It was weightless in his large hand.

It looked like a cannon to them.

With the temp still at eighty-three degrees, Midnight was broiling in the cheap wool facemask, long sleeves, and skin-tight nitrile gloves.

Jack and Coke compelled Gibson to think he had a set of balls. A 153-pound, tattooed, scraggy badass. He stepped in front of Lea Lea, got into the intruder's space, gave a forceful push on Midnight's chest with his right hand.

"Ged da fuggg outta here, Jack."

Gibson's skull fractured as the pistol smacked the side of his head. He dropped hard to the gravel. Unconscious.

Lea Lea's gut wrenched tight. Too stunned to holler. Midnight touched the barrel to her forehead, gently. "Scream and I'll blow your head off your shoulders."

Pee drained into her panties.

10

12:50 A.M. MIDNIGHT'S van eased down the sandy, two-track path deep into piney woods just outside of Black Point, Alabama, forty miles from the beach bar. Remnants of a logging road used decades ago. He entered the rear side of the property off a rock-and-tar country road.

The parcel approached 200 acres. Although close to town, it carried a desolate feel. The open fields were wild with overgrown brush. Low-slung palmettos and a carpet of pine straw encircled the timber.

A small, sixty-five-year-old ranch home, the homestead, fronted Colony Street. It had sat empty for the last seven years, decaying in place, since old lady Washington passed away.

The woods closed in the farther Midnight drove, headlights shining into a pitch-black vortex, easily bringing on claustrophobia for those so inclined.

A bright flash shone in the distance, 250 feet in, like sunshine glinting off a foil gum wrapper. The truck came to a stop next to a shiny aluminum thirty-one-foot-long travel trailer. Its edges were curved like a loaf of bread.

It was a 1969 Airstream Land Yacht. Midnight had bought it for $5,900 off eBay and had it shipped south from Michigan. He wrapped the inside with stainless steel, impervious to escaping contamination.

Six brass drains had been inserted into the floor. When opened, liquids could drain through an airtight passageway into kill tanks below the trailer. The containers were one-third full of sodium hypochlorite. Lethal to viruses.

Parked ten feet from the Land Yacht was an old sixteen-foot Airstream Bambi. It was a staging area for Midnight to suit up.

Inside the Land Yacht, there was a stainless-steel exam table with stirrups and studio-grade lighting.

Everything was powered off a large battery bank. No generators to clatter through the soft night woods.

A vivid yellow sticker was glued onto the doors of a small refrigerator and tiny freezer. The center of the sticker held a high-contrast black symbol. A circle encircled with three incomplete circles. Some called them flowers. Some called them claws.

The design was eerie. Scientists knew this symbol as U+2623. The biohazard symbol.

This wasn't a family campsite in Yellowstone.

11

FOCUS, he told himself.

This was dangerous work. And he was one of the relatively few people on earth who had actually worked in a Biosafety Level 4 Lab.

Vaccinations? He'd had them. Ebola. Q Fever. Rift Valley Fever. Eastern Equine Encephalitis. Venezuelan Equine Encephalitis. Anthrax. Botulism.

But he didn't have a vaccination for the sub-microscopic life form waiting in the trailer. The little monster sleeping in cool darkness. It originated from somewhere in the Congolese rainforest in central Africa. Somewhere in over five hundred million acres spanning six countries.

Midnight didn't know exactly what he had. Nobody knew what it was. *Nobody.*

But he knew what it *did.*

Camptown ladies sing this song, doo-dah, doo-dah ...

12

LEA LEA'S EYELIDS JIGGLED open sixteen minutes after a short-acting sedative shot. She was naked, strapped to the stainless exam table, back raised thirty degrees, legs spread, feet in the stirrups. Bright light fired into her eyes.

She tried to make sense of this. Naked on a cold table. Couldn't move. Her eyes scanned the stainless-steel room. Biohazard warning stickers on the fridge and freezer glared back at her. Two five-gallon containers of bleach abutted the wall. Her eyes shifted upward. Mounted on the ceiling was a fume hood with a double-HEPA-filtered ventilation system. Vent pipes reached toward the heavens from the roof of the Airstream.

"Are we in a hospital?" Her tone was softened after the midazolam.

"Not quite, queenie. More of a laboratory." He pronounced it la-BORE-atory. Midnight sat in a metal chair, fighting to control his enthusiasm, sipping on a cold bottled water.

The door was closed, no air conditioning, humidity high.

He stood, stepped to a cooler, extracted a bottle of water from the ice, walked over to her, unscrewed the cap, and pored. All over her face, first, then her breasts and belly. Her eyes widened at the cold insult. A sharp scream erupted.

Now she was awake.

Midnight was shirtless. He watched her eyes study his powerful chest.

"What do you want, what? Don't hurt me. I've got money. My daddy has money, we can pay you." Trying everything to appear calm, but her tone rode the outskirts of hysteria.

"Don't need money. Don't need anything. I'm in a giving mode. Gonna give you what women like you need. Something that runt boyfriend couldn't provide."

Midnight stepped to the end of the table, looked straight up at her, between her legs, over her vagina, past her breasts, into her eyes. He unhooked his shorts, let them drop down over his powerful thighs onto the floor. He put his hands on his hips, felt his erection creep to life in his briefs. "Look between my legs. A present for a haughty woman. Your sissy boy didn't have anything like this, did he?"

Her eyes fell to see his crotch. His penis was swelling, twitching inside the underwear. "No, please no. Money, we have a lot of money. Please don't do this. Don't get yourself in trouble." Tears flooded.

"Trouble? I've been in trouble since I was a little boy. All of it from a woman like you. A controlling woman, bless that dead bitch's heart."

He slid his briefs off. He touched himself, bringing his phallus fully erect. "This is what a *man* looks like. You ever had a real man?"

"Please, God, no. Please, I beg you, no." Her head shook side to side. "Take me home, I'll never mention this, never, I swear."

He shot her a hard stare, eyes full of vile. "You're right about that, you little skank. You'll never mention it."

Her hands and legs jerked against the restraints. Resembled seizure activity.

A leather belt circled her waist, with her wrists locked tight to her sides in metal wrist cuffs. Two-inch-wide nylon straps went around each ankle, then cinched to the stirrups. Her movements were futile.

"Relax, baby doll, don't believe you're heading anywhere."

He walked back to the caddy, pulled out a stainless-steel funnel and a quart container of liquid. Back to Lea Lea, he placed the jug on the floor.

"What is that? What the hell!" Eyes reddened with tears, wide with fear.

Her body quivered. "Queenie, it's nothing but a little evil remover. Time for the doctor to do a cleansing. All that negative juju harms your chi."

"You're not a doctor, you sick fuck."

Midnight's eyebrows raised in glee. "Well, not a very ethical one, at any rate."

"Let me the fuck out of here! PLEEEASE! Let me go." She was tight, lean, and young. Every muscle fiber rippled with anger. The table rocked with her struggle. Movements became frantic. Knew she was fighting for her life.

Midnight held a funnel with a three-inch-long spout with an opening circumference of over an inch. Plenty of highway for gushing fluid. She whimpered under squinched eyes, groaned as he slid the funnel into her vagina. Tried to expel it with her pelvic muscles.

"In deep, queen, it's not coming out."

"What are you doing, you crazy shit? My father will have you killed. You're dead, you bastard."

"You'll see what I'm doing. Oh, and don't worry. I'll call him when we're done. Let him know I purified his satan child. You don't have any sisters, do you? I offer a family plan." Laughed at his joke.

He bent and lifted the jug, twisted off the cap. Lea Lea's eyes locked on the container. He noticed, turned the jug so she could read the label.

"Hydrochloric acid," she said. A wave of terror marched across her face. "Hell no, no, please, no. Just screw me. I thought that's what you wanted. Just fuck me! What the hell are you doing? No, no, nooo, don't put that in me."

He placed the bottle over the funnel, began to pore. With the funnel full, he placed the container on the table, label in view of the camera, stepped back, began rolling video on the GoPro.

Vaginal mucosa melted away as if hit with a blow torch. The exam table rocked like it wanted to walk across the room. Metal clanging on metal. Her skin blazed red, morphed to whale-belly white, then liquefied. White, swirling fumes arose from between her legs.

But the screams. Oh, dear God, the screams.

Midnight sat in the chair, picked up the lubricant and applied it to himself, and went to work, violently. His eyes burned red, blazing on Lea Lea, his face contorting in pleasured rage.

"You made me do it, mama! You did! You evil bitch!"

Two minutes. Midnight was done. Lea Lea had stopped fighting, nearly passed out from the pain. Covered with sweat.

He toweled himself off, put on his briefs and shorts, washed his hands with sanitizer, finished the bottle of water he started, threw it in the caddy.

He emerged with a container of Formalin, a disposable scalpel, a pack of gauze, and duct tape. He slid nitrile gloves on his hands.

Apprehension in her eyes, Lea Lea spotted the scalpel. Apprehension rocketed into horror.

"What the hell? Don't. Wait. No. We'll pay you. Oh, hell, anything, anything!" The room exploded with her stress.

He unscrewed the specimen bottle, placed it on the table. Looked her in the eyes. He lifted her left breast, jiggled it up and down. "What are you, queenie? B-cup?"

She watched his hands, adrenaline blowing up her pupils.

The surgical blade slid through breast tissue like it was steak fat. He held her areola and nipple in his hand, placed it in the Formalin.

She shrieked like angry monkeys.

"Need a vacation souvenir, queenie, like buying a T-shirt in Gatlinburg." It was over in a flash. He grabbed her right breast, quickly carved off the areola. He placed two four-by-four pieces of gauze over the wounds. They quickly reddened.

"Not quite done. Need to sign my work, like Van Gogh." He stepped back to the caddy, grabbed another syringe of midazolam. Lower dose than the first time. Back at the table, he jabbed it in her thigh.

He gave it four minutes, then stepped to the table. She was down. His hands were gloved. He placed a #11 scalpel on the table. He watched her chest rise and fall with respirations, slow and soft. He unlatched her left hand, then her chest strap, and eased her onto her side.

She was posed at an odd angle, but he felt he could do it. He possessed sharp vision and steady hands. He picked up the blade, this one with a sharp point, and began to carve an "M" and an "N" onto her back.

Eyes closed. Lea Lea moaned. Pain seeped through the effects of the sedative.

Strips of meat were dropped into a lab specimen bag.

Straps were reattached. Midnight stepped back, studied Sloane's body. Vivid, fresh blood drained onto the table from her back wounds. Two squares of gauze on her breasts. Blowtorched vaginal tissue.

"You're sure a sight, queenie!" Thought he heard a groan.

"Almost showtime, girl. Gotta wake the boogieman."

13

OUTSIDE THE AIRSTREAM, Midnight sat in a fold-out camp chair under a half-moon. With his eyes closed, he soaked in the sound of tree frogs and crickets on this splendid evening.

Midway through a cold Powerade, he felt his energy pulsing, and it was intense.

The universe had no idea of the horror on tap.

Twelve years ago, he had smuggled Red X-81 into the United States. It was a lethally hot Biosafety Level 4 virus. The act alone was unthinkable. The highest breach of scientific ethics.

The tiny vial of Victoria Ngoy's blood likely held a billion particles of Red X-81. Back in the States, Midnight placed it into a facility freezer. It was stored at minus 130 degrees centigrade. One month ago, the vial was thawed. A sample of Ngoy's blood was mixed with serum from a cynomolgus monkey, an animal with up to 93 percent genetic similarity with humans.

This sample was placed into a $70,000 viral bioreactor, a machine that could amplify the virus into *billions* of copies.

But there could be a glitch. Midnight knew this. Freeze-dried virus lost viability over time. Midnight's gun might have no bullets.

He was about to find out. Very carefully.

The murder weapon was twenty feet away.

In a refrigerator.

AT THE REFRIDGERATOR, the biohazard warnings reinforced his paranoic apprehension. *Better be paranoid,* he thought. He wore a bright orange Racal biohazard suit. The hood employed a battery-operated air purifying system utilizing HEPA filters.

He bent, opened the door, watched the bulb shine on a single six-by-six-inch Lexan container. Inside, a small tube of blood and an empty 3cc syringe were packed in blue egg-crate-shaped foam. An eighteen-gauge needle was attached to the syringe. He placed the container on a stainless instrument tray.

Sweat popped out of his pores, he felt it under his arms. Wished he could mop his brow. His mind chased all the ways he could screw this up.

His left hand picked up the vial. The blood was very dark, almost black. He swirled the vial left and right. A viscous fluid flowed in each direction. Unclotted. Good.

He uncapped the needle on the syringe. *You've been waiting ... but careful ... extremely careful.* Looked at his fingers. Dead calm. Steady. He gingerly sliced the needle through the rubber stopper on the container, pulled up a single cc of blood. Not much.

But it might hold a hundred million particles of the hot virus. *Might.*

Red X-81. Ready to launch.

Standing at Lea Lea's side, her face burned with redness. Looked like she couldn't breathe. Syringe in full view. Her panic ripped into him. Words silently screamed from her mouth. He read her lips. *What the fuck!*

Her pupils dilated to the size of dimes, mouth desert dry.

Rocking, kicking, swinging, screaming. Lea Lea threw everything she had at the restraints.

He put his hand on her left knee, leaned sideways, pushed the knee down against the stainless table, firmly.

His eyes marked a target high on her thigh, eight inches from his left hand.

His right hand tremored. *Careful, you son of a bitch.* Eyes remained on the target. *Wham!* He jammed the needle in her leg up to the hub. His thumb plunged the blood into her muscle.

Midnight walked the needle back to the Lexan container like he held a detonator for an activated IED.

Red X-81 might be worse than an explosive device.

14

SIXTY-TWO MINUTES after inoculation, Lea Lea appeared to be resting as peacefully as a woman could after having her body mutilated. Fight or flight cooled down. Her chest gently rose and fell.

He wondered about the incubation time. Could be hours. Or days. Or a week.

Or never.

The rhythm of her breathing was hypnotic. The swoosh of air in his suit became soothing white noise.

What if nothing happened? How long should I give it?

His lids slowly closed as he mulled Plan B. Strychnine. It was the poison he had used on sixteen-year-old Sunshine Gage, twenty-seven years ago, on this same property.

He reminisced with the memory. *God, it was beautiful.* Sunshine was victim number two.

A scream ripped through the trailer.

Midnight jerked, eyelids busting open.

SEVENTY-THREE MINUTES after the needle left her thigh, apprehension overcame Lea Lea. *What's happening? What's in me?* Agitation gripped her.

A spaceman was sitting fifteen feet away, facing her. His eyes were closed.

She felt it, knew it. Her body was reacting. *To what?* Her brain didn't know. The train was gaining speed. *It's coming,* she thought.

He's murdering me.

A flash of heat flushed through her. Two minutes later, cold. Chills. She was naked. The steel table felt like ice. A bloom of exhaustion circulated down her body in a wave.

Energy zapped, like when a circuit breaker blew.

Sharp pain raced through her joints. Muscles began to ache. Agony marched up her spine deep into her head. The anguish settled behind her eyes.

Her skull was about to explode.

Her shrill scream bounced off the stainless-steel walls.

"My head!"

Midnight jumped at the scream, stood, watched for a moment. Stepped closer so he could hear.

"My head! My head!"

He moved into her personal space. His faceplate was three feet away from her mouth. Clear mucus ran from her nose. Heat flushed her skin, undulating down to her feet.

"What's in me!"

And her eyes. Oh, Lord. The orbs appeared ready to fire from the sockets.

Bliss ran through Midnight's nerves. *It's happening.*

Red X-81 was *alive* in Lea Lea Sloane.

Demons were present. He stepped back five feet, unable to take his eyes from her anguish.

He backed up, grabbed the chair, pulled it closer, sat, and watched. He knew what happened. It took two minutes for the capillaries in the muscle to dump the virus into the veins. In only moments, the heathen struck the heart and lungs. Sixty seconds after leaving the heart, the lethally hot virus rode the blood flow into every organ of the body.

The heathen clocked in. Then it went to work. Amplification. A thousand times smaller than a cell, the virus particle overcomes the body's immune system to invade the cells and hijack its systems to replicate into thousands of copies of itself. Over and over and over.

Armies of demons.

Midnight picked up a temporal thermometer and walked to her side.

He noticed small purple dots forming everywhere on her. Tiny hemorrhages under the skin. He placed the thermometer at her temple. It read 103.4 degrees.

Droplets of blood began pulsating from each nostril. Every heartbeat pumped out a flow. Her tongue snaked out, slid across her slippery upper lip gathering red ooze, and hypnotically pulled it into her mouth.

Lea Lea watched his eyes through his face plate. He watched back. The whites of her eyes were reddening.

Both were scared of each other.

Lea Lea began to shake her head and holler. Sledgehammers bashed through her skull. Her brain cells swelling with millions of virus particles.

Blood leaked from both ears. Brain cells were exploding. Every viral-filled drop looking for a host.

Midnight stepped away, terrified, stood against the wall.

Lea Lea coughed. A dry cough. Again, one more time, with her head wrenching forward. Another cough, this one drawn out, ending with a gagging sound in the throat.

Then it was quick.

A cannon load of vomit shot out of her mouth, covering her abdomen, flying between her legs, down onto the floor.

Hundreds of millions of hot virus particles hitched along for the ride. Midnight's fingers scrambled to hit a switch on the wall. Four ceiling fixtures came alive with ultraviolet light. It destroyed the genetic code of a virus, eliminating replication capabilities.

She continued to retch. Friable tissue from the GI tract began to infiltrate the bloody vomitus.

The virus was destroying her intestines.

Petechiae on her skin enlarging into purple contusions across her belly and legs.

Beyond doubt, he thought. Red X-81 was one of Africa's hemorrhagic fever viruses.

Four hours later, Lea Lea Sloane's face was a passive mask. Dry heaving ceased ninety minutes ago. Eyes open now, dilated, unmoving. A sign of brain damage.

He studied her chest ... maybe he saw movement ... maybe. No noise for over an hour. *Has to be dead,* he thought. Totally dehydrated. Bone dry. No blood to feed the organs.

He watched. And let the GoPro cameras record.

Forty-five minutes later, the sky edged from black into gray daylight. Stars blinked out. The moon fading into day.

Midnight was exhausted. He stood after sitting on the floor. The movement caused a startle response from Lea Lea. A shriek followed a sharp jerk.

Alive. *How?*

She opened her mouth, slowly. Red eyes fixed on him. Blood caked her teeth. *Was she smiling? Was it a silent scream?*

Midnight picked up a thermometer, stepped gingerly through drying vomit to her side to take a reading. Blood leaked slowly from her tear ducts into a thin stream down her cheeks. Each weak heartbeat initiated a blip in the flow.

A raw grunt filled the trailer. The sound was powerful, deep, like a large animal going down. Her body shook violently. Blood squirted from both ears. Pupils disappeared deep into her head. Arms and legs fought the straps. Skin around her wrists ripped open like tissue paper.

Pools of blood flushed from her vagina. Her rectum belched out a fetid, bloody, green liquid.

The stench was indescribable.

Her damaged brain was gripped in a grand mal seizure. Frenzied shaking scattered blood everywhere. Midnight's face was inches from her with a thermometer in his hand.

Blood rained across his face shield. Vomit struck his chest.

He dropped the thermometer, backed away rapidly, eyes wide, terrified.

And then her vibrations stopped cold. A switch turned off.

Back against the wall, he stood still for five minutes, trembling. Watching. He couldn't look away.

Dead? Has to be.

Covered with sweat inside the suit, he moved toward her. Slowly. Wanted to check her carotid pulse. Lightly, he placed his second and third fingers on her neck. Nothing. Difficult to pick up with gloves.

At ten seconds he pushed a little harder, searching for a beat. Not a hint of a thump. Nothing to pump. All blood drained from her body.

Done.

He turned to leave, not seeing her pupils move. Slowly, lizard-like. Barely two millimeters.

Her body seized. Snapped with nerve current. He turned toward her. Blood poured over her bottom lip. Her crusted teeth clicked and snapped.

Trying to bite him.

Racing away, his rubber boots slid on the slick floor, feet coming out from under him. He fell flat on his back. Propelled by his hands and feet, he rushed toward the exit in an upside-down bear crawl.

At the door, he forced himself up. His back was covered with blood, vomit, and stool. The putrid goo was speckled with tattered gut lining.

He prayed there was no break in the suit. Air pressure wouldn't fend off this slime.

Opening the door, he looked back one more time.

A smile slowly ceased his face

Camptown ladies sing this song, doo-dah, doo-dah ...

15

POINT CLEAR, ALABAMA

KIM CAWTHON'S FRONT bicycle tire blew seventy feet from the bridge over tiny Cottonmouth Creek. She was covered with sweat, her legs pumping madly, shooting for a personal best through the broiling heat.

The rubber left the rim. The bike wobbled. "Going down!" She screamed. Her lithe body launched toward the pavement. She hit on her side and tumbled eight feet.

It looked bad.

Sixteen bikes stopped behind her. Kim had been kicking their ass.

Ragged road rash to arms and legs. Bloody gravel-marred skin. Face okay, still beautiful. Brought her hands to her mouth. Teeth okay. She laughed through tears. Her first words — "And I was winning." She was six miles from the finish at the Pro Cycle shop in downtown Black Point.

After resting five minutes, Kim was helped up. No apparent bone damage, some bruising, significant skin tears. One of the riders, Kelly Stark, was an ER nurse. They'd catch a ride to her house to clean the wounds, apply ointment and bandages.

"Guys, do I smell that bad?" Kim's eyes squinted as she scanned in the direction of the odor.

Midnight Man

A stench permeated the air. It was 12:50 p.m. on a Saturday. High of ninety-three degrees in another hour, zero clouds in the sky. The bikers were completing a sixty-five-mile round-trip ride from Black Point to the beach. All country backroads, a canvas of soybean fields, sweet corn, and sod-grass farms.

Two women, wearing colorful, sweat-soaked performance gear, walked to the bridge, peered over the edge.

They screamed.

16

DETECTIVE BILLY STARR, JR., was at Lyrene's, a meat-and-three joint in downtown Black Point, when the call came in. Hints of fried catfish hung in the air. Glen Campbell singing "Wichita Lineman" from ceiling-mounted speakers. Billy had already eaten two of the three ham biscuits on the plate with creamed corn and lima beans.

There was a tepid argument going on at the table between Billy and his lunch partner. Alabama football. Jovial Asa Carnley, a short, round, early-seventies man with a thick white beard, ran a local feed store. He also treated lunch with the reverence of a First Communion.

"Asa, look man, I know you've been following the Tide thirty years longer than I have, but there's no way in hell Bryce Young's gonna have a bigger year than Mac Jones did last year."

Asa dabbed a cathead biscuit in a pool of gravy, pointed it at Billy, shook his head. "Wrong. That's Saban's highest-rated quarterback recruit … *EV-VER*. Look, this is how crazy it is, Billy." He took a small nibble of the biscuit, taunting him, talked while he chewed. "The kid already has deals approaching a million bucks this year in that name, image, likeness horseshit, *and he hasn't even started one game!*"

Billy's phone, lying on the table, rang. He picked it up, spotted the dispatch number, answered. "Whatcha got, Arlene?" He listened for twenty seconds, while his stoic face stared over the top of Asa's head. "Okay, I'm rolling now. Leaving from Lyrene's."

Billy glanced at his plate like he was saying goodnight to a cheerleader. "Dammit, Asa, gotta run."

"What? We just got here. Ain't nobody dead, man."

Billy stood, downed his iced tea in three gulps. "Wrong. We got a body. Tell Ms. Lyrene to box my cobbler. I'll run by later to pick it up." He dropped a ten and two ones on the table, made for the exit.

Cecil watched through the plate glass as Billy hopped in a black Yukon, fired on the light bar, backed out into traffic, screeching the tires as he headed west. He fought a powerful urge to run out, follow him sneaky-like, get some early scuttlebutt on the crime. *But, hell,* he thought, *there's way too much chicken-fried steak to be eaten to make that rash decision.*

TWO BLOCKS WEST on Black Point Avenue Billy cleared the last of the downtown buildings. He hit the siren. A quarter-mile later he had a view of the city pier from the bluff, spotted a haze of heat hovering over the bay. He sliced left onto Great Bay Road. Cars edged out of his way.

Three minutes from there to the Magnolia Hotel. Two minutes from there to Cottonmouth Creek.

Hot dammit, he thought as he arrived. Bunch of bikers in tight-ass clown suits. He knew this crew had already posted shots of the scene on every social media site in the known universe.

Billy pulled right to the side of the bridge, edging the lookee-loos out of the way. Hopped out. "Get back people, get back fifty yards. Show some respect! Put your phones up!"

Pike Tatum, the Black Point police chief, pulled up right behind Billy. Two more patrols behind Pike. He hollered to his men, "Block both sides of the road. Plenty ways down."

Billy looked down at the mud. Froze. Not possible. *Déjà vu.* It was exactly what had tickled his mind on the way over.

Pike ambled to his side.

"I don't believe it, man, I just don't believe it. Look at this shit, Pike. This looks exactly like that murder me and Jase found when we were boys. Thin white chick. Blond hair. Look at the back, same divots sliced out. Nipples sawed off. Same friggin' blowflies. Same spider crabs. Seriously, *same damn shit!*" He ran his hand through his thinning blond hair.

Pike had rushed to the scene straight from the city rec center, where he was playing pickup basketball with a crew of Black Point High School players. He was just shy of fifty, had a full head of dark hair with strands of salt sneaking in, was still wearing his baggy gym shorts and sleeveless T-shirt. Almost three decades ago he'd been a six-four shooting guard at Ole Miss. Scored more sorority babes than points.

He crawled back in his pickup, cranked the engine, clicked HIGH on the AC, hit call on a phone contact. He was on hold for several minutes with the Mobile office of the Alabama Department of Forensic Science before he got a guy who could pull the trigger.

"Dirk, it's Pike Tatum over in Black Point. I hate ruining your Saturday, but I have to."

"No big deal. Whatcha got?"

Pike heard a wheeze as the man spoke. "A dead female lying in low-tide goop, two miles south of the Magnolia, on Great Bay Road."

"Got it." Pike heard a lighter fire up a cigarette, then an exhale. "I just finished cutting the grass. Let me call in a team, grab a shower, and I'll see you in forty minutes. You know I live in Silver Hill, close. The team will take at least two hours to grab the truck and make it across the bay from Mobile."

"No problem, and thanks." Pike pulled an iced sports drink from the small cooler he'd taken to the gym, took a long swig. In the rearview mirror, he spotted a white van from a local news affiliate, just on the far side of a squad car. The long transmission antenna was jacked into the sky. A cameraman, late twenties, in shorts and shades, was leaning on the van, holding his camera at his side.

And there she was, Kate Dallas, stepping out from van's shotgun seat. He watched her, knowing she was wondering if he was here. They've dated about twelve times over the last eighteen months. There was an organic attraction between them, but they chose to remain defiantly single. At thirty-four, Kate was still shooting for a large-market gig.

And Pike? He just wanted to do what Pike wanted to do.

He watched her do a two-minute spot on camera, imagining what she was saying. Afterward, she slid on a pair of dark aviator shades and stared in his direction. Glasses looked sharp with her dark hair. He stepped out of his truck, moseyed her way with the easy swagger of an athlete, his eyes locked on her white smile.

Kate stepped away from the TV van, out of listening distance of her cameraman. Didn't matter, he crawled back into the truck's air conditioning.

"Well, Pike, aren't you a ragged sight. Whatcha got on a hot August day?"

Pike kept an acceptable businesslike distance from her, stayed out of her personal space, because any sane adult would read their body language, know they were bangin' each other. But he could still glimpse an aroma. Delightful.

She wore a pale, marine-blue linen top, a slightly asymmetrical turquoise necklace drawing the eye to a hint of cleavage, snow-white cotton slacks.

Pike made a point of letting her see his eyes ogle her cleavage before he focused on her question.

"Well, Kate, not sure yet." He cocked his head to the side. "Could take hours to get a handle on it."

"Well, Chief, let me *tell you* what you've got. And I have plenty of photos, thanks to your biker friends. You have a young, blond dead woman. My guess is that it's Lea Lea Sloane, a twenty-four-year-old sophomore medical student at Vanderbilt. Her father is a wealthy car dealer in Atlanta, and she grew up in the ritzy Buckhead section of town, close to the governor's mansion. She and her on-again, off-again, boyfriend were staying in daddy's penthouse condo at Turquoise Place in Orange Beach. Four nights ago, she and her boyfriend left the Flora-Bama, late. Got jumped. Last anyone saw her."

Pike's eyebrows scrunched. "Huh. Is that what you think I've got? A rich girl from Atlanta?"

"Yeah, buddy, I do." Her lips almost said, *kiss me.*

"Well, dang. That's exactly what I was going to tell you. However, this situation calls for more discussion, especially in dissecting your keen criminology insights. How 'bout this? I could run down to Greer's, grab a couple of thick fillets, some red wine, and we could enjoy them while we watched the sunset at my condo. Could even take a swim after dark." His eyebrows rose. "If you want."

"Well ... it would probably take us to midnight to solve the case."

"Oh, sure ... easily midnight."

"I can make that work."

"Pertinent to the investigation, Kate, I need to take down the name of that scent. Put it in my report."

"Chance by Chanel. Hints of grapefruit, jasmine, and white musk. You like?"

Midnight Man

"By the time we break the case, what'd we say, midnight, you'll know my answer."

17

DIRK ODENDAHL STEPPED out of a bland state vehicle, moseyed over to Chief Tatum and Detective Starr, shook hands, and said, "Well, I made it. Where's the vic?"

Odendahl was tall and rail skinny, had a ruddy complexion, and smoked Camels like they were safe.

Tatum gestured with his head, said, "Come on. Let's take a look from the top." They walked to the bridge, looked down.

"Believe you nailed it, Pike, you and the detective. That's a body, likely dead," said Odendahl, straight-faced. He took a couple of pictures with his phone. "Something odd about this. Hold on a minute."

Odendahl went to his car, popped the trunk, pulled out some hip waders, pulled off his shoes, and slid into them.

"Damn, that's rank." It smelled like rotting meat, bowel gas, and ten-day-old boiled cabbage. The odor assaulted them. Dirk pulled a blue bottle of Vicks from his pocket, dabbed a generous portion at the opening of his nose. "Anybody else?" Dirk held out the bottle. Pike and Billy didn't hesitate.

"Thanks, Dirk. Didn't know how much more of this I could take," said Pike.

"Let's get a better look." Dirk led the way as they tramped down the bank through marsh grass, getting close to the body. Tatum and Starr stopped when they hit mud, about five feet from the body.

"Heck, Dirk," said Starr, "I'm in dress loafers. Close as I'm going."

Odendahl said nothing, eased into the muck, edged up to the woman. He shot six or seven more photos from various angles. He shooed the blowflies away, leaned down, and put his finger on the body, gauging the composition. "Ya'll were right, she's dead." Tatum and Starr didn't laugh.

Odendahl stood, flicked a Camel out of a pack, torched a lighter to it, inhaled deeply, and stepped into the water. The body was on its side, a couple of inches deep in the mud. He took one more step backward toward the center of the creek and almost went down. It was a drop-off. "Holy hell!" The murky, stagnant water came within an inch of filling his waders.

"Dirk, get your tail over here. We don't want to have to pull you out and do CPR on your ass."

Odendahl laughed. "Think you're right, Pike."

"Hold it, don't move, Dirk. Look." Billy Starr was pointing. "Thirty feet, in the grass." The head of a gator, looking straight at them.

"The hell I'm not moving, get out of the way." Odendahl made it out of the creek and climbed straight up the bank. He looked back toward the still gator. "That's a big 'un. Looks like eight feet of grass tamped down behind him. We'll have to watch him when the team gets to work. I don't think that fella will come into a crowd but let's get an officer with a rifle guarding my crew."

Odendahl flicked the stub of the Camel in the water, tapped another out of the pack, lit it, and inhaled deeply.

"Guess y'all saw it, right? What's odd? An unusual blood presentation."

18

"**BILLY, TELL US** what you remember about that murder here back in the day," said the chief. The air was dead still, mid-afternoon, not a wrinkle on the bay water. "Hotter than Bolivia out here. I was sweating less playing basketball. Let's go sit in my truck."

"Hold on a sec, Pike, be right with you," Billy said.

Odendahl and Tatum walked fifteen feet to a big four-door pickup. "No smoking in my truck, Dirk, got it?" Dirk laughed, hopped in the back seat. Pike hopped in the driver's seat, fired up the engine, pored the coal to the AC.

THE WHOLE SCENE was surreal to Billy Starr. *Is this really happening? Again?* In his mind, he was transported back to that day. He remembered exactly what he'd been wearing. He remembered nobody answering the door at the home next to the creek. They had to go to two more houses before they could make the phone call to the police. And he remembered being pissed they didn't get to fish off old man Garney's pier that afternoon. A fishing opportunity lost to eternity.

Billy walked to the edge of the bridge, looked down at the body. By his recollection, he was exactly where he'd stood when he spotted Sunshine Gage twenty-seven years ago, pictured his bicycle right behind him on the ground. He knew that was the day he was smacked in the face that life wasn't all starlit nights and baseball games.

He pulled out his phone, snapped a picture. He walked eighteen feet to his left, crossing over the thin thread of water passing under the bridge. He sighted the body, enlarged the view, snapped another pic.

Pike tamped the horn in his truck. Billy looked up, saw Pike gesturing with his hand through the windshield. "I'm coming."

Billy pulled up a name under his contacts, attached two photos. He dictated a message. "Jase, this is RIGHT NOW! Can you believe this shit?" Hit send.

"THE KILLER WAS never found," said Starr, sitting in the truck's front passenger seat. "I got my daddy on the phone and he and a couple other guys got here fast. Pretty sure they were eating a burger down at the VFW. Daddy was thirty-eight then, a year older than I am now. Died three years later of a heart attack chasing some piece of garbage down Black Point Avenue who'd just heisted two pounds of ground chuck from Greer's. Dead over freakin' hamburger. It'd almost be kind of amusing if it was somebody else's daddy."

Pike had heard the hamburger story at least twenty times. He pushed on. "So, no suspects, or what?"

"I was only ten. I didn't get the details. Mostly I think the chief then, Ham Mosley, blamed it on a drifter, somebody passing through. At home it sounded like Daddy didn't buy it, the drifter angle. He said it had to be a local. The girl lived only a quarter-mile south of the Magnolia, on the bay."

"So who was she? Who are we talking about?" asked Odendahl.

"Her name was Sunshine Gage, abducted after her sixteenth birthday party. The party was at the pool at the Magnolia, just up the road here. And she was gorgeous. I mean I was only ten, but I knew she was a looker. Tall and blond." Billy pointed toward the creek. "Very, very similar to the girl in the mud, best I can remember."

Odendahl spoke up. "I remember hearing about that deal, I think. Prominent family, her dad was a doctor, right?"

"Yep. And still is a doctor. Pike, you know Kimbo, the vet, he takes care of the department's shepherds? That's Sunshine's brother."

"Oh, sure, I know him. I know I've only been in town three years, but I'm surprised I didn't hear about that case."

Billy looked away, out over the bay, as he spoke in barely a whisper.

"Pike, it was the kind of evil Black Point wanted to forget."

19

THE CRIME SCENE unit's van zipped right up next to Pike's pickup. He jumped, still thinking about Gage murder. The van was sleek with a swept-back windshield, like something carefully crafted in a wind tunnel. "Alabama Department of Forensic Science" was written on the truck's side, above "Crime Scene Unit."

Two people hopped out. One Native American woman. One an Indian American of East Asian heritage.

Billy Starr took a gander at them. "What the hell is this?" Starr's worldview came to an abrupt halt at the county line.

"Easy, detective," said Odendahl. "Each of them is three times smarter than you using only half their brain."

Chief Tatum barked out a laugh at that. "Let's go meet 'em." Pike killed the engine. The men hopped out of the truck.

"Chief Tatum, Detective Starr," Odendahl cocked a thumb at each person as he spoke their name. "This is Dakota Nightwind — she goes by Dak — and Kazmi Ramesh." They all shook hands.

Dak walked to the edge of the bridge, looked down, saw the body in sloppy goop. "Oh, hell." She turned around, looked at Starr. "I think Kaz and I will be able to get the corpse on the detective's shoulders, have him trudge up the bank while we push him from behind." Serious look on her face.

"Huh?" said Starr.

Dak walked past him, patted him on the shoulder, said, "Screwin' with you, detective. We got this."

Kazmi held two Canon DSLR cameras.

"Shoot the scene, Kazmi, stills and video," said Dak. She slung open the side door on the van, grabbed two pairs of chest-high waders.

"It's a dirty scene, Kazmi, skip the Tyvek, just waders and gloves."

Pike already had an officer standing by, holding an AR-15. He pointed over to the gator in the weeds. "One of the neighbors."

"He won't be a problem," she said. Kazmi's eyes squinted. Not sure about that.

Pike watched Dakota suit up over khaki shorts and a navy T-shirt identifying her as state crime-scene personnel. She had muscular legs, a broad chest, short black hair, and a round face. In his estimation, she was a woman who could crack a beer bottle over your head in a bar fight, then let you pick up the glass.

"Kazmi, cover the overhead shots. Get some 360 video. We need shots from the other side of the stream, too, grab some measurements, including the exact distance from the top of the bridge down to the body, then get your tail down here with me."

With her waders on, she negotiated the creek bank as nimbly as a Sherpa descending Everest, careful to keep her camera from scraping the mud.

Billy Starr's phone chirped. A text. He stepped away, pulled it up, read it.

Are you serious? Today? Cottonmouth Creek?

Jase Loggins was sitting on his micro-balcony at his overpriced studio apartment in Venice, California. No humidity, seventy-three degrees, a mild cooling zephyr sweeping off the

Pacific Ocean. Best weather in America.

Jase was a fair screenwriter and a bit-part actor, mostly when the role called for a Deep South accent. His income barely covered the bills.

Billy responded: **Yes, today. At the scene now. Will get back to you.**

Jase texted back: **There's a book here, Billy. Or a crime episode. Guarantee you.**

DAK AND KAZMI meticulously studied the body, both using magnifying glasses. Dirk stood behind them, watching.

"Look at these wounds, Dirk," said Kazmi. They had to cock their heads to see the back. "Ultrasharp edges, no ripping, couldn't have been done in anger."

"Something strange," said Dakota. "Petechiae everywhere." She pointed to the head. "Dried blood in the ear canal. Look here." She bent sideways to glance at the eyes. "Dried blood around the eyes. Bizarre."

Starr, puzzled look on his face, said, "What's that about?"

"Don't know, Bubba," she said without looking at him. She reached out with a nitrile-gloved hand, pushed the lips a little farther back. "Good gosh. Her teeth are caked with blood. Detective, do you remember anything like that on the other girl?"

"Nope. But I didn't get close enough to see."

"Okay. We're going to have to dig up the case files on the Gage girl. Detective Starr said there were wounds on the back. But he was a kid then, didn't see them up close," said Chief Tatum.

Dakota and Kazmi had been informed of the similar murder scene found here decades earlier. "Absolutely," replied Kazmi. "Is there any way these could be initials? Look closely. It looks like an M and an N."

"I agree, has that look. Or maybe nutjob hieroglyphics?" The wounds were bold, individual lines, one inch in width with squared-off ends, unconnected when they changed direction — rectangular lesions with whole slices of flesh removed.

"Think that's all we're getting," said Dak, holding a clean plastic bag. "Three fibers, one black, two red. Likely nothing." They'd been tweezed off the girl's shoulders and placed in the bag.

"Well, I think we can move the body now. Let's get her on her back," said Odendahl, who had one of the Canons strapped around his neck.

The chief and detective watched from the bridge, the body not more than twenty-five feet below them.

With effort, Lea Lea Sloane was turned onto her back. Black goo lathered on the anterior of her body, covering her breasts.

"Dak, you mind scraping some mud off one of her breasts?" said Starr.

"Why?"

"You'll see why, I think."

Dak dabbed her gloved hand in creek water, gently removed some mud.

They all saw it. The areola was lanced off.

Chief Tatum looked at Dirk, who blipped his eyebrows, then said, "Twenty-seven years, huh? Starting to get interesting."

20

PIKE SPOTTED KATE'S news van, knew he had to head on down to Greer's and pick up steaks, potatoes, and asparagus.

He also wanted to get his hands on the Sunshine Gage murder book. They'd be on microfiche. *They better be on microfiche,* he thought. He'd tell Billy to get down to the station, dig them up, make several copies. Billy was standing next to his Tahoe.

"Hey, Billy, hold up."

Pike walked over, was about to speak when Billy got the jump on him. "I'll tell you a little interesting tidbit, Pike. It came to me when they were loading the body. You remember Jake Montoya, the FBI agent who was down here when Wild Bill got killed?"

"Of course I do. Why?"

"Sunshine Gage was his girlfriend. He was at the birthday party that night. Daddy took me to the Black Point High School games, always said Montoya was a helluva ball player."

Pike felt like he got slugged. "Come again. Montoya?"

"Yep. Sunshine Gage was Jake Montoya's girlfriend. Small world, right?"

Pike tried to absorb that. He glanced out toward the bay, thinking. "Well, that's interesting." Pike immediately decided he wanted to see the old case files before Starr got his hands on them. "Look, I'm going to dig up the files on that case in a minute. I want you to get in touch with Orange Beach PD, let them know we have a strong contender for the missing Sloane girl."

Pike started walking toward the TV van, thinking he'd give a raincheck on the steaks tonight.

It took fifteen more steps to regain his sanity. *Only a certain type of lunatic would pass up an evening of antics with Kate Dallas.*

He wasn't that type.

21

"**CHIEF TATUM, IT'S** Dakota Nightwind." Tatum answered on the second ring. He'd just stepped out of the shower, his head swimming with erotic thoughts about an evening with Kate Dallas.

"Yes, Dak, anything yet?"

"Yep, wanted you to know. We have a solid ID. Jim Stone, Lea Lea's father, and her boyfriend, Gregg something or other, came by the morgue. We called them after we cleaned her up. We had the ID ourselves from the moment we received the pictures from Orange Beach PD. But they confirmed it."

"How'd they take it?"

"The dad was stoic. He'll crash when he gets back to his wife. She couldn't bear to make the trip. The boyfriend, Gregg? Kind of a flake if you ask me. He spent the night in the hospital from a concussion. The perp slugged him with a pistol, left him unconscious."

"Were you able to ask the boyfriend about the guy?"

"I did, actually. Asked him how many were there. He said one guy. Big guy. Wore a mask, a ski mask. Happened fast … and he and Lea Lea had been overserved at the Bama. I didn't push it."

"Good work, Dak, thanks. I was able to dig up the records on Sunshine Gage's murder from years ago. Might want you,

Dirk, and Kazmi to review some things. Similarities and whatnot."

"We'd be happy to. Let us know."

"Oh, hey, do you mind calling the detectives in Orange Beach, let them know we have a positive ID on their abduction case?"

"Will do."

Pike was towel-drying his hair when Jake Montoya popped into his thoughts. It would be an uncomfortable phone call, but after he reviewed the Gage case, he'd make it.

He brushed his teeth, swished around some mouthwash and spit, pulled on some clean underwear and walking shorts, buttoned up a blue, cotton shirt, and picked up his phone. Tapped Billy Starr's contact.

"Detective Starr."

"Billy, you don't have to say that when my name is on caller ID. Listen, positive ID on Lea Lea Sloane by her dad."

"Figured so."

"Here's what I need today. The uniforms knocked on doors this afternoon out at the creek. Nobody saw anything. Have them go back tonight and ask again. Try to cover three-quarters of a mile north and south of the creek."

"Got it."

Another forty minutes until Kate Dallas arrived for drinks and dinner. Pike lit several rosewood candles in the living room and kitchen, jasmine for the bedroom and master bath, and remade the bed with fresh cotton sheets.

He spotted the manilla envelope stuffed with the Sunshine Gage investigation. He mixed a quick gin and tonic and went out on the deck, sat in a fading white Adirondack, envelope on his lap.

A light westerly breeze teased his hair, the dropping sun popping in and out from a slow-moving lavender cloudbank.

Midnight Man

He left the envelope alone. Much too nice an evening to ruin it with the evil of man.

22

DETECTIVE STARR DROVE Chief Tatum three blocks from the station, eased into the parking lot next to Lyrene's. "Be right back, Pike, grabbing us some chow." It was 7:20 in the morning, truck windows down, a pleasant morning at this point.

Pike was responding to an email on his phone when Billy slung open the driver's door. He had a brown lunch sack holding four hot, country-ham biscuits wrapped in foil, and two large coffees.

Billy cut right at the light off Black Point Avenue onto US 98. Passed the hospital and Burger King, then kicked up the speed. The four-lane was wide open heading south toward the Gulf.

Both downed their first biscuit before any conversation. Radio on low, Elton John singing "Levon." Billy steered the Tahoe with his left hand, unwrapped his second biscuit with his right, took a bite, then a swig of coffee.

"Yep," said Billy. "This thing's well thought out. Nab a girl an hour away at the Flora-Bama, find someplace to torture her, drive her to the creek, an hour away. Nothing random about it."

They reached the light at County 32 in Point Clear, polo

field on their right lined with perfectly shaped leafy trees spanning the highway side. The truck cut left through light traffic and a green light.

It took fifty minutes to reach Orange Beach PD. Starr shut the truck down, dumped their breakfast trash in an outside receptacle, and entered the building with Tatum.

The chief spoke up. "Chief Pike Tatum to see Mackey Lee."

"Good to see you again, Chief." Pike was looking at a woman standing behind bullet-resistant Lexan. She was maybe five-five, silky black hair pulled back in a bobbed ponytail, dark eyes, minimal makeup. Attractive. Well, as attractive as you can be in a loose, tan cop uniform. Pike's mind was spinning. *Do I know her?*

She saved him. "I'm Ginger Smith. We danced at my daughter's wedding at the Magnolia, two summers ago."

"That's right." Pike waggled a pointer finger. "Your daughter, Lida — I love that name by the way. Married John Lafferty. I play golf about twice a month with his father, Jerry. They're a good-looking couple."

"I shouldn't say this about my own daughter, but Lida married up. John dumped that silly English degree and has started a ski-lift company in Grand Junction. Business is good and they're loving that Colorado lifestyle."

"Glad things are going well for them. Jerry told me they were out there."

Ginger continued, "Yes, great memories from that wedding night. Breeze off the bay, honeysuckle in the air. And the dancing was wonderful. Under the party lights, barefoot in the grass. Mmm." She shook her head. "You know, Pike, sometimes a woman needs a man with strong hands to hold her while she moves her body," she said with a smile of impurity.

It all rushed back to him. Stunning black dress, pearl necklace overexposed cleavage, and seductive perfume. Ginger's husband was about her height, short for a man, and carried the huge watermelon belly of a southern frat boy gone to seed. He was at the bar the whole night talking college football while Ginger rubbed every bit of her body on him during the slow songs. He knew all he had to do was ask ...

"That was a beautiful evening, Ginger, it really was." He glanced at her hand. Still wore a wedding ring.

"I'll say." Her eyes sparkled. She buzzed the door. "Come on back, Pike. Go to the end of the hall, the conference room."

"Thanks, Ginger."

An Italian look about her, he thought, a look that was just right. Wondered how far he might bend his ethics. *Her train definitely hadn't left the station yet.*

CHIEF MACKEY LEE and another man stood as Tatum and Starr entered the conference room. The light gray walls were sprinkled with colorful beach photography, a large whiteboard hung on one wall opposite a fifty-five-inch HD television screen. The carpet had the smell of a just-vacuumed living room.

Mackey extended a hand. "Good to see you, Pike. And this is Detective Jernigan."

Pike cocked a thumb at Starr. "Detective Billy Starr." Handshakes all around.

"Take a seat," said Chief Lee.

Pike slid a manilla envelope across the table to Lee. "Photos from the scene."

Lee opened the envelope, glanced at three pictures, shook his head. "Oh, dear God. And her daddy had to see that ... ah, hell. That family will never find peace."

Lee slid them to Jernigan. He scanned them, rubbed his hand across his mouth, shook his head. "I've got twin thirteen-year-old daughters." He glanced out the lone window a moment, quiet, like he was picturing violence coming upon his girls. None of the other men spoke. Jernigan turned his head back, locked his eyes on Tatum and Starr. "We gotta grab that son of a bitch."

"We'll get him. We'll nail that piece of garbage," said Billy Starr, with audacious confidence.

"Yeah," said Chief Lee, with the realism of scant confidence. He glanced at a clock on the wall. "The boyfriend will be here in five minutes. We didn't get much in the first interview. The boy got clocked with the guy's pistol, busted his skull, was in the hospital overnight with a concussion."

"Mackey, we've got some background here you're gonna find mighty interesting. It goes back a way. Fill him in, Billy."

"Well, it's some shit, I'll tell you that. I was ten years old when ..."

23

LEA LEA SLOANE'S BOYFRIEND, Greg Gibson, was escorted into the conference room wearing the look of a guy who had lost a week's beach tan in two hours. His head was shaved on the left side, displaying twelve metal staples holding together a three-inch-long gash. Eyes red, gray halos beneath them.

With imagination, you could sense a hemp aroma seeping off his Zac Brown T-shirt.

"Greg, this is Chief Tatum and Detective Starr from Black Point. They'll be handling the lead on Lea Lea's case since she was discovered there, with our assistance, of course, on anything we string together in Orange Beach."

Greg nodded at the men. "Yes, sir." His tone was calm, words slow. Pike would put odds on both dope and lack of sleep.

"Greg, deeply sorry about Lea Lea," said Tatum. "Thanks for meeting us today, we just needed to hear from you about the events of the evening."

"Do y'all have anything for a headache?" asked Greg. "Tylenol, aspirin, anything? They say I'm going to probably have headaches another two weeks."

Jernigan hopped up. "I'll grab something. Y'all get started."

"Well, we left Nashville on a Thursday night, drove to Atlanta, to Mr. Sloane's house, stayed until Saturday morning.

Then we drove to the beach." Greg spoke with a flat affect, didn't make eye contact. "Lea Lea had two weeks of break from med school. We were going to be here a week, then drive to 30-A for a couple days, stay with some friends of ours at Alys Beach. It's a cool spot." He stopped talking for a moment, looking dazed.

He continued. "Things were going so good here." Eyebrows up, head shaking, but still a little lost in space. "Lot of beach time, great weather, no stress. Went parasailing one day, did a half-day charter fishing, drank a lot of tequila, ate out lunch and dinner ... just good times ... really, really good."

Tatum thought Gibson appeared shell-shocked. "Greg, we want to focus on the evening at the Flora-Bama. Let's start there."

Jernigan was back with a bottle of Tylenol and a cold bottled water, slid them to Greg. "Thanks, man." He looked at the label. "Two tablets. Screw that." It came out as a mumble. He tapped out four, tossed them into his mouth, twisted the top off the water, downed three slugs. "That'll help."

"Okay. The Flora-Bama. I don't know, got there maybe 7:30, something like that. Packed. The place is always packed. We parked way down the road, seemed like a hundred yards, next to a big construction dumpster, a red one, on the canal side of the road. Nowhere else to park. We had to wait an hour to eat at their restaurant on the waterway, the River Grill, or something like that, had some fish and oysters, started in on the drinking. After that, we went across the street to the Flora-Bama, listened to some music a couple hours, couple different bands, danced drunk ... ah, hell, man, it was fun ..." He threw his hands up. "And that was it."

"Greg, we're getting close to done here. Just hang on. We need to hear about who assaulted you. First off, how many were there?"

Greg's head flopped forward. He rubbed his temples as he spoke, ignoring the question. "She told me, man, Lea Lea told me. I should have listened." His voice was weak, sounding like a breakdown was on the way.

"Told you what?"

"Told me we should call Uber. She was always responsible, careful. She's in medical school, man, she's smart, she knows. We were both drunk on our ass, could barely walk. But I wouldn't have it. I didn't want to come back for her car the next day. Might even be towed by then."

"And?"

"I convinced her. Told her I could handle it." Greg's fist slammed the table. The cops jumped at his unexpected intensity. Flat affect gone. It came out as a shout, a harsh tone. "Why the fuck did I do that? It was my fault! I should have listened!" He looked down at the table, shook his head, let the fingers of his left hand trace gently across the staples in his head. His voice dropped barely above a whisper. "Why, why, why, man? She was always right. Always. Just call fuckin' Uber. All I had to do."

The cops kept their mouths shut a moment, glanced at each other, uncomfortable watching a man disintegrate before them.

"So," Greg continued, "it was dark when we came out. It was late, eleven something, maybe midnight, didn't seem like a single car had left. We had to stop and think a minute, where's the car? We laughed about that until we almost fell to the ground. Anyway, we remembered we said when we got out of the car, 'We're on the Florida side,' started walking that way. I think we were holding on to each other, stumbling along, like kids, really. It seemed like two miles. We finally got to the car ... and there he was, in the dark. Just one dude."

"Tell us about the guy, Greg," said Starr.

"All we saw was a shadow. He stepped up as we were about

to unlock the car. It was dark, no close streetlight. His arm was out, holding a gun, pointed at us." Greg shrugged. "It happened so fast. Totally unexpected ...and we were so drunk. I mean *drunk*."

"What did he look like?" said Billy.

Greg lifted his hands, palms up. "No clue. Wore a mask, you know, like a bank robber, it was dark-colored, black probably. Long pants ... and I'm pretty sure long sleeves. It was very, very fast, everything. Just not much to tell." He looked the cops in the eyes. "Sorry, guys ... oh, I think he had on blue gloves. Probably those medical gloves."

"You're doing good, Greg," said Starr. "How close was he to you?"

"The end of the pistol was maybe three, four feet from me. It was close. I think the gun was black. I don't remember anything chrome."

"Good. Okay, he's close. Let's talk about his size. Bigger or smaller than you?"

"Bigger, definitely. I'm five-eleven ... guy had to be six-two, six-three. Easily over 200 pounds. But, still, those are rough guesses."

"What'd he say to y'all?"

"'Holler and I'll kill you.' That's it, nothing else. 'Holler and I'll kill you.'"

"What about his voice? White guy? Black guy? Sound Spanish?"

"Not Hispanic, almost positive. White or black, I couldn't tell you. I didn't immediately think Black, I know that."

"Deep voice? Soft voice? What?"

"Man, I've thought about that constantly, what he sounded like. Just a guy, nothing special, well, wait, he didn't sound young, you know, nothing like early twenties. Sounded like a fully grown man, his voice a little deep. Could be early thirties up to, hell, I don't know, fifty."

"What'd you do when he said, don't holler?"

"All that tequila made me think I was Superman. I stepped right up to the pistol, one step, told him, 'Get the fuck out of here.' And, man, that ain't me. I'm passive."

"What'd he say?"

"Nothing. That pistol slammed into my head so fast I didn't have time to so much as jerk. It was like red lightning bolts raged through my skull. My next memory was being loaded into an ambulance."

"So, nothing else you can think of?"

"No, nothing." Voice full of dejection, head shaking.

Starr looked to Tatum, Lee, and Jernigan. "Can you guys think of anything else?"

"Yeah," said Detective Jernigan. "Greg, when y'all parked, were there any other vehicles on that lot, cars, pickups, vans?"

"Nope. We drove out until there weren't any cars. Specifically drove another sixty or seventy feet to get on the far side of the construction dumpster. Lea Lea said she didn't want any drunks sideswiping her car."

"Okay. When you went back. Anything parked next to y'all's car?"

"Nope. Well, hold it ... no, I don't think so. We were just focused on finding her car. I don't remember seeing anything."

Pike Tatum weighed in. "Greg, since you've been at the beach, did you or Lea Lea have any words with anybody? Any scuffles of any sort?"

"No. Everything was chill."

"In the Bama, did Lea Lea dance with anyone else? Or did you see any guy checking her out, maybe laid a long look on her?"

Thought a moment. Shook his head. "Nuh uh, no."

"Who'd you talk to at the condo?"

"Nobody, really." Greg snapped his fingers. "Wait. Lea Lea did talk to a guy at the pool on two different days. He told her he was a doctor, a dermatologist at UAB."

"Anything at this point strike you as suspicious about him? The way he looked at her? Anything sexual in the conversation?"

"Not really. His wife was right there when they talked. Had a couple of kids, maybe eight or ten years old. And the guy definitely didn't have the heft of the guy at the Flora-Bama. More of a studious white guy."

"Okay, thanks."

Detective Starr stood. "I think that's it for now, Greg." He pulled a business card out of a shirt pocket. "Thank you for coming. Here's my contact. Cell phone on the card. If you think of anything, call immediately. I don't care if it's three in the morning. We're gonna get this guy."

Greg took the card, slid it in his jeans pocket, turned to leave, turned back to the men at the conference room door. "Know what we were talking about? Stumbling out to the car? Baby names. She wanted to name a boy Jesse."

The conversation had turned poignant. Surprised the cops.

"What name did you like?" asked Starr, losing the asshole cop tone.

Greg harrumphed out an abbreviated laugh. "I quoted Blake Shelton. You name the babies, I'll name the dogs." A sad smile crossed his face as he left the room.

Billy sat back down. The cops were silent a few moments.

Mackey Lee cleared his throat, said, "I'm losing the stomach for this stuff."

24

TWENTY MINUTES PAST ten at night. Pike Tatum lounged comfortably in a cushioned teak chaise on the balcony at his condo, thinking. The small table next to him held a copy of the murder book on Sunshine Gage, the Black Point High School annual from Jake Montoya's senior year, and two empty beer bottles.

Mellow from the alcohol, he stared blankly in a northwest direction across Mobile Bay. Clouds blacked out the stars, the breeze was picking up, citronella flames whipping in the wind, fighting away bugs. Reports said heavy rains from the west arriving by midnight. His eyes gazed over the end of the Black Point pier, settling on the lights of Mobile, fifteen miles in the distance. A gauzy conglomeration of sparkles blinked back at him.

A thin pedestal lamp shot a cone of light over his shoulder.

A quiet night on his bayfront balcony was Pike's favorite time to read. He'd read Gage's murder book at the office earlier in the afternoon. He read it again, slower, tonight after dinner.

Billy Starr's daddy chased his tail on the case. Never had a solid suspect. Interviewed every employee of the Magnolia Hotel, two, three times each. Focused mainly on those who'd worked the restaurant and bar that night. Nothing. Starr brought in the state bureau to investigate. Just more people chasing their tails. The case never solved.

The horror and agony of it all slowly eased out of the town's memory, shocking as it was.

But there was one promising bit of evidence. The skin under Sunshine Gage's fingernails. The state crime lab had no DNA matches. Neither did the FBI CODIS system.

Priority number one was decided earlier today. Get with the state lab and locate that tissue.

One thing struck Pike. He never saw any mention of anybody going by *Midnight.* Another thing tugged at him. The flesh carved out of Sunshine Gage's back. There was no mention of the symmetry and precision of the wounds. He studied the photos. The flesh was removed with clean incisions, carefully, not the slightest hint of a ripping wound, no frantic slashing, something that might be found in an attack. On a cursory glance, Lea Lea's wounds looked similar to Sunshine's.

On a more detailed look, the eviscerated flesh excavations looked *exactly* the same.

No mention by Starr of recognition of an M or N. *Why should there be?* It was like popsicle sticks were laid on the ground creating the shape of an M and N, only the sticks never touched. Looking at one corpse only, it would likely appear to be a random removal of tissue.

There was a list of all the hotel, restaurant, and bar employees in the murder book. Nobody with the initials M.N. Many positions were seasonal. For some, an entry-level job. How many were dead by now?

There was one particular difference in the bodies. There was no overt blood on Gage. No petechiae. No contusions. Lea Lea Sloane had dried blood at every orifice, and massive amounts in the vaginal and rectal regions. *Why?*

Who's still on the job? Who's still in town? Who's going to reveal themselves?

Feeling bushed, ready to hit the hay. About to stand up when his eyes hit the high school annual. He picked it up and started flipping through it. The Black Point Pirates. Blue and yellow. Happy times, hopefully. The last four years before real life.

Class photos. Ninth grade. Tenth grade, eleventh. Senior class. Found Jake Montoya and Kimbo Gage. Thought they hadn't aged much. Spotted a good dozen people he'd seen around town in the years he'd been chief.

Skimmed back to the tenth grade. Sunshine Gage. He'd thought Sunshine was a nickname. It was her given name. She was blond, tan, and beautiful. Perfect name for the girl in the pictures, he thought. Pike skipped to sports. Saw her in action shots playing volleyball. Tall with tomboyish muscle, looked like an athlete.

She'd put up a fight. She would.

Jumped back to the football team. Oh boy, a loud and proud bunch of chest-beaters. Undefeated, nobody even close all season. Claimed they were the best Alabama team in history. Mythical national champs.

Demolished Dothan 72-6 in the state championship game. Zeke and Eli Washington in the backfield. Both ran for over 200 yards, two touchdowns apiece. Photo of Jake Montoya, hot and sweaty after the game, holding his helmet, arms around his adoptive parents, Bonnie and Ed. Pike read the caption under the photo.

YOU THE MAN!

Jake Montoya ran the opening kickoff back eighty-nine yards for the first score. Took one punt return fifty-seven yards for a score. Followed that with four interceptions, two for touchdowns! Get ready to Roll Tide. The Jake Train arrives in Tuscaloosa next year!

Holy smoke, thought Pike. *Now he's in the NFL Hall of Fame.*

Silent lightning flashed on the western edge of the bay. A few fat raindrops slapped Pike, redirected his thoughts. Needed to run background on hundreds of male students. Had to track down old Magnolia Hotel employees

Had to tell Jake Montoya his girlfriend's killer was back.

25

SAN FRANCISCO

"OH MY GOSH! That was amazing." Annika Johansson was out of breath with a sheen of sweat on her completely nude body, lying on a king-size bed at the Westin near San Francisco International Airport.

It was eighteen minutes past noon. Blue skies with blustery winds off the bay.

Annika was the beautiful daughter of beautiful Swedish parents. She was classically Scandinavian, tall and slender with high cheekbones, Nordic blue eyes, and blond hair.

"You always look like you stepped out of a photo shoot. Your skin just glows." Jake Montoya was on his side next to her, fingers of his left hand gliding over her chest.

A silent smile raised her lips at the compliment.

Montoya was six-three with lithe, ropey muscles and broad shoulders. His Italian-Cuban heritage gifted him with olive skin, dark eyes, and black hair. He was the kind of man people noticed.

"Know what's fascinating? Sex with you, Annika, is like a sport." Jake laughed. "And I think you always win."

She pushed Jake onto his back and threw a leg across to straddle his abdomen. "What can I say? Swedish women fuck back."

They both laughed at that remark. Naughty talk from a beautiful woman.

They'd met during the winter after Jake's last season with the Washington Redskins at Phil Knight's palatial home in Aspen. Annika's father did some occasional legal work for Knight. She ran track at Oregon, just like Knight. Jake had an endorsement deal with Nike.

Jake and Phil clicked over their mutual love of books.

With her hands on his shoulders, Annika leaned down for a kiss. Jake's hands moved to her breasts.

"How is it you're so gentle for a football brute?"

"Annika ..." playful ice in his tone.

"Oops, forgot. Football was another lifetime. You're in the FBI now."

"Yes. So let's look out of the windshield, not into the rearview mirror."

Her hands went to his chest. "You don't have one of those bulked-up muscle-head chests. You're flat, tight, and hard, kind of like a swimmer. That, my man, I like."

Jake's hands slid over her thighs. He gave her a light squeeze then rubbed her runner's muscles.

Annika saw his eyes staring between her legs. She was confident in her nudity.

He cocked his eyebrows. "Well, know what I like, you work of art?"

"I think I do." Playful sparkle in her eye.

"Your intelligence and that sleek, narrow nose."

She punched his chest, smiled with the whitest teeth he'd ever seen, said, "You drive me crazy, man." She leaned down for a kiss.

Jake's phone rang.

She broke the kiss, shot him a look that said *need to answer that?*

He shook his head.

Annika leaned back down, took Jake's face in her hands. "I don't mind you teasing my nipples while I kiss you ... if you were wondering."

Three minutes later a chime sounded next to the bed. A text hitting. Jake ignored it.

"Okay, Jake. An unexpected call from you this morning. I canceled two very important client meetings. And now I'm naked in a hotel room on a weekday at lunchtime. Care to tell me what's going on?"

"It's highly confidential."

"Look, buddy, I'm a partner in my father's law firm. I think I know how to maintain a confidence."

"Okay." He nodded. "A big break. The second suspect in the legal extortion case has been spotted in Indonesia." She and Jake had discussed the case on several occasions. It had been a huge national story.

Eighteen months ago Jake had worked a case where two men extorted over $100 million from several American trial lawyers. Four lawyers were brutally murdered. One man, an MIT-trained computer wizard, was in prison. The second suspect, a former Navy SEAL, killed an FBI agent while eluding capture. He was presumed dead from a plane crash.

"Lucky Hendrickson, the SEAL, is alive. He had plastic surgery in South America. In six hours I'm leaving San Francisco for Korea, then to Jakarta." Jake spoke with the confidence he felt. "Lucky is sailing around Indonesia and has been spotted by a very reliable source. It's uncanny—"

Jake's cell rang again. "Ahh, man."

"Take it." Annika grabbed the phone and gave it to him.

He eyed the caller ID. Pike Tatum, the police chief in Black Point, Alabama.

Jake edged Annika off him, stood, and answered. "Pike, is my mother okay?" His words were laced with concern.

"Oh, she's fine, Jake. I saw her at Publix yesterday, had a nice chat. Calling about something else."

"Oh, thank God. What's up?"

"Why don't you sit down?"

Jake felt the air leave him. He took a seat in a leather chair, sat on the edge, apprehension ramping up.

He listened to Chief Tatum for four minutes before ending the call.

A thunderstruck look crossed his face. His eyes went blank, staring into nothingness.

The Indonesia trip was dead.

26

BLACK POINT, ALABAMA

JAKE LEANED HIS old mountain bike against the red brick of the Black Point Police Department, a one-story brick structure in downtown Black Point, across the street from a pizza and Mexican joint. He arrived at his mother's house last night, late, after a flight from California to Atlanta to Pensacola.

It was 7:10 in the morning, dew still lingering on the grass, a pleasant early morning coolness in the air, downtown mostly empty at this hour. The ride was just over a mile from Bonnie's bungalow at the bottom of Fels Avenue, which sat about 150 feet from the high bluff overlooking the waters of Mobile Bay.

"Special Agent Jake Montoya here to see Chief Tatum." He spoke to a woman of maybe twenty-seven, boyish blond haircut, broad shoulders, wearing a collared law enforcement top with two large, button-closed pockets on either side of the chest.

"Yes, sir, Agent. He's expecting you."

She buzzed him inside and he got a better look at her. Taller than he thought, heavy through the hips and thighs. Figured her for a cleanup batter on the department softball team. *A chick who could tear the hide off the ball.*

Pike Tatum stood outside his office on recently mopped tile

that smelled of eucalyptus and lemon. He wore a black polo shirt with stone-colored chinos, low-top hiking shoes on his feet.

"Mornin', Pike."

The chief extended his right hand for a shake. "Great to see you again, Jake, but damn I hate the circumstances." He gave Jake the once-over. "Like the new Bureau uniforms."

Jake wore a black tee advertising Capital Mixed Martial Arts, Washington, DC, over gray hiking shorts and running shoes. The temple bar of a pair of Wayfarers was folded over the top of the tee. No badge. No gun.

"Not on duty. Yet."

"Come in, have a seat." Pike took a seat behind his desk, Jake sat in a heavy wooden chair, crossed an ankle over a knee. Very low-volume jazz off a satellite station drifted out of a Bose radio.

"Care for anything? Coffee? Coke?" asked Pike.

"I'm good. Lay it out."

Pike pursed his lips, exhaled, leaned onto his desk with both forearms. An earnest look crossed his face. "Dammit, Jake, we've got some ugly business here. First, let me say I'm so sorry about that ... situation with Sunshine Gage. Hell, I don't know what to call it."

"Yes, you do. It was a brutal murder. Call it what it is. That's what it was when it happened. That's what it is today."

"Okay, sure." Pike's jaws tensed at Jake's bluntness. "Well, we've got another one, a murdered young woman. For all the world it looks like basically the same MO as Sunshine. Body in Cottonmouth Creek, same back wounds, same ... same desecration in the vaginal area, nipples sliced off." His eyes focused on the desk while he shook his head. "I hate to even mention the details."

"It's okay, Pike. Go on."

"Did you meet Detective Billy Starr when you were here on the Burnham case?"

"I think so, briefly when we ran the warrant on Johnny Earl Shedd."

Pike nodded. "Yeah, he was there. But he was the kid, he and a buddy, that found Sunshine's body all those years ago. He was ten at the time."

"I knew some boys found her. I didn't know him. He was about eight years younger than me. We've never talked."

"He'll be here at eight. Want you to speak to him."

"Sure."

Pike stood, walked around to the front of the desk, plopped half his butt on the corner, looked down at Jake. "The woman's name was Lea Lea Sloane. Twenty-four years old, just finished her second year at Vandy's med school, dad's a car dealer in Atlanta. She was on vacation at the beach with her semi-dim-wit boyfriend from Nashville. Spent the evening eating and drinking at the Flora-Bama and had arrived at the car to leave when the abductor showed. The boyfriend got clocked with a pistol, spent a night in the hospital. Lea Lea was gone. Found four days later in the creek mud."

Jake was stone-faced when he said, "What do you have on the guy?"

"Not much. No video. Pitch dark. They had to park a long way from the Bama, in a construction area. Boyfriend says the guy was bigger than him, over six feet, over 200 pounds. Not Hispanic, unable to tell if black or white. Thinks the voice could be a guy in his late thirties to about fifty. Both the boyfriend and Lea Lea were blitzed. Boyfriend says they stumbled to the car after leaving the bar."

"Well, my money is on a white guy," said Jake. "But, could it really be the same guy?" Shook his head. "What's he been doing all these years? Could it be a copycat?"

Pike threw both palms in the air.

"The file we have on Sunshine is on microfiche. It's locked up. Only me and Starr have access. If anybody wanted to see it, they had to come through us, and I've not had a single soul go into the files since I've been here. So where would they get the details?"

"Huh." Jake bit lightly on his bottom lip. "That's interesting. So what about Starr? Very bizarre. Ten years old. He found Sunshine."

"Yeah, Starr. His dad, Billy Starr, Sr., was the lead detective on the case."

Jake snapped his fingers. "That's right. I knew that name sounded familiar. He spoke to me several times about Sunshine. For a while, I thought he was trying to implicate me somehow. Left a bad taste in my mouth."

"Doin' his job, I guess."

"I can't remember, Pike. How big is Billy, Junior?"

"Over six feet. Over 200 pounds."

There was a tap on the office doorframe.

"Well, there he is now, Detective Billy Starr."

27

"HECK OF A career, Jake. I mean, unbelievable," said Starr, holding a magazine in his hand. He was six-two and well-fed, with pointy bitch tits poking through his polo, dirty blond hair thinning back from a shiny forehead, wearing metal-framed glasses. "NFL Hall of Fame. Damn."

Billy and Jake just shook hands, and the detective was starstruck sitting in Pike's office with the former All-Pro. "Wanted to speak to you at Shedd's place, but no time. Listen, my daddy took me to all the Black Point games, including the state championship. He had season tickets to Bama. Think I saw you five or six times in Tuscaloosa. And here you are. Oh, hey, would you sign this for me?" Billy handed the magazine to Jake. "I've had this in my office for years."

It was a shot of Jake on a *Sports Illustrated* cover dunking the ball over the goalpost crossbar after a pick-six in the Super Bowl. A legendary photo around Black Point.

Jake took the magazine, looked at the picture a few moments, almost felt embarrassed by the ask. He avoided football bluster. Some players disintegrate when the stadium lights flicker off. Not Jake. "Seems like a long time ago, Billy," he said with a courteous smile. "Glad to sign it for you." Jake took the thick-tipped Sharpie from Starr, scribbled his name.

"One question, Jake. Want your opinion. Last year was one

of the best Bama teams ever. We had Mac Jones at quarterback, had better numbers than Tua, like that was even possible. Smith, Ruggs, and Waddle at receiver. Played like they had glue on their hands, caught anything that was even reasonably close. Najee Harris chewing up the turf, running the ball. All those guys are in the pros, now. My question. New quarterback, Bryce Young. Think we'll run the table this year?"

Jake's face had the same look he'd have if someone asked him about physics. His shoulders shrugged as his hands went out to his side, palms up. "No clue, Billy. I haven't watched a Bama game in probably twelve years. Never met Coach Saban. On Saturdays in the fall I'm kayaking or mountain biking, usually both."

Billy's face squeezed out a wry smile, thinking Jake was jerking his chain. Realizing he wasn't, his eyebrows arched in astonishment. *Twelve years? Sacrilege.*

"Let's get rolling, guys. I'm here unofficially, but from what I'm hearing the FBI will likely need to be brought in on this. I think I can swing it with two murders, both with the same characteristic signature. What do you have so far?"

"Shit. That's what we've got, Jake, pure T nothing but shit," said Starr. "One clue. The perp was likely over six feet tall and over 200 pounds. And we have a murder that looks like a carbon copy of Sunshine Gage. Well, close anyways. There's some strange bleeding on the Sloane girl

"What strange bleeding?"

"She had dried blood around every orifice. Mouth, ears, vagina, rectum. Nothing like that on Sunshine." Starr caught a look from the chief.

"Oh, hey, sorry about that, Jake. Sunshine was your girlfriend. Hope I didn't sound flip about it."

"Not a problem, Billy. She's been dead almost thirty years. Two days never go by without me thinking about her. But now we have a chance to catch the guy. And, by God, I want to catch the son of a bitch." Jake's tone like sandpaper grit.

"I agree with you about bringing in the Bureau. We don't have the manpower to run down our background suspects. Should we call the Mobile office or can you jump in on the case?"

"Oh, I'm jumping in. Count on that. And I already know three people from the Mobile office. Met them on the Burnham case."

"Great."

"You guys have any direction you want to start on this?" said Jake.

"Sure do. From reading the murder book on Sunshine, I think there was only a cursory glance at the high school students that may have been at the birthday party," said Tatum. "Billy's daddy talked to many of them, but the reports are terse, mostly people saying they didn't see anything, didn't know anyone that had it in for her, and basically were as shocked as everyone else in town. Likely a zero chance a female student had anything to do with this."

"Right," said Montoya.

"I think we need to run down every male from the ninth to twelfth grades, see what they've been up to for the last twenty-five years," said Tatum.

"I agree. That'll take some manpower. We've got that at the Bureau."

"And the hotel employees, too," said Billy. "My daddy hit them the hardest. I believe, but I'm not sure, that Daddy thought it was someone from out of there. I was only ten back then, so he never pulled me into the living room and said, 'Here's where we are, son.'"

"Absolutely, Billy."

"Jake, Dad did confide and discuss the case with someone

else."

"Who?"

"My mother. She's seventy-one, lives right here in Black Point, mind's sharp as an icepick. She works three days a week at the Page and Palette Bookstore. Guarantee she has memories of this."

"Great. I'd love to meet her."

"Jake, I've got everything on the Sloane case and the Sunshine Gage murder book loaded onto a cloud site for you and the folks in DC," said the chief. "We'll be adding names out of the high school yearbook and the Magnolia Hotel staff." He handed a Black Point PD business card to Jake. "These are the sign-in credentials."

Jake took the card, looking like someone handed him a bomb. "Fellas, I won't be looking at the file on Sunshine. Not now. Probably not ever."

Billy and Pike said nothing, looked toward the ground, nodded their heads with understanding.

"Jake, one more thing. Some bad news I learned this morning."

Jake inhaled. "Shoot."

"Sunshine had a tissue sample under her nails. The ABI ran the tissue for a DNA match, twenty-seven years ago. Nothing. But here's the problem. I called the state to locate the tissue so we could run it again."

Jake listened, a skeptical look on his face. "Yeah?"

"Sixteen years ago there was a fire at the state lab. Wires shorted or something. Significant portions of their archive refrigeration units were destroyed."

Jake's head dropped. "Ahh, man." He looked up, shook his head, fixed his eyes on Starr.

"I need to know everybody who had access to Sunshine's murder book and autopsy. That means going back twenty-seven years. Black Point officers. Crime-scene crew. Pathology staff. Bureau of Investigation. Funeral home personnel."

"We've got some work, guys."

Jake's face went taut, steely. "Something's gnawing in my gut. Really bad feeling. Tip of the iceberg kind of thing."

"What are you talking about?" said Pike, eyebrows scrunched down with concern.

"We likely have a serial killer in Black Point."

28

LEAVING THE STATION, Jake waved three fingers at the woman at the desk. "Thanks." He received a quick chin nod.

It was 8:17, and he'd been in the office an hour. He pulled out his phone, sat on a concrete bench, tapped a contact. Dog days of summer, dead-still air. Dew already dried on the grass.

Answered on the third ring, in downtown Washington, DC. "Thought you were on vacation." It was Randy Garrison, Jake's boss.

"Well, yeah, I was. A week is all I can take," Jake lied. "Then I get restless. You have a minute?"

"Got me at a good time. I just left one of those horse-crap Bureau meetings with the director and a few department heads. I mean, damn, Jake, is one of the requirements to be director that you have to be a clueless political imbecile?"

Jake laughed. "Wonder if the guy's ever even arrested anybody?"

"Doubt it. What's up?"

"Need you to assign me to a case." It took Jake ten minutes to describe the Lea Lea Sloane murder and the similarities to Sunshine Gage.

"Ah, man. That thing with your girlfriend ... unbelievable and sad. Sorry. But wait a minute. Are you saying *twenty-seven years?* Same MO and same signature from the killer?"

"That's what the locals are telling me. I met the chief over a year ago on the Burnham case, fellow named Pike Tatum. He's a solid guy, a former Dallas homicide detective, serious about his work. He knows in a small department he's overmatched here."

"But twenty-seven years. What's this guy been up to? Has he been on a spree across the country, and we missed it? Or maybe he's been in prison." Garrison leaned back in his executive chair, placed his feet on his desk, getting comfortable with the story. "Definitely run the recent releases of the long-timers."

"We'll check that in a day or two. But, Randy, it could be a copycat."

"Yeah, yeah, there's that. Well, hell yeah, we'll get you on it. With an exact duplicate, plus the uniqueness of the signature, I think we've got a basis to bring in the Bureau. The nipple excision and the vaginal thing really creeps me out. Angry, sexual, has to be a woman hater. And we'll need to bring in the crew at the Mobile office. You need to get any files from Black Point, get them to Behavior Analysis, see if the voodoo witch doctor gang can give us a solid profile to chase down."

"I've already got a cloud site with the files from Sunshine and the other victim. Her name is Lea Lea Sloane. I'll text you the sign-on credentials in a moment. I'll call Mobile in a little while. I worked with a few of them on the Burnham case."

"Sounds good. Don't forget the daily reports. And, Jake, I know you don't need the job but try not to go too rogue."

"How about a little rogue?"

Garrison lowered his voice, spoke like a teenager hiding pot from his mother. "You've got to, man, you've just got to. That was your girlfriend, for crying out loud."

JAKE THREW A leg over his bike, pushed off, headed south on Colony Street. Three blocks put him at Del La Mare. Page and Palette Bookstore on the corner. Thought about Billy Starr's mother working there. Might be smart to pick her brain before her son got to her.

Spotted people in the coffee shop section. Leaned his bike on the wall, walked into Latte Da. The smell of coffee and cinnamon and raisins washed over him.

Jake's eyes landed on the sign going into the bookstore section. Open 10 a.m. *Too early.*

A blond woman with an air of officiousness, wearing a tropical-blue sleeveless top over slacks and practical heels, was tapping a note into her cell phone. She spotted Jake and seemed to recognize him. Jake had been in a few months ago and had bought a couple Rick Bragg books.

"Sir, may I help you find something? I'm Karin Wilson, the owner."

"Well, I see the bookstore doesn't open until ten. I'll probably run by later and pick up a book or two. Oh, by the way, is Mrs. Starr coming in today?"

Karin averted her eyes from his angular facial features, glanced at the wall clock. "No, Elaine will be in tomorrow from noon to closing."

"Thanks, I'll be back." He turned to leave then turned back. "Oh, hey, do you know if you have that book in by Opie Taylor?"

"Opie?" Puzzled look.

"The red-headed kid from Andy Griffith. Ron Howard. It's about Ron and his brother, can't think of his name."

"Absolutely. It's called *The Boys.* Want me to put a copy behind the counter for you?"

"That'd be great. My name's Jake Montoya. See you in a day or two."

AS HE MEANDERED out of the building, Karin's eyes locked

in on his broad shoulders and carved, muscular legs.
Bet he never gets lonely, she thought.

29

JAKE PEDALED A block down to Fels Avenue, cut right, gave the bike several strong kicks on the pedals, then sat up straight, hands off the handlebars, and coasted. Exactly like he did as a boy. The road was a twenty-degree downhill slope to his mother's house, a half-mile away.

At Summit Street an image appeared in his peripheral vision from a small cottage to his left. He shot his eyes that way. Barely a glance. *A Boston Whaler?* He grabbed the handlebars, squeezed the brake levers, twisted a U-turn in the middle of the road, pedaled back past two houses to reach the cottage, a classic Black Point bungalow, built decades ago.

An American flag was attached to the home and a lush pindo palm was the focus of the front yard. *I like the look*, he thought, *tropical*. He cut right on Summit Street to reach the driveway, where the boat sat on a trailer, covered.

He leaned the bike against a tree, glanced around, thinking he probably looked like a thief. To the side of the drive was a micro-beachy party area. Two bright-colored Adirondack chairs sat on beach sand under three sabal palms, strung with a string of party lights. Helluva spot for a glass of wine on a pleasant evening.

The house looked empty. Didn't see anyone outside in the neighborhood. He crept up to the boat, which was backed up to the door of a small garage. Outline sure was a Boston Whaler, the Montauk model, sixteen feet, six inches of center-console runabout that was unsinkable. Had a newish-looking Yamaha bolted on the transom.

After glancing around once again, he pulled up the boat cover. *Ahh, geesh.* Baby blue cockpit. Mahogany console, gleaming with varnish. A restored 1960s boat. He eased the cover down, cinched it tight, glanced into space, thinking, *Rare. Gorgeous.*

He stepped to the side of the garage, glanced around again, then put his face to the window of a Dutch door, hands to the side of his temples, blocking glare.

Gotta be kidding, he thought.

Jammed together inside, like a Manhattan parking lot, was a Porsche 911 and a Jeepster with two paddle boards on a rack. A truck that Martha Stewart would have been proud to have at her place on Nantucket. And a screaming-yellow dune buggy. And multiple Ducatis. And bicycles. And a cool vintage black-and-white photo of a blond-haired kid on a '60s minibike.

Disneyland!

"Any way you could help me get that crap out of here?"

Jake jumped at the voice, turned around, sheepishly. Standing before him was a woman, maybe five feet, maybe a hundred pounds, brown hair, a summer tan, wearing extremely short lemon-colored shorts, a matching racerback top, and running shoes. With his ultrasharp observation skills, he happened to notice her toned arms and lean, shapely legs. Thought she could have been a model for Title Nine.

Thankfully she was smiling. "Yeah, if I could get all that crap out of there, I'd have some room for my stuff, like a new sewing machine."

"Look, I apologize for my nosiness. I was riding by on my

bike and spotted the boat. I love old Whalers."

"No problem. You're not the first. You ought to see what happens when Bryan pulls all that junk out and starts washing it down. A crowd develops."

Jake laughed. "I bet. Look, I'm just visiting from Washington. My mother's house is at the bottom of the hill. Name's Jake."

"I'm Dayna. Nice to meet you." She was smiling, soaking him in. She seemed to like what she saw.

"Well, Dayna, gotta shove off. Thanks for not calling the cops on me." Said it with a sparkle in his eye.

"I would have, but too much paperwork." She smiled back, holding it.

He walked back to his bike, turned it toward the street.

"Hey, are you a runner? You look like it."

His face slackened and his head cocked back. "Yeah, on occasion."

"Well, we've got a group that meets on Saturday morning at seven for a ten miler. We start at the bluff overlooking the pier. Come join us."

Pedaling in a circle, Jake said, "Seven would work. Might do that. Doing some martial arts with Woo Chow on the bluff at five-thirty. Thanks for the offer. Oh, hey ... do you really sew?"

"Hell no, man, I shop."

30

THE SPRING SCREECHED as he pulled the screen door open. Wood slapped back against the doorframe as he stepped into his mother's house, a small jonquil-yellow cottage with a tin roof, built in '36. The sound was homey and nostalgic, always reminding him of the Deep South.

Walking into the dead silence caused a hollow feeling, lonely. Bonnie was at work managing the grill company.

He stopped in the small living room, glanced around, inhaled the familiar scent of his childhood. Ed's chair hadn't moved an inch since he last sat in it, reading the *Mobile Press-Register,* drinking a beer after a day on a construction site. Same photos on the wall. Same knickknacks scattered about.

He stepped into his bedroom, a room that once belonged to Ed and Bonnie's biological son, Chuck. The memory tormented him every time he returned to this room.

Chuck's last day. Almost thirty-five years ago.

The boy died in a bicycle accident on the last day of the third grade, riding home to start the great American summer. Jake and Kimbo rode behind Chuck on their bikes, racing downhill on Fels, intentionally letting Chuck win. Bonnie was on her knees planting fresh zinnias around the base of her mailbox. All three watched Chuck shoot through the stop sign at Great Bay Road.

The front end of an old Bel Air driven by a retired pastor was waiting for him.

Jake's eyes zipped across Chuck's old fishing rods leaning in the corner of the wall. A small plastic tackle box rested on the floor beside them. He took a moment to look at the picture sitting on top of the bookcase, between a few Matchbox cars. Chuck with Bonnie and Ed at Disney World. A smiling, happy family.

A residue of guilt swept through him. He'd finished growing up in this room. Chuck didn't. *Why? Why? Why?* Chuck was uncoordinated, not a hint of athleticism. Jake let him win the race coming home from school. Thought it'd make Chuck feel good.

And it got the boy killed.

Jake formally introduced himself to Bonnie and Ed five days after the accident. Only nine, he knocked on their door like a man to apologize for Chuck's death. He'd suggested the race, he told them.

No, they said, through tears, that wasn't his fault. That was life happening.

Bonnie and Ed also learned that day that Jake was two weeks away from being placed in the foster system. His grandmother, his guardian, was losing her mind to dementia.

Suddenly the house closed in on him. He had to get out of the room, get out of the house, get some air. He found what he was looking for on the bottom shelf. His twelfth-grade high school annual. He grabbed it, walked to the kitchen, placed it in a backpack with a legal pad, a couple of pens, and his laptop, pulled a water out of the refrigerator and three Fig Newtons from a package on the counter, and walked out the front door.

Approaching mid-morning there was still no wind. Jake strolled out onto Billy Rigdon's dock at his bayfront home, an eight-minute walk from his mother's cottage.

Under a tin-covered roof, Jake twisted an aging, weather-beaten, wooden chair around to face west, looking across the bay, took a seat. The glassy water was backlit with the sun still firing its light from the east. The morning was pure serenity.

He powered up his laptop, typed in Billy's Wi-Fi code. Bang. He was on. He pulled the card from his pocket that Chief Tatum had given him. Cloud credentials for the Sunshine Gage and Lea Lea Sloane murder books. He signed on, made sure he didn't click anything on Sunshine, dug into the Sloane case.

In twenty minutes he'd read it twice. It was thin. The dictated interview with the boyfriend, Greg. Pathology reports with photos. Tox screen with no blood alcohol, but high levels found in the hair. And the bottom-line cause of death. *Exsanguination, shock, and multi-organ failure.*

Huh. No poison. Unlike Sunshine. There was a dictated note with a lot of medical jargon from the pathologist. The last line caught Jake's eye.

We can find no plausible medical explanation for the extensive internal physical degradation suffered by the decedent.

He studied all the photos, beginning from the initial shots of Sloane in the muck of Cottonmouth Creek. A pale, naked body.

He studied the closeups of the back wounds. Exactly like Billy Starr said, no shredding, just precise tissue removal.

The blood was evident in the close-up photos. The tiny petechial hemorrhages spotting the skin. The crusting at the orifices. Even in the eyes.

He jerked as a loud splash hit the water, forty feet away. Looked out to see the body of a pelican, head underwater, searching for a snack.

Went back to the computer. He could see it. The letter M. The letter N. Starr said it was exactly the same as on Sunshine. Initials for the killer? Who could be that precise? Ideas raced through his mind. A surgeon? A taxidermist? A pathologist? A vet? A grocery store butcher? Hands accustomed to precision cuts on meat.

Cheek retractors opened the mouth. Dried blood caked the teeth like scabs.

Then the anterior photos. Areolas sliced away. Vaginal tissue boiled off. Speculated it was from acid. *Indescribable pain*, he thought.

He averted his eyes back to the bay, a tranquil blue heaven. Spotted the outline of a freighter, five miles out, heading into the port of Mobile. Three kayaks headed north, fifty yards out from the shore, steaming along at a good rate, paddles moving rapidly in figure-eight patterns.

He got back to work. He placed the computer on the table, pulled out the high school annual, started flicking through some pages. Lots of signatures. Read some of the inside jokes. Smiled at a couple of them, wondering where the heck some of these people were. Flipped back to class photos. He started with his grade, seniors.

It didn't take long to reach the first asshole. Billy Burbank. A prick in the first grade. A prick in the twelfth grade. He was always after Sunshine. And she basically pissed in his face.

"Are you the guy, Billy boy?" said Jake on the quiet dock. *No, you wouldn't have the balls.*

After a quick spin through his class's pictures, he glanced over the water again. Nothing like the Washington, DC, chaos going on this very moment. A formation of pelicans glided by, had to be eight of them, wings outstretched, headed south.

He thought about that a moment. Yeah, Black Point *was* a nice place. The Gages had been working on him for years to give up law enforcement. "Come home," they said, "live off your investments, run the grill company, give up the deadly game of crime."

And rot on the vine? Nope. Not yet.

He picked up the phone, tapped Pike's contact, stood, and walked into the sunshine.

"Pike. It's Jake. Look, I just ran through the Sloane book. Not much there. Also glanced at my twelfth-grade classmates. I'm sitting on Rigdon's dock, on Great Bay Road. It's killing my motivation."

"I bet. Nice morning."

"Yeah. There were probably a thousand kids in the high school back then. Cutting that in half leaves us with roughly 500 boys to look into. We need to compile a list."

"Already have it. Anybody you want me to send it to?"

"I do. Ross Tolleson, my analyst in DC. The guy's a crackerjack and sneaky smart. He pulls some important crap out of his rear on almost every case I work. Stuff nobody else sees. Upload it to the cloud site, plus send the list to his email. I'll shoot the address to you when we hang up."

"Great."

"I'm going to take a ride down to the Flora-Bama. I want to get a feel for the abduction scene. Oh, one other thing about the list. Throw in all the male teachers, custodial staff, and cafeteria folks."

"Good idea. Talk soon."

The morning heat over the water felt good. He pulled off his tee, tossed it into a chair, punched in Tolleson's number, letting the rays wash over him.

Answered mid-ring. No "Hello, how are you."

"What do ya got?" said Ross.

"Nothing, yet."

"That's some bizarre, heavy stuff." Tolleson exhaled deeply. "The same guy or a copycat? Interesting question."

"Yeah. Garrison has agreed to let me float in on the case.

Only two vics, but extreme similarities. We're going on the basis it's serial. Well planned. Distinct signatures. But we're keeping the Bureau's interest quiet at this point."

"Sure. What do you need?"

"I want you to create a team to look into some people. I need to know where they are now, what they've been doing over the last twenty-five years, any criminal records, the usual tight background check."

"Got it. How many?"

"Guessing here. Somewhere between five and six hundred. Well, wait a minute, maybe seven hundred or more if we take in hotel employees at the time."

Nothing but silence on the phone. Jake looked up and down the shoreline, waiting for Ross to speak.

"Ross, you there?"

"Jake, what month is it?"

"August."

"Right. And what do Ross and Sally Tolleson and their two amazing children do in August? Every August."

"Buy school clothes."

"NO! We take ten days on Hatteras!"

Jake heard the ice, scrunched his face, didn't say anything.

"Ever heard of Rodanthe? It's about thirty miles south of Nags Head, on North Carolina 12. Middle of dang nowhere. Standing in the middle of the highway you can practically piss in the Atlantic on one side or Pamlico Sound on the other ... without taking a step. Sally invited two other families and their seven kids. One guy is a fascinating dog groomer. The other is a taxidermist. There's no goofy golf. No go-cart tracks. No roller coasters. No amazing restaurants. No beautiful hot chicks like South Beach. Just women in mom suits with coverups, nine lazy kids, fish bait, ten gallons of potato salad, and plenty of time to try to digest why the wives say no sex with all the kids running around."

Jake laughed. "Let me see what I can do."

"Please, Jake, anything. Get me out of that nightmare. Make it two thousand people if you have to."

Hung up with Ross. One last call. Andy Grissom, the Special Agent in Charge of the Mobile, Alabama, field office. No answer, then a text popped up: **Call you in 5**.

Jake's eyes cut over to the kayaks, thought, *No better time.* He hoisted one off the rack, moved it down the three-step ladder to the swim platform. Headed to grab a paddle when his phone rang.

"The legendary Jake Montoya. How are you, man?" Andy Grissom and his agents were involved in the takedown of Theo Fuller, the digital mastermind behind the extortion of some of the richest litigators in America.

"Doing well, Andy. Have some news to share. I'm working on a possible siting of Lucky Hendrickson, the dude who killed Agent Switek."

"If he's alive, we need to get all hands on deck, get that son of a bitch. Wonder how Switek's widow is doing? Have you talked to her? Hope the poor woman is hanging on."

"Funny you should bring that up." Jake coughed out a chuckle. "I bumped into her at a charity golf tournament. She's doing more than hanging on. Five months after her husband was killed, she married a guy five years younger than her that owned a bunch of tire stores. The guy's making a killing. Has the missus living in high cotton."

"They always say FBI wives have to be resilient." Humor in his tone.

"Well, let me tell you, Andy. The tournament was at Avenel Farm in Potomac, where she said she was a member. The woman has dropped thirty pounds, changed her hairstyle, spends her days either shopping or playing golf. She's the prototype for resilience."

Grissom was laughing at that as Jake got serious. "Andy, here's why I called. I'm in Black Point right now. A few days ago we had a murder that is a complete look-a-like to one that happened twenty-seven years ago. A young blond woman. Desecration of the vaginal area, possibly with acid. Flesh carved out of her back. Breasts carved on. Dumped in the mud in the exact same place, a tidal creek running in off the bay."

"Well, how's the Bureau coming in on that? Two local murders."

"It's unannounced at this point. We're tiptoeing in, gathering some background on a large group of people. But with the unique signatures, we think we can get away with calling it serial. Need your help from the Mobile office. If you remember, we had Benton, Allen, and Wills helping out on the Fuller case. Did a great job."

"Things changed, Jake." Grissom sighed. "I got demoted seven months ago. I'm now sitting in a small office in Williston, in western North Dakota, middle of absolute nowhere."

A bewildered look swept Jake's face. "What? Screwin' with me, right?"

"Unfortunately, no. Here's what happened. Had a clown in the Mobile office named Chandler Harlow. The prick liked to be called *Chan*. His worldview of himself was something like two steps above James Bond. Always flirting with the staff, he began to get bolder after his wife left him over his antics. I'd told him to cut the crap on a number of occasions. Even wrote him up twice. When his wife pulled up stakes, he began drinking more, which caused him to lose most of his filter. Then came the Christmas party."

"Oh, yeah. I hear trouble." *The office Christmas party.*

"Yep. So we have a convention room rented in the Riverview

Plaza Hotel, nicest place in Mobile." Grissom started laughing, thinking about it. "It'd be funny if my ass wasn't sitting in Williston, North Dakota. Anyway, we had an open bar, fantastic finger food, a little three-person trio. Beautiful evening. Until Harlow gets into his third scotch. Little by little, he starts hitting on every woman in the place, asking them to slow dance, all that crap. Three of our clerical staff arrived together, attractive young women, late twenties, unmarried. They all three went into the restroom at the same time, like women do. They didn't know it, but Harlow was there in a stall, taking a leak, I guess thinking he's in the men's room. He heard them. He completely took off his shoes and socks and pants. Walked out wearing his sport coat, oxford shirt and tie, looked all three of the women in the eye with his tallywacker flopping in the wind, and said, 'Which of you ladies wants my dick to propose to you tonight?'"

Jake howled. "That's hilarious!"

"Next thing came the sexual harassment suit from one of the women. Harlow was canned. I was demoted to North Dakota. And the woman filing the suit was promoted. I've got to keep my nose clean, hopefully get out of here in a year or two."

"Who's running Mobile?"

"Nia Cruz. She's an interesting woman. Definitely a cool customer. Very qualified. She's biracial, Hispanic and Black, grew up someplace over around New Orleans. Joined the Marines out of LSU, was military police. Got another degree online in criminal justice. Got out of the Marines, went to Hollywood to try to become an actress, got a law degree at night from, I think, Loyola. Scrubbed acting, applied to the Bureau. She's smart and moving up fast. Through the grapevine I heard she's getting an online MBA."

"Huh. Motivated. Is she the type to file a sexual harassment suit? Or sexual discrimination suit?"

Grissom barked out a laugh. "Definitely not. She's the type to drag you out of the building, invite your friends to come watch, and beat your ass into the next month. She's six feet, maybe six-one, lean and built. She was a second-team All-American on LSU's basketball team. And she's married to the sweetest little white homemaker you could ever want to meet, Mary."

"Huh."

"Yeah."

31

THE SETTING WESTERLY sun peeked through the trees as Jake drove his Land Cruiser south on Great Bay Road, cruising at a lazy thirty-five, windows down, shades on, elbow resting on the door sill. Three miles from town, at the Magnolia Hotel, he slowed, he glanced at the boats at the marina before twisting through the S-curve.

Still thinking about that vintage Boston Whaler he'd seen earlier. Made up his mind he was going to do it—meet for the ten-mile run on Saturday, ask if there was any way on God's green earth they'd sell that boat. He thought a Whaler clamped to the ass end of his Land Cruiser might make his life complete.

He drove for another mile past bayfront estates, cut left on County 32, took it to Colony Street, sliced right, drove not even a mile, turned into the crushed-oyster-shell drive. The sign said Refuge of Hope, An Animal Sanctuary. The large two-story home and office was an eighth of a mile down a gauntlet of majestic live oaks, like a scene from Faulkner's Mississippi.

A quarter of the way down the drive Jake spotted Moses standing still as a statue, clandestinely watching six horses. The donkey was twenty-three, had been found wobbling down a Mississippi highway, starving. Now he was rejuvenated, back on the job, running off evil-minded coyotes.

Crushed shell gave way to pea gravel as Jake reached the

circular driveway in front of the house. He pulled his tan Cruiser up behind Hope Hiassen's glossy black '80s Porsche 911. The ragtop was down, the license plate said RESQ.

Two of the organization's vice presidents stood on the front porch and yapped out happy barks, tails whipping their rear-ends side to side.

Jeep and Arlo. Free-range golden retrievers.

Three minutes later, the front door opened while he rubbed the ears of both dogs.

A tall woman with dark hair reaching just below her ears bounded off the porch, put her arms around Jake's neck, and gave him a quick kiss. Her smile looked like a toothpaste ad.

"That's what I like in a woman, needy."

Hope, five-eight, wore a short blue Nike tennis skirt under a white racerback top, revealing the arms and shoulders of a woman who was familiar with a weight room.

"You didn't call. But, boy, I like the surprise." She continued beaming, "What's going on? Thought you were deep in a case somewhere."

"More business. I'll tell you about it later."

"Any pleasure?" Playful glint in her eyes.

"Anything's possible. Look, I'm heading to the beach, gonna grab a bite while I decompress in a sea breeze, then run a business errand. Wanna ride?"

She punched his arm. "And you have to ask? Let me grab a shower. I just gave two lessons." Hope began playing tennis at age seven in Dana Point, California, and became a top collegiate player at the University of Virginia. Besides running the animal sanctuary, she occasionally taught tennis at the Colony Club.

"Let's take the Land Cruiser, great night for it," said Jake.

"Not a chance, buddy. We'll take the 911. I'll let you drive. Let me get going on the shower, I'm hungry."

Jake gave it five minutes, then told Jeep and Arlo he'd see them in a little while. Walked into the house and up the stairs to the second floor and heard the sound of shower water splashing from the master bathroom. Thought he heard Hope humming an Adele tune. He slid off his clothes.

The only light in the bathroom came from a mixture of lavender and vanilla candles. Hope wiped the steam off the glass as he approached.

"Oh my, the plumber. I called you a week ago, didn't I?"

"Still need the service call?"

"I believe so." Hope opened the shower door, a lathering of body wash covering her small breasts. "I apologize, I just didn't have time to dress."

AN HOUR AND a half later, the plumbing problem was solved. Jake, driving the Porsche 911, cut left through a green light across Highway 59 onto the Beach Expressway. Wide-open road, radar detector on. He shoveled some muscle to the accelerator, Hope tapping off a classic rock station to KSJ Country out of Pensacola. Caught a song in the second verse.

"Turn it up," said Jake.

"Oh yeah, love this," she said. Old Crow Medicine Show. "Wagon Wheel." They joined in.

Hittin' a buck-ten in a top-down 911, buttery three-quarter moon surrounded by pinpoint starlight spritzing from a coal-black sky. Hope butt-dancing in the seat, Jake keeping time with his palm on the steering wheel. The euphoria of sexual afterglow.

Fifteen minutes 'til oysters and beer.

Fine night to be alive.

32

A GULF BREEZE DRIFTED across their table at the Gulf Restaurant. The joint was a beach dive constructed out of old, maritime shipping containers perched next to the jetties at Perdido Pass. Cold beer, fried shrimp, raw oysters, and a long-haired dude strumming out Buffett, Taylor, and Eagles covers practically held them hostage.

TEN FORTY-SIX p.m. Two-and-one-half miles east of the restaurant, Jake edged the 911 up next to the construction dumpster situated near a two-story, pastel-colored, island-style home on Key Largo Place, almost a hundred yards past the Flora-Bama beach bar.

"You lost? Why are we stopping?" Hope said.

Jake killed the engine. "Hop out, let's take a walk."

"It's kind of dark, Jake." Car lights streamed past the site, slowed because of the busy bar. The dumpster, coupled with a dark, late night, was just far enough off the road to would make it almost impossible to spot a predator lurking.

Jake walked around the container, thinking, walked out to the highway, stopped, looked down the road both ways and at the condos across the street, facing the Gulf.

In a slow stride, he moseyed down Perdido Beach Boulevard, toward the Flora-Bama. "Come on, Hope." She caught up with him, started asking questions. He put up his hand. *Not now.*

He scanned the utility poles and buildings for cameras. Spotted a few, but night wasn't the best time to take an inventory. Chief Tatum told him Orange Beach PD combed through the area gathering footage. Had nothing, they reported. He made a mental note. He'd come back in the daytime, walk the area with a detective, spot all the camera locations, and review the footage himself. Take as long as it takes. *Impossible that the cameras caught nothing.*

They stopped at the entrance to the Flora-Bama. Summertime. Eleven p.m. is not close to late in a beach town. Still had ballpark-sized crowds coming and going. Decided he wasn't going in slinging questions around, not yet. If he flashed his FBI identification it'd make it into social media and to the local press in fifteen minutes. People know some big stink is happening when federal agents arrive.

Back at the car, Hope folded her arms across her chest, spoke to Jake through the darkness. "Alright, mister, what's going on here?"

He held up a hand once again. "Give me a minute." Jake walked quietly in tight circles in front of the dark beach cottage. Lost in thought, almost a trance.

Crime of opportunity? Long way from the bar. Boyfriend said between eating, drinking, and dancing they were at the Bama for four hours. Could somebody have spotted them in the bar and raced out ahead of them? He would have had to know where they parked. But wouldn't they see him walking in front of them? Falling down drunk. Maybe not. Maybe someone followed them to the bar, saw the outlying spot, and liked the chances. Thought back to Sunshine's birthday party. She had less than a mile's drive to get home. Virtually no traffic. He never felt that was just some unplanned, unfortunate act in the universe. Lea Lea Sloane. So similar to Sunshine in looks. No way somebody sat lying in wait in the dark for hours whiling away the time hoping a straggler that looked like Sunshine would stroll by.

No possible way, Jake thought. *Lea Lea Sloane had been stalked meticulously by a cunning predator.*

Doom gripped him. They were dealing with a smart guy, operating with an intricate blueprint.

Back in the moment, speaking in ambient light, he explained to Hope.

"A twenty-four-year-old woman was abducted right here. She was attractive, from a good family, and a medical student at Vanderbilt. Had life by the horns." Jake raked his hand through his hair, shook his head, slowly.

"Is she okay?"

"She was tortured and murdered."

33

JAKE CHECKED THE three-day forecast on his phone while he waited. Still a bleak sky but westerly breezes had blown out most of the rain, leaving nothing but dense humidity. It was early, before seven in the morning, and he sat in his Land Cruiser, windows down, radio on, in the parking lot of Sweet E's Pork Chop Biscuits, facing busy US 98. CVS was behind him in the shopping center, and Walgreens had the corner nailed down across the street. Busiest traffic spot in Black Point.

Humming along to "Lyin' Eyes" when a bland, four-door sedan pulled up next to him. It was black and so was the driver. A tall woman stepped out, wearing dark slacks and a white polo shirt with "FBI" stitched over the top of "Mobile Field Office."

His eyes caught her buff arms protruding from her short sleeves. *Definitely fit.* A tight, short haircut, a serious but attractive face.

She launched a sharp look at him that said, "I'm in charge," to set the tone.

He thought to himself he could picture her in Hollywood, maybe in a Bond film, or kickin' ass with the Rock. *What happened?*

"You Montoya?"

Jake smiled, figured her for thirty-seven, thirty-eight. "I am. Are you SAC Agent Cruz?"

"All day, baby, all day. Call me Nia, I don't have time for all that tribal language." She glanced over at Jake's ride. "What's this thing? I kinda like it."

"It's a Toyota FJ-40 Land Cruiser, an old '76 model. Stopped making new ones for America in the '80s." He said it with a touch of smugness.

"Bet you get some looks in this thing, don't you?"

"All day, baby, all day." He smiled. She smiled. "Let's grab a quick bite, then hit it."

Jake had introduced himself over the phone to Agent Nia Cruz yesterday. Told her they might have a serial murder brewing, needed her in on it. She practically jumped through the phone. "Oh, hell, yeah."

Inside, they ordered at the counter, took a seat. Took only five minutes to have the meal delivered on a tray to the table. Same thing for both. Two pork-chop biscuits, bowl of cheese grits, and large teas. A trio of hot sauces sat on the table. "This place just opened in the last month or so," said Jake. "I wanted to try it. Belongs to an old high school football teammate, Elijah Washington."

"He was a pro, right?"

"Yep. Played at Auburn, got drafted by Arizona, played a couple years in Atlanta, finished up with the Dallas Cowboys. I think he's got over seventy of these places in Texas, doing extremely well, I hear. It's been some years since I've seen him."

Nia watched Jake lift the top off his biscuit, pop a few drops of Texas Pete on his pork chop, replace the top, and take a bite. Bliss crossed his face. "Oh, yeah."

"You know, Jake, some Black women in the Bureau would call the CDO and report you for inviting them to a pork-chop biscuit shack. Probably say you're orchestrating a passive-aggressive diminution of our natural worth in order to place yourself atop the pedestal of our relationship."

Holding his biscuit, a blank look crossed his face. "I might have to go back to college to understand that diminution thing. And who the hell is the CDO?" He ate a spoonful of grits, took a long slug of tea.

"The Chief Diversity Officer, in DC." She teased a little hot sauce onto her biscuit, took a bite. "Whoa, damn, this *is* good." Said it while she chewed. "I'm thinking I might insist on some sensitivity training for you to advance your wokeness."

He held another spoonful of grits in his right hand, wagged his left pointer. "Uh uh, won't fly. I'm so woke I never sleep. See, I've *dated* Black women, and more importantly, a buddy and I sell the finest grill in America at unthinkable low prices to African Americans so they can hone their skills in the great craft of barbecue artistry."

"You date Black women, huh? Bet every one of them were models." She smirked playfully as she placed her lips around a straw, looked into his dark eyes, soaked down some tea.

"Now, hold on, Nia, they weren't all models. Some of them were nothing more than run-of-the-mill, high-profile on-air newswomen in New York and Boston."

Nia snorted a laugh, waved him back with her palm. "You're too much, man. Now I see where all that humor comes from on the Big Jake Grill commercials. I see your face on those SEC games almost as much as that Yella Wood guy. And he ain't funny."

Both ate fast. Jake said, "Let's head on down to Cottonmouth Creek, show you where the Sloane girl was found, then down to Orange Beach. I'll review the case on the way."

"Sounds good. Give me your keys, I'll drive."

"Careful, now. I could fall in love with a woman who likes

Land Cruisers."

"Jake, I'm gay."

"Nia, I'm woke. Anything's possible."

She snickered. "Glad I met you, Jake." Nia hopped in the driver's seat, hooked her seatbelt, fired up the engine.

Jake shook his head, smiled. *Chicks dig old Land Cruisers.*

34

TWENTY MINUTES LATER, after eyeballing the still, murky water of Cottonmouth Creek, Nia hopped back in the driver's seat without asking. "Kind of like this prehistoric truck. Slow as hell, but fun. I think we're picking up even more looks with a Black woman at the wheel. What do you think?"

"Without a doubt."

On the way to the creek, Jake had filled her in on the case, including his relationship with Sunshine Gage. Nia knew enough to leave that wound unopened, at this point.

From the creek they drove south on leafy Scenic 98 that ran parallel to the bay for three miles, then the road curved inland. They proceeded east, headed to Foley, then Orange Beach.

They were approaching old downtown Foley. "Go straight through town, cut right on the Beach Express a couple miles out. I've got to make two calls."

He dialed the FBI office in Atlanta first. He explained who he was, got kicked between a couple of people until he was put through to Supervisory Special Agent Dennis Hopkins, a seasoned, fifteen-year veteran at the Bureau. Jake explained the situation that Lea Lea Sloane had been brutally murdered in Alabama.

"Dennis, I say this very reluctantly and only to put some fire under you. There was a case virtually identical to this some years back. There is the possibility that this is a serial case. Right now we want no media in on it, none. What I do need is some background discussions with people that knew Sloane well, high school and college. Who could have it in for her? She went to the University of Georgia, undergrad. Attractive, well-to-do. Almost certainly in a sorority. Track down some of her sisters. I'm gonna have Nashville look into the med school scene up there."

"Got it. I'll start with the parents first. Then the friends, pick up some names. Shoot me their contact info."

"You got it, Dennis. And thanks. Get back anytime day or night with anything interesting."

Jake dug out his notes, texted the contact info to Hopkins.

He dialed Nashville as soon as he fired off the text. Same thing. Phone dance until he reached Angie Beckwith, a supervisory agent. Went through the background.

"Agent Beckwith, I need you to look into Sloane's friends at Vandy's med school. Her boyfriend is Greg Gibson, lives in Nashville, does some kind of behind-the-scenes work with a country band called the Flat Top Tractors." He heard her chuckle. "Yeah, great name. Need you to really dig into him and his music pals. Some of that world can get a little dark. Get me all of your contact info."

Jake received a text in three minutes. He stored her contact in his phone, shot her the names Lea Lea Sloane and Greg Gibson, with his number.

Nia listened to the conversations. "Hopefully, they'll find somebody with a grudge, and we'll slam this case shut."

Three minutes later, Nia swung the Land Cruiser into a Shell station, oddly situated in between the northbound and southbound lanes.

"Gotta pee?" asked Jake.

"Nope. The Cruiser's running on fumes."

At the pump, Jake pulled a credit card from his wallet, handed it to her. "Fill it, please. I do have to pee." Jake was fifteen feet from the truck when he stopped, walked back. Nia had the gas nozzle in her hand.

"Nia, just so you know, those calls were purely perfunctory, procedural horseshit. Total waste of man-hours. Sloane was in the wrong place at the wrong time. Period. Nobody from Atlanta or Nashville had a thing to do with this. Bet my life on it. Nobody there knew a thing about the Sunshine Gage case."

Nia removed the gas cap, inserted the nozzle, began pumping. "Okay." Continued listening over the traffic zipping past.

"The Sloane woman stumbled into a killer's backyard. This guy's an ambush predator and right now that man is within thirty miles of us. Guarantee you."

FIFTEEN MINUTES LATER they were introducing themselves to Chief Mackey Lee and Detective David Jernigan in the chief's office of the Orange Beach Police Department. The appointment was for 8:30. Jake and Nia were ten minutes early. The plan was set up. Detective Jernigan would drive Jake and Nia to the scene. See everything in the daylight.

Thirty minutes later they had a list of cams to compare to what OBPD previously found. They also established a search perimeter. Playa del Rio RV Park to the east. Wind Drift condominiums to the west. A half mile out from the abduction site, each way.

Back at the station, Jake said, "Chief, here's what we need. Info on all the homeowners in this one-mile span. Who was in town, who wasn't. Plus all the renters when Sloane was abducted."

Jernigan heard this. "Jake, I agree, but we just don't have the manpower for that kind of thing."

"No problem, no small-town force would, David. The Bureau

will handle that."

Jake stretched, swept his hand through his hair. "David, would you have any room here to stage, say, fifteen guys? All we'd need is some folding tables and Wi-Fi. I think it'd be a couple of weeks, max."

"No problem. We've got two conference rooms. Should work fine."

"Great. Let me grab that video footage you guys pulled, and we'll get out of your way."

SEVEN MILES SOUTH of Black Point, rolling north on US 98, Nia pointed to an old, weathered barn 200 yards off the highway. Oak Hollow Farm. "Went to a wedding reception there eight months ago. Best barbecue I ever ate. Oh, hey, reminds me. My wife Mary is a terrific cook, but everything's inside. I wouldn't mind some smoked meat on occasion. I'd like to set up an outdoor space, get some nice furniture, lights, a fire pit, a grill, that kind of thing. How easy is it to use the Big Jake?"

"Basically, it's idiot-proof, especially with smoking."

"Well, what about the cost on those babies? Is there a friends and family rate?" She drove like Jake, with her left elbow on the door sill, breeze blowing her hair. She glanced toward him, lifted her shades as she asked.

"Not sure. We have to ask my mother."

"Your mother?"

"Keep driving. Her office is three miles up ahead."

Moments later, the Land Cruiser pulled up to a brick-fronted façade of what was nothing more than an industrial metal building. A national-park-sized flagpole flew the logo flags of the Black Point Pirates, Alabama Crimson Tide, and Washington Redskins, all below the stars and stripes.

Jake's adoptive mother, Bonnie, was seated at a large desk behind three computer screens, talking on the phone, a cold tumbler of Coca-Cola beside her. Her desktop was a disaster scene. Purchase orders, staplers, pens, tape dispensers, calendars, and bills she had to pay. Like a desk at a small-town hardware store in 1966. She held up a pointer finger when she saw them.

"Yes, sir, Pastor, they'll leave the factory today. And God bless you, too." She hung up. "Oh, Roll Tide, Pastor. Oh, shoot, he's off the line." She cranked out a smile at her own humor. "Shipping two grills up to a church camp in Blue Ridge, Georgia. Said they need them when they watch the Bulldogs lose on TV to Nick Saban." She barked out a laugh.

"Mama, this is Nia Cruz. She's the Special Agent in Charge of the Mobile office. She wants to know if we have a friends and family rate on grill pricing."

Bonnie was five-four, strawberry blond, and had the figure of a woman who enjoys fatback in her green beans. "Uh-huh. Well, it depends. First things first. Nia, any way you can fire my son from the Bureau? I don't like him working around all those guns. First, it was football. Now it's guns. I'm a walking embarrassment for good mothering."

"Not sure, Ms. Bonnie. But I can start with some highly negative evaluations in a performance review."

"That's a good start. Like the way you think. Make him look like a total incompetent so I can get him back to this grill empire. Now, what model, son? We have the Cheerleader, the National Championship, and the Super Bowl."

"Mama, start with the Super Bowl model and work down."

Bonnie started moving paper around her desk, looking. She opened a spiral notebook, started flipping through pages, occasionally stopping for a brief gander. "Where is that dadgum price sheet? Only three products, you'd think I knew the prices by now." She placed a pair of half-frame readers on her face, looked up at a computer monitor, started tapping on the keyboard. Turned in her chair, glanced at another monitor.

"Okay, got it." She took off her glasses.

"That model's free."

35

EIGHT DAYS LATER. No summer squalls for several days, blue sky under wispy clouds, humidity tolerable. It was seven-twenty in the morning and Lyrene's was full of the breakfast crowd. Patsy Cline singing "Walking After Midnight" in the background.

Jake and his mother sat in a booth in the back, Jake with his back to the door. They were both working on buttermilk waffles and sausage patties when Jake heard a voice.

"Well, lookee here. Bonnie, this boy still trying to pretend he ain't legendary, hiding his rump back here in the weeds?"

Jake stood. "Miss Lyrene, come here girl, I need a hug." Lyrene, eighty-nine years old, was five-two in Walmart work boots and a flour-covered apron, gray hair over bone and gristle, smelling like Marlboros and Oil of Olay.

After a big squeeze, she said, "Jake, I'd have married you right out of junior high school like I did my first husband. That man bedded me every night for ten straight years. Wooo-eee was I into you wild animal types."

Lyrene had told most folks she'd swore off chasing men and dancing once she hit eighty-five, so don't come calling unless you only wanna throw back a couple shots of Wild Turkey.

"Jake, you need a little more butter on that waffle, son. It'll put lead in your pencil. Holler at y'all later, gotta get on back to the stove."

Jake, grinning, took a bite of waffle, then a forkful of sausage. "Mama, that woman is some piece of work, but boy, can she cook." His phone vibrated on the table. Tolleson, in DC. He took a quick swig of tea, answered.

"Mornin', Ross." Bonnie stood, signaled she had to run.

"Hold it, Ross."

"Gotta get to work. Talk to you later, son."

"Okay, I love you. Remember, we're eating at Woo's tonight. Hope's joining us."

Jake was back. "Eating breakfast with my mother. Okay, where are we?"

"I'm about to put the first hundred backgrounds in the cloud for you on the same site Chief Tatum used, as long as you want them to have access."

"Definitely. Anything stick out?"

"Nope. We'll call you if something hinky pops."

"Good work on that."

"Thanks. From now on we're putting them up in real-time. You guys check multiple times daily."

"We're going to be pushed to hit them face to face," said Jake. "I want an alibi for the night of Sloane's abduction, to clear them. Might have you guys do some phone interviews, but not yet. I'm checking out video footage from the beach. Talk soon."

Jake was pulling cash out of his wallet, thinking about the volume of interviews. *Lot of man hours.* Tolleson's crew would handle a substantial portion through phone calls. Jake would use agents out of the Mobile office, a couple of detectives at Black Point PD, and Cruz had eighteen agents shipping into Orange Beach from different field offices.

Jake stared into space a moment, fighting back his worst thought. This ghost has been underground twenty-seven

years.
   We may never grab him.

36

HIGHWAY 30-A, SEASIDE, FLORIDA

NOTHING BUT BLACKNESS due south, save for some lights flickering from a few shrimp trawlers. East and west, in the distance as far as the eye could see, lights twinkled from Gulf-front condo towers. Sunset was an hour ago. Twilight seeped through pinks, reds, lavender, and indigo before seeping into the coal black of night.

Midnight's eyes cautiously stole looks at a blond sitting at a two-top table. She was alone. Unusual for this time and this environment. Tried to hold back the hard stare. *Damn if she didn't look like Sunshine Gage.*

If Sunshine was alive today, he thought, she'd look like this woman. Early forties, full blond hair to her shoulders, tall, maybe five-eight, five-ten, trim arms exposed in a sleeveless, chambray shift. *Flattering on her*, he thought.

MARY JANE MARKHAM stared into the night at the black Gulf water, reflecting. Tequila massaged her thoughts into almost not giving a shit. It was only *almost*. Over and over and over, her mind kept seeing the words from the anonymous email sender on the computer screen.

Sandy is fucking his office manager.

Six words bulldozed her perfect life off a cliff.

Out of high school, Mary Jane received a full academic scholarship to Alabama, pledged Phi Mu, and through sheer will, athleticism, a stunning figure, and exceptionally generous donations to the school by her father, she became a member of the cheerleading squad. An SEC school, not too shabby.

Mary Jane found her guy. Sandy Hopkins. A sleekly built, tall, dark-haired KA who also swam for the Crimson Tide. One fine specimen. And he was accepted to UAB's dental school. A tall, beautiful blond and her taller, handsome husband, *a doctor.*

In Dothan, Alabama, Mary Jane and Sandy lived in an expansive brick home fronting the course at the country club. They had a boy and a girl who could be *Town and Country* cover children. Their 401ks were swelling up. Everyone was healthy and happy.

Until the email.

Was it real? Can't be. Sandy teaches eighth-grade boys Sunday school.

Mary Jane did what well-to-do women do. Hired a private investigator. Google found her a man in Tallahassee, close, but not too close. He was a retired homicide and white-collar crime detective, a wily son of a bitch who was dead certain everybody on the planet was lying.

He worked fast. Oh, it was real, he said. But it wasn't one woman.

The detective found twelve.

MIDNIGHT DIDN'T COME here for action; he came for dinner. *But now ... life was happening. ...* Sunshine all grown up. Like, somehow, it was only a dream he killed her as a teenager.

The sight of the woman caused spasms in his gut. Hate was cranking. So hard to control. It burned like a blue-flamed torch. He glanced around the room as he took a sip of wine. *Can anyone tell?*

His thoughts drifted back. *Sunshine's sixteen-year-old body. Never had he seen anything so beautiful. She cried, she begged, she fought.*

Right now he was on the rooftop bar of Bud & Alley's, a trattoria perched on a dune overlooking the Gulf. Of Mexico. Wafts of a gentle sea breeze twisted the candlelight. With a little imagination, one could get a whiff of pecan and oak wood burning in the pizza oven, sifting through the sound of Van Morrison singing "Into the Mystic." Everybody on the deck in some room of their happy place.

He knew he should leave. Knew it. But he couldn't. Pressure bolted him to his seat, watching her. She'd picked at her salad, mostly staring toward the water. Lost in thought.

Alone.

A thin, gold necklace with a single large diamond encircled her neck. Gold open-loop earrings drew attention to feminine ears. A watch hung loosely on her left wrist, a trio of bracelets on her right. The watch had some heft to it, the band stainless and gold. Had to be a Rolex. *Cartier nonsense,* he thought, *all of it.* With the watch, could be twenty-five grand worth of jingle on her.

A controller. Had to be a whore to get all the bling.

The dining area was saturated with them. Rich bitches coming to Seaside. All rolling around in their Mercedes or Range Rovers, spending money, getting their way.

And here was grown-up Sunshine.

And she was ... all ... alone.

37

MIDNIGHT COUNTED THREE margaritas. Only a single slice of pizza along with the high alcohol intake. Wouldn't have a bit of fight in her. Felt her weakness in his groin. Squeezed his thighs together, massaging his power.

Thought about stepping over and talking to her. *Why all the contemplation, princess?*

Why not? The restaurant was crowded, everybody soaking in their own sense of importance. Nobody gives a damn about anyone else. Who'd really notice?

Cameras are why not.

He'd spotted four.

Midnight made the first move.

He paid and left.

A HYPERWRINKLED OLD BALD man sat in a happy red Adirondack chair, directly across the street from Bud & Alley's, working slowly through a shaved ice called "Nuclear Waste." He wore an untucked, blue-checked button-down shirt under a British driving cap.

Midnight needed the ice. The mask went over his neck and down under his shirt and was hot as hell. Had to cool down. When he left the restaurant he went straight to his car, drove it a hundred yards away, parked in some shadows on a side

Midnight Man

street, changed shirts, added the mask and cap, speed-walked back. A small backpack was at his feet.

His brain was tangled with desire, neurons sparking off energy shocks like fireworks. Felt it in his chest, under his arms. Dampness. Sweat caused his shirt to stick to the chair.

A platoon of whimsical Airstream trailers was parked in a row behind him, repurposed as food vendors. On the amphitheater lawn, behind the Airstreams, a hundred or so people sat listening to three directionless beach hippies strum out acoustic cover tunes. "Horse With No Name" in the air. America. The crowd sang along.

Seaside, Florida, was a fairy-tale experience. Cottages and stores and restaurants were huddled close together, seemingly in an intimate way, like you could wrap your arms around it, hug it. The lone beach road, County 30-A, tiptoed between the beachfront and "downtown" Seaside. People treated it as a wide sidewalk. Traffic was thinning at this hour, rolling barely faster than people walked.

One worrisome thought raced through his brain. Did she leave when he moved his car? *Wasting time?*

He almost left but didn't.

Oh, oh ... There she was.

Blondie walked seventy feet from the restaurant, stopped at the road, looked both ways, began moving after a Jeep and a Bentley passed.

Midnight couldn't take his eyes off her. Light bounce of her breasts with her loose stroll. Legs lean but firm. Pictured her in a spinning class or yoga or Pilates or whatever the hell, in Buckhead or Mountain Brook. Maintaining the power-bitch body as she peeked over the fence at middle age.

She walked right by him, glanced down with an insouciant smile, didn't break stride. He spotted the tiniest of lines around her eyes. *Too almighty to mumble a "hello," are you?*

A light scent of jasmine and sea-spray perfume trailed her. *Naturally. Seducing hapless men as your prey.*

Adrenaline rushed through his body at the smell of her. Made him feel like a Viking home from the sea.

Gonna hurt you. And oh will I love it. Pressure continued to build between his legs. His eyes monitored nearby stragglers as he slid his hand across his crotch.

She was forty feet past him when he stood. The backpack was in his hand, one he retrieved from the trunk of his car.

He locked his eyes on her and thought he saw a lilt in her stride. An alcohol wobble. *Oh yeah, mama.* Felt lightning shoot down his spine.

Seaside was a quirky agglomeration of over 400 unique, pastel-colored beach cottages. Everything was picket fences, bicycles, ice cream, clear-blue water, white sand, and beautiful children with beautiful parents. A living, breathing Hallmark movie.

And so deliciously perfect for a murder.

Seaside would leave anyone with the impression they were in the safest place on the planet. But, oh no. No. No. No. Midnight knew by the end of the evening Quentin Tarantino would be directing the film and he'd be Samuel L. Jackson. Satan in the flesh.

Ain't that right, MUTHA-FUCKA!

38

MIDNIGHT AMBLED ON with a carefree stroll, slowly following the woman's indecisive meandering from a distance. Blondie weaved deeply into the web of streets and alleyways like she wasn't sure where she was heading, past cottages with playful names like "PB&J" and "Stairway to Heaven."

Smolian Street to Grayton Street to Forest Street. Walking past eight houses on Forest, she twisted loosely down a gravel walkway to reach a guest suite behind the main home.

Midnight walked by, barely a sideways glance at the place. No lights on in houses flanking the cottage, nor the main home. *Perfect.*

All systems GO! Squeezed his eyes tight, fighting a scream. Felt like he'd been doused with lighter fluid and torched off with a thick-wooded fireplace match.

Three couples walked behind him, two houses away. Conversation loud, all boozed up, carefree. Certainly, he thought, they weren't focusing on him. He picked up speed, increasing the distance.

Think, think, think. Finish it in the house ... or take her on the road? Didn't have the van. *So what?* Cops were what. Bad karma was what. *Flat tire. DUI check. Fender bender. All bad.* Settled it. The house.

Four houses later, the voices behind him died as they wound off the street and onto the porch of their cottage. Midnight heard a screen door slap, glanced back. Nobody.

Dead silence and starlight.

He walked to the far reaches of streetlamp glow, where the shadows begin, and cut through the yard of a dark cottage.

Behind the row of homes was a natural brush mangrove of scrub pine, palmetto, wax myrtle, pine straw, and railroad vines. It was thick, thorny, left to grow wild. *Awww, hell.* Made him think of rattlesnakes coiled under the palmetto, ready to strike.

Heart hammering with desire, he thought, *Screw snakes.*

Wished he had safety glasses for this jungle march, but he didn't. The woman was nine houses down. He kept count. In the brush, he began to move slowly toward the cottage, very slowly, hand in front of his face, eyes dilated, soaking in what little ambient light there was. Jumped occasionally at the bite of a briar. Heard his feet crunch the dry brush as he walked, sounding like a bobcat slinking out of the woods.

Reaching the cottage, he stood dead still, watched, and listened in the dark.

A dangerous black shadow.

Lights were on. Blinds open. He spotted her placing a glass into the refrigerator door, filling it with ice. She wore the same dress. Figured she might have relaxed into her pajamas when she walked in the door, but no.

He unzipped the backpack, pulled out a yellow T-shirt and red hat. He'd bought them before leaving the restaurant. Didn't know he'd be wearing them tonight—he just liked T-shirts. He unbuttoned his shirt, removed it, stuffed it in the backpack, pulled the T-shirt over his head. The shirt had a graphic silhouette of a dog, Bud, and a cat, Alley.

Bud & Alley's. Good Food. Good People. Good Times, it said.

Good place to meet your killer.

39

MIDNIGHT WAITED. WATCHED. Water weeds in the brush, full of flying insects. With a whiff, he blew them away from his face. Mary Jane was talking on her cell, a serious look on her face.

"Fran, thirty minutes ago I made up my mind." She was FaceTiming an old friend, a Phi Mu sister, now living twenty-five miles from her in Abbeville, Alabama. In her mind, Fran Morelock was the sanest woman she knew.

"I'm dumping that perverted cocksucker."

Fran grimaced at Mary Jane's vulgarity. She'd never heard her talk like that. It was the alcohol, was all.

"I'm about to ram a rod so far up Sandy's ass he'll think he's in prison." Fran smiled at that one, said nothing.

"Listen to this." Mary Jane laughed. "Oh, this is so priceless. Monday morning, four days from now, I will arrive at the dental office fifteen minutes after Sandy starts his day. My attorney will be with me with divorce papers. A cop friend of his will be with him *in his friggin' police car, lights flashing.* A locksmith will be with us to change out the locks. His helper will be at my house changing the locks. I own the dental building. There's no lease. Every bit of Sandy's crap will be thrown on the street."

Fran's mind spun at this drunken revelation. The Christian

part of her soul wanted to say, "Wait a minute, Mary Jane, let's really think this through. There're children to think about." The less Christian part of her said, "Tear his ass apart, girl."

"Now, here's the fun part, Fran. I'm about to call Uber, have them drive me over to the Red Bar in Grayton Beach. With any luck, a hot young guy will be screwin' my eyeballs out in two hours."

Get off the phone ... get off the phone ... get off the phone. Midnight's body shook, he couldn't wait any longer. Testosterone had him feeling like was going to crash through the window, destroy the room.

Mary Jane heard a tap on the door.

"Fran, I've got to run. Uber's here. Call you in the morning."

Mary Jane grabbed her purse. Ten steps later, at the door, she thought, *I don't even remember using the Uber app.*

"Who is it?"

"Ma'am, it's David Daniels, a manager at Bud & Alley's. You forgot your credit card."

She glanced quickly through the blinds, saw an old man wearing a yellow Bud & Alley's shirt. A red baseball cap covered his head.

She placed her fingers on the deadbolt, unlocked it with a twist. Two thoughts raced through her alcohol fog at that moment.

I know I have my credit card. How do they know where I'm staying?

The door slammed into Mary Jane's face.

A bear-claw-sized hand seized her throat while two raging eyes bored through her skull.

"There you are, Sunshine."

MARY JANE TRIED to scream. Nothing. Not a wheeze. Not a baby's breath. Not a whistle. Airway slammed shut. Midnight winched down his grip on her throat.

He kicked the door shut with his heel, then flicked his fingers across a wall switch, dousing lights in the living area. The suite was tiny, a little efficiency attached by a portico to the main unit, a two-story cottage painted a tranquil lavender, named *Sweet Dreams*.

Mary Jane was caught off guard by the intrusion. Now off-balance, Midnight easily shoved her fifteen feet back to the kitchenette area. She grunted as her back slammed into the edge of the counter.

Midnight pulled out drawers until he found the knives. He discovered a fillet knife, a utensil with a thin, curved, nine-inch blade. It was an appalling weapon.

He directed the point right under her chin at the edge of her throat with just enough pressure to release a drop of blood. "If you scream ... this knife goes all the way into your brain ... do you understand?" Midnight's deep voice reverberated through her bones. He had eight inches in height and ninety-five pounds on her. She was tiny under his heft.

She nodded.

He released his grip on her throat, slowly. Her head slumped forward. She coughed several times, tried to stop.

"Why are you doing this?" She spoke hoarsely, through fearful tears. "Don't hurt me, please don't hurt me. I have two children. They're amazing and beautiful. They need me." She couldn't stop shaking. *This happens to other people.*

"You're amazing and beautiful. Why wouldn't they be?" He softened his tone. But inside? He was coiled like a cobra, ready to strike. Wished she'd make a move.

He dumped supplies from his backpack and quickly wrapped duct tape over her mouth and around the back of her head.

Her face flushed with horror. She pushed against his chest,

feeling thick muscle. He didn't budge. She bolted to his side, tried to slip past. His fist slammed into her right cheek like a brick, sending her to the floor.

Bruising appeared immediately. She was disoriented, moaning, semi-conscious.

Midnight's gloved hands slipped inside her dress at the top of her cleavage. A strong tug ripped apart the chambray, exposing her bra and panties. He ripped until the dress was completely open in the front.

"You're a trim little mommy bitch." He put his fingertips in the top of her panties, tugged. She flailed as they left her legs.

He flipped her, ripped her open dress down her arms, tossed it behind him. She flinched, reorienting herself.

"Be still, bitch." Fast as a lightning strike, his right fist flew down in a roundhouse arc, smashing into her kidney. Searing pain caused her to vomit. But her mouth was taped closed. Yellow bile shot from her nose. Smelled like wine and salad dressing.

He unhooked her bra, pulled it like he was starting a lawnmower. She flipped onto her belly. Nylon flex-cuffs were slipped over her wrists and ankles.

He pictured his mother, all those years ago. Her filthy, spooge-filled twat had looked like she was dripping bacon lard after whoring sessions. What she made him do! Clean it. *Git yo fat ass down and lick it, boy. Kiss it all clean.*

His rage caught fire.

Ten minutes later. Now Miss Mary Jane was strapped down on a queen-sized bed. Her arms were pulled back over her head, still in flex cuffs. Parachute cord stretched from the bedposts to her wrists, locking down her arms.

He uncuffed her ankles, ready to spread her open, tie her to the bedposts. She rolled, kicked, and fought. Midnight picked up the fillet knife, made sure she saw it. He lifted her right breast, placed the razor-sharp blade at the base.

"Your titty ain't no match for this blade. You want a breast reduction, or do you want the rope?"

She stilled her legs. He splayed her thighs open to the point she could easily deliver a child, cinched her ankles to the bedposts with rope.

He hopped off the bed, spotted a satellite radio on the dresser. Four small speakers in the room. He turned it on. "Nice." He popped around some of the SiriusXM preset channels. Stopped on *Symphony Hall.*

He glanced back at Mary Jane. "That's better. I like working to music. This should comfort both of us." He bumped the volume. Violin Concerto No. 1 in A Minor, B.

"Bach. Excellent."

Everything went bright. Vivid colors exploded in his brain. He felt like he was outside his body, watching an IMAX film. Like something terrorizing from Wes Craven with that Freddy Krueger psycho. Dangerous as hell. Smiled at that, *Freddy Krueger.* He swayed with the violins as he dug into his backpack. A brown glass bottle emerged in his hand.

Lab-grade hydrochloric acid, 100 milliliters.

Next, he removed two 10-milliliter syringes and two 18-gauge needles. Then two small vials containing 10 milliliters of clear liquid. Insulin.

He drew one full vial into each syringe with the 18-gauge needle. One-hundred units in each syringe. He laid both syringes on the bed.

Midnight picked up the bottle of acid, humming along with the melodic string music as he unscrewed the cap. He got on the bed, on his knees, looking down intently at Mary Jane's vagina. Smooth as a baby. He held the bottle in front of her face.

She read the label, started bucking. Tried to roll over.

Midnight Man

"Look who's here, mama, your boy, little fat fuck." Midnight's voice changed, raised an octave. "Remember me? Remember all those bad names you called me? Well, I ain't fat anymore. Here, lessee if we can clean you up some. Get your little bald tuna smelling all sweet again."

Forgot the funnel. "Damn." He tweaked her lips open with his left hand. *Careful now. Careful.*

Springsteen's words came to mind. Midnight had hundreds of songs locked in his head. Mumbling like sheets soaking wet and a freight train in the middle of your head, or some such.

Vaginal tissue so thin, so delicate, completely exposed to this corrosive acid.

Mary Jane couldn't control her tremors. A terrible cold wave flushed through her. The whole bed rumbled. Midnight removed his left hand, began covering the outer lips with acid. The skin reddened, jumped at him, like a crab boiling on the stove. He emptied the rest of the bottle covering an area two inches outside the vagina.

In minutes the tissue degraded into a third-degree chemical burn, the caustic contents raging deep into the dermis.

"Getting' clean, now, mama. Gonna kill all that demon seed in you. Getting you all spic 'n' span, wash 'n' wear." Fumes of acid misted off the tissue.

He retrieved a chair from the kitchen, placed it at the side of the bed, sat, and thought about the insulin. It was a fast-acting insulin. Peak onset in fifteen minutes.

"Insulin, mama. A miracle in small doses. Murder in large doses." He winced. "Got you a nice large dose." He emptied a full syringe into the fat on her thigh.

He took a seat, rubbed a hand over his crotch, felt the rage. Heat thrummed through his body. His fingers vibrated as they tugged his zipper down. He took hold of himself, feeling uncontrolled exhilaration.

In seven minutes, perspiration covered Mary Jane's body. Her eyes were open. "Dizzy. What is it?"

Midnight didn't answer. He watched. And glowed. And knew he was a master of the universe.

Eleven minutes. "Head hurts, can't see."

He smiled. *"Aren't you glad, mama? Aren't you glad I'm your sweet little fatass?"*

Nine minutes later, her words were garbled.

Thirty-four minutes after the injections, she began seizing. Convulsions followed, her muscles wrenched in pain. Eyelids twitched. Pupils darted.

"Getting' the picture, mama? Things ain't gonna work out."

Convulsions came and went, their intervals lengthening.

At sixty-seven minutes, Mary Jane's body was still. Eyes open, pupils fixed. He felt her carotid pulse, first the left, then the right. Thought, *Maybe a blip.* He pulled a stethoscope from his backpack, placed the ear tips in his ears, listened to her chest. Heartbeat faint, barely discernible.

Comatose. Caused by desperately low blood sugar.

Huh. Glanced at the time on a clock radio. This could take a while.

Do it.

He pinched her nostrils closed with his left hand. Placed his right hand over her mouth. Held firm for four minutes. Let go. Listened with his stethoscope.

Dead.

Two-twelve in the morning. *Long night,* he thought. *Almost over.*

He removed two plastic tissue-sample bottles. They held Formalin.

Midnight deviated. He left her back intact. With tissue forceps in his left hand, he clamped onto the ravaged left labia majora. With the fillet knife in his right hand, he carved the tissue away from the body. He did the same with the right. Placed the samples in the fluid.

Lanced off the areolas, too.

Thought about his tissue collection stored in the dark, dry closet at home.

Hey girls, meet Mary Jane.

Midnight slid out of town as silent as night fog. No credit card usage. Cash only. No battery in his phone. No signals pinging cell towers. His digital footprint was like stepping in water. Small splash, then gone.

Nobody there.

40

JAKE'S EYES FELT strained, like he'd been staring into the sun for three straight hours. He squinched them closed, hoping to force out the fatigue. Since 7:00 a.m. he'd been studying video from the Flora-Bama area. Stopping and starting, replaying, scribbling notes onto legal pads. Everything about it was exhausting.

He sat in his mother's kitchen, ambient piano music streaming in the background, the soft, sweet smell of African violets coming from atop the windowsill. Diet Coke bottles, energy bar wrappers, a cell phone, and three legal pads lay scattered across the table. He glanced at his watch. Three-ten in the afternoon. He had hours to go, maybe days. Exhaling wearily, he said to no one, "This is getting old."

His eyes spotted the single white pill on the table. Ten milligrams of amphetamine. It was prescribed to be used as needed, mainly for the heat of the hunt, when sleep is a luxury. Right now there was a maniac on the loose. Time is life. Had to get through the video.

Nia had spotted four cameras the Orange Beach Police missed.

Popped the pill in his mouth, took a swig of Coke, stood up, and stretched. Needed a break. Kayaking, or a run? Both, he decided.

He walked into the bathroom, brushed his teeth, splashed cold water on his face. Felt better already. Already in hiking shorts and a T-shirt, he sat and pulled on socks, tied on running shoes.

His phone began to ring, he grabbed it, looked at the number. Local, no ID. "Hello."

"This is Elaine Starr, calling from Page and Palette Bookstore. I'm trying to reach Jake Montoya."

"I'm Jake."

"I just wanted to remind you that your book is here behind the counter, *The Boys.*"

"Mrs. Starr, I completely forgot. My Opie Taylor book. I'll be there in ten minutes."

"That'll be just fine."

Pleasant voice, he thought. His mind crafted an image of a teacher, history, maybe English. A tall, exceedingly thin woman with a long, graceful neck, permanently encircled by a stylish chain holding her eyeglasses. Always in a dress, modest heels, and her gray hair pulled into a bun.

JAKE PARKED THE Land Cruiser in an angled spot at the front door of The Black Point Store, a place selling caps, tees, and gear advertising the town. He killed the engine, shutting down Seger and "Night Moves," walked across Del La Mare Avenue, opened a door and walked into the Black Point landmark.

Violin music in the background. Scent of rosemary in the air. Suddenly the world was a better place. He walked twenty feet up to the cashier's space, caught the eye of a twenty-something, bookish female with a pencil behind her ear and a tattoo on her neck.

"I'm looking for Mrs. Starr." The young woman pointed to a lady straightening a display table.

Jake approached her. "Mrs. Starr?"

She turned. "Yes?"

Jake was looking at a late-sixty-something woman with a broad bottom, wide shoulders, and a fleshy face, a woman who had never invoked jealousy in other females. A cheerfully colored top and easy smile lent a small-town friendliness to her.

"I'm Jake Montoya ... here to pick up the book."

"Of course."

At the counter, Starr ran Jake's credit card, placed the book in a bag. "I have to tell you—I took a peek inside when I had a free minute. I liked what I read. I grew up on Andy Griffith and loved little Opie."

"Looking forward to it. Listen, Mrs. Starr, I'm in the FBI, working a case here. It has some bearing on one your husband worked years ago. Could I make an appointment to speak with you for a few minutes?"

Mrs. Starr looked at the watch on her wrist, a fading, gold Timex that had probably cost nine bucks thirty years ago. "I opened this morning and am due for lunch. How about now?"

"Perfect."

"Follow me." She grabbed a brown bag and a tumbler of tea from below the counter and walked him to another room labeled the Book Cellar, a room with a bar and ample space for author signings.

The room was empty. They took a seat at a table. Mrs. Starr pulled a chicken salad sandwich and a baggie of grapes from her sack. Jake was patient as she started on the food. After her first bite and a sip of tea, she got the jump on him.

After dabbing a napkin daintily across her lips, she said, "Jake, I'm so happy to meet you. I've known who you were since you were in the ninth grade, playing on the high school team. My late husband Bill took me and Billy to every game, and he watched every Bama game he could on TV if he wasn't in Tuscaloosa with our son." She smiled at the memory. "Bill used to say, 'I like this Montoya kid, always plays it smart.' He thought you were incredible. Wished he was here with us right now."

The smile faded, leaving only wistful nostalgia in her voice. Jake saw the lasting love for him in her eyes.

"Wow. Thank you so much for those kind words ... and that memory." Jake changed gears with his tone. More businesslike. "I wish he was here, too, Mrs. Starr. I could really use his expertise. We've got a bad situation out there."

"I know what it's about. Sunshine Gage. And that Sloane woman. Just a tragedy. Billy told me y'all wanted to talk to me."

He nodded. "That's right. Need to dig into your memory. Would you mind telling me what you remember about the Gage case?"

Starr put down her sandwich, looked at Jake with sad eyes. "Bottom line, I can tell you this. The sweet girl's death also killed my husband. I mean literally. I'm one hundred percent sure of it."

Her son hadn't expressed that thought. He let her talk.

"See, Jake, Black Point had almost no murders. Just a peaceful town, you know that. Then Sunshine. Bill was the lead detective and he'd never seen anything like that. Neither had Ham Mosley, the chief at the time. The Gage girl was from a prominent family, I know you're close with them, you know that. But it was the pressure, it was tremendous. Bill couldn't sleep, started drinking every night ... then his heart ..." Her hands went up in defeat. "Bill took it too personally, like he was the only one that could break the case. His heart couldn't take it ... just couldn't handle the stress."

Jake saw the moisture in her eyes. He didn't expect this, the widow's pain after all these years. Decided to cut the interview short, come back, and visit with her later, probably with her son, Billy.

Jake knew Bill Starr had worked the case hard because he, Jake, had been interviewed intensely on two occasions, getting roughed up verbally, like he had been in on killing his girlfriend. His memory of Detective Bill Starr was of a peckerwood asshole. Jake had an unbreakable alibi the whole time. He was with Sunshine's brother and father.

New facts from Elaine Starr reshaped his opinion. Bill Starr was the consummate cop, eating, sleeping, and breathing the case until it came back and ate him alive.

"Mrs. Starr, Billy said your husband would talk to you about his cases."

"He did," she nodded, "to let off steam."

"Ma'am, I apologize, this wasn't the best time to talk, while you're working. But I was wondering, what's your bottom-line take on things, as Bill explained them to you?"

Elaine Starr regained her composure. She looked across the room at the bar, thinking. Her eyes then glanced through the plate-glass window, in a trance, not even seeing the cars flow by.

She shifted her gaze back to Jake. "Okay. Bottom line. Bill thought it was one man, or maybe two, and they weren't from Black Point. He interviewed every single employee of the Magnolia Hotel multiple times. He couldn't pin a hint of suspicion on anyone, and worse, nobody saw a thing. Nobody."

Jake thought, *Bullshit. Somebody knows something. Saw something. They just might not understand what they saw.*

"Your husband interviewed me, very thoroughly, I might add. Did he mention any other students he may have interviewed? What they may have said?"

"No. But weren't you there for the assembly? Bill went to the high school and spoke to the student body."

Midnight Man

He snapped his fingers, pointed at her. "That's right! I completely forgot about that. Honestly, Mrs. Starr, I've tried to forget all of it over the years. But, yeah, I remember that. He instructed everyone to write down a phone number. He called it a hotline, or a tip line, or something. Said everything was anonymous."

"Bill never thought it could be a student. Just wouldn't happen in Black Point, he said. But, *IF*, if it was a student, he was sure somebody would blab about it. Said nobody could keep a killing secret, no high school kid, anyway."

"What came in?"

"Malarkey, that's what. Pranksters. Some female said the principal did it. Happens that he was at Disney that weekend with his wife and kids. Another girl called and said *you* did it. Well, you checked out. And some boy called and said a mad scientist did it. That's all I recall."

Jake's mind was on the girl for the moment, naming him. *Had to be Tonda Whitworth.* She was always pissed he didn't ask her out. *Out of proportion pissed.* Told him once she might accidentally have sex on the first date if he took her to Pizza Hut. He had already been under the mistaken impression that all girls put out on the first date, whether it was Pizza Hut or the bowling alley.

"Mad scientist? What was that about?"

"I have no idea. Bill didn't either. He felt it was just some punk jerking his chain. A smart butt."

"Huh. Jerks everywhere. Well, Mrs. Starr, I better get outta your way. Thanks so much for your time."

They both stood. "It was so good to meet you, Jake. I sure hope you and Billy can run this guy down."

"We're bringing some big heat in. Two similar cases make this a very different situation. Sadly, Bill didn't have access to what we'll be bringing."

JAKE WALKED OUT of the bookstore into a wall of Gulf Coast humidity, hustled across Del La Mare, hopped into the Land Cruiser, twisted the key. Jagger blasted out of the speakers. He killed the sound. Cat feet tiptoed across his brain. *Something.* He couldn't pull it together. *Think.*

He waited on three cars to pass, then drove the Cruiser out of the space. He eased down to the stop sign at Church Street. He cut left and drove sixty yards to an old Black Point school built in 1925.

And the haze cleared.

A mad scientist.

The bodies were assaulted with bleach, hydrochloric acid, and poison.

A mad scientist.

Did the caller *know* the mad scientist?

Or was the *caller* the mad scientist?

41

"JAKE, IT'S MARK Benton. Can you take a ride with me?" It was 6:50 in the morning. Montoya was sitting at his mother's kitchen table with a plate of scrambled eggs and two toasted waffles in front of him. Thirty minutes earlier he'd been working out with Woo Chow on the bluff overlooking the bay.

It was Woo who had introduced Jake at age twelve to Jeet Kune Do, Bruce Lee's hybrid martial art.

"If you're calling this early it must be important. But, yeah, I can go. What's cooking?"

Benton was mid-thirties, a ten-year veteran of the Bureau, based in Mobile. "Back in high school, do you remember a teacher named Leonard Bascom?"

A puzzled expression crossed his face as he put his fork down. "Yeah."

"I was going through Tolleson's latest uploads. Bascom's file hit about midnight. Looks like Tolleson's crew is putting in long days, popping up files in real-time."

"They better be. I was going to log on in about twenty minutes. Eating right now."

"Looks like Bascom would have been approaching age thirty or so at the time of the Gage incident. Do you have any recollection of him attending the birthday party?"

Jake picked up a glass of Diet Coke, took a swig, winced at

his girlfriend's murder referred to as an *incident*. Forcing the thought away, he stepped back into his memory bank. Heard Sunshine singing at her party. Smelled dope smoke drifting over the pool. Pictured Dr. Gage in a Hawaiian shirt, flipping burgers on the grill.

"Don't remember seeing him. Got a couple of people I can ask, see what they recall. Why?"

"Bascom has quite a history. The latest is, he was released four months ago from Santa Rosa Correctional in Milton, Florida. Three-year stint for aggravated sexual assault. Listen to this. He doped up a woman with ketamine at some beach bar over in Fort Walton Beach, took her to a hotel, stripped her down ... and that's all she remembered. But, but, but ... she woke up the next day completely naked, with spray paint on her."

"Spray paint?"

"Yep, this freak painted concentric red circles around her vagina. The circles extended down onto her thighs and belly. Like a bullseye."

"Raped?"

"Nope. She went to the ER. No semen, no hair on a rape kit. No vaginal trauma. Her pocketbook was in the room, but her driver's license was gone. A souvenir, I guess."

"Address for Bascom?"

"Yep. Some apartments, just off 29 in the Ensley area of Pensacola, about a mile north of I-10. Reportedly has a job at a hardware store a couple of miles away."

"Hell yeah, let's take a ride. There's a Hampton Inn at the Highway 98 exit in Daphne, on your right as you pull off. I can be there at 7:45."

"See you there."

In a daze, Jake took his plate to the microwave, reheated it, took it back to the table. He picked at his food, thinking.

Makes sense. But is it going to be this easy? Leonard Bascom? Skinny Lenny. Tall guy, around six-five, thin but with a natural fitness about him. Had prominent veins in his forearms, and big hands, he recalled. Mousy brown hair, mousy brown mustache, metal frame glasses. An odd duck. General reputation as a squirrelly geek.

But smart.

Taught chemistry and biology. Made it difficult. Had a cockiness to his knowledge. Took his job seriously.

Bleach, hydrochloric acid, strychnine. And ketamine.

A mad scientist.

Needed to speak to Kimbo. Jake glanced at the time. Still early, 7:10. He cleaned his plate, brushed his teeth, shaved, jumped in the shower.

Twenty-five minutes later he was at the light at Morphy and 98, next to the hospital. He tapped Kimbo's contact on his phone. Answered as the light turned green.

"Good timing, I just finished neutering a goldendoodle. Those hybrids are taking over the town."

"Got a question for you that I hate to ask."

"I can handle it. Shoot."

"The night of Sunshine's birthday party. Did you see Leonard Bascom there, the chem teacher?"

Twenty seconds of silence. "You there?"

"I'm here. Thinking. Skinny Lenny. Yes, he was there. I know that for an absolute fact."

"Why are you that sure? I didn't see him."

Kimbo chuckled. "Remember how we used to joke he was probably banging Mrs. Beck, the English teacher?"

Jake laughed. "Jane Beck. Yeah, but she was at least twenty years older than him."

"No, no, ten to twelve at the most. But, man, she had those

long legs, always strolling around in heels. Skinny Lenny always seemed to be sniffing around her. And he was supposedly married, but nobody ever saw his wife, not that I remember. Maybe he wasn't married. But I saw him talking to her that evening, Jane. Definitely in her space as he chatted."

"You know, it's starting to come back. I think I remember her there. But this is important. Are you 100 percent positive Lenny was there?"

"Yes, here's why. He spotted me watching them, broke away, just for a moment. Like nothing was up. Asked me if I was going to Tulane or Auburn. And he said I was damn good in science, knew I'd do well, wouldn't have a problem getting into vet school. Schmoozing me, taking my mind off him and Mrs. Beck. It was the compliment, mainly. You don't forget compliments, and that meant something coming from him. He was weird, but he seemed brilliant. So what's the deal? Why are you asking?"

Jake was braking at the red light in front of Target. "Lenny did three years for aggravated sexual assault in Florida. Got out six months ago. Don't know much more than that. Another agent and I are going to speak to him right now."

"What? You don't think ..."

"Don't know, Kimbo. Taking a fresh look at everything."

"Well, look closely. Oh, I was going to call you today. I ran into Elijah Washington at Ace Hardware yesterday."

"No kidding. Funny you mention him. I just put some money in his pocket. I had breakfast at Sweet E's Pork Chop Biscuits. Good stuff."

"Looks like he's kicking it with the pork-chop gig. I invited him over to eat Saturday night. Told him you were in town. He seemed excited to hear that. How about you and Hope joining us?"

"I'd love to. Is he bringing his wife?"

"Not married, he said."
"Okay. Text me a time."
"Will do."

He rang off, tapped up Hope Hiassen's number. Texted: ***Dinner at Kimbo and Jan's Saturday. Old buddy who played high school ball with me joining us. He played at Auburn, finished up a pro career with the Cowboys.***

Response in two minutes: ***Love me some football players.***

42

AGENT BENTON, A fresh-faced man with olive skin, a tight, dark haircut, and an angular facial structure, pushed the government Ford up to eighty on I-10. The eastern sun was in the air, a harsh white ball.

"Thank God for the guy who invented sunglasses." Benton looked like he was born to wear dark aviators.

"I didn't have time to scan the file. What else was happening there?" said Jake.

Benton pulled out a pack of Juicy Fruit, held it up to Montoya. "Gum?"

"Sure. Thanks."

Both men unwrapped the foil, tossed a piece in their mouth. "Bascom has been married and divorced twice. Both divorces were quick and uncomplicated. No children, both women worked, no assets to fight over. Looking at a timeline, the first divorce was about a year after the Gage murder. Bascom moved to Auburn, Alabama, took a job teaching science at Opelika High School."

"Why'd he leave Black Point?"

"Not sure. We only have the basics, but there's something below the surface, I feel it. Look, back to the wives again. We need to track them down. Wife number one, married three years, went silently in the night, as far as we know."

"She might still be in Black Point."

"I hope so. Married to wife number two for eighteen months. This was in Auburn. Three domestic calls to the residence. Files said, somewhat vaguely, he wanted her to participate in what she referred to as unnatural sex acts." Benton looked over at Jake. "You know, the kind of stuff you're into."

Jake laughed. "Huh. Getting interesting." Jake tensed, thinking about Bascom touching Sunshine. Rushed the thought out of his mind.

"Definitely. Anyway, wife two moved out, got a restraining order, and filed for divorce."

"Any addresses for them?"

"Nothing we know as current."

"Give me a minute." Jake pulled out his phone, tapped Tolleson's contact. Fast answer. "Ross, how's life in DC?"

"I'm on the Outer Banks right now. Hot, but a great breeze off the Atlantic."

"Getting along with your housemates?" Jake laughed at the question.

"Everything's good. One of the guy's is a great cook. We're doing a little surf fishing in an hour or so, then chartering an offshore trip in the morning, leaving out of Hatteras Harbor."

"Won't hold you. Need your guys on something, today if possible. The file on Leonard Bascom, a teacher, hit about midnight. The guy had two ex-wives. Need you to locate them, get me some contact information."

"I'll shoot the team an email right now."

"In a few minutes, a Mobile agent and I will be speaking to Bascom."

"He look good for it? Bascom?"

"Definitely has some qualities. Gotta run."

They blew past a Cracker Barrel, several hotels, and a Waffle House. Seconds later, Benton steered the sedan off the interstate at the Highway 29 exit, turned left at the light, Pensacola Boulevard, headed north.

It was a commercial corridor with the usual suspects: fast food, banks, car lots, pharmacies, and nail shops. At two miles they passed a grocery store, an auto parts store, a quick oil change spot, and another auto parts store.

Morton's Building Supply was on the left. Benton swung into the parking lot, killed the engine. The place was a tan metal building with a seedy warehouse look to it, not even half the size of a Home Depot. There was a lumber yard behind the structure with a forklift operator zipping across the yard carrying a load of framing lumber.

"Kinda looks like a dump, but they're doing a hell of a business," said Benton. Mostly pickups in the parking lot with a scattering of mommy SUVs.

"Family operation, has to be. This place goes way back. It's the kind of spot I'd use. Now, put on your cop face, Mark."

In the building, Montoya went straight to the closest cashier, a woman with tattoos on both forearms, boyishly cut bleached-blond hair with a glaze of neon green on top, and a build that looked like she could tote a stack of two-by-tens on her shoulder. Nametag read "Serenity."

"Ma'am, we're looking for a manager."

Serenity's eyes took a walk over both men, then focused on the badge and pistol both men wore on their hips. "Call me a fuckin' palm reader or whatever, but I'm guessing y'all are cops."

"FBI."

"Good timing, for me that is." She popped her eyebrows up. "I was thinking about applying with you guys. I can knock a deer down at two hundred yards. And I could blow someone's drawers to shreds with my Ruger 9 at forty feet."

Benton and Montoya looked at each other, a glint of a smile in their eyes. Benton fielded the inquiry. "The Bureau's always looking for top candidates. And we take great pride in firearm accuracy. Just go online at FBI.gov, apply digitally."

"Heck, I'll do it tonight. Maybe upload a couple of pictures of me in camo."

"That personal touch will pull you to the front of the line."

"One question. Any chance my irritable bowel syndrome would hold me back? I have to hit the can a lot. I mean, *a lot.*"

"Not if you can shoot," said Jake. "Plenty of bathrooms out there. Now, Serenity, how about pointing us to a manager."

She placed two fingers between her lips, let out a shrill whistle, yelled "JEB!"

A doughy man, with a fleshy pink face and prematurely thinning blond hair, arrived out of nowhere. Couldn't have been more than five-eight, late twenties.

"Serenity, how can I help these gentlemen?"

"Thought that was your damn problem to figure out."

Jake eyed the nametag. Jeb Morton. Figured a third-generation family member, likely to bankrupt a fifty-year-old business in twenty-four months. "Jeb, I'm Special Agent Jake Montoya, this is Agent Mark Benton. We're from the FBI. Need a moment of your time."

"Okaaay." Concern in his eyes. He walked them to an unoccupied aisle, just past the grass seed and lawn sprinklers.

"We need to speak to Leonard Bascom. Is he in?" said Benton.

"Why? What'd he do?"

"Jeb, let's not make this uncomfortable," said Montoya, popping some authority into his tone. "We've got a busy day, so let's get with it, okay?"

"Sure, sorry. No, he's not in. Probably seven, eight days ago he clocked out, never returned. I called his number probably ten times, never an answer, mailbox full."

"What'd he do here?"

"Paint guy. And excellent, too. He picked up the system quicker than anyone we've ever had and was fast at knocking out orders."

"Did he have any problems with the customers? Or employees?"

Jeb glanced over a stack of garden hoses, thinking. Started shaking his head, "No, none."

"Can you think of any reason why he would have left? Maybe another job?"

"I'd say that was likely it, but nobody has called for a reference. He definitely let me know he felt underutilized, like he needed to be higher up the food chain. Told him we didn't have anything, not at the moment."

"Jeb, can we get the address and phone number he gave you?"

"Sure, in my office." They walked to the other side of the store, entered an office through an unmarked brown door. They found a woman sitting at a desk with a cup of coffee in her hand.

"Wait a minute, guys. Oh, this is my Aunt Mitzi. Mitzi, what did you say about Lenny Bascom to me? Probably a month ago."

Mitzi, early fifties, blondish hair with streaks of silver creeping in, careful makeup, had her eyes on Montoya and Benton. "What's going on, Jeb?"

"FBI guys, want to speak to Bascom."

"What'd he do?" Mitzi's tone was suspicious.

"Ma'am, we don't know that he did anything. We'd just like to speak to him. There's no more detail to share."

"Well, he did something, else you wouldn't be here. Makes

those looks more concerning now."

"What looks?"

"Hard to describe. He'd come to the office to ask me something about his paycheck, something that wasn't really even a question. And if he saw me near the paint department, he'd stop and come over with some other stupid question, always squeeze in close to ask it. You know, in my personal space."

Jake eyed the ring on her left hand. Married. She had a pleasant voice with a southern lilt. Easy to see a man wanting to speak to her.

"I didn't think much of it at first, but later I mentioned it to Jeb. Bascom's eyes, when we spoke, were intense, like there was a plot behind them. Sounds stupid, I know. And then, I probably shouldn't say this, you'll think I'm conceited or something, but I got the impression he was picturing me naked, or in some kind of sexual scenario. That's crazy, don't know why I felt that way."

Jake smiled inside, suppressed the urge to tell her that most every man she ever met pictured her naked. Including her preacher. And probably Benton.

Benton looked at Jeb. "You run any kind of background check on Bascom?"

"No, I didn't. Look, I've got seven open positions right now. Can't find anybody to work, I mean no damn body. He walked in and filled out an app. We chatted, he was dressed neatly, shaven, nice haircut, seemed sharp, said he was sick of teaching and retired a year ago. I just hired him on the spot."

"Mitzi," said Jake, "likely a smart read on Lenny. One piece of info. He was recently released from state prison after sexual assault. At this point I'd be extra vigilant, let your husband know, maybe get some security lights and cameras for your home."

Mitzi slid open her desktop drawer to her right. Instantly, a small 9mm auto was in her hand. "Sig P365. Travels everywhere with me."

"Keep it close," said Benton. "Jeb, how about that info? We've got to run."

MONTOYA AND BENTON drove straight to Bascom's place. The address was the same one as in the cloud file. The complex was a low-slung white brick building of maybe twenty apartments. Lawn was more mowed weeds than mowed grass, grills out on most patios, parking area a quarter full, most vehicles fading with miles.

"Might have been nice fifty years ago."

Benton pointed. "Yeah, when the pool had water, not dirt." In the middle of the courtyard, the concrete, decorative-stone pool coping formed a neat rectangle. The pool had been filled in with dirt, covered with grass.

"Help you?" A dark-complected Black man exited the office, toilet plunger and tool caddy in his hand, "Navy Retired" cap on his head.

"Yes, sir. Looking for the manager."

"Well, you're done looking. I'm the head honcho, Horace Sellers."

Benton introduced themselves as FBI agents, told Horace they were looking to speak to Leonard Bascom.

"Hadn't seen him. Car's been gone five or six days."

"How was he as a tenant?"

"Well, he paid his rent, didn't make no noise, didn't bother anybody, not that I know of. So, I'll call him a good tenant. He hurt anybody?"

"We just need to speak to him. Do you happen to have the make and model of the car he drove?"

"Sure do. Got the plate number, too. Be right back."

Jake looked at the info Horace handed him. Neat penmanship on yellow, junior legal pad sheet. Did the math, "Seventeen-year-old Camry."

"Yep, just broke in then, you know them Toyota's run strong," said Horace, coughing out a laugh.

"One last question," said Benton, knowing Horace likely watched the tenants like a private eye. "You ever see any women with Bascom?"

"Yeah, couple of blonds on different occasions. Wouldn't mind grabbing a blond for myself, know what I'm saying." Had one eyebrow raised.

"I hear that," said Benton, going along. "Say," eyes catching the plunger, "didn't you get a call about a drain problem in Bascom's apartment?"

"No, no, no. Myrtle Beemer. Toilet backed up."

Montoya liked Benton's play. "Horace, you probably missed it. Maybe it got erased on your answering machine. Bascom's got a drain clogged with hair." Cocked his head at Horace, with instruction in his eye.

Horace's eyes narrowed into slits, a wily smile crossing his lips. "Damn glad you reminded me, tired of Bascom calling all times day and night. Drain problems. That crap haunts me."

They entered the hot apartment with a musty smell in the air. Air conditioner off. They found a cheap double bed, a four-drawer dresser, a couch covered in brown polypropylene fabric, a kitchen table with two chairs, silverware for three settings, and a faux-wood credenza holding a thirty-two-inch television.

"All this stuff from Goodwill. I saw the truck bring it," Horace said.

Jake scavenged the bedroom and bath. Nothing. No clothes, no toiletries.

"Jake." Benton had the cabinet open below the kitchen sink, pointed as Jake walked into the room.

Two gallons of concentrated sodium hypochlorite. Bleach.

Jake pulled a business card from his pocket, pushed it toward Horace. "Horace, lock this place tight. Don't come back in, don't rent it. We'll be back."

Leonard Bascom was on the run.

43

BENTON DUMPED JAKE back at the Hampton Inn in Daphne. Montoya glanced at his watch. Twenty-five minutes past eleven. He leaned in before closing the door. "Good work, Mark. We should have something on the wives by mid-afternoon, hopefully. And I'm betting we'll get a location on Bascom in forty-eight hours."

"Hope so. I'm heading back to review what's dropping in from Washington."

Jake filed a "Be On The Lookout" call for Bascom as he rode back from Pensacola. Needed for questioning. Full physical description of Bascom. Make, model, color, year of car. Six-five in height makes an ID easier.

Jake opened the door to the Land Cruiser, lowered the windows. Had to be a hundred degrees in the truck. *Note to self ... buy a damn AC ... fast.* He fired up, pulled onto the access road, spotted Foo's 150 yards away. *Chicken fingers will work*, he thought. Pulled in. Grabbed the book he brought with him.

He read while he ate. He was a third of the way through *The Boys*. Found it interesting, and surprising, all the love in Ron Howard's family. Nobody dead on dope by age thirty after overbearing parents forced them into a torturous childhood as a child actor.

Finished lunch. Rabbit-eared a page in the book. Was about

to push off when his phone rang. Virginia number, no ID.

"Jake Montoya."

"Agent Montoya, this is Dr. Ai Zhang calling from the Behavior Analysis Unit at Quantico."

Jake thought he'd heard the unaccented voice say "Eye Jong." A Chinese American? Second thought, her SAT score was probably a tad higher than his.

"Well, hello." Jake pushed his trash across the table. "Is your first name 'I'?"

He heard a giggle. "That's right. Let me spell it. 'A-I' is my first name. Last name,' Z-H-A-N-G.' 'Eye' Jong. Easy to mispronounce."

Her voice was soft, pleasing. *Has that common Asian calmness*, he thought. And of course, she's erudite, she's at the BAU.

"Lovely name, Ai. Hey, curious, what's your doctorate in?"

"Medicine. MD from the University of Washington. Residency and fellowship from USC. Undergrad, dual majors in psychology and organic chemistry. How about you?"

"I have a graduate degree in fracturing skulls." He laughed. She did too, and it was genuine.

"Thank goodness you're on my team. Anyway, Jake, your case was passed to me to analyze. I have sent a report to you via email, but I wanted to introduce myself. Answer any questions you might have."

"Sure, Ai. Run through the high points if you don't mind. I only check email on my birthday and July 4th." Jake heard a raucous laugh, belying the delicate Asian lady he pictured.

"I knew you'd be funny. The other night my husband yelled for me to come into the TV room. Your grill commercial with the runaway cheerleaders was playing. Jason was doubled over laughing, tears in his eyes."

"Kind of you to share that." A prideful smile ripped across

Midnight Man

his face. He wrote that one.

"So let's start at the top," said Ai. "I have no idea if you have any suspects, but please reveal nothing to me. I need the freedom of neutrality. I start with a blank slate, only looking at the evidence."

Here it comes, he thought. BAU operated six stories underground at Quantico. Jake pictured a Serbian-voodoo-witch doctoress in the bowels of a crumbling 120-year-old building in the New Orleans French Quarter. Dim lighting from a Tiffany lamp shrouded with hanging tassels. Scarf on her head, oversize hoop earrings, poofy pleasant blouse over bright flowery calf-length skirt, coins hung around the neck, wrists covered with jangling bracelets, bad teeth, and barefoot.

He already knew the first thing she'd say. *White male, 30s.*

"Absolutely. Fire away, Ai."

"Okay. White male, twenty-eight to mid-forties, but likely early thirties, especially if this is the first murder." Jake rolled his eyes, glanced around the restaurant, wanted to scream "Would you listen to this bullshit!?"

"He's in the organized category for sure. Everything is precise, no evidence of an uncontrolled rage during the killings. He's comfortable in the night, likely respectable looking, non-threatening in appearance. Definitely doesn't look like a monster."

"What do you see with the desecration of the vagina?"

"This is likely the key indicator of his motives. Almost certainly he has failed relationships with women. High likelihood he is not married, or if he was married it would have been short-lived. If currently married, he likely torments his wife with systematic abuse, and, likely, nonconsensual sexual practices."

"Like what?"

"Forced anal penetration would be at the top of the list."

"Okay. Keep going."

"He would want to have reassurance he was viewed as dominant, would likely instruct his wife to refer to him as King or Master or Daddy."

A smile. *Daddy.*

"By the same token, he would verbally denigrate his wife with terms like whore, bitch, slut, and the C-word."

"Interesting."

"Back to the desecration of the vagina on Ms. Sloane. That most assuredly shows a hatred and contempt for women. There is an emotional need to denigrate. Almost certainly the perpetrator has suffered abuse in his life. Sexual and emotional, less likely purely physical. This man has trouble performing in what we would consider a normal sexual encounter like traditional intercourse. He may have a prescription for an erectile dysfunction drug like Viagra or Cialis. But even they may be of no benefit, because of his mindset."

"As you know, Ai, we have no evidence of rape or penetration or ejaculation. But you think he's getting off sexually."

"I absolutely do. He likely achieves erections as he inflicts punishment. He may orgasm to the sound of a woman's screams. He may orgasm at her death. It would be extraordinarily rare not to have a sexual component. And listen, we don't know he didn't penetrate her. We just have no physical evidence, related to the dousing with what is likely acid."

"Right. Let's talk about the acid and poison."

"Certainly. But let's go back for a moment to the determination of 'organized.' It's not likely this guy grabbed the first woman he saw on the street. He's cautious. Calculating. Strong chance he identifies a woman, then studies her pattern of life. He learns her milieu, her surroundings. Knows the escape routes. Likely has a few plausible excuses ready to roll off his tongue if anyone encounters him during his surveillance stage."

"Makes sense, I suppose."

"Okay, the chemicals. Hydrochloric acid and bleach. This man has some education in science and chemistry. Likely college educated. But a high turnover in jobs. He harbors a deep anger. That can surface at work and make others uncomfortable, leading to a dismissal. It's a factor in how well he can wear a well-controlled public face."

"Okay. What about the bleach?"

"Likely used to cleanse the impurities in the subject. At least in the killer's mind. The vic is dirty, full of evil. And certainly, it would be devastating to the vaginal tissue. He would enjoy that."

"The acid?"

"This is for full-on pain and torture. He knows this will destroy any residual evil untouched by the bleach. And he knows, if the woman doesn't die, she is unlikely to have painful intercourse for the rest of her life. The autopsy revealed significant damage to her cervix. He has destroyed her womanhood."

"I see."

Ai continued. "Hydrochloric acid is used primarily in industrial environments. Used in many manufacturing processes. Chem lab usage of course. At home, its primary use is for swimming pools. It really knocks out the algae. Some other home cleaners may have a touch of HCL, but that wouldn't be what he used here."

"What do you make of the cuts on the back? And the nipple excisions?"

"Yes, that. The nipples. More pure anger against women. For the back, the autopsy photos showed high precision around the edges. Nothing ragged or performed in a rage. Could make you think of someone comfortable with a scalpel. A vet, a surgeon, a taxidermist, maybe even a meat-shop butcher. Through my imagination, I see the letters M and N. But there's no other body to compare it to. So it's probably happenstance that it came out that way."

"Yeah, Ai, I can read it that way myself."

"Look, Jake, that's a lot of bluster for a one-off murder. This could be a scorned old boyfriend tracking her down to the beach. He watches her and the new boyfriend, snatches her, kills her, gets rid of the source of his pain, and now his life is all better again. Heck, who knows, maybe his name's Michael Neeland. M and N."

Blood. Why isn't she talking about the blood?

"Ai, you're dancing around something. The blood. It was present in large quantities at every orifice. Even tear ducts. Petechiae and bruising on the body. What's the deal?"

"Jake, that's very puzzling. Extremely so. That's not what Behavior Analysis solves. I understand pathology is without answers on what caused that. It has to be instituted by the killer to bring an otherworldly level of suffering to the victims. This killer has quite a bit of scientific knowledge. A frightening amount."

"Well, Ai, I agree with that. But I held back on you on the one-off murder, just to see what you came up with. Here's more info. This is actually the second killing. Both blonds, both young, both with vaginal desecration, both dumped in the same spot of a brackish creek flowing in from the bay. This is in the small Alabama town of Black Point."

Ai was silent, soaking in the information.

"The first girl was killed with strychnine." Jake added that last detail.

"An Agatha Christie plot. More science at play," said Ai. "What's the time differential?"

"Twenty ... seven ...years."

"We've got a problem, Jake."

44

NIA CRUZ EDGED her car into a parallel parking spot on Colony Street in downtown Black Point. Montoya's Land Cruiser was parked across the street, almost at the front door of Black Point PD. It was thirty-five minutes past eight in the morning and the rain had eased back to a drizzle.

Wearing a light parka, she popped out, spit her gum onto the street, thought about that a moment, picked it up, and slow-jogged to the building entrance, her right hand holding a messenger bag at her side. She slid out of her damp jacket as she announced herself, flicked the gum into a trash container.

In only a moment she was in Chief Pike Tatum's office, a room with a large window that looked out on a concrete-block retaining wall. There was a whiff of carpet cleaner in the air and *The Dan Patrick Show* on low in the background, speculating on the Atlanta Braves' chances to make the Series. Tatum and Detective Billy Starr both sipped from cups of coffee. Jake held a tumbler of iced Diet Coke.

Tatum and Starr stood. Jake introduced Nia to the men. "How about some coffee, Agent?" The chief pointed at his cup.

"Too hot for that, but thanks."

"Got water, Coke, and tea if you care for any. All cold."

"Ever had Joe Tea?" Starr said.

"Never heard of it."

"Hang on. Think you'll like it." He scampered out of the room, grabbed a bottle from the breakroom fridge, was back in twenty seconds.

The bottle's label had a vintage truck on it. Nia studied it. "Reminds me of Snapple."

"Better. You'll see."

"Thanks." Nia patted her messenger bag, glanced at the men with concern in her eyes. "Have some information. *Alarming information.* I think we're walking in quicksand."

"Oh, hell. Let's move to the conference room. More room at the table," said the chief.

Nia pulled a laptop and cable from her bag as she settled into her seat. She signed on to the department's Wi-Fi. She connected the HDMI cable to her computer and the projector on the table. "Think we're good to go."

Montoya, Starr, and Tatum each had a legal pad in front of them. "Guys, I have everything in a file I'll send you. Take notes if you want to."

They nodded.

"In conjunction with several agents at Quantico, I've been reviewing the Violent Crime Apprehension Program files." She smiled. "I wanted to say the whole name, so you know that I actually know what VICAP stands for. As you know, VICAP collects significant data on homicides, sexual assaults, missing persons, and other crimes. We went back thirty years, three years prior to the Gage case, and started looking, using the characteristics of the Gage and Sloane murders. And we know, those two are for all intents the same."

"Did you set some geographic boundaries?" said Tatum.

"Yes, Chief, we did. Initially, it was Alabama, Florida, and Mississippi. We quickly stepped out wider, covering the whole South, from Texas to Virginia, including Kentucky. Then, seeing the results, we looked at the continental US." Nia bumped her forehead toward the screen. "Let's start here."

A photo popped up, a custom wooden road sign with a colorful planting of flowers at the base that read "Welcome to Auburn, Alabama—Loveliest Village on the Plains."

"When I played basketball at LSU, we had games in Auburn. Never saw much of the town. Looks to be a great little spot ... except for things like this."

Another photo hit the screen, a beautiful sandy-blond-haired girl with perfect skin and a Miss America smile. All apple pie and Chevrolet.

"This is Allie Abrams, a junior at Auburn University. She was from Fort Valley, Georgia, a small town where they grow a lot of peaches. She played in the band, majored in forestry. An outdoorsy girl, she rode horses most of her life."

"Sorority?" said Starr.

"Nope. GDI."

"GDI?"

"Gosh damn independent."

"Oh yeah, right."

"What's the timeline?" said Jake.

"Three years after Gage. Here's the skinny. She was last seen as she finished a shift at a Western Sizzlin Steakhouse on a Friday night. The restaurant's long gone now. She was found on a Monday morning at the Fisheries Center, part of the College of Agriculture, on AL-147, outskirts of town."

Jake's muscles tensed when he heard *three years after Gage*. Leonard Bascom had lived in Auburn at that time. He kept his mouth shut for the moment, wanted to hear Nia out. First thing after the meeting, he'd put some heat under the BOLO for Skinny Lenny. *We've got you, dude.*

But he kept thinking, *Couldn't be this easy, could it?* He ruminated back to Bill Starr, the original detective. Surely he had interviewed the high school teachers. Right? Bascom taught chemistry and should have been the first guy Starr spoke to as far as teachers go. Or maybe Jim Lamb, the girls' volleyball coach. He was around Sunshine all the time. Lotta young flesh in his face daily. Did he have an eye for it? Feel like he needed a taste? There were whispers he liked to be mighty close to the locker room when the girls changed.

Back to Bill Starr. Jake knew the detective was missing a piece of the puzzle—Bascom hadn't done time yet for sexual assault.

Montoya tuned back into Cruz as she popped another photo on the screen. It was the back of Allie Abrams. The carvings. Hypothetically, an M and an N. "I will skip the photo of the vagina. It's ugly. Severe chemical burns. And Allie was poisoned—that was the cause of death."

"Strychnine?"

"Nope, ethylene glycol. Antifreeze." She looked down at a pad beside the computer and read. "Causes neurological symptoms, seizures, muscle twitches, elevated heart rate, elevated blood pressure, elevated potassium, muscle spasms, metabolic acidosis, lactic acidosis, and after three days, kidney failure." She glanced up with a look ... *Got all that?*

"Hell, that sounds bad," said Starr, eyes furrowed into confusion. "All I understood was muscle twitches."

"Well, there you go, gentleman. We've identified three extremely similar cases in relatively close proximity. I think we can safely conclude we are dealing with a serial killer."

"Son of a bitch," said Tatum. "But twenty-seven damn years?"

Cruz added, "Reportedly, Chief, there is no burnout rate on serial killers. They can have the appetite for it until they die."

"Folks, I may have some good news," said Jake, with a troubled look that defied a favorable report.

"Hold up, Jake," said Nia. "Unfortunately, there's more bad

news. All of this is in the files I'll email you. Let's get the bad news out of the way, then we'll finish with good news."

"More bad news?" Jake twirled the pointer of his right hand in a circle. "Stay the course, captain." *But I've already solved the case,* he thought.

"I'll make this quick, fellas. Strap on your seatbelts. You can read the reports at your leisure."

"Now, murder and mayhem. You'll like this." Her dark eyes zeroed in on each man. A fizz of tension seized the room.

"Twenty-two years ago, murders in Phoenix and Seattle. Eight weeks apart. Twenty years ago, a murder in Charlotte. Nineteen years ago, a murder in Jacksonville, eight weeks later a murder in St. Louis. Eighteen years ago, a murder in New Orleans."

"Were they all—" Starr tried to shove in a question.

Cruz held up a finger, not taking her eyes off her computer screen. "Detective, let me finish, then questions." Thumped him with authority.

"Seventeen years ago, a murder in Tampa, eight weeks later, a murder in Minneapolis. Sixteen years ago, a murder in San Francisco, six weeks later, a dead woman in Baltimore. Twelve years ago, murder in Philadelphia. Eleven years ago, another murder in New Orleans. New Orleans is the only duplicate city, as far as I can tell. Ten years ago, a murder in Kansas City."

Cruz looked up at the men. "*Thirteen* murders. From what we could dig up, murders with that same MO stopped cold ten years ago, until the Sloane woman in Orange Beach."

The energy in the room vibrated at this news. Tatum's eyes caught Montoya's gaze. He saw alarm in Jake's eyes. And maybe a flash of excitement.

Jake thought, *No way Skinny Lenny knocked all those out, could he?* "Run over the MO, Nia."

"All victims are women ranging from twenty to thirty-six years old. All blonds, slim and attractive. All with chemical vaginal desecration. All died from poisoning. All had the signature carvings on the back. All had their areolas excised from their breasts." Nia leaned back in her seat. "This prick scored tissue souvenirs from his victims."

Starr whistled. "That's some gruesome shit." Had a face that looked like he'd stepped in cat poop.

"Okay," said Tatum, "we have strychnine in Sunshine Gage. Antifreeze in the girl in Auburn. Anything else?"

"Several were killed with botulinum toxin, which my research says is the most toxic poison in the world, or close." She glanced down at her notes. "Aerosolized, one gram can kill a million people. It only takes *one-billionth* of a gram to kill a human." She looked up at Jake. "So Jake, make sure your plastic surgeon is dosing your Botox correctly. It causes muscle paralysis, and when your respiratory muscles get paralyzed, you stop breathing and then, you know ..."

"Where would you get this stuff?"

"Just briefly looked at that. I found commercial labs that sell it to the pharmaceutical industry. We'll get Jake's analyst in DC to dig in on this."

"Will do," said Montoya.

"Next, we have a little beauty called sodium fluoroacetate. It's the active ingredient in a product known as Compound 1080."

"I've heard of that," said Starr. His face took on a puzzled look. "I mean I think I have." Put his palm up. "Sorry for the interruption, Agent."

"No worries, Detective. To me, this stuff looks perfect. It's sold to kill predators. Very limited use now, mostly in the West. There's a significant movement to ban the substance, related mostly to accidental poisonings of unintended animals. It was easier to buy when these killings occurred than now."

"Perfect? Why?" Jake said, just before a sip of Coke.

"It's colorless and odorless and potent. One teaspoonful can kill a hundred humans. It would be easy to slip in a drink. And it causes a slow, ugly death. Hallucinations, convulsions, hyperextended limbs, intense pain. Following convulsions, it causes organ failure, nervous system failure, and respiratory arrest."

"Good God," said Tatum. "Hey y'all, hold on a sec." The chief hustled to his office to get the box of donuts he'd bought before heading to work. He plopped it on the table, flicked open the top, nabbed a jelly-filled for himself. "Help yourselves."

"Are you serious, Chief? What a damn rube cop cliché," said Cruz.

"Didn't mean to hurt your feelings, Agent," he said through his first bite.

Starr and Jake both quickly snatched a donut from the box.

"More for us, Pike," said Jake, as he bit into a chocolate glazed.

"Ah, the hell with y'all." Nia reached into the box, left with *two* in her hand.

With a full mouth, Tatum said, "What else is the guy using?"

Nia held up a finger, finished chewing her first bite, a big one. She downed a swig of Joe Tea, scraped the back of her hand across her lips. "Fellas, I apologize. These things are decadent. Okay, he used insulin, cyanide, and amatoxin."

"Insulin? Medicine?"

"Yes. Too much insulin drops your sugar very low. That can cause insulin shock and death. Full description of the effects in the reports."

"The hell is amatoxin?" mumbled Starr.

"A toxin from mushrooms. It causes a lot of ugly things to

happen that ultimately cause liver and kidney failure in about seventy-two hours. So, Pike, you and Billy take a look at this stuff if it interests you, but rest assured, the Bureau is about to go apoplectic on this. Ton of work to do."

"Looks like we've got one smart, dangerous son of a bitch out there. He's a traveler, he seems meticulous, he's deadly with chemicals. He's leaving signatures—why hasn't the Bureau been on this?" said the chief.

"I think the story is this," said Cruz. "Besides New Orleans, there has been only one of these killings in a specific jurisdiction. And they're all big cities. Those departments are flush with other murders they're dealing with. This guy does the deal, hits the road. Like the year he did one in San Francisco, then six weeks later in Baltimore. Nobody has more than one case. No connection. And even if they jump on VICAP, that may mean more work for them in the long run. Just another big city murder filed in the unsolved cases, growing colder by the day."

"I agree," said the chief. "Sometimes the locals don't want the friction of working with the feds anyway. My research indicates the Bureau feels there are twenty-five to fifty serial killers operating at any time. Most of them seem very random, no signature attached. But we've got a good footprint on this guy. Hell of a lot of work to be done for sure, but we may get him. We know he's been in our backyard lately."

"Okay, my turn. I have a positive lead going." Jake went into the background on Leonard Bascom—he was at Sunshine's party, his release from prison, the visit to his apartment, now empty with two bleach containers in the kitchen. "He's in the wind. We have a BOLO on him. But it makes me wonder; did he just murder someone? Is he leaving town for a while? He's got two ex-wives we want to talk to. We're chasing them down from Washington."

"Sounds good," said Tatum.

"My interest in Bascom just ramped up, based on what Nia told us."

Nia looked at him, a question in her eyes.

"Bascom was living in Auburn at the time the student was murdered there. Three years after Sunshine Gage," said Jake.

Starr snapped his fingers. "That's right."

"That's great work, Nia," said Jake. "How about you speaking to agents in those cities, give them the rundown on what we know. We're going to need them to get their hands on the murder books from the local PD, dig into them. Also, any info for Bascom being in the cities at the time of the incident."

"I'll work on it when I get back to the office."

"Billy, I'd like a meeting with you and the ten agents I'm bringing up from Orange Beach," said Jake. "We need in-person interviews with every teacher, student, and former Magnolia Hotel employee still living in the area. Could we say eight here tomorrow, at the station?"

"Absolutely."

"Jake, I'm going to send Benton and Marcia Allen over, too," said Cruz.

"Good idea. I'll see you in the morning. Right now I want to locate Bascom's ex-wives."

Everyone stood. "Guys, we're ignoring the elephant in the room." Chief Tatum looked at their puzzled faces.

"Lea Lea Sloane. No poison. Nothing on tox screen. All major organs deteriorated into goo. Blood dumping from every pore in her body."

"*What the hell killed her?*"

45

MONTOYA AND CRUZ walked out of the station together. They were ambushed by a wall of humidity left by the rain. Intense mid-morning sunshine, not a cloud in the sky. "Talk soon." Nia scatted across the street in front of ongoing traffic.

Jake hopped in the Cruiser, dropped the windows, had his hand on the key, ready to start. Thought about what Nia reported. The cities. Tampa. Green Bay. Charlotte. Philadelphia, New Orleans. Baltimore. He'd been to all of them, playing football for the Redskins.

NFL cities.

Huh. Like that matters. Big cities are just perfect jungles to kill folks.

He pulled out his phone, tapped his mother's number. "Big Jake Grills ..." She laughed. "I mean, hello, son. It's a habit when I'm in the office, even though it's my cell. What's up on this fine Black Point day, with football season minutes away? Oh, oh, oh, wait. I think this came to me in a dream or something, a new tagline. 'Game Time is Grill Time.' What do you think?"

"I love it. I say copyright that or whatever you do. Now, how 'bout I bring you a box lunch from Lyrene's?"

"Absolutely. Surprise me."

"Will do."

"Don't care what they say, boy. The legendary Jake Montoya is a pretty good son." She chuckled.

Jake laughed. "Love you too, Mama. Gotta see a man about a horse, first. Be there in an hour."

Game Time is Grill Time. Liked it, he did.

Jake found a hole in the traffic, eased onto Colony Street, popped 92 ZEW on the dial. Buffett singing "Twelve Volt Man." Jimmy had told Jake at a local bar it was one of his favorite songs. He turned it up.

He drove three blocks south, parked in front of Page and Palette Bookstore. Hopped out, window-shopped a moment, spotted Rick Bragg's new book, something about a dog and his people. Hadn't heard of it. Quickly walked in, grabbed a copy, paid, and went back to the task at hand.

Outside the store, he walked south, cut down a walkway into the French Quarter, spotted the steep stairs that rose to a space that looked like a three-story broom closet. Sign said "Wirebenders." The organization was in the glamorous business of making orthodontic retainers. One of those off-the-grid, cash-cow outfits.

Jake took a breath, steeled himself.

Climbed the stairs like he was taking a gallows walk. Had to entice Jones to sell his Boston Whaler.

46

THE ADS CARPET-BOMBED the region: **$1,000,000 For the Arrest and Conviction of Individuals Involved in the Murder of Lea Lea Sloane.**

They blitzed the area between Mobile, Alabama, the Gulf beaches, and Pensacola, Florida.

Radio. Television. Billboards. Facebook. Instagram. Twitter. *Mobile Press-Register. Pensacola News Journal.*

Even the most unplugged, off-the-grid individual would get a sniff of the million-buck opportunity.

Jake, Hope, Kimbo and his wife Jan, and Elijah Washington were sitting at the end of Kimbo's pier. It was dark, candle flames twisting in a light breeze, Boney James' smooth saxophone swaying off a playlist through two tiny Bose speakers.

Kimbo's Lowcountry boil had been a hit.

Jake and Eli steered the conversation out of football, a subject they'd long grown tired of.

"Listen, Eli, I'm tired of talking about sports," said Kimbo. "Let's talk about pork chops. Jake and I have eaten at Sweet E's. It's killer, man. I want to know the grand plan for the company."

"I moved back to Black Point eight months ago and set up an office. Dallas slap wore me out. Lured my top two lieutenants with me. We opened Black Point six months back. Just recently opened Orange Beach and Destin locations."

"Sounds like pedal to the metal," said Kimbo.

Eli, hiding 290 pounds under an oversize Bahama shirt laughed, big white teeth lighting the night. "It is. I've got my foot on the gas. I never thought things would go this well. Approaching about eighty restaurants. Texans are chop-eating fools, I can tell you that. I have two in New Orleans that do really well. Gonna throw out a few more, outside of Texas. If those sell some chops, I'm going to franchise. I already have seven retired ball guys who are ready to jump in."

Jake's phone rang, and he glanced at it. Pike Tatum. Tapped accept.

"Shit's hit the fan, Jake."

"Hold it, Pike." He glanced up at the group. "Be right back." He walked off the pier, stopped in the backyard. "I'm back. What happened?"

"Another murder. Over in Seaside, Florida, right next to Destin."

"I know the place."

"Blond woman, attractive, early forties, found in a guest cottage. Had been dead for a couple of days. Same vaginal deal. Nipples sliced off."

"Poisoned?"

"Don't know. Running tox screens. And they'll dig in, they know about the Sloane woman."

"Dammit, Pike, this guy's right under our noses."

"Absolutely. But there's something else," said Tatum.

Jake exhaled loudly. "Not another one."

"No. It's Lea Lea Sloane's father, the big-shot Toyota dealer in Atlanta. Today he started blanketing the area with ads for a million-dollar reward for the arrest of his daughter's killer. Phone numbers for Orange Beach and Black Point PDs. Plus the FBI tipline number."

"Ahhh, jeeez, a million? Are you serious?" Jake stared into the blackness of the bay, spotted the shadow of a large freighter miles out, headed south to the Gulf.

"Yep."

"We'll be underwater with crackpots. We've got to talk to him, quick." Another call was coming in. Tolleson, Jake's analyst. "Hold it a minute, Pike."

"Ross, I'm putting out fires. What's up?"

"I'm back in DC. The Hatteras trip went better than expected. Calling to see who's running the ads on Sloane. I've been alerted to eight calls on the tip line in the last ninety minutes."

"Sloane's old man is behind it, just came to my attention, too. Look, I have to get off. I'll call you tomorrow."

"Pike, I'm back. That was DC. Eight calls to the Bureau already. Did you ever meet Sloane's father? You need to give him a call, tell him to shut that crap down."

"Never met him. I think it'd be better to get that message from the FBI. He'll think we're a bunch of yokels."

"Probably right. Text me any detective contacts you have for Walton County, Florida. And send me Sloane's number. Need to speak to them."

"Will do. You'll have it in five."

Walking back out onto the pier, Jake popped up the time on his phone. 9:40 p.m. That'd be 10:40 in Atlanta. Decided to wait until the morning for Sloane. Let the man get some sleep, if that was even possible.

"You okay, Jake?" Jan asked.

"Not the best. This is all public information, so I'll mention it. Another woman found over at Seaside, Florida—Destin, basically. Same body type, blond, early forties. Looks to be the same MO."

"I heard about that one down at Cottonmouth Creek.

Whatcha got on suspects?" Eli looked Jake in the eye.

"Can't really go into that, Eli."

"Yeah, yeah, right. This stuff's interesting. Scary, but interesting." He took a slug of beer. "Man, that's good beer. This guy sounds slippery, like some kind of hitman."

Jake took a quick slug of beer. "Yeah, you're right, E. And I'm sure you'll catch wind of an ad. The Sloane girl's father is advertising a million dollars cash reward for information leading to the arrest of a killer. I just learned this. That'll throw a lot of mud in the water. Every nutjob with a phone will be calling." He tossed the rest of his beer in the trash can.

Fatigue raked his voice as he said, "Hope, I'm kind of drained of the party mode. Mind if we hit it. Sorry about this, guys."

Her brow furrowed "No, Jake, sure, that's fine." Glanced at Jan. "See you tomorrow at three, Jan. We'll work on your volleys."

NINETY MINUTES LATER. Jake and Hope were naked in her bed at the animal sanctuary. Two vanilla candles flickering on a dresser. On low, Diana Krall sang "The Look of Love," a song that'd make any sane man want intimacy. Jake had little interest. Not tonight. Distracted. Thinking.

Hope was lying on her back, eyes closed, arms above her head, small breasts exposed. She was a woman comfortable with nakedness, totally at ease and confident letting Jake explore her body.

He was on his side, resting his head on his hand. He let his eyes glance all the way down to her toes. Five feet, eight inches of sleek, fit woman. Feminine muscle defined and toned.

The fingers of his left hand began tracing over her smooth skin. First, down her upper arms. Slowly around her neck, over her cheeks, around her lips.

"Beautiful lips," he said. She said nothing. *Asleep*, he thought.

His fingers reached the top of her chest, swirled lightly. He felt her heartbeat, watched the gentle rise and fall of her chest with soft breathing. His fingers whirled around her nipples, then traveled outside her breasts and down to her tummy, teasing around her belly button, went south, tiptoed around her pubic area before reaching her thighs.

He reversed course. Back at her breasts, with the lightest touch possible, he focused on her nipples. In the faintest whisper, he said, "Body of a goddess."

"I'm not asleep, mister. You've set me on fire."

"Is that right?" Starting to feel a twitch between his legs, himself.

"How do you do that? How do you make those strong hands have the touch of a feather floating through the air?"

47

THE NEXT MORNING, Jake prepared himself for blowback. He had his cell phone in his hand, the number for James Sloane pulled up, ready to tap call. An empty bowl and plate were in front of him on the table, just emptied of oatmeal with cinnamon, three frozen waffles, two strips of bacon.

Sitting on the back porch of the home office of the Refuge of Hope, he glanced downrange, spotted a red-bearded older man driving a Gator loaded with feed for large animals. A large white barn, acres and acres of green pasture, groves of oaks, and a twelve-acre pond. A paradise for man or beast.

It was just after seven in Point Clear, the peaceful early coolness of the summer morning about to be shattered. *Don't want to but have to*, he thought. He tapped call.

Four rings later an answer. "This is Jim Sloane, please leave a message." Jake did. Told him it was urgent they talk.

Wondered about the man. Running twenty Toyota dealerships. Big business, over a billion dollars in sales. Maybe a steely, arrogant son of a bitch. Probably back at work. He didn't picture a guy gone frail, lying in bed zonked on Xanax with an ice pack on his head. The wife, yeah, maybe, but not the dad.

Jake was typing a text message to Sloane when his phone rang.

"Agent Jake Montoya."

"You better be calling with the name of the person I'm making the check out to." Deep voice, commanding, brusque almost to the point of anger.

"Is this James Sloane?"

"Yes. And who the hell is Jake Montoya?"

"Sir, I'm one of many FBI agents on your daughter's case."

"Are you going to tell me you got the son of a bitch?"

"Not yet, but we're making progress."

"Well, how about getting your ass back to work. Stop wasting time calling me with nothing but babble."

Yep. An arrogant son of a bitch.

"I'm not babbling, sir. I have something important to tell you." He consciously said *tell you,* not *ask you.*

"I'm listening."

"Take the ads down. They're hindering the investigation."

"Hindering? You gotta be fuckin' kiddin' me. That might be the only thing that gets this solved." Sounding more like a street brawler than a guy upgrading your Camry to leather interior. "According to my research, Montoya, forty percent of murders are unsolved. *Forty damn percent!* Not my little girl. No sir. This guy's going down. Very few people can spend what I can spend to make it happen."

Sloane was pushing Jake's buttons. He pictured his right hand gripping Sloane's throat, eyes filled with fire boring into the man. He took a breath, brought contrition into his voice.

"Mr. Sloane, seriously, at this point the ads will hinder the investigation. Currently, we have some leads and are digging into them. We're making progress."

"Well, you're about to have more leads, Agent. Somebody knows who did this. And you know as well as I do, everybody cracks with the right dollar figure."

Jake decided to put some ice in his tone. "It's a hindrance

right now. It's too much bullshit flowing in. It jumbles everything. Chasing too many directions at once. I'm telling you, sir, stop running these ads."

Jake heard a smug laugh. "You know the problem, Montoya, is you don't know how it feels. You don't know how Lea Lea's mother feels. I'm a CEO. I'm a strong man. But you haven't felt it personally. We're crushed, absolutely destroyed." Sloane ramped up his irritation. "So don't be calling me telling me what the hell I can or cannot do."

Jake did know how it felt. Sunshine Gage. He'd watched Sunshine's mother, Marin, go to pieces over it. Tender moments with her daughter at the sweet sixteen birthday party, never to see her only daughter again. Sunshine's father was a surgeon. A big man. A strong man. He wasn't seen in public for three months. Kimbo told Jake years later that his father went on antidepressants. Tranquilizers were the only thing that kept him going.

"I want you to listen to me, Mr. Sloane." All irritation left his voice. "I do know how you feel. I'm going to tell you how I've felt for the last twenty-seven years. Got that? I said twenty ... seven ... years."

James Sloane shut his mouth and listened. Jake poured out the hot pain of his soul like he was talking to a pastor. He described what he saw in Dr. and Mrs. Gage. He described picking up the pieces slowly, a long process. He revealed the newest murder in Destin. And then dropped the bomb. There might be *many more* by the same man.

"Mr. Sloane, nobody, I mean *nobody,* wants this son of a bitch more than I do. We need three weeks. Just give us three weeks to pursue our own leads. Then we can revisit the ads, and if we're stalling, maybe the ads would be a good thing. Can you do that?"

"Agent Montoya, I never dreamed I'd hear a story like that.

Yes, on one condition."

"What's that?"

"Keep me apprised every step of the way. On everything. Everything you say will be confidential, just between you and me. It'll make me feel I'm doing something. The last thing I can stand to feel is helplessness."

"I can do that, sir." A truce.

"Call me Jim, Jake. We're two men in the same foxhole."

"Yes, sir, Jim. We are."

JAKE TOOK HIS dishes to the sink, rinsed them, placed them in the dishwasher. He walked into Hope's office. She was wearing a pair of cheap drugstore readers, pouring through email proposals from prospective manufacturing facilities for her dog and cat food. Carole King's album *Tapestry* played in the background.

"Well, got that done," said Jake.

"How'd he take it?"

"Went okay. We have an understanding at this point." He glanced out the window. "Nice morning. I'm going to get in a run, there was maybe a little more stress on that call than I thought."

"Good idea."

He climbed the stairs, walked down the hall to the master bedroom. Changed into running shorts and a navy T-shirt advertising Brumos Porsche, out of Jacksonville. A shirt that Kimbo gave him.

He sat on the bed, grabbed his phone, scrolled through his contacts, tapped call.

An older woman answered in a slow but pleasing southern drawl. It was a voice that had comforted him for the last twenty-something years in Washington. Sarah Bradley. Jake had lived in a cottage at her Georgetown estate since his first year with the Redskins. He pictured her cheery smile and Q-tip white, short, chic haircut.

"Son, when are you coming back? I'm missing you up here."

"Missing you too, Ms. Sarah ... I just wanted to hear your voice ..."

48

AN ELECTRONIC CHIME sounded as Jake stepped through the office door. He was clean-shaven, wearing a crisp, blue chambray shirt over black slacks. Badge hooked to his belt as well as a holstered .45 automatic.

Tolleson had given him the woman's name as well as her employer, home address, and cell phone number. Grace Keeler. She was the office manager of a prominent insurance agency in Foley, Alabama, a small city twenty-one miles from Black Point.

The office lobby had a couch, four chairs, and a few travel magazines on a table. Light from four windows brightened the room. Potpourri scent in the air. Gino Vannelli singing about nights in Montreal, in the background.

A blond woman, early twenties, wearing trendy glasses, glanced at him from behind a curved receptionist's counter. Jake stepped up, placed his forearms on the polished granite.

"How may I help you, sir?" Gleaming teeth. He could smell the cinnamon in her gum.

"My name is Jake Montoya, from the FBI. I'd like to briefly speak to Grace Keeler."

She noticed the badge and gun. Her face was a mix of curiosity and suspicion. "Is there a problem?"

"No, no, no. Just want to see if Mrs. Keeler can provide some info on something from long ago. Definitely no problem."

She walked down the hall and returned with a woman who appeared to be somewhere in her mid-fifties.

"Ma'am, I'm Special Agent Jake Montoya of the FBI. May I speak with you for just a few moments?"

Jake intentionally hadn't called for an appointment or to interview Keeler on the phone. It was 11:40. He wanted to catch her near lunchtime, hoped she wouldn't be with a client. Plus he wanted to get candid responses, nothing that could be contrived with hours of thought about an upcoming interview. And he needed to see her eyes. Truth detectors.

Keeler had fixed herself up about as well as a plain woman could. Neat, low-maintenance haircut, a few gray strands slipping in. Modest makeup. Dark skirt. Conservative white blouse, wearing a cross on a thin gold chain, displayed over a chaste cleavage view.

"Have a seat, agent. Care for coffee, tea, Coke, or water?"

Jake spotted a multitude of family photos. Kids, husband. At Disney, in ball uniforms, on a boat, the beach. Kids growing older through the pictures. Happy faces in all of them.

"No thanks. I don't want to take a lot of your time, but I do have some very important questions. I need your insight."

"Oh, goodness. About what?"

"Leonard Bascom."

Jake watched her face freeze into a mask of tension. He waited for her to respond.

"I don't know why, really I have no idea why, but I had an intuition you were going to ask about him."

"Have you seen or talked to him recently? Why did you think that?"

"Heavens no. Not for over twenty years. But why would I think that? He's a bad man, a bad person. I had no clue who I was marrying. He was a chameleon." She pinched her lips, raised her eyebrows, shook her head. "The mistakes of youth."

Jake commiserated. "We all have them. Were you aware he was in prison recently for sexual assault?"

Looked like she didn't want to answer, then nodded. "Yes, a friend said she saw a posting on Facebook about it. I don't do social media. Too much hateful dialogue spewing around. I can't bear to read it."

"I want to go back twenty-seven years."

Keeler inhaled deeply. "Goodness, okay." She adjusted her skirt over her knees.

"Do you remember when a sixteen-year-old girl was murdered after her birthday party in Black Point? Leonard was teaching at the high school."

Keeler shook her head as if to say no, but instead said, "Oh, dear Lord, yes. What a tragedy." Her eyes looked at the desk. Processing. "Wait. Do you think Lenny had anything to do with it?" Her hand went to her mouth.

Jake lifted his hands, palms up. "I don't know. Did he ever mention her to you?"

"I can't believe this. After all these years. I can't. Lenny? That was so horrible and brutal."

"Think carefully, please. Did he ever mention Sunshine Gage to you?"

Keeler glanced out the window. Cars traveling on a side street. Looked back. "Well, I'm sure we talked about it after the murder. Who in town didn't? I'll have to think about it. Right now I don't remember him talking about her in any specific way. Do you know if she was in one of his classes?"

"She wasn't. She was tenth grade. Would have had biology with him the next fall."

"Goodness, Lenny. Oh my God." Shaking her head. "Why are you here now, Agent? What has happened?"

"There's been a second murder. Identical to Sunshine Gage.

Body found in Cottonmouth Creek in Point Clear. Same place as Sunshine Gage."

"I heard about that. But I didn't see any mention of the Gage girl, that there was a connection. Okay, but why Lenny? Why now?"

"The FBI is in on this now. We have a lot of resources. Far more than the local police had back in the nineties. We're interviewing everybody we can find from the high school. All teachers. All the students, males, at any rate. And Lenny was released from prison in the last eight months."

Jake saw something in her eyes. A look that said she could see the possibility of this with her former husband. He appraised her, had known girls like her in high school. Quietly made good grades, shy, likely not in with the popular crowd, maybe never asked to the prom, probably in church Sunday mornings and Wednesday nights. Sheltered.

"Mrs. Keeler, here's another thing. We just received a report of another woman's murder over near Destin. Very similar circumstances. Acid and bleach poured on the vagina. Parts of the body carved away. Poisoned. Don't have official confirmation on that from Destin, yet."

Keeler's face went ashen. "Good gracious." Came out in a mumbled whisper.

"Mrs. Keeler, I want to be perfectly clear. Regardless of what happens, you will not be brought in in any official capacity. This will likely be the only time we speak, so everything you tell me will be confidential. And I'd like you to honor the confidentiality of this meeting, yourself. News of this type travels fast."

"Okay, I understand. But what can I tell you? I don't know anything. And you can call me Grace, if you'd like. It'd seem a little friendlier to me."

"Ok, thank you, Grace. The main reason I wanted to speak to you is to get some deeper insight into Leonard. The FBI has a sophisticated group of profilers that look into characteristics of crime scenes to attempt to paint a picture of characteristics of possible suspects."

"Yes, I know. I watch reruns of *Criminal Minds,* and I saw *Mindhunter* on Netflix. It's quite interesting. Can't say I understand it all, though."

Jake smiled. "It does have a kind of voodoo feel to it. Let's get into a couple of questions then you can get back to insuring cars and condos."

"That, I understand." Said it with a thin smile. Loosening up.

"After you married Leonard, was your sex life normal? At least as you perceived normal?"

"Oh, gosh, Agent. That's so personal." She averted her eyes.

"Please, Grace, I need background."

She stepped from behind her desk, closed the office door, sat back at her desk. Clearly uncomfortable. "No. I had no real sexual background when we married. Not sure what I expected. Maybe intercourse twice a week, in the dark. Lenny wanted it every day. Lights on, fully exposed. I know we were married, but I'm shy."

"I understand. I'm going to skip over questions about oral sex ..."

"You don't have to. I felt that was dirty. He was very forceful making that happen. He made me, really. I hated it. That's the beginning of when I started to despise the man."

"So it would be correct in saying he made you subject to things you resisted?"

"Yes, And if I didn't ... let's just say he had a temper."

"Did he hit you?"

Grace looked out the window again. Jake began to feel bad asking this delicate flower these questions.

"Yes, he hit me, but not like a wife beater. No black eyes or broken bones." She looked down. Jake waited.

"One day I found some magazines in the garage. They were filthy. Bondage sex or whatever you call it. Total perversion. Masks. Whips. Tying women up. It was all very frightening to me. I never mentioned I spotted them, just hoped that behavior wouldn't come into my home."

Had to ask. "Did it? Come into your home?"

"Two years, maybe almost two and half years after we were married, it did. It was a Friday night. In bed, dark. Always had to make love on Friday. Everything happened quickly. He pulled my wrists together and I felt something soft slide over them. It was velvet rope or something. Same things on my ankles. I was tied up. I started screaming. Lenny put a gag over my mouth, told me to shut up, he was going to expand my horizons. He was thin but very strong. He stepped off the bed, turned on the lights. He was wearing a black mask, had a small whip in his hand. I'd never been so scared in my life. Why did I marry him? Why, why, why?" She began to cry, grabbed some tissues from a box, stood, looked away out the window.

He gave her time to recompose. She turned back to him, eyes dry, slightly red. "I apologize. Difficult memory."

"You are doing very well, Grace. This is very important information. One last question and then I'm gone."

"Okay."

"What exactly did he do to you that night?" Looked away as he asked.

49

GRACE KELLER TOOK a deep breath, ended it with a sigh. Eyes looking anywhere but into Jake's. "I hate to talk about it. I've forced this from my mind for years. Can you promise I'll never be in a courtroom talking about this?"

A look of gravitas settled across Jake's face, his tone soft, reassuring. "Grace, I absolutely promise. I'm taking no notes, no recordings."

"If you're lying, you would really damage me. I wouldn't want my husband to know, and God forbid, not my boys. They're teenagers."

"I promise." Seeing her concern, he knew he wouldn't even tell his colleagues. Black Point and Foley are small towns. He'd keep this to himself, deep background.

She looked away as she began to speak. "He whipped my breasts first. It hurt. Really hurt. I told him to stop. Begged him to stop. I felt like a rapist, a monster, had broken into my house, not the man I married. He didn't break the skin, but it left bruises and red streaks. He uttered filthy, nasty things, called me a whore and a slut. He sounded angry as he said it, but I could tell he was enjoying it, sexually, I mean. He flipped me on my belly then started whipping me on my bottom, this time hard. He cut the skin. I was screaming. He just laughed. He pointed to his penis, said look how excited I made him. To me, that was as bad as it could get."

"I'm so sorry." Jake hid his anger.

"But it got worse."

Jake said nothing, fuming. She was delivering the goods.

"He flipped me on my back. He started spanking me ... between my legs, my lady parts. It was so sick. Through the pain, I kept thinking, *how did I marry this freak?* Such a pervert. I knew I was going to be bruised ... down there. It hurt ... hurt so much." She started crying again.

"Take your time, Grace."

"Then he went into the kitchen, returned with a can of Crisco. He rubbed it all over the handle of the whip. He turned me back on my stomach." A big sob. "He pushed it into me, into my bottom, it went in and out repeatedly. It hurt so bad ... "

Jake fought the thought. Lenny Bascom holed up someplace doing that to Sunshine. *Stop, stop, stop thinking.*

Grace stepped away from her desk and went into the small restroom adjoining her office. Jake heard sink water running. Pictured her placing drops of Visine in her eyes, if she had any.

She returned five minutes later, looking better, only barely. With some strength in her tone, she said, "He untied me, told me that's what married couples do, and that soon I'd consider it the best sex we could have." Shook her head, thinking about the absurdity of the thought.

Jake nodded, like a counselor taking everything she could deliver. No interruption.

"The next morning he was out riding road bikes with friends, a Saturday ritual. I moved fast, packed some clothes and toiletries, and took off. I drove to an old friend's home in Birmingham. She was a nurse. She begged me to go to an ER. I didn't. I wanted it to all be a bad dream. She photographed me, extensively. I had her write down every word as I described the experience. We went to a mailbox store, and I had my signature notarized on the document. I had some sort of record and her as a witness. The following Monday I contacted a divorce attorney. We filed papers."

"And he took it without a fight?"

"Yep. He was informed by my attorney that everything was recorded with photos and verbal documentation of the event. Insinuated that information would go to the school board and the Black Point police. He took the liberty of saying it was verified at an ER although it really wasn't. My nurse friend says the hospital encourages filing a police report. The divorce went through without a peep. I was on antidepressants for three years, had therapy also … suicide was on my mind for months." She shook her head, trying to lose the memory.

Jake pointed to a bookshelf. "Grace, these are beautiful pictures of your family. I don't know you, but I can say I'm proud of you. You've made a nice life."

She touched the cross hanging on the thin gold chain around her neck. "I'm protected by the armor of Jesus Christ. Oddly, I now look back at that situation as ultimately my greatest blessing. I'd never been in church in my life. But I was placed in the fire … and I met Jesus. That situation has steered me to eternal life."

50

JAKE SPOTTED A Five Guys location on 59 after leaving Grace's office. The Land Cruiser swung in on its own. He picked up his phone from the passenger seat. Tapped call for Chief Tatum. Pike answered after the third ring.

"Happy lunchtime, Jake. What's the latest?"

"You eating?"

"Yeah. I'm putting the cuffs on a coupla fried chicken breasts at Lyrene's. Just about done." Pike took swig of tea. "Fire away. Whatcha got?"

"Just met with Bascom's first wife. Not much there. At the most, she felt he was a weirdo, no compatibility. He didn't want children, she did, so she did the right thing, moved on. She has a terrific family now."

"Huh. You would have thought she'd have a tale or two. Must have been too early in his deviancy." Pike laughed at the phrase.

"One last thing. James Sloane. We had a good chat. He agreed to kill the commercials … at least for a few weeks. The guy loves his daughter, naturally, he just happens to have the kind of money to stir up a calamity."

"Good job on that. I thought he'd blow you off."

"Well, me too. But, you know, he can be a resource. If we hit dead ends it might be nice for him to plow the countryside with cash. He's right about one thing; enough money and people start talking. Think about those cases where somebody has been watching the movements of a perp, maybe not even on purpose, and then something hits them and they make a call to the cops, say something like, 'I don't know what's going on, but *something's* going on.'"

"Absolutely. The accidental observer."

"Gotta run, Pike. Talk later."

JAKE WALKED OUT of Five Guys, situated the lunch in the truck, pulled out, cut left on County 20 at the light, heading down the backroads toward Black Point. Radio off. Thinking. *Had to be Bascom.* But these other places, the major cities, could he hit those? *Sure he could.* He'd have vacation time. Could easily fit in one murder a year. Wondered if the murders were on the weekends. Lot of groundwork to do. Lots.

The Cruiser was rolling at a modest fifty miles per hour between flat fields of sod on both sides of the road for as far as you could see. Bucolic countryside. He was done with the burger, was scarfing down the rest of the salty fries. He pictured Grace's face, just before he left. She had a look of contentment, after breaking down at the awful memory. Bliss after bringing up Jesus and eternal life.

The open country road invited contemplation. He let his thoughts drift.

One hand on the wheel, breeze blowing in, his mind sifted back through the dust, pictured walking into the Black Point Presbyterian church with Ed and Bonnie. It was the first Sunday he was with them. They went every Sunday until he graduated high school.

He stopped going to church when he reached college. If people said, 'Let us pray,' he bowed his head. He even prayed on his own for Sarah Bradley when she had cancer. At some point, he didn't know when, he felt like he didn't know who he was talking to, or who was listening, if anyone.

If asked, he'd say he believed in God. But he'd never had the lightning bolt, life-changing Jesus moment like Grace Keller.

He'd wrestled with some thoughts over the last couple of years. His life was charmed. He had everything he needed and wanted. Was healthy. Was wealthy. But on a deeper level, he wondered, *Is this all there is?*

Something, *something,* was just out of his grasp.

The Land Cruiser crossed the short bridge over the Magnolia River, coming into the lush hamlet of Magnolia Springs, a place river homes get their mail by boat. He couldn't get past Grace mentioning being "placed in the fire."

At Jesse's Restaurant, he cut left onto Oak Street, drove languidly under majestic canopies of ancient live oaks, widely regarded as the most serene, beautiful residential street in Alabama.

The visual tranquility did nothing to ease back a troublesome thought.

What fire out there is waiting to burn me alive?

51

THE OFFICE WAS cold, AC down low. *Nice*, he thought. It was ninety-two degrees outside when Jake walked into the building. He was on North Royal Street in downtown Mobile, sitting in an FBI conference room talking with Nia Cruz. Their eyes were fixed on a wall-mounted, sixty-inch monitor.

"Bascom's the guy, Nia. Has to be." Jake held a cold water in his hand.

Nia's chin rested in the palm of her left hand, left elbow on the desk. Her fingers teased across her mouth. "I agree. But why does it have to be such a cliché? I mean ... a white van? Come on, man."

Jake laughed. "You know, I agree with that. *Anybody* would be focused on vans. Why not throw the body in the trunk of a Hyundai? That van's gonna help get this guy the death penalty, I hope."

They'd been running and rerunning video footage of a Ford van on the road in front of the Flora-Bama, from the night of the Sloane abduction.

The truck arrived minutes after Lea Lea Sloane and her boyfriend parked. The van didn't stop, kept traveling into Florida. Likely passed the couple as they walked toward the restaurant fronting the canal.

"What's your gut feeling, Nia? Was this guy trailing them

from their condo or did he just happen to pass by as Sloane and her boyfriend walked away from their car?"

"I think he followed them there. Saw them, somehow, at the condo, or maybe spotted them at a grocery or convenience store or something, and followed them back to the condo, watched their pattern of life. He knew they'd go out to eat. And he was ready."

"But he was damn lucky they parked in an isolated location that night."

Nia nodded, took a swig of her Coke. "Yeah, for sure. But he could have followed them back to the condo. Grabbed Sloane there. But he just got lucky at the bar."

In the daylight footage, they had a clear view of the tag ... and it was all but worthless. It was partially covered with mud, revealing only the letter A.

Cameras catching the vehicle approaching indicated a single occupant, the driver. Large trucker cap pulled low, oversized shades, looked like the kind old folks put on over their regular glasses.

"Dark face," said Jake. "Masked up."

"And the plate. No other mud on the truck, Jake. Slick, but revealing, the attempt at deception," said Cruz.

"It's the guy," said Jake, twirling a pen in his fingers. "I think you heard this. Once the agents in Orange Beach ran the truck, 'white Ford van, letter A on the tag,' they found out every midsize van tag in Alabama has an 'A' on the plate."

"I heard. But, whatever. I think Bascom sounds good for it."

Jake started nodding. "The Bureau profiler said he was an 'organized' killer. Well, they nailed that simple part. Bascom's sharp, a science geek, I knew that back in high school. We'll pick him up soon."

JAKE DROVE EAST on the causeway leaving Mobile when the

call hit. He was approaching Felix's Fish Camp, fronting Mobile Bay on his right. Windows down, Mellencamp turned up loud, singing over the breeze about little pink houses.

Looking south, the bay extended as far as the eye could see.

"Montoya."

"Jake, it's Steven Morelock, in DC."

"Hold it." Jake swung the Land Cruiser into Felix's parking lot, coming to a stop next to a decaying, wooden, commercial net boat that had the appearance of a shipwrecked vessel.

"I'm back. Now I can hear you."

"You may not remember, I met you in DC and again in Miami, on the Andie Chen kidnapping."

"Of course, I remember. In Miami, we talked about you growing up in Abbeville, playing baseball at Troy, your kids. Enjoyed our conversation. Steven," he said with a light tone, "I don't forget people from Alabama."

"Good to hear. I'd love to catch up on some of your war stories sometime. But look, Tolleson put me on this financial transaction search for Leonard Bascom, but I don't have much to offer."

"Don't tell me that."

"Yeah, so DOJ squeezed a quick subpoena out of a judge for bank and credit card records. Everything over twenty years old is wiped, gone. But regarding the cities in question, I've got nothing, no credit cards, and checking going back up to twenty years. No airlines, no hotels, no car rentals, no restaurants. Not a hint of Bascom, financially, in those cities."

"Son of a bitch." Tone was a mix of surprise and disappointment. His brain said that had to be wrong, but what next? "So, it's not him? What do you think, Steven?"

"Jake, I'm your numbers guy." Steven had left Troy University with a master's in forensic accounting. He spit-shined his resume by picking up an MBA at the Wharton School of Business, in Pennsylvania.

"But," Steven continued, "Bascom in no way is ruled out in this. You can pay for everything with cash. You can buy prepaid credit cards with cash and use them. The biggest issue with that, as I see it, is an ID. Keep his real name out of it. But you can buy pretty damn good-looking fake IDs online. Hotels probably pay almost no attention. I saw Bascom's photo. Clean-cut guy, glasses, has a meek look about him. My feeling is hotels and rental agencies could care less. I see the issue being the airlines. They'd look closer, particularly with a cash customer."

Jake listened carefully over the whirr of cars speeding down the highway. "That sounds right. The thing we're linking right now, Tolleson's team, is where exactly is this guy during each of the murders, over the years."

"Right. And that shouldn't be that hard ... as long as he's working. You need his base, then travel out from there."

"That's right. Good work, Steven. Call me anytime with any new info, ideas, whatever."

"Will do."

Jake almost ended the call when the thought floated in. "Hey, Steven."

"Yeah?"

"We've grown up with a lot of similar experiences, seen the same sights. If I could scare up a date, would you and your wife let me buy you dinner in Georgetown?"

"Tara's my wife, and we'd love that. Call anytime."

Pulling back onto Battleship Parkway, heading toward Black Point, he thought about the invitation. At this point in his life, he'd spent half his time in the Deep South and half in Washington. He had friends from all over the country, good friends, fine people.

But the red-clay South was mixed into his blood. He knew the land, knew the people, knew how they lived, how they thought, loved the food, loved the hot weather, and the cadence of the drawl was sweet, pure music.

Up to speed, he said it out loud, to no one. "Yep, glad I asked."

Popped on the radio, switched from rock to country. Tim McGraw singing "Meanwhile, Back at Mama's."

The afternoon sun spilled through the windshield, warm on his face.

Felt mighty nice.

52

DRIVING BACK FROM Mobile, Jake decided he needed some exercise. He popped up Dayna Jones on the phone, wanted to see if she and Bryan might be interested in a run.

She answered from the dental lab. "Bryan's not here right now. But I'm up for it, and I'm almost positive he'd be interested."

"Great. Y'all wanna meet me on the bluff by my mother's house at six?"

"Sounds good. You still interested in the Whaler?"

"Better believe it."

"Don't mention it to Bryan, but I want it gone. We've got too much crap, ninety-eight percent of it his. Dune buggy, Porsche, VW, Jeep, boats, kayaks, Ducatis, Suzukis, Hondas, Toyotas ... something's got to give. I can't think straight."

Jake laughed at her surreptitious tone of voice like she was planning a coup. She continued. "A piece of advice. Let Bryan beat you on a run. It might help your cause."

"Beat me on a run?" A tinge of improbability in his voice. He chuckled again. "That's actually harder than it looks." Laughed again.

"Fake a sprained ankle or something." She giggled.

"I'll try. See you at six."

CARRYING A BAG of snacks and a drink, Jake walked from the cottage to his buddy's bayfront house. He settled into a wooden chair on the dock, popped open his laptop, signed on to the Wi-Fi.

Quickly found what he wanted. A digital folder of interviews conducted with people still living in the vicinity of Black Point. Within that folder was another folder: Magnolia Hotel Employees. There were thirty-two names. Only four were still with the hotel. Grizzled veterans, he thought.

He pulled up the first name. Marc Ethridge. Jake remembered him, a guy about six years older than he was. Played basketball at Black Point. Eyes hit on the line "Currently: CEO of a twelve-store pharmacy chain started by his father."

Stopped reading. Pulled a banana out, peeled it, coated it with a layer of peanut butter, took a bite, started reading again. Ethridge had a finance degree from Florida State, no pharmacy degree. Jake thought, *Okay, the leader, the vision guy.* Didn't know the difference between 500 mg of aspirin and 500 mg of metformin ... but good at—A burst of breeze snapped across his face, breaking his focus. Felt good in the humid air. He looked up from the screen, saw clouds bunching in the distance, morphing into a darkening gray, while a small chop blew up on the water. You could count on a quick afternoon squall most summer afternoons. Hoped it would come and go before his run.

He finished with Ethridge, went to the second name, and then the third, and the fourth.

Every report was filled with endless detail, minutia. All worthless bull hockey. Wondered if the agents and cops were being paid by the word.

He started skimming, figured if there was anything of note the interviewer would surely highlight it, right?

He reached interview number twenty-eight. Talmadge Jenkins. Currently was a resident at Oak Acres for the last seven years. Age, ninety-one years old. Jake had seen the place years ago, a small nursing home just outside of Black Point, nestled in a lovely grove of pines, oaks, and magnolias. Peaceful spot to finish out life.

His eyes quickly spotted a yellow highlighted sentence.

"I seen him."

The interviewer was an FBI agent, so he was well-taught, experienced. His notes indicated that he pounded further questions back at Mr. Jenkins about that statement. Nothing of relevance emerged. Notes indicated many of his answers were incorrect or nonsensical. Asked where he worked, he said, "On a ship." He had actually worked in the kitchen at the Magnolia Hotel for forty-nine years. Jenkins said he had no children. He had eight. According to the Oak Acres staff, several of his children visited weekly.

Jenkins was in the Alzheimer's unit. All interviews had date and time. The interview began at 4:35 p.m., ended at 4:50 p.m. It was the agent's last interview of the day.

Jake took a deep breath, something buzzing around his mind over what he just read. *The time of day.*

He'd finished both bananas. Reached in the bag, pulled out several cookies, started eating. A whiff of ozone in the air. A gray wall had formed several miles out on the bay.

Rain.

He slid his chair to the very middle of the pier's picnic area, covered by a tin roof. Five minutes later fat raindrops began pounding the tin, sounding like rocks. Sharp cracks followed the lightning.

In a daze, watching the rain batter the bay, he tried to remember the name of the term. Couldn't think of it, tapped up

Google. Typed in "dementia." Found a long list of mental deficits. There it was. *Sundowner's Syndrome.* An enhanced confusion often started late in the afternoon lasting into the evening. Double-checked the time on the agent's report. 4:50 p.m. *Huh.*

He pressed on to finish a quick read through the last four interviews. Nothing caught his eye. The rain slowed, becoming a gentle shower drumming out a tranquil beat on the roof. Glanced at his watch. Fifty minutes until six o'clock. The weather would blow out before the run.

He was about to close his computer but spotted another file. Labeled "Reward Tip Calls." Had time. He opened the folder and found seventeen reports. Each was a verbatim transcript of what was reported to the tip line. *The cranks calling in.* Looking for $1,000,000 for dropping a name. Indications were that three people had been interviewed.

Jake didn't feel like delving into the sludge right now. Maybe take a glance at it tonight. Yet he let his eyes race across the words, while he began to have thoughts about letting Bryan Jones out-run him. *Aw hell,* he thought, *he'd break a leg to buy that Boston Whaler.*

About to sign off when two sentences jolted him. "*My daddy is Talmadge Jenkins. He knows the killer.*"

Jake took a long slug of Coke.

The nursing home guy.

53

8:02 A.M. Jake sat in the driver's seat of his Land Cruiser at his mother's cottage, dialed the insurance office of Gracie Keller. They opened at eight. He'd wanted to call her cell last night but didn't. Needed to keep this away from her home life.

The receptionist recognized Jake's name from yesterday and he was put through to Mrs. Keller.

"Gracie, sorry to bother you so early. This will only take one moment."

"Okay." Jake read her tone. She thought she'd washed her hands of this ugliness.

"Just a question. Did you or Leonard know anyone named Talmadge Jenkins?"

"Talmadge Jenkins? That name sounds familiar. Let me think."

"Talmadge was a cook at the Magnolia Hotel for decades. Perhaps you two ate there and met him."

"We didn't have the kind of money for that place. I don't know. I can't say I recognize the name. What'd he do?"

"Nothing. He's ninety-one years old and lives in a rest home with dementia. We have an unverified report that he may have seen the killer years ago."

"Sounds like a good lead."

"Well, you know, dementia. It'll be sketchy. I hope this is

the last time I bother you, Gracie. Thanks for taking my call."

"Wait, wait, wait. Is Jenkins a Black man?"

"Yes."

"Something is coming back. Leonard and I had a small wedding. My father paid for everything, although it was very modest by today's standards. I think ... no, I'm almost positive, that he hired a man who worked at the Magnolia to cater it. As I remember the food was very good. My father knew the man."

"How can I reach your dad?"

"Well, you can't. My parents are deceased."

JAKE REACHED OAK ACRES at 8:27 in the morning. Right on time. A woman and man sat in rockers on the front porch of what looked to be an old two-story farmhouse, now the facility's office. The setting felt comfortable, homey, clean, with white paint and red shutters, and trimmed shrubbery edging up to the porch. Summer flowers lined the short sidewalk, inviting visitors inside.

A tall, regal Black woman stood from a rocker as Jake topped the steps. "Are you Agent Montoya?" She had a pleasing smile on her face, the kind you get when a million bucks are about to hit your bank account.

She extended a hand first. "I'm Sheena Milroe, the oldest of all the kids. Mom and Dad had eight of us."

"Mrs. Milroe, thanks so much for the call. As you know, we're up to our necks in dirty laundry." Jake pegged her at late sixties, maybe seventy. Dark-complected with the smooth skin of a forty-year-old.

Jake leaned down to speak to Sheena's father. With his hand extended for a shake, he said, "Mr. Jenkins. Thank you for meeting with me. My name is Jake and I work for the FBI." Jake felt a solid grip from Talmadge's right hand, the old man still carrying some grit.

"I'm ready to go, Willy. Ain't been fishing in some time. We goin' down ta Weeks Bay?"

"No, Daddy. No fishing today. This is Jake, not Willy. He's a policeman." Sheena had her hand on her father's forearm, looking him in the eye as she spoke.

"We buy some bait, we can still go fishing."

"Agent, I'm sorry. You just need to speak to Daddy, ask questions. Call him Tally, that's what his friends called him. Something meaningful might pop out between the confusion."

LAST NIGHT AFTER the run, Jake had called Sheena. Immediately, he was impressed by her apparent desire to catch a killer. She didn't even speak of the money, initially. She said her dad first mentioned something about fifteen years ago when he was seventy-five. Dementia was in its early stages. He recalled the murder of the Gage girl. "Told us he saw the killer," Sheena said. "Said it was a doctor. Called him George."

"Okay, but a question for you. Did your dad ever do catering on the side?"

"Oh, sure. He did weddings, birthdays, events for ball teams. Sure did. It was all word of mouth, not a real business."

"Any records in existence on the events?"

She smiled. "Oh, shoot, no. He never kept records, ever. It was all cash, probably never paid a penny in taxes on any of it. But keep that to yourself." Smiled again.

JAKE SLID A rocker up close to Jenkins, had a manila folder in his hand containing two eight-by-ten color photos. He slid one out.

"Tally, did you know this girl?" It was a shot of Sunshine, waist up, smiling, wearing a T-shirt.

He studied it with tired, rheumy eyes. His head began to bob, slowly. Was that just a tremor? Talmadge's hands shook the whole time Jake had been there.

"Waitress."

"Waitress? Where was she a waitress, Tally?"

"At the dentist. Cleaned my teeth."

Jake looked at Sheena, frustration tightening his muscles.

"I know, it's difficult. Agent, he's said that before about the waitress. My niece Angie worked at the Magnolia in the summers, also in the kitchen with Daddy. The Gage girl worked at the pool. Angie said Sunshine took food orders from guests at the pool and ran them over to the kitchen. They'd call her to come pick up the food."

"So Angie thinks Tally thought of her as a waitress?"

"Yes."

"Makes sense." Jake leaned closer to Mr. Jenkins. "Tally, this girl was killed. You know the man who did it. You told Sheena you saw the killer. I need to know who it was."

Jenkins looked at his daughter, confused.

"Daddy, you told us you know who killed the waitress."

"Probably catch some specks today. Fry 'em tonight. Le's go, Willy. Need some beer, too. Cain't do no fishing without beer."

Sheena scrunched her eyes. "Sorry, Agent, it's difficult."

Jake was looking at Sheena when the photo was pulled from his fingers. Tally focused his eyes on Sunshine Gage's photo when he spoke.

"Dr. George. New moon," said Tally, his lower jaw flapping up and down.

Jake's eyes cut back to Sheena. She nodded. "That's it, that's what he says."

"Tally, did George kill the girl?"

"Peanut doctor." Tally raised his hand high.

"Sheena, what's that mean? Peanut doctor."

"Don't know. He just says peanut doctor. But I think he

raises his hand because the man is tall."

Jake slid another photo from the envelope. A yearbook shot of Leonard Bascom in his chemistry lab, from the year of Sunshine's murder. Several students were around him. It was easy to see the man was very tall. *And Tally raised his hand ...*

"Is this the doctor, Tally?"

Tally grabbed the photo, studied it. Pulled it close to his eyes. His lips trembled.

"Is that the doctor, Tally?"

Jenkins let loose a frightening holler as he stood. Jake felt the man's strength as he pushed past him. He reached the steps, started walking down, wobbly, agitated, arms flailing. Jake reached him, attempted to stop him.

Two nursing assistants rushed out of the building. It looked like a fight to them. Tally trying to beat back a big white man. Tally's daughter in the middle of it.

The nurses, anger in their eyes, pushed Jake away. "Get back, Ms. Sheena. Is okay, Tally, everything okay. Let's get some cookies and Kool-Aid." Both aides had their arms around Tally's back, firing disgusted looks at Jake.

"Goin' fishin'. Me and Willy goin' fishin'."

"Later on, Tally, later on," said one of the aides.

"Sheena, I'm so sorry. I apologize for causing that."

"Wasn't you, Agent. That happens with us, too, his own children." Her eyes welled up; she wiped her cheek as the first tear rolled down. "It's just so hard seeing Daddy like that."

"I understand." He pressed his lips together, shook his head before he spoke. "Again, I'm sorry I provoked him."

Sheena composed herself. "Before you ask, we don't know any doctor named George. We've looked into that. At least there's no doctor or dentist in Black Point, Foley, or Robertsdale named George."

"Any idea about peanuts?"

"Well, a little. Daddy used to grow peanuts back then on five acres a friend let him use, a rich white farmer that used to eat at the Magnolia. Daddy harvested them and boiled them in a large pot over an open fire or with propane. He had teenagers sell them at stands around the county. It was more a labor of love than a money maker. It tickled him to death to have people telling him he cooked up the finest boiled peanuts in Alabama."

"Making me want some. I love boiled peanuts."

"He called them Tally's Top Secrets. Claimed his recipe sat in a bank vault, like Coca-Cola." A smile edged across her face. "Wasn't nothing more than a concoction of salt, shrimp-boil seasoning, and Budweiser."

"Do you know this man?" Jake handed Sheena the picture of Bascom.

"Don't know him but I know who it is. Used to be a teacher at the high school. You think he did it? Killed the girl?"

Jake hesitated for a moment. "I can only say he's a person of interest … and he's tall. Look, I better be going. Thank you for the call. If anything comes out of the information you've provided, I will do what I can to get some money your way."

"Coming from the daddy of the girl killed in Orange Beach?"

"That's right."

JAKE TURNED OFF the radio as he pulled out of Oak Acres. He took one turn to reach County 48, turned west. Heading into Black Point, windows down, the sound of rubber on the road. Forty miles per hour on a country road. Thinking time.

He reached the Walmart at 181, cut into the lot, stopped outside the tire department, kept the engine humming.

Pulled up Google on his phone, typed in GEORGE DOCTOR PEANUTS. Boom. A split second at the most. He was looking at a picture of Dr. George Washington Carver, an esteemed Black scientist at Tuskegee Institute in Alabama. He read a few sentences. Carver pushed the idea of crop rotation. Cotton depleted soil nutrients. Peanuts restored soil nutrients. Carver became known as the Peanut Man after developing hundreds of uses for the nuts.

Eased the truck back onto 48, flicked on the radio, punched on a classic rock station. The Guess Who blitzing through "American Woman." Tried to sing along inside his head

But still. *George* and *Peanut* and *Doctor* stabbed through the music into his brain. It felt like needles.

That old man knows ...

54

JAKE CUT THE engine after pulling into a parking spot situated between a CBD shop in an old gas station and the library. Made a note to ask the owner about CBD to cool off a high-strung dog. Rowdy, his service Mali, had some inbred tendencies that caused him to go postal at times. Not a bad thing ... at the right times.

He hustled into the library, messenger bag on his shoulder, nodded at the librarian behind the counter, and set up on a table in the fiction section. A group of Clive Cussler novels was lined up like soldiers behind him on a shelf.

Using the library's Wi-Fi, he pulled up the cloud site holding all the case files. He briefly looked through some interviews with former students from the Gage era, now living elsewhere. Men forty-one to forty-five years old or so, today. Some photos had guys looking ten years older. Bald with glasses and jowls will do it. He remembered a few, but mostly it seemed like he could have been looking at names and faces from a school he never attended. Just didn't remember the people. Mostly average Joes slicing through life one minute at a time. A lot of excessively useless information in the reports.

He popped open the file on Leonard Bascom's timeline. It began with the Gage murder, twenty-seven years ago.

Black Point, AL: Year 27–26. Teacher Black Point H.S. Divorced from (now) Gracie Keller. Resigned from H.S., moved to Auburn, AL.

Auburn, AL: Year 25–18. Lived in Auburn, science teacher at Opelika H.S. Resigned. Moved to Albany, Georgia.

Albany, GA: Year 17–16. Science teacher at a very small private school named Greenfield Academy. Abruptly left job in the middle of the week. FBI contact with a former teacher from that era said he was sexually harassing a divorced secretary that worked in the office. Bascom resigned and agreed to leave town to avoid police intervention. The woman in question had remarried. Contacted, she refused to speak of the issue. General impression was the episode was quietly brushed under the rug.

Panama City, FL: Year 15–11. Worked two years at a small military base named Naval Surface Warfare Center. He was a civil service entry-level IT specialist. Left to take a position in road sales with MedChem America, based out of Minnesota. Bumped his salary by $35,000 a year. He sold laboratory agents used in cytology and pathology. Traveled Jacksonville, FL, to Mobile, AL, and into south Georgia and lower Alabama. Visited independent labs, colleges, and hospitals. **OF NOTE:** Left the job and moved to Niceville, FL, after he was assaulted at his apartment in Panama City. He was beat up by a brother and the father of a woman he dated who worked at a hospital lab in Tallahassee. Cammy Biddle. We spoke to her. She reported Bascom became "weird and scary" after a couple of nice dinner dates. Allusions to rough sexual practices. Said Bascom showed up at her house wearing a black leather mask around 11:00 p.m. on a Tuesday. She told him to leave and not call again. He didn't listen and began stalking her. She says Bascom knew who beat him and didn't file a police report.

NICEVILLE, FL: Year 10–8. Worked at Publix Supermarket. No issues reported. Excellent employee. Became an assistant manager within twelve months. Left to take a position at a Publix in Perdido Key, FL.

PERDIDO KEY, FL: Year 7–4. Fired after an arrest for sexual assault.

MILTON, FL: Year 3–6 months ago. Incarcerated at Santa Rosa Correctional Institution.

PENSACOLA, FL: 5 months ago. Employed by Morton's Building Supply.

Well, he ain't at Morton's now.

Jake studied the geography. Bascom had made a loop over the last almost thirty years. Black Point to Auburn, Alabama, then over into Georgia, finally dropping back down on the Gulf Coast. Last stop Pensacola, fifty miles from Black Point.

He tapped up a Pensacola map on the web. Wanted some color in his head. Pecked the minus sign a few times, expanding the perimeter. *Mary Jane Hopkins, murdered in Seaside, Florida.* Eyeballed Niceville, Florida. Right across Choctawhatchee Bay from Destin. Checked the distance. Thirty-two miles to Seaside. Mid-Bay Bridge to 98 in Destin, east to 30-A. Simple trip. Bascom knew that, surely, he did.

Lea Lea Sloane, grabbed at the Flora-Bama. Seven miles from the Flora-Bama to the Publix where Bascom worked.

He leaned back, squinched his eyes closed, forcing out the fatigue caused by the computer screen. Kept them closed, thinking.

How could it not be Bascom?

His cell phone rattled on the heavy oak library table, ringer off. He picked it up, spotted the name Amy Cox. Jake stored a contact. Amy was Bascom's second wife, from Auburn. They had an eighteen-month marriage, over twenty years ago.

"Hello, this is Jake Montoya." Jake stood and hustled

quickly past the newspapers and magazines and out the front door of the building. The librarian stopped checking someone out to eye him suspiciously.

"I wanna know why somebody's blowin' up my phone. I don't need one more bullshit sales call."

"Ma'am, I apologize. I'm with the FBI. I want to set up a meeting to speak to you."

"About what?" Her volume rose, irritated. "All I do is work my ass off and pay my damn taxes. I didn't break any laws."

"No, no, nothing you've done. I need to discuss Leonard Bascom."

A few moments of silence. Then the call dropped. Cox had hung up.

He smirked, glanced across Black Point Avenue at a scrum of students talking on the lawn at Coastal, a small community college. They had backpacks slung over their shoulders, one had a cigarette dangling from his mouth.

Jake's phone vibrated again. *Good, she's calling back,* he thought. Looked at the number. Nope. Area code 850. Florida.

"Jake Montoya."

"Is this FBI Agent Montoya?"

"Yes."

"This is Detective Ed Stubbs in Apalachicola, Florida. We got him."

"Who?"

"Leonard Bascom."

55

JAKE PULLED THE Land Cruiser door closed, dropped the messenger bag on the passenger seat, and slid the key in the ignition. He tapped Nia Cruz's contact number in his phone.

Two rings. "How's it shaking, Jake?"

"It's shaking out pretty well. They grabbed him—Bascom."

"Where?"

"Apalachicola, Florida. Heading over. I can wait an hour for you if you want to come."

"Hell, yeah, I'm coming."

"Good. Meet me at the Hampton Inn, I-10 at Hwy 98."

"I know the place. I'll be there in forty."

"Great. I'm going to see if Chief Tatum wants in."

"Sure. See you shortly."

Jake was scrolling up Tatum's contact when his phone rang. Amy Cox, Bascom's second wife again.

"Agent Montoya."

"Agent, this is Amy Cox. Let's just get this crap over with. I don't want to think about this ... whatever's going on, or hear back from cops, got it?"

"Yes, ma'am. We should be able to handle it in one call. I'm looking for early background on Leonard."

It was broiling hot in the truck. He stepped out, walked toward the shady portico of the library, speaking as he went, providing a succinct version of why he was interested in Bascom. He mentioned Sunshine Gage and Lea Lea Sloane. Informed her of Bascom's recent prison time.

"Think back, Ms. Cox, did Leonard ever mention a high school girl getting killed the day she turned sixteen? This would have been in Black Point, a few years before you married him."

"No, he didn't. I would have remembered. Now, wait a minute. Are you shittin' me? Lenny's a killer? I know he's a f-ing perv."

"We're in the middle of a large investigation. Your former husband is a person of interest."

"Well, holy mother trucker." Little bit of excitement in her voice, the kind you get before saturating social media with scandalous information. "You think one of them TV shows, you know, those true crime ones, will interview me? Heck fire, it'd make my year getting on *Dateline* or something."

Jake looked at his watch. "Ms. Cox, let me ask you a few questions."

"Hell, anything. I'm glad I called back. I married a wild-eyed serial killer and lived to talk about it. I might get a freakin' book deal out of it."

"Did Leonard ever have any lab chemicals at home?"

She snorted. "Sure as hell did. He had two card tables set up in a spare bedroom. Looked like some ten-year-old boy's chemistry set. He told me not to go in there. Said there was acid and poisonous stuff. And I didn't—go in there, I mean."

Jake perked up. "Are you sure those were the words, acid and poisons?"

"Two hundred percent positive."

"Did he mention hydrochloric acid?"

"Could have been vinegar for all I know. Can't remember what kind. All I heard was acid."

"What about names of poisons?"

"Mmmm. Don't remember names, even if he said them. Lenny thought I was dumb."

"Strychnine, arsenic, cyanide, amatoxin. Ever heard of things like that from Lenny?"

"No. I've heard of arsenic and cyanide, but not from Lenny. That beanpole psycho could have killed me, couldn't he? I knew he was a bad seed."

"One more thing, really quick. His sexual proclivities."

"His sex who?"

"What he liked to do during sex. Did he ever hurt you, sexually?"

"Well, yeah, every time."

"How so?"

"Well, ole Lenny had a pecker on him like a red-headed donkey. Wanted to put that thing everywhere, if you know what I mean. And hell yeah, it could hurt."

Jake snorted a quiet chuckle. "Did he ever hit you, or beat you?"

"Yeah. He started spanking my ass during sex, maybe about six months into our marriage. And I ain't gonna lie, kinda revved my crank at first. I liked it. Took me to a whole different level of hot. I mean, man, it turned me into juicy fruit." Her voice changed. It slowed, took on a deeper timber, serious. "But then things went deeper, escalated is the word I want. You've heard the term 'he beat my ass.'"

"Yeah."

"Well, he beat it. Violently. It wasn't a little spanking redness, it was bruising, serious black-and-blue bruising. I couldn't sit down. But it got worse."

"How?"

"He started tying me up. Then he took to spanking my front part."

"Your vagina?"

"Yes. He's sick. He's a perverted mother. My theory is, he hates women. But when he started whacking on my tuna, that's when I left. I can take a playful pop on the ass, but the cooter? Hell no. I moved from Auburn to Charlotte, North Carolina. He was at school, and I boogied. Never directly spoke to him again."

"Why didn't you file charges?"

"I thought he might kill me. He didn't say it, but he didn't have to. He wasn't no mild-mannered chemistry teacher. I sure found that out."

"Ms. Cox, thank you. You've been very helpful. Save my number in case anything comes to mind." *Probably a mistake telling her that,* he thought ... his phone might start ringing all the time.

"Sure. And if any of those TV people start snooping, give 'em my number. I'm gonna bone up on that poison stuff. Never know when my mind will catch fire with a memory."

Jake hung up, jogged back to the truck. Knew he was late. He fired up the Land Cruiser, headed through downtown. Needed to pick up his badge and gun at his mother's house. At the light in front of a small deli, he dialed Chief Tatum.

Answered after four rings. "Chief Tatum." Jake heard some fog in his voice.

"Pike, it's Jake. They grabbed Bascom in Apalachicola. I just found out. You want to ride over with me and Cruz?"

Pike laughed. "Sure, if I can pin a badge on my hospital gown. I'm in recovery at the hospital. Just had a colonoscopy. Nothing's up, just routine. How 'bout this? Call me tonight when you're driving back. Soon's I get out of here, I'm heading over to Lyrene's for some fried perch and vegetables. Haven't eaten in a day."

"Absolutely. This is the guy, Pike. I feel it in my bones."

56

AT HIS MOTHER'S house, Jake changed shirts, washed his face, and brushed his teeth. He grabbed a bottle of cold Diet Coke for the road.

Heading east, up the hill on Fels Avenue, he dialed Nia Cruz.

"Where are you, man? You're late."

"Bascom's second wife called. I'll tell you about it."

"And I'm starving. Have you eaten?"

"No." He hadn't stopped thinking about the perch and vegetables that Tatum mentioned. It would take only a minute to pick up some to-go boxes. "Any ideas?"

"Yeah. Swing by Sweet E's and grab us some pork-chop biscuits. I'll take an order of slaw and a large tea."

"Good idea. I'll be at the restaurant in five minutes. Oh, make sure your tank is full. Taking your car."

JAKE WAS PULLING his wallet out when he heard his name. He'd just ordered six chop biscuits, two slaws, and two teas. It was a deep voice coming from a big man. And he knew who.

He turned to see Elijah Washington. "Eli, whatchu doing on the front lines? Thought you'd be in some office mapping out corporate strategy and studying market data."

"I'm a man of the people, Jake, you know that." Eli put his

Midnight Man

hand on Jake's wallet. "Put that back in your pocket. Your money is no good at Sweet E's." He told the girl at the counter, "I'll get that straight with you in a minute.

"But, yeah, Jake, just chatting with a manager, discussing our standards." Eli wore a little-too-tight polo shirt with the Sweet E's logo, a paunch showing just above his khakis. How 'bout you?"

"Grabbing some good chow and heading to Apalachicola. We picked up Leonard Bascom."

"Bascom? You mean Skinny Lenny, the tall science geek?"

"Yep."

"Why?"

"He's a person of interest in these murders."

Eli squinched his eyes. "That's interesting, but I can picture it. Sunshine's too?"

"Yep. You probably saw him that night. He was at Sunshine's birthday party."

Eli's whole face scrunched, thinking. "Don't arrest me after the fact, but I think I accidentally smoked a tad too much of Zip Streetman's weed. But I do remember seeing him. He was always chatting up that teacher, what's her name ... Mrs. Beck."

Eli continued. "Jake, this is interesting, man. I knew Skinny was dangerous. Saw it in his eyes. They were beady ... and always glued to some girl's ass ...oh wait, that was you, my bad." Both had a laugh. "I'd love to know how this is shaking out. Hope you nail him."

"Thanks, Eli. I can't say too much about this now, but it's interesting ... and it's a big deal."

"Haul him in, brother, put this behind us for good." The food was up quickly. "Speedy service, too," said Eli, lightening his tone. "Spread the word."

Jake grabbed the bags. "Thanks. Let's get together soon. I'll be around for a while."

At the truck, Jake put his shades on, glanced back at the restaurant after loading up. Spotted Eli looking at him. A look of contemplation? Look of worry?

Something felt a little off about Eli's interest. *I never had an inkling Skinny Lenny was a perv.* Knew he shouldn't have opened his mouth about Bascom. He got loose and stupid with an old friend, like he was a teenager again.

He eased the Land Cruiser onto US 98, headed north toward Daphne through a blazing afternoon, a sweat stain forming on the back of his shirt.

He drove in a daze, only hitting fifty on the four-lane, cars racing past. Lost in thought. After four miles, he glanced over to his left. Spotted the almost-new Tractor Supply store. He wasn't really seeing it—he was pulling out a thought. A crazy thought.

Elijah Washington recently moves back to Black Point. He opens a restaurant in Orange Beach. Then there's a dead girl. He opens a restaurant in Destin. There's a dead woman at Seaside. *Huh.*

A blast like a train horn sounded behind him. He glanced in the rearview mirror and was looking into the grill of a jacked-up, ass-kicker F-250. Looked at his speedometer. Driving twenty miles per hour below the speed limit. Put his foot down on the accelerator, tossed an apologetic wave out his window.

Eli Washington. Huh, must be the heat.

57

APALACHICOLA, FLORIDA

THE BLACK GOVERNMENT sedan edged to a stop at a small, gray stucco building with a standing-seam metal roof. It could have been a machine shop, but it was the Apalachicola, Florida, police department.

They hopped out, stretched, and headed past three tall, lonely, sabal palms sprouting through some sparse, dry grass.

"About to get interesting." Jake held the door for Nia. They both approached the female officer sitting behind bullet-resistant glass.

"FBI Special Agents Montoya and Cruz here to see Detective Stubbs. He's expecting us."

She nodded, picked up the phone, tapped a couple of numbers, said, "They're here."

Stubbs arrived in only a moment as if he'd been anxious since speaking to Jake earlier. He had thick, dark hair swept back and cut short, a rough-hewn, pock-marked face, and a brush-cut mustache. Throw six inches on his short legs and a Stetson on his head, and you'd be looking at the Marlboro Man.

"Come on in, guys, come on in." He opened the door, shook both their hands as he introduced himself. Stubbs eyed the six-foot African American woman wearing black slacks and a black polo shirt with a heavy Glock holstered to her waist. Jake, six-three, broad-shouldered, wore a white polo with his cut, hard arm muscles emerging from the sleeves.

"Gotta say, you two almost look like you'd wish a little violence would break out today."

"I sure as hell wouldn't mind," said Nia. Her expression said it was the truth.

Jake looked at her, barked out a laugh. "She's gotten a little cabin fever on the ride over, Detective. Great work picking up Bascom, by the way. Where'd you nab him?"

"Well, we aren't going to take too much credit here," he chuckled. "He called us."

Nia snorted. "He did? Why?"

"He was staying at a little motel about a mile from here, down on 98. He woke up this morning, said he was gonna head out to Dolores Sweet Shoppe for breakfast." He flicked a thumb toward the side of the building. "It's right next door. Anyway, he found somebody had smashed out his driver's window. Said they stole some clothes that were in a couple of big trash bags, you know, like the type for leaves. Had a stereo in the trunk. Said it was gone. Of course, we ran him when we took the report. Ex-con. Spotted your BOLO." Stubbs threw his hands in the air, palms up. "And here we are, thinking we're Kojak." Grinned a yellow-toothed smile.

Jake and Nia laughed. Stubbs told the story with some theatricality, knowing he was making fun of himself.

"What was his reaction when you told him you were taking him in?"

"Surprise. Truly. I was called over there to the hotel. I told him we were holding him. Bascom said something like, 'Just got out of prison, ain't gonna do anything to get me back in.'"

"Where is he?"

"Come on." Stubbs walked them down the hall, stopped at

a metal door, and slid a key into a heavy commercial lock, opened the door. "You have visitors, Mr. Bascom."

"Thanks, Detective, we've got this," said Jake. Montoya and Cruz walked in, closed the door.

Bascom was seated at a utilitarian metal table in a fifteen-by-twelve, gray-walled room. Concrete floor, four-bulb fluorescent fixture on the ceiling throwing out too much light, a couple old *Time* and *Sports Illustrated* magazines on the table to help pass the time. No handcuffs.

"Mr. Bascom, I'm FBI Special Agent Jake Montoya, this is Nia Cruz, Special Agent in Charge of the Mobile, Alabama, field office. I made a B in your chemistry class and an A in biology."

Bascom's eyes went from concern over seeing their guns and badges and hearing "FBI" to what could possibly be read as relief.

"Oh my God, I don't believe this." Bascom stood, stepped around the table, hand extended for a shake. He smiled like he was reuniting with one of his old frat buddies from college.

Jake felt a large paw grab his hand with a strength greater than he would have thought. *This guy could easily manhandle a woman.*

"Jake, I followed your career at Bama and with the Redskins. It was unbelievable, man. I was so proud to have known you. I told everybody you'd been my student." He held his grip as he said that. Jake eased his hand loose.

"Please have a seat, Mr. Bascom." Jake had none of the hale-fellow-well-met tone in his voice.

"Jake, call me Lenny. But what's going on here? Somebody broke into my car ... *my* car ... and now I'm in a police station. But hey, you made the hall of fame a few years back. Just incredible, Jake."

Jake responded with a modest nod. Didn't go there.

"And look at those guns." Bascom felt Jake's upper right

arm with his hand. "Looks like you could still play."

Jake's eyes caught Nia's. He imagined her thoughts. *Textbook psychopath. Manipulative. Highly intelligent. Easy, superficial charm.*

"Lenny, we need to ask you a few questions," said Jake as he eased his chair up to the table, looking straight into Lenny's eyes. Nia pulled a chair back to the wall, allowing Bascom to focus on Montoya. Jake pulled his phone out of his pocket, turned it on *Record,* placed it on the table.

Bascom's eyes looked at the phone, a skeptical look in his eyes. "Lenny, it's just easier to record your answers rather than trying to write things down."

"Okay, sure. But what's this about?"

Jake spoke the date, time, and location of the interview. Also stated he, Cruz, and Bascom were in the room. "Just some background, that's what this is about. Lenny, do you know where the development of Seaside, Florida, is?"

Eyes squinted, puzzled. "Well, sure. Over near Destin. Why?"

"Have you been over there in the last month?"

"The last month? No. I haven't been around there in *years.* I think I went by there one time on a Saturday. Again, man, years ago. Walked around, bought a snow cone or a taco or something, watched the crowd, and left. The place was packed with people. That's not my thing, crowds. Why, Jake, what's going on?" Concern in Bascom's eyes.

"Lenny, how many times did you go to the Flora-Bama Lounge? Whether you lived in Black Point or Pensacola or wherever."

"The Flora-Bama? Wait a minute. Why?"

"Lenny, please answer the question."

"The Flora-Bama is just like Seaside. I went one time and one time only. I used to work at a Publix on Perdido Key. The store was about six, eight miles from the bar. Close. This was the year before I went to prison. Of course, you know about that. There was a produce manager there, a guy named Jon Pierce, a total music nut. He dragged me over there one time to see an Allman Brothers cover band. Jon loved southern rock. You could look up the date on that ... or call Jon, he'll tell you. I never went another time. Why?"

"In the last month have you been near the Flora-Bama? Or just driven by?"

Bascom began shaking his head. "No. Nowhere close. The last time was the one I just mentioned. Jake, I just got out of prison. Whatever happened, I didn't do it. I swear to God. Now what's this about? I didn't do a damn thing, but you're making me nervous with these questions."

Jake shot his eyes to Nia. It was quick, only a flash, then he locked them onto Bascom's face.

"Lenny, just one more question."

"Good. Because I didn't do anything. I just want to get back to the motel and get my car window covered."

"Sure. Lenny, this goes back to my senior year at Black Point. Do you remember those years?"

"Sure do. Good years. State championship in football. I'll never forget it. You had the game of your life that night, outshining Eli and Zeke Washington. I have a good memory, even remember the score. Black Point 72, Dothan 6. Sent those kids packing."

"Lenny, you do have a good memory. I'm not surprised one bit. You know there was a rumor back in school in those days."

Jake saw Lenny tense. But he couldn't resist asking. "What rumor?"

"You were the smartest person in the school and way more intelligent than the principal."

Bascom's muscles relaxed. "Well, you know ..."

False modesty, thought Jake. He couldn't disguise his arrogance.

"I bet you remember the night of Sunshine Gage's birthday party."

Bascom was silent a moment. Thinking. Jake wondered, *Structuring an answer?*

"Of course. How can anyone forget that tragedy?"

"You were at the party, right?"

Bascom leaned back, looked toward the ceiling. "Lemme think."

Jake caught Nia's eyes again while Bascom looked away. *Here we go ... the lie.*

"You know, I don't think I was. No, almost sure I wasn't. Why do you ask?"

Jake leaned across the table, easing into Bascom's face. Nia stood, took two steps to the table, stood next to Bascom, looked down, her black eyes full of menace.

"Lenny, we have more than one witness who put you at the party. Remember Jane Beck? You were always sniffing up her skirt. You were working her pretty hard that night."

Bascom's face hardened. Getting pressed, his eyes dilated. Jake spotted his forearms tense as his hands balled into fists.

"But Lenny, we're not concerned about Mrs. Beck. We want to know what you did after the birthday party."

"After?" His head leaned left as his eyes squinted. "Guess I went home."

Jake shook his head, let a cocksure grin ease across his face. "No, you didn't. You met up with Sunshine Gage. She had that blond hair, that tall, tan, athletic body ... she was some kind of fox."

Bascom's chair crashed behind him as he stood abruptly. Eyes filled with rage, he leaned into Jake's space.

"I want a lawyer. I mean, what the fuck is this?"

58

HEAT WAVES UNDULATED off the runway. Watch them long enough and you'll think you're dehydrated, traipsing through Death Valley.

Jake sat behind the wheel in a white Suburban. Engine off, windows down, the truck was parked on the tarmac at the Black Point Airport. He faced the flight approach to Runway 1.

He was thinking about the old man with dementia. Talmadge Jenkins.

George. Doctor. New Moon. Peanuts. That's what Tally said at the nursing home.

He strained his memory to recall the weather the night of Sunshine's party. Late April. It had been a cool spring up to then, wonderful days. His mother remarked on that. Low humidity, little rain. Must have been warm. He didn't need a sweatshirt. Sunshine wore shorts and a tank top. A lot of very loud rock music from the band before Sunshine and Kimbo sang a few acoustic tunes.

Jake laid his head back on the headrest, closed his eyes, thinking deeper. Cookout smoke mixing with a zephyr of weed fumes. A cacophony of happy voices. A few weeks left in the school year. Bug candles flickering around the pool.

But the moon? Didn't remember. Tally had to have seen George in the new moon. A big-ass full moon spraying light on the dark spring night.

The kind of brightness that would hit the face of a killer like a spotlight.

He opened his eyes, picked up his phone. A web search brought Jake to the phases of the moon. Started reading. *What?* The new moon is not a full moon. It's the opposite. It sits between the earth and the sun. Blends into the night sky, unseen.

No light. How could Tally see George? *Must be wrong about the new moon.*

He Googled the Farmer's Almanac recordings of that night, twenty-seven years ago.

New moon.

And Tally saw George. *But how?*

A GLINT OF light flicked. He glanced through the windshield. Something out in the distance. Tiny. Moving. He locked his eyes on it. Getting bigger.

It was Sarah Bradley's $10 million Embraer. Twin jet engines attached up high near the tail pushed the plane to a 520-miles-per-hour cruising speed coming in from Montana. Gear down, the plane roared past Jake in seconds, touching down as gently as laying a baby in a crib.

A spark of excitement zipped through him. Happy as hell to see Ms. Sarah and Dr. Bud Smith. And Rowdy was on the plane. The dog had saved his life in a standoff in Virginia Beach a couple of years ago.

Four minutes later, Jake, leaning on the Suburban, watched the plane come to a halt on the tarmac. The air stair floated down.

The black head of a Belgian Malinois came to the door, scanned left and right, always appraising, focused.

Jake blasted a shrill whistle from his lips, screamed,

Midnight Man

"Rowdy boy."

The agile dog took one step down, then launched onto the pavement. He raced wide open to Jake and jumped onto his chest. A seventy-five-pound missile. It took Jake five steps backward to regain his balance.

Jake wiped the dog's saliva off his face after putting him on the ground. "Sit." He slid two chicken strips into the dog's mouth.

Jake hugged Ms. Sara, shook hands with Bud Smith. "Great to see y'all. Whoa, let me help, Steve." Jake hustled over to take a couple of suitcases from the pilot's hands.

In the Suburban, Bud and Steve flanked Rowdy in the second seat, luggage in the back.

Loaded, the truck eased onto County 32. Jake said, "Steve, we've got a bayfront room at the Magnolia Hotel for you. Hope set up a golf foursome for the morning with the pro and a couple of local guys. Two nice courses, terrific food, a great swimming pool. You'll love the place."

"Thanks, glad to be here."

"Ms. Sarah, Hope's gonna drown you in all of her animal plans. So get ready."

"I can't wait. This is so fun." She wore a ball cap that said Bradley Farms over a pair of large, dark sunglasses and a plaid range-wear top she bought in Bozeman.

"Bud, we've got to get in some offshore swim training. Gulf Shores will be just like the upcoming Ironman in Panama City."

"Absolutely. You're quite the host, Jake. Now, when you're working, can I get the keys to the Land Cruiser? I want to do some exploring."

Jake went silent, focused on the highway, thinking about someone else at the wheel of his truck.

"Bud, I might not quite be the host you think I am."

59

"BABY IT." Jake tossed the Land Cruiser keys to Bud, reluctantly.

It was after eight-thirty when he walked out the front door, brain edging into cop mode. He hopped in the 911, popped in the key, twisted. A deep rumble vibrated through his seat. Revved the engine a couple of times. Nice. He eased the top down and slow-rolled down the long, crushed shell drive.

A quarter of a mile down Colony Street, driving north, he slid on his shades, punched on SiriusXM. Classic Vinyl station. "Jessica" by the Allman Brothers. Betts and Leavell ripping through an instrumental that would have blown Mozart's mind. He pumped the volume, laid some weight on the accelerator. Rolled up fast on an aging Jeep, blew around him at eighty-five.

Glanced in the rearview. Grinned.

Feeling the speed.

HE WAS ONE of four people standing at the door when the librarian unlocked it. It was nine o'clock sharp. He twisted through the bookshelves to snag one of the small study rooms. The space was featureless with no windows and bland, sand-colored paint on the walls. Dead quiet. No distractions.

He closed the door, dug into the files in the cloud. Lots of data from the big city murders stretching back years.

Over the past five days, reports had been posted. Two agents in each city had been given high-priority assignments to get copies of all files, including photos, and speak to the investigating officers from years back.

Current detectives had nothing to add. What was in the report was what was in the report. The original cops were fading into the mist of time.

The reading was tedious, and to a certain extent, repetitive. Various suspects had been picked up and questioned in each case, but no solid evidence emerged on anyone.

Two guys, detectives now retired, one in Baltimore, one in Tampa, picked up on similar murders in Charlotte and Seattle. Contact with other city departments went nowhere. Nobody sounded an alarm for a serial case. Too much distance. Not enough personnel. Too much daily wreckage in their own backyard to start looking at events in cities hundreds or thousands of miles away.

Every case dead-ended. Unsolved. *One smooth killer. Smart.*

The agents put on a full-court press of showing photos of Leonard Bascom to close friends of the deceased as well as individuals who had last seen the victims. They were only able to locate a little more than half of these people, most were in the wind, or dead. Nobody remembered Bascom. The agents stressed his physique. A very tall white man, six-five, beanpole thin.

Still nothing.

After three hours of staring at a computer screen, Jake leaned back, closed his eyes. *Not a damn thing.* Nothing from the field agents on Bascom.

Morelock, the forensic accountant, had already reported finding no transactions of any type from Bascom in these cities on the dates in question.

But still ... *that freakin' Bascom ...*

He loaded up his laptop, marched out into the library lobby, grabbed a swallow of cold water from the cooler, and walked outside into a blanket of moist heat that felt like a virus coming on. Looked at the time. Almost noon. He dialed Hope.

She answered quickly. "Hey there, guy, have you eaten?"

"That's why I was calling. You and Sarah up for a pork-chop biscuit from Eli's?"

"I'll ask, she's right here."

Jake heard Sarah say yes. "How about we meet you there in thirty minutes?"

"Perfect. See you there."

A few minutes to kill. Jake fired up the Porsche, turned off the radio, eased west on Black Point Avenue, heading downhill toward the bay, light traffic. The stunning view hit at the intersection with Magnolia, the elevated California-style vista over Mobile Bay. The seascape made the town.

The murder cities buzzed through his mind like a fly you couldn't kill. Tampa, Charlotte, Kansas City, New Orleans, Philly, St. Louis. They were all big American cities.

And they were all *NFL cities*. The football aspect was unavoidable static in his mind. *Why?*

Reaching the pier, he cut the 911 to the right, headed for the bayfront park, a leafy, narrow strip of land bounded by the cliff face of the high bluff and the tannin-colored bay water. He eased to a stop in front of an empty swing set, shaded by the fat green leaves of an oak. He killed the engine, let his eyes gaze over the water.

It was quiet. He spotted hundreds of gulls occupying a weather-beaten wooden dock like they were waiting for a bus. Blue sky out past them for a million miles, not a single cloud.

He dropped his head back to the headrest, closed his eyes. A wisp of breeze carried the smell of the bay over the car. Brain in neutral.

A day that felt damn good.

He gave it ten minutes. *You better head to Sweet E's.* He placed his hand on the key—

And there was that thought again. Sweet E. Elijah Washington. Eli.

The right time period. Eli had played in the NFL during those years. He would have visited some of those cities.

Which cities? What dates?

Two new Gulf Coast restaurants. Two murdered women close by. He'd thought of that once, but now it was more real after hitting dead ends on Bascom.

And Eli had been at Sunshine Gage's birthday party.

All facts.

60

AFTER LUNCH IT took three minutes for Jake to arrive back at the library. He parked in the lot across the street, picked up his cell. He tapped Pike's number.

"Chief Tatum."

"Pike, it's Jake."

"I know that. I saw your name." Humorous tone. "Solve this thing yet?"

Jake swept his fingers through his hair. "Making progress, seriously. Listen, this morning I met Sheena Milroe at the rest home where her father lives. His name is Talmadge Jenkins. Sheena was one of the callers to the tip line. She said her father saw Sunshine Gage's killer."

"Yeah, yeah. I saw her name in the reports, didn't pay much attention. Figure a money grubber with a horse-crap story."

Jake shook his head at no one. "After meeting her, I don't think so. Anyway, Jenkins is ninety-one and has dementia. He worked in food service at the Magnolia Hotel for decades. And I checked this, too, from the original investigation by Billy Starr's daddy. Jenkins was working in the restaurant the night of Sunshine's birthday party."

Jake went through most of the conversation, including the key terms the ancient man had tossed out. George, doctor, peanuts, and new moon.

"Well, sure sounds like dementia. Old fella's talking brain waves."

"I think Talmadge saw the guy. I do. I believe he thinks the guy's name is George. And I checked, the night Sunshine went missing there was a new moon, which I figured was one of those hyper-bright moons, looks like they're running on nuclear power."

"Nope."

"Well, I now know it means there is no visible moon. I first thought he caught the guy in the moonlight, you know. Made sense."

"Right—if it had been a full moon."

"But doctor and peanuts? That's where it goes off the tracks. Just for the hell of it, I web-searched George-Doctor-Peanuts as a single term."

"And?"

"First thing that pops up. Dr. George Washington Carver, the scientist at what was then called Tuskegee Institute, not far from Montgomery and Auburn. He died in 1943. Carver came up with a bunch of uses for peanuts."

"Well, what the hell does that—"

"Don't know. But here's another kink. On the side, Jenkins grew his own peanuts on land some farmer loaned him, boiled them in what he called a top-secret formula, and had kids sell them at stands around the county. Had a big reputation as the best boiled peanuts in the state."

"And so ..."

"Well, I don't know. But anyway, I'm sitting in the car, burning up. I need something from you."

"Shoot."

"Get Billy Starr and another guy or gal and check into any county extension agents back in that time period to see if there was anyone named George at the county agency. First or last name."

"Got it."

"Also, check with any seed place or whatever that may have sold peanut-seed kernels for planting. And maybe any peanut farmers. You know, ask around for anyone named George. We need that son of a bitch. Oh, one other thing. Any students at Black Point High named George, double-check them. Do that first."

"Will do."

"Gotta run. Talk later."

Jake hopped out of the 911, sweat on the back of his oxford-cloth shirt, more under his arms. He tossed his Wayfarers onto the passenger seat, felt the breeze toss his hair, looked up. Clouds racing, afternoon rain coming.

He raised the top and the windows. Locked the car. He fast-walked to the street, looked, sprinted across North Bancroft in front of an oncoming city truck, bounded up the steps and into the library.

The place felt like a grocery store cooler. *Thank God.*

61

TWO LIBRARIANS AT the checkout desk, seven people signed in on the public computers, and one librarian, a man wearing a pair of scholarly glasses, was at the reference desk. Pleasant smell of books in the air.

Jake strode past all of them to the study room. Occupied. Looked like a tutoring session in action. He walked a little farther until he found an empty table snugged between two shelves. One shelf housed books on do-it-yourself projects, the other, travel.

Time for research. He purposely hadn't mentioned his theory to Pike Tatum or Nia Cruz or Billy Starr. They'd think he was nuts.

On a legal pad, he had written the dates, locations, and victim identification for all the big city murders.

Have to do it. Where were you, Eli Washington?

He began chronologically, starting after the Auburn student's murder. He knew where Eli was then. *In Auburn, playing college ball.*

September 13, 1999. Philadelphia, Pennsylvania. Katie Turner. Twenty-eight-year-old dental hygienist. Blond. Divorced four months. No children. Last seen in the historic Old City vicinity, a popular nightlife area.

Full battery on his laptop. He pulled up Google. Stopped.

Finger tapped the table. Pulled a stick of spearmint gum from his shirt pocket, unwrapped it, tossed it in his mouth, flicked the foil into a metal trashcan.

Thought about things for a moment. Made his decision. *I don't want to be right.*

His fingers started typing: **Arizona Cardinals 1999 Schedule.** It was Elijah Washington's first year in the NFL.

Hesitated once more. Had to do it. Tapped enter.

It was instantaneous. The lineup of sixteen games.

September 12, 1999. Arizona at Philadelphia Eagles.

Hell no! A day apart from Katie Turner. *Eli was there!*

His gut hollowed, felt like he was falling down an elevator shaft.

He pushed his chair back, walked as fast as he could back through the atrium and into the lobby. Went straight to the men's room. Splashed cold water on his face from the sink.

No, no. Hold on. Has to be a fluke. Can't be right, can't be ...

Jake walked back into the atrium, began a controlled walk to his research hidey-hole, felt eyes on him. People had just watched him frantically zip through the room.

He sat down. Everything where he left it. Looked at the legal pad.

November 20, 2001. Phoenix, Arizona. Lori Thorne. Twenty-five-year-old graduate student in computer science at Arizona State University. Blond. Last seen after tutoring five students at night in the engineering building.

He pulled up the web result for the Cardinals 2001 schedule.

November 18, 2001. Cardinals vs. Detroit Lions. Sun Devil Stadium. *In Arizona.*

The murder was two days later. *Eli was in town!*

He thought, *How could he do this?* **Why** *would he do this? Is this a coincidence? Not a coincidence he was at Sunshine's* *birthday party.*

Jake looked further down the kill list.

December 21, 2003. Tampa, Florida. Kayla Mills. Twenty-eight-year-old schoolteacher. Blond. Married. Two-year-old son. Out on Christmas break. Car located in the parking lot of WestShore Plaza mall, where she told her husband she was going for last-minute shopping.

Eli played for Arizona, then the Atlanta Falcons, then finished his career in Dallas. Kayla Mills died during Eli's first year with the Falcons.

Jake pulled up Atlanta's schedule for that year.

December 20, 2003. Atlanta Falcons at Tampa Bay.

Jake's head flopped. He rubbed his brow. Eli was there.

Eli Washington was in Tampa!

This ain't coincidence. No way, he thought. He closed up his laptop, tossed it and his legal pad in his messenger bag, speed-walked out of the library, shaking.

Had to speak to someone. Fast.

62

LENNY BASCOM SAT for two days in the Black Point jail and was close to being sent to Pensacola to be charged. He'd violated Florida's sexual offender statute related to a change in residential address.

Montoya needed time with Bascom. Another interview, and quickly.

Spence Geiger, Bascom's lawyer, was standing in the lobby of the Black Point Police Department when Jake arrived. Jake saw a five-nine man, heavy in the gut, blocky head, wearing cowboy boots.

After a quick introduction, Geiger said, "Agent, Mr. Bascom said he'd answer questions, but I will step in immediately if I think it's in his best interest." He said it like his client was on death row ... because he might be, soon.

"Got it, counselor."

Montoya knew that they had nothing on Bascom tying him in proximity to Lea Lea Sloane and Mary Jane Hopkins other than he'd been in the vicinity of the Flora-Bama Lounge and Seaside, Florida, *years ago*. Nothing tying him to the big city murders. *And* ... things were getting interesting on Elijah Washington's status.

Jake wanted one last shot before Bascom was shipped back to Pensacola.

Bascom was in the interrogation room when Jake and the attorney entered. The lawyer shook hands with Bascom. "Look to me, Lenny, before answering anything."

"Mr. Geiger, I have nothing to hide. I was guilty of assault of one woman in the past and did my time. I haven't done anything since. And I won't do it again. Ever."

Hearing that, Jake felt Bascom's tone was the Gospel. It's what he came to verify. He kept thinking about Bascom's surprise in Apalachicola. Bascom *was puzzled* at the accusations. Nothing shifty in his answers. *But.* Psychopaths can pull that off.

Everyone sat, pulled chairs up to a table that was bolted to the floor. Cool glow from harsh fluorescents in the room. Smell of disinfectant in the air. Jake pulled a small digital recorder out of his shirt pocket. "I'd like to record this session if that's okay." Turned on the recorder.

"I'd prefer it," said Bascom. "Don't want anybody coming up with lies about what I say."

"I agree," said Geiger. He pulled his own recorder out of his briefcase, turned it on, spoke the time and date and participants in the room. Jake's machine picked that up.

Jake wanted to focus on the Seaside and Flora-Bama murders … and touch again on Sunshine Gage.

"Here's what's interesting, Leonard. And I know you're a smart man, always did, way back in high school. Lea Lea Sloane was killed a few weeks ago. She was abducted from a parking spot about a hundred yards from the Flora-Bama. Her boyfriend was clubbed with a pistol, knocked unconscious."

"Don't know anything about that. Never heard the name. Never saw her. Wasn't near the Flora-Bama." Bascom shaking his head with the look of a preacher on his face.

"Let me finish. This young woman was twenty-four, blond

and tall like Sunshine Gage. She was killed in a similar fashion. Vagina desecrated. Skin carved up. Nipples sliced off. This is twenty-seven years after Sunshine." Jake leveled hard eyes on Bascom.

"Hold it," said Geiger. "Is that a question?"

"It's okay, Mr. Geiger. I have nothing to hide because I wasn't involved in anything like that. Never have been. Only a sick maniac would do that. That's not me." Tone calm. Confident.

"Exactly like Sunshine. And you," Jake pointed at Lenny, "you were at Sunshine's birthday party. You know exactly where the Flora-Bama is. You've been there. You told me that."

Montoya and Geiger both jumped as Bascom's large hand slapped the metal table. Sounded like a gunshot. Bascom's finger was six inches from Jake's face, anger in his eyes. Calmness left the room.

"Let's get this crap straight right now, Montoya!"

Geiger reached over and gently eased Bascom's hand down. "Easy, Lenny, easy. Let's get your hand down."

"Hell with easy, they're not trying to put you in prison for murder. I don't know anything about it. Got it? Nothing! That crap's from somebody else. I couldn't even dream of that sick nonsense."

The most common defense, thought Jake. *Some other dude did it.*

"Convince me, Lenny." Jake leaned forward on the desk, resting on both forearms. "Help me believe you."

"Okay, I'll help you, starting with Sunshine Gage. I'm like everybody else was in town. Shocked at her murder. It was gruesome. A sick monster was behind that ... and that other girl, Sloane or whatever. Another freakin' monster."

"Lenny, you've been in prison for sexual assault. Some people might call you a monster."

"I DID THAT! *I did.*" Bascom yelled briefly. "I did do it." Voice softening. "But it was nothing even close to what happened to those girls. Not close. Not in the same universe."

Jake scrunched his lips into a disingenuous smile. Wanted to show Bascom some doubt.

Lenny Bascom continued. "Okay, look. Sunshine Gage. I've never had to say this because I've never been accused of Sunshine's murder. I've got an alibi. Rock solid. You're right. I was at the birthday party. And I *was* talking to Jane Beck. She was an attractive woman, you know that. I believe she taught you English. Her husband had died a year or so before that. Cancer. I went home with her that night, after the party. I was there at her place until ... hell, maybe two-thirty in the morning. Then I went home, to my place."

"She was what, ten, twelve years older than you? Did you bang her?"

Bascom's tongue rolled under his lower lip, getting pissed.

"She was eleven years older than me, forty. I didn't *bang* her. We made love. Damn, Jake, she was beautiful, you know she was. Don't tell me you've never found an older woman attractive."

Definitely not going to tell you that, he thought.

"But you were married, right, Lenny?"

Bascom exhaled. "Yes. When I got home it was World War Three. A lot of screaming."

"Did you spank Jane Beck?"

Geiger put his hand on Bascom's forearm, looked him in the eye, shook his head.

"It's okay, Mr. Geiger. Yes, I spanked her, but that was later. I didn't hurt her."

"Did you beat your wife?"

"Things got rough in the bedroom, the night before she left me. But I didn't *beat* her. When I got home late after Sunshine's party, I told Gracie about Mrs. Beck. I told her we made love. I didn't care. Our marriage, although short, was miserable."

"What'd she say? Your wife."

"Said I was the biggest mistake she ever made. She left me a year later."

Gracie Keeler didn't mention that in the insurance office, Jane Beck after the party. Why?

Jake looked at Bascom a few beats, looked at Geiger, their eyes met. Geiger was neutral in his expression.

"Well, Lenny, I think I'll speak to Mrs. Beck, see if she remembers."

"She'll remember. Guarantee that. After that night I went to her house after school twice a week for almost a year. Ask her about those pops on her rump. She was hungry, very hungry, sexually. I didn't hurt that lady, she liked it. Older women, man, you wouldn't believe them."

Yes, I would, actually.

"Another thing. Ask Gracie. Ask her about that argument the night of the Gage party. She's too straight to lie ... I hope."

"Okay, hold it then. Be right back," said Jake. He left the room, took a quick pee. Lot of tea at lunch. He grabbed three bottled waters from the break room. Still thirsty from the salty pork at Eli's.

Walked back into the interrogation room, placed the waters on the desk. "Drink up, gentlemen. Got a few more questions."

Jake unscrewed the cap, took two heavy swigs, replaced the top, sat down.

"Okay, Lea Lea Sloane ..."

Lenny Bascom was unwavering in his answers. He looked Jake dead in the eyes with each answer. Not so much as a twitch. Appropriate blinking, no fixed stare. No looking away at crucial moments. No excess pauses to craft a lie. Every answer was quick and forthright.

I didn't do it. I wasn't at the Flora-Bama. I have not stepped foot in the state of Alabama for years. I was not at the Turquoise Place condominiums. I have never had strychnine in my possession in my life. Yes, I have used hydrochloric acid but only in laboratory settings. Oh, oh, oh, I did have some at home in Black Point but just for preparing projects for the high school. Never eaten at Bud & Alley's in Seaside.

Jake stood, walked in slow circles around the interview table, thinking. Bascom's and Geiger's eyes were on him, probably wondering, What's Montoya going to do?

Jake processed the last twenty minutes in sections. Bascom was a smart piece of garbage, but he believed him. And if he didn't do Sunshine, he likely didn't do Lea Lea Sloane. He'd check with Jane Beck. He'd call Gracie Keeler, one more time.

"Leonard, thank you for speaking with me. Mr. Geiger, thanks for your time. Let's get Leonard over to Pensacola."

Jake glanced at his watch.

Had time.

63

JAKE DID THE math. Mrs. Beck was sixty-seven years old. He coughed out a laugh at the thought. *How do you ask an almost seventy-year-old woman if she likes to get her ass spanked during sex?*

A quick web search of her name on his phone gave up her address.

Her place was only ten minutes away. He checked his watch. Coming up on four o'clock. Typical subtropical afternoon. Humidity almost a living thing.

He popped the engine alive on the Land Cruiser, eased into the traffic on Colony Street, right behind the spewing gray smoke from an old '60s Ford. Two lights down, turned right on Black Point Avenue, heading west, cut south on Great Bay Road.

The breeze waved up a light chop on Mobile Bay, off to his right. Singing along in his head with Paul Simon as he explained fifty ways to leave your lover. At the boat ramp, he turned east onto Pier Street, heading up a modest incline.

He spotted Jane's house a quarter of a mile up, a charming tin-roofed craftsman-style cottage painted dark gray with vivid white trim, likely built in the years around World War Two. Beck's name on the mailbox, flowers at the base. A thick-trunked Canary Island date palm was the yard's statement

Midnight Man

plant. Everything about the place felt down-home and comfortable.

And there she was, in the yard wearing a straw landscaper hat, garden hose in her hand, watering some camellias.

Jake pulled into the drive. Killed the engine. She turned. He saw curiosity on her face, wondering who—

Jake slid off his sunglasses, ran his hand through his hair, slid his pistol under the seat, popped out of the truck.

A twist of a bay breeze tossed some fronds in the palm. Grass manicured, green as a PGA course.

"Mrs. Beck. You probably don't remember me. I'm Jake Montoya. You taught me English way back when." He tried not to look like a salesman.

She dropped the hose as a broad smile crossed her face. She walked toward him with a lively step. "Oh my goodness, what a surprise!" He felt her cheer. Jane was about five-six, trim, wearing jean shorts, a black tank top, with a gardener's tan on her legs and arms.

Skin surprisingly taut. *One well-preserved woman.*

"Jake, a teacher never forgets her favorite students. And you were definitely a favorite. Everybody probably thinks you're just a football ruffian." She grinned. "I bet they have no idea of your love of words and stories."

He returned her smile, happy she remembered him. "You're right about that. Not a single soul has ever come up to me to talk about Holden Caulfield or Atticus Finch."

She laughed at that. "I bet not. Jake, it's treacherously hot out here. Let's go inside. I have sweet tea and lemonade."

"Sounds good." Following her toward the house, he realized he was getting older, and felt his nature accommodating time. Couldn't believe how attractive he found her. Amazing legs. Her calves danced as she walked. *Sixty-seven.*

On the stoop, he said, "Oh, Ms. Beck, you won't believe this.

I have a master's in literature from Georgetown."

She stopped, looked him in the eye, gently grabbed his forearm with both hands. "Nooo." Eyebrows raised. "That's so impressive! I want to hear all about it."

She was close, in his space. Over a light sheen of perspiration on her skin, he smelled a delightful aroma, clean and botanical. *Citrus?* Appealing ...

Sipping tea and lemonade, they talked for over an hour. They hadn't seen each other since Jake graduated. She fired the questions but still did most of the talking. His life. Her life. Her second husband, who also died of cancer, just like the first.

She found his life story compelling. Had followed his football career, she told him. NFL Hall of Fame. Big Jake Grill Company. Federal agent. Lastly, their favorite books and crime writers they loved.

"Jake, you're such a delight to talk to. Know what? This just hit me. I think you should teach. I do. There's such a magnetism about you. You would captivate students. We need these kids to read."

He smiled, locked onto her brown eyes. "Very, very kind of you to say. But right now I'm in the bad guy business. And that's what I'm here to speak to you about."

"Now this is really getting fun," She took a quick sip of tea, leaned toward him on the couch. "True crime. Can't make that stuff up. But how in the world could I possibly help you?"

"Leonard Bascom—"

Jane's eyebrows raised. "Ohhh."

64

IT WAS A PLANNED seduction. Jake had called Jones earlier in the morning to see if he and Dayna wanted to put in six or seven miles when they got off work. Said he wanted them to meet a buddy of his, a former veterinarian from the DC area who was down for a visit.

Jake was having night sweats about Jones' old Boston Whaler. Vivid dreams of the boat being put up for sale without his knowledge. He drives by their cottage. Driveway cleared. Had to get that vessel away from Jones by any means necessary. Problem was, he found ole Jones was a likable guy as well as a pretty interesting character.

But Jones was a nocturnal web crawler, familiar with deals done in the dark. A dude a little too clever.

Worrisome, he thought.

His ace in the hole was the wife. Dayna. Clearly a sensible woman, pragmatic compared to Bryan's gunslinger approach to web purchases. But she was dead set on unclogging the driveway.

JAKE AND BUD SMITH were parked near the pier when the Joneses arrived on mountain bikes. After introductions, they chained their bikes to the Land Cruiser.

"Let's do it," said Dayna, looking fast and sleek in her shorts and racerback top, just standing still.

They began a slow jog, heading south along the bay. Looking down from the bluff, they could see the water was glassed off. Not a sniff of wind.

By the time they'd reached the VFW Lodge, Dayna and Bryan were both deep into conversation with Bud, first about dogs, then about his uncountable bicycle trips. Another mile and a half had them in front of the Magnolia Hotel. By the time they rounded the S-curve, Dr. Bud was inviting them to go with him to the Patagonia region of South America for two weeks.

The last words Jake heard Bud say were, "Most stunning landscapes on the planet."

He was lost in thought, Jane Beck on his mind, and what she'd had to say. She was guarded at first, and curious. Why Lenny Bascom? Why now? Jake told her everything, probably more than he should have.

She wasn't aware that Lenny had spent time in jail. At first, she seemed both disappointed and surprised, but the more they talked, she admitted she could see him going too far.

Jane displayed no shyness as she discussed her relationship with Bascom. The one thing, the only thing Jake really had to know, was this: Did Leonard Bascom go home with her after Sunshine's birthday party?

He did.

"Mrs. Beck, are you a hundred percent sure about that specific day? This is critical."

"Yes. Positive." Her eyelids dropped a little. "Just like with my favorite students, a woman never forgets her first time with a man." Her voice ran husky as she spoke, talking about sex.

"I was a dry desert, Jake. Lenny reawakened me. It was unexpected. No, it was more than that. It was indescribable. This is only between me and you." She leaned in, lowered her voice. "I had three orgasms that night. *Three!* He touched me and pleased me in ways my husband could never dream of. Do you know what that's like?"

Is that rhetorical? Or does she need an answer?

They were sitting on her couch. She'd crossed her legs, waggling her bare foot absentmindedly as she spoke. A glint of her red nail polish caught his eye.

A dainty foot. Hypnotic in its movement.

He steered away from her question, had what he needed, knew he should go.

But he didn't.

"This might be a little delicate, but I feel I should ask. You know, in the name of justice." He raised his eyebrows. It certainly could have been described as playful. "We are dealing with crimes of a violent nature."

But he didn't ask. He made a statement. "Lenny said he spanked you."

She looked him in the face. All he saw were deep pools of big brown eyes. Clean citrus scent in the room. Tan legs.

"He did." Her voice deepened an octave. Her eyebrows raised, ever so slightly. "It surprised me at first. But boy. Boy, oh boy, oh boy. It sent me. It was deep, deep ... and intense." She didn't look away as she spoke. "The orgasms, I mean."

My old English teacher!

He watched her suck in a deep breath.

He felt a smidge of nerves, the good kind. A quick thought ... student/teacher fantasies. They were real, he knew that. But mid-forties and sixty-seven years old? Unheard of?

Reined in his self-control. No way. Not a chance. He just couldn't. *But kind of almost slightly a chance.*

"So what happened?"

"We met like lovers at the dark end of the street for, gosh, almost a year." She made two fists, said, "Ummmph. It was deliciously hot ... every single time."

He felt something stir in him. *Keep it professional.*

"How did it end?"

"Lenny never said it, but I think he may have found someone else. Plus, he moved to Auburn." A reminiscent expression floated down her face. "But don't feel sorry for me. If I need to not be lonely, I just go to one of my online matchmaking sites. Have you ever done that?"

"Ummm, no, I haven't."

"I guess not." Her eyes roamed down his body, invitation in her eyes.

"It's surprising, even the sites that appear very conservative are nothing more than funnels for sex. I mean you just would not believe how active it is. Truth be told, I need more than most women. Didn't know that until I was forty or so. I like it aggressive, but not rough. Call it high intensity. The spankings blasted things into another galaxy. Lenny taught me that. I'm sure I scared a couple of men I met from the Christian sites." She glanced away, giggled at the thought. "My gynecologist plants a little pellet in my arm. Testosterone and estrogen. Let me tell you, that keeps the fires burning." Brown eyes saying, *Come on, touch me.*

"Huh." He could not believe she was dumping this level of intimate information on him. He felt the invitation, thought about it, fought the urge, stood.

"Well, look, it has been great reconnecting with you. And, trust me, you have provided a critical piece of information."

"My pleasure. And I do love that term, 'RE-connecting.'" She held her look.

"I could really picture something with you, Mrs. Beck."

"I was hoping you would."

He smiled. "I take that as a great compliment. But I'm talking English and literature. You would be a tremendous writer of romance novels."

"Would be? Let me show you something." She walked Jake into the den, held up a single open hand to her bookshelves. "Fifty-three books and counting. But it's not romance, Jake, it's erotica. My writing has some teeth in it."

He pulled one from the shelf. The cover was a shirtless, ultra-ripped guy wearing jeans and a cowboy hat. "*Bronco Buster* by Ava Wild," he read out loud. "Love your pen name."

"Every one of them is available on Amazon."

"When I'm back in DC I'll definitely download one. I'm curious and impressed with your productivity. Fifty-three books! Well, I think I'm stealing too much of your time. Thank you so much, Mrs. Beck."

"Jane. Call me Jane."

"Sure. Jane, you've helped out Lenny, and me, a lot."

"That's good to know. And if you ever have any free time, stop by, and let's brainstorm." Cheshire cat smile, eyebrows teasing. "Always looking for new material."

Driving back to the animal sanctuary, sun low in the west, shadows slicing through the trees, he wondered. His mind's eye pictured the tip of his index finger and thumb an eighth of an inch apart. *I was that close.*

Cutting east onto County 32 off Scenic 98, he pulled to the side of the road. He had one thing left to do.

He dialed Gracie Keeler.

JAKE WAS TOLD Mrs. Keeler was in a meeting with a customer.

"I'll hold, it's important."

"Sir, it could be a while."

"I'll hold, thank you."

"Hello, Agent Montoya, I'm told it's important." Keeler made Jake wait eleven long minutes through droning insurance minutia in the on-hold recording.

"I'll make this quick, Grace."

"Okay."

"Leonard told us that after Sunshine Gage's party, he went home with Jane Beck, the English teacher. He said he got home and told you they made love and you two had a big fight over that. Is that accurate?"

"Yes, it is. It's the truth." She was matter-of-fact, no bite in her tone.

He thought that might stoke some anger. Her life was now much too comfortable to revisit those harsh feelings. Another lifetime to her. But yet, she didn't divulge that information when she had the chance. He knew why ... he thought.

She was humiliated.

65

SHEENA MILROE ANSWERED on the fifth ring. Jake hoped 9:40 at night wasn't too late, but *screw it*, he thought. There's a killer out there. And likely just around the corner.

"Sheena, sorry about the late hour. It's Jake Montoya."

"No problem. Just watching season three of *The Crown*. I never had any interest in the royals, but this is quite fascinating. Hold on, let me pause it ... Okay. What's going on?"

"Just thinking about your dad and what he said."

She laughed. "What part? Fishing?"

Jake laughed with her. "Yeah, he was ready to go, he sure was." Another blip of a chuckle. "The part about George and the peanuts and the new moon. I was a little ignorant about the moon. I thought that would mean a bright, full moon, but it's not. Barring stars, it's a dark night. I thought he might have seen the George fellow in the light splash from the moon."

"Nope. No moonlight that night. I thought the same thing. I had to look it up, too."

"Getting back to George. Are there any kids out there you knew working the peanut stands named George? That Tally knew?"

"No. All of us talked about that. None of us remember any George." Jake heard her take a sip of a drink.

"Huh, okay. Question. About the peanut stands. Did Eli or

Zeke Washington work at the stands?"

Sheena was quiet for a few moments. He gave her time, knew it was deep in the past.

"I don't think so. I don't remember it, anyway. The last year or two he ran the stands, it was his grandchildren running them. He has twenty-one of them. That man wanted to start his own nation."

Jake barked a chuckle. "Sounds like it."

"But why Eli or Zeke? They were in your grade, right?"

"Yes. We graduated together. Played ball together since middle school. It's nothing really. Eli has moved back to town. He's running his pork-chop chain out of Black Point. Thought I might ask him about George ... particularly if he or Zeke worked a stand."

"Good idea. I just can't pull out a memory of seeing them."

"Okay, thanks, Sheena. Call me if something pops into your head."

ELEVEN HOURS LATER, Jake met with Chief Tatum, Agent Cruz, and Detective Starr in the conference room at Black Point PD. He updated them on Bascom's alibi from Jane Beck. Told Tatum, and Starr in particular, to not reveal that info. Mrs. Beck was a nice lady still living in the community.

"Jake, you're a little slow on the uptake about her," said Billy. "The whole town knows she's making boatloads of money writing those sex stories. Rumors of over a half-a-million bucks a year." He laughed out loud. "Hell, my wife reads them on her Kindle, says she'd like to be a fly on her bedroom wall—if our minister wouldn't find out." Barked out another laugh. Tatum and Cruz joined him.

Jake smiled. "I've been away too long. Before yesterday, the last time I saw her was at the end of the twelfth grade, turning in my book report on *Animal Farm*."

He also informed them that Bascom's wife at the time verified that version of the story.

TATUM, STARR, AND Cruz were informed about the meeting with Talmadge Jenkins. It was murky, he told them, conversing with a dementia patient. "Jenkins said George was the killer."

Jake scratched his left forearm. "Now, this is why I wanted to meet. I slipped up on something interesting, but disturbing, especially to me personally. Eli Washington."

"What?" said Starr.

"Yep. He and I played ball together in high school, known him for years. He moved back to Black Point maybe eight months ago. Running his pork-chop company out of here. Nia and I ate at the restaurant."

"Tasty, too," she said.

Pike said, "I used to eat at one of his joints in Texas at least once a week. Good stuff. Busy spots."

"I've been out to the one here on 98 probably five times. Now if we could just get a Chick-Fil-A in here, we'd be set," said Starr.

"Okay, it's settled," said Jake. "We all like pork-chop biscuits. But listen up. Eli Washington was at Sunshine's birthday party. That's indisputable, but not surprising. It was an open invitation to anyone who knew her. Now, guys, focus on what I'm going to tell you." He looked each one of them in the eye.

"A couple of years after Sunshine's death, a coed is killed in Auburn. Same basic MO, different poison, antifreeze. Who's living in Auburn? Eli Washington. The body was found two days after the Georgia game. I looked up the stats. Eli had a good game, 126 yards."

"Eli Washington?" Billy Starr's voice went high, both hands

raised, palms out, his facial expression indicating nonsense was in the air. "What the hell?"

"Hold it, Billy." Jake shot him a look. "So Eli Washington arrives back in Black Point. Builds two restaurants on the coast, Orange Beach, Alabama, and Destin, Florida. Now we have a dead woman visiting in Destin and a dead woman visiting Orange Beach." Jake glanced at their faces, hoping to see some excitement.

Nobody was electrified, particularly Starr. "Come on, man. Are you serious?"

Jake had pegged Starr as a rube the first time they met. "Well, okay, Starr." Ice in his tone. "This is a good time for me to stop. Bring it to us, Billy, what do you have? Let's review your list of suspects."

Jake's sudden irritation shook the room. Pike and Nia picked up on it, both of them easing back in their seats, eyes widening.

"So, whatcha got, Billy?" Jake's harsh glare pierced the detective sitting straight across the table from him. "Let's hear it. We've got a madman outside our window, practically in arm's reach. You see him? Who're you looking at?"

Starr shrunk in his chair, sheepish look on his face. "Well, can't say I really have anything. I'm reviewing interviews daily from the students and the employees at the Magnolia Hotel. But nothing solid yet."

Jake gulped out something that sounded like a cough. "Let me get this straight, Billy. We've got what, 330 million people in the United States, right? And you don't have one single suspect. Even with a list of hundreds of former students and hotel employees and you have zero. ZEE-ROW. That right, Billy?"

The air vibrated with tension.

Starr looked down at the table. Tatum and Cruz looked down at the table. Nobody wanted to meet eyes.

"Jake, look, I apologize. In no way did I mean to denigrate your work, your suspicion. On second thought it's starting to sink in about Eli. I apologize for interrupting your presentation." Starr, a large man at six-two, although soft everywhere, looked like he was about to cry.

Jake noticed, lightened up. "Billy, you gotta understand. This animal, whoever he is, killed my girlfriend. I've lived with this for twenty-seven years. We need to be on the same page, that's all. Look, this case is huge, something way bigger than two young women found in Cottonmouth Creek. We've got a traveler. And this piece of garbage has been doing his thing for almost three decades."

"Continue where you were headed, Jake. We're interested," Agent Cruz said.

Jake twisted a cap off a grape sports drink, downed three big slugs. "Okay. What I'm about to tell you might coalesce some things for you, but I want your opinion."

Chief Tatum nodded, holding a Danish in his left hand. "Fire away, man, you've piqued my interest." Took a bite of the pastry.

"Okay. I studied all the murders in the big cities. The ones Nia dug up off VICAP from the Bureau. In every single instance but two, Eli Washington was in those cities within twenty-four hours of the killings. How do I know? Here's how. His team was there playing an NFL game. All of those cities are NFL cities. He was the starting fullback in each game."

"Muh-ther-hugger," said Starr. "Pure genius, Jake. I'm a stupid piece of crap saying what I said a few minutes ago. Damn, man, I'm sorry. This is Sherlock Holmes stuff, it is."

"Wow," said Nia, leaning back. Eyebrows raised. "So, wait. We've got Eli at the scene of the very first murder. He's also at murder two, in college at Auburn. Two new restaurants in the last couple of months, two dead women from the vicinity."

Starr was so onboard he sounded like it was his idea. "Exactly, Nia, exactly. Got this guy, we do." He stood, did a little jig around the conference table, firmly cementing the fact he was a dumb rube.

"So what's next?" said Tatum

"We're gonna put a tail on him, twenty-four-seven. Nia, I want you on that. You might want Stan Wills over here. Think that was his name. He did a great job surveilling the law office on the Lucky Hendrickson case. But whoever it is, they need to be shadows."

Pike stood, stretched. "What can we bring to the table?"

"Back up Nia's team when she needs it. You got any cops that don't look like cops?"

"You mean besides Billy?" Laughs all around, including Billy.

"I'm going to speak with Justice in Washington. This has to be done by the book, picture-perfect the whole way. We need to get into Eli's computers, plus all his texts and phone calls, as well as credit card and banking info."

"Crawling up his ass. I *LIKE* it," said Starr.

"And I've got one more thing up my sleeve."

"What's that?"

Jake stood. A cunning smile twisted across his face.

He walked out of the room.

66

"**HE'D LOVE IT.** At least I think he would," said Sheena Milroe. She was in the produce section of Piggly Wiggly, picking out zucchini, when Jake called. "He definitely loves some pork chops."

"Be good to get him out, too. I'll pick you two up at eleven, tomorrow morning," he said.

"Wonderful. And thank you. Oh, I didn't mention this to you. After you left the other day, he mentioned your name. Some way, somehow, through all the backroads and short circuits in his brain, your name came back to him. That man loved his football. And he mentioned the holy trinity, too." She laughed. "Can you believe that? What they called you and Zeke and Eli in high school."

"Did he mention Eli and Zeke specifically?" Black Point locals had begun to call the football stars Montoya and Eli and Zeke Washington the holy trinity their senior year in high school.

"Oh, no, no. Just the trinity."

"Interesting. Well, okay, see you tomorrow, Sheena." Jake rang off, thought about the mystery and complexity of the human mind for a moment. Tally would be seeing a second member of the trinity tomorrow, Eli Washington. *That*, he thought, *will be interesting.*

Jake hatched a plan with Dr. John David Gage, Kimbo and Sunshine's father, a man he'd been close to since becoming friends with Kimbo in the first grade. Yesterday, they met over a beer on the dock at Gage's Point Clear home. A couple of beers, actually.

The doctor had a stake in the case. A hell of a stake. Someone killed his only daughter.

After Gage heard the story, he was skeptical. "Eli? Man, I just don't know about that." He compressed his mouth, skepticism in his eyes. "Hard for me to wrap my arms around it." Took a last swallow of beer, twisted the top off another. "But I'll do anything you suggest. You know that."

MONTOYA, TALMADGE JENKINS, and his daughter walked into a wall of cool air as they entered Sweet E's Pork Chop Biscuits. Zac Brown singing through the sound system.

"Feel good in here," said Tally, steady with his cane, wearing baggy khaki pants and a loose summer-weight button-up shirt. A Magnolia Hotel golf cap was on his head. "Want greens with my chop. And mac and cheese." They'd discussed the menu on the ride over.

"Yes, sir, Tally, coming right up," said Jake. Looked at Sheena, spoke softly. "Lucid today."

Walking to the counter, Jake spotted Dr. Gage sitting at a table with Eli. Far corner, deep in conversation, papers scattered on the table between two drink cups and greasy wrappers that held biscuits fifteen minutes ago.

The scheme was simple. Dr. Gage was to speak to Eli about franchising opportunities. They'd meet in the restaurant so Gage could sample a biscuit. He knew Eli but hadn't seen him for over twenty years. And the meeting made perfect sense. It was known in the community that Dr. Gage was an active investor and a very wealthy man. He'd made his real money off condominium developments on the redneck Riviera stretching from Panama City to Gulf Shores after selling off three thousand acres of Bay County farmland, left to him by his grandfather.

Fifteen years later, Gage bought every single acre back. Swore he'd never sell a square inch of it again.

Eli Washington was excited to meet with him. He knew Gage could buy and sell restaurant franchisees with the excess change in his pocket.

Food on the table, and Tally dug in like he hadn't eaten in a month. Jake watched his face. A satisfied man, long disconnected from the worries of the world.

Tally pointed at the biscuit. "Lard. Knows what they doin'." He sprinkled hot sauce on his greens, dug in like he held a shovel.

"Man knows his food, Jake. Always said lard made the better biscuit. Never wanted to switch over to butter." She forked some baked beans into her mouth, eyes combing the restaurant. Dabbed a napkin across her lips. "I think that's Eli over there," she pointed, "in the corner talking to Dr. Gage."

Jake's head swiveled. "Think you're right, Sheena. We'll stop by their table after we're finished, say howdy."

Jake finished up quickly, took several swallows of tea, wiped his mouth. Sheena was right behind him.

Tally had one more bite of biscuit. "Good, real good," he said. Took the last bite, shot 'em a comical grin. Not a tooth in his head.

"Daddy could chew the bark off a pine tree." She smiled. "Sure could. And I'll tell you, he liked this food. He's mighty stingy on food compliments."

Jake felt his nerves start to sizzle. Showtime. The stage had been set.

Tally's lucid ... for the moment. Come on, man, just keep the wires clear ...

"Tally, let's go meet the cook. Let him know we liked his food." Jake pushed out of his chair, walked around the table, helped Tally up, placed the cane in his hand. "Right over here, Tally, let's say hello. Tell the cook you liked that biscuit."

"Where? Buying bait? Shrimps be good ... go fishin' today."

Jake looked at him. *Oh hell. Not now, please not now.*

67

DR. GAGE HAD been stealing peeks out of the corner of his eye, hoping they'd hurry over ... before he actually threw money down on the table. Eli laid out the past, present, and future of the company. And it was slickly enticing. There were eye-popping returns, on paper.

But Eli's ask surprised him. Came at Gage from a different angle, acutely aware of the doctor's financial wherewithal. Suggested Gage buy a piece of the *parent* company, grow it fast, let the franchisees pay him. Eli and Gage ...partners.

Gage wasn't stupid. He was a medical man first. He parsed out a few qualities of a psychopath. Eli was charming. Collected and cool in their conversation. The numbers were too good, almost assuredly trumped up, he assumed. And the manipulation. Gage could practically feel Eli's hands on him ... pushing, pushing, pushing ... smile on his face the whole time. Driving him to the pit.

Gage's ire built as they spoke. Eli chirped along, not recognizing a thing. Quickly, the meeting with Jake on the dock crossed his mind. Montoya had told him every detail they had.

This son of a bitch was in almost all locations women were killed. *He's the guy.* Gage knew it.

Gage's hand rubbed over his right pants pocket. He felt the steel outline. *The answer to twenty-seven years of pain.* At home, he'd fought the right decision. He lost the fight.

A black hammerless Smith and Wesson .38 caliber revolver rested in his pocket. Three short feet from Eli Washington's face. He'd smiled at Eli, listened intently, said the right words that indicated strong interest in this new venture.

Gage's hand eased into his pocket. The pistol grip slid comfortably into his palm. His right index finger maneuvered into the trigger guard, coming to rest on the curved trigger. Trigger touch was light as a feather. Five rounds in the gun. Hollow points. It wouldn't take him six seconds to empty the weapon. Three in the chest. Two in the face. Screw the blood. He was a surgeon.

Slowly, very slowly, Gage eased the gun from his cotton pocket.

Jake's hand popped solidly on the doctor's right shoulder. "John David, looks like you enjoyed your pork chop." Locked his eyes on J.D.'s face. Gage knew he'd spotted the pistol.

The doctor stood, ghostly pale for only a moment. He packed away his malicious intent.

"Well, Jake, hello. And Mr. Jenkins, hello, sir." Shook their hands. Gage knew Jenkins and his daughter. Treated Tally for a bowel obstruction in the late '90s. "Sheena, good to see you getting your daddy out. And how about this food? Man, it's something. I'm here talking to the original chef of this organization."

Before Jake could say a word, Tally looked at Eli. "George, you smart boy, always smart. Lard in the biscuits. Smart with peanuts, too."

Electricity sizzled through Jake's nervous system. Identified. Wanted to scream. *We got you!*

Gage froze, wondering if he'd heard right.

Eli was standing now. Knew he was looking at old man Jenkins. Mind probably Jell-O by now.

Midnight Man

"Glad you liked it, Mr. Jenkins. But, sir, I'm Eli. Eli Washington." Eli's eyes flicked across Jake's and Sheena's faces, sympathetic to the man's mental status.

Tally's hand raised, pointed at Eli. "Know you, son. You George." Tally pulled back his hand, pointed at his own head. "You smart, boy. Them peanuts."

Suddenly, the light left Tally's eyes. He looked around. Confusion in the surroundings. Turned toward his daughter, Sheena. A look of fear on his face.

"Who're you?"

68

A TWELVE-MINUTE ride to return Talmadge Jenkins back to Oak Acres. Little conversation on the way. Jake thinking, *You're done, Eli.* Sheena Milroe was lost in her own world, calculating the split of a million bucks between her and her siblings.

Jake pulled to a stop at the memory facility, helped Tally get to the front door, Sheena right with him.

"Tally, thanks so much for having lunch with me."

"Take my nap, then we'll go fishin'. Get the shrimps. We'll fish."

"Yes, sir, we will." Looked to Sheena. "Thank God you called us. We've got a lot of work to do. We'll be pulling out every resource to put the puzzle together. And it's a huge puzzle. Almost twenty murders over thirty years, Pennsylvania to the West Coast." Jake sighed at the magnitude. "What worries me, Sheena, is lots of times we know the killer but can't nail the evidence. That won't happen this time. We're going to take down Eli Washington. I promise you that."

She shook her head. "I just can't believe this. This insanity happens other places. Eli was a good boy, always popular. He was friends with my children growing up. Everybody loved him. It's just so sad ... and frightening"

"I'm as shocked as you are. Seriously. Now this is critical, I mean critical. Don't mention that lunch and George and whatever to anyone. I mean nobody. And that includes your brothers and sisters. Your kids, too. It could blow the case."

"I won't. I won't. Getting this close scares me. Eli saw me."

"Sheena, just be glad you're not a twenty-two-year-old blond, white girl." Said it with a straight face.

She laughed. He followed it with a snort.

"Remember. I want big money rolling into your bank accounts."

Sheena zipped her fingers across her lips.

WHAT WAS J.D. THINKING? Leaving Oak Acres, Jake eased onto the county road, bore down on the gas pedal, slinging a wash of breeze over roadside wildflowers. He tapped a contact on his phone. John David Gage. Five rings. Voicemail.

"John David, this is Jake. Where are you? We need to talk." Rang off. Concerned. Reached County 48, turned left, heading into Black Point. Spoke out loud to no one. "Where are you, J.D.?"

Jumped the truck up to sixty-five. Figured he'd check Gage's home in Point Clear, twenty minutes away. He needed to speak to Nia and Pike but was too agitated to call. Priority one was John David.

Idling in the left turn lane next to the Walmart, foot on the brake. *Come on, come on, change.* Light turned green. Phone rang. His eyes hit the screen.

"John David, where are you? Let's talk."

"Easy, partner, where's the fire?"

Jake heard an untroubled tone. "You okay? Don't think I didn't see what was happening in the restaurant."

"Well, I'm downtown at Ace Hardware. I was okay until Tony told me he was out of stock on the PVC elbow joints I'm looking for. Working on my irrigation system this afternoon."

Jake exhaled, relieved. "You gonna pull a pistol on him, too? Tony."

"Listen, son." Dr. Gage had been calling him son since he was six years old and was almost a surrogate parent. "I'd never do that, Jake, never. It was pure fantasy, killing the man that took your child. It wasn't going to happen. On my worst day, I'm not capable of murder. Getting that close, knowing I could take the man, fulfilled my fantasy."

Jake understood, harboring his own fantasy. Nothing so clean as pistol shots. His involved knives, mutilation, broken bones. Prolonged agony. Carving every shred of skin from Eli's body. And he *could* do it. And he would do it if the right circumstances arose.

"Okay, John, good to know. You call me if those thoughts overtake you."

"Will do, son. Thanks."

Jake rang off the call, U-turned, rolled back to the light, turned left to get back on 48, known as Black Point Avenue at that point. Heading toward downtown, to the Black Point PD.

He dialed Agent Cruz's number just before the roundabout at County 13. While it rang, he popped up the AC fan, Hope's Suburban was full of late August heat.

Four rings. Answered. "Don't keep a lady waiting. Whatcha got?"

"He's the guy, Nia. Eli Washington is the damn guy." Said it like he was out of breath.

"Tell me."

Jake recounted the scene, beginning to end. "First thing the old man said was 'George,' looking Eli Washington right in the eye the whole time."

"I mean, whoa, that's just unbelievable. Can't believe you strung this together. But we've got a problem."

"Lay it out."

"What, you suffering from that NFL concussion business? It's obvious. We have a ninety-one-year-old man with dementia talking about a crime from almost thirty years ago. And he doesn't even know *his own daughter* standing next to him."

"There's evidence, has to be. Serial killers like souvenirs. Might have photos, video, who knows."

"I'd bet on tissue samples, nipples, maybe," she added.

"Absolutely. It's there, we just have to find it. We need to get into Eli's place. Tolleson is already in touch with justice. Now we have a little more ammunition with this verbal George ID."

"Jake, they're gonna laugh you out of the Bureau with that *George* malarkey. Can't nobody even find *anybody* named George. Just a name out of the freaking blue."

"Working on it, Nia. More than ever, we need a tail on Eli."

She laughed. "Uh, dude. While you were enjoying lunch, Stan Wills and an agent named Palmer were in two separate cars, watching the restaurant. We got this, baby."

"I didn't see them."

"You ordered shadows. You got shadows."

He was a block from the PD when he hung up. Downtown was overparked with cars, too many people. He got lucky, a woman backing her minivan out of a spot just to the side of Provision, an eclectic coffee and wine shop. He eased the Suburban in

Jake found Pike Tatum and Billy Starr in the conference room, a box lunch from Lyrene's on the table, the smell of fried chicken grease in the air.

"Sometimes we eat a late lunch, Jake, try to catch a little of the Paul Finebaum show on ESPN."

Jake looked at the big screen mounted on the wall. Saw a thin, bald guy, late sixties, glasses. "Never heard of him. Who is he?"

"Seriously?" said Pike, a dubious frown crossing his face. "Best college sports show in America. Focused on the SEC."

Jake shrugged. "I'm out of the loop."

"Oh, man, you know what would be hilarious, Pike?" Billy Starr slapped the table, face beaming. "Have Jake call Paul, tell him it's Jake Montoya, and that he'd never heard of Finebaum."

Pike barked a laugh. "That *would* be funny ... super funny His audience would be laughing their asses off. Do it, Jake. Right now. You tell the screener it's Jake Montoya, former Bama All-American and NFL Hall of Famer, they'll put you right through, no doubt about it."

"Shit yeah, they will," said Starr, talking over a mouthful of greens.

"Another time. I wanna update you on Eli Washington and George."

"Oh, hold it, Jake," said Starr, wiping his mouth. "Did you review our report we uploaded? On people named George?"

Shook his head. "Uh uh, hadn't seen it."

"Okay, really quick. Not crap, man, nothing interesting. Farmer down in the south county for years. Ikie George. Farmed peanuts and soybeans. Died about six years ago. Another guy working at the farm supply store over in Robertsdale where they sell that peanut seedling stuff. Name of Johnson George. I mean his dadgum last name is already a first name. Did his parents think that was funny? Giving him a last name for a first name?"

Jake nodded. "Speed it up, Billy."

"Okay, I talked to Johnson, he's slow, you know what I mean?" Starr tapped his head. "And he's only thirty-three. Just a boy when all this started. One other guy. George Yoder. He's Amish or Mennonite or some such. Long beard, a straw hat with a band around it, pants with suspenders. All those guys dress alike, ya know. Lives out near Elberta. Sixty-six years old. Has farmed peanuts for over forty years, still farming. Raises goats and donkeys, too. Over at the feed store in Robertsdale, I asked about him. They said he knows more about peanuts than anybody around. I talked to him for maybe ten minutes." Billy shook his head. "Nah, man, can't picture it."

"Yeah, thanks, Billy. An Amish serial killer for thirty years." Chuckled. "It'd probably fly on *Dateline*."

Jake filled them in on the lunch. Told them Eli was the guy, to keep that tight until they locked down some solid evidence.

He popped a stick of gum in his mouth, spearmint. Held the pack out to Starr and Tatum. "Hope to have a warrant in a day or two. Gonna tear Eli's house apart. Same thing for his place in Dallas. He still has a house there. Rip through his computer files, financials. Look for any storage units. Be ready to rock, boys."

Leaving the station, Jake checked his watch. 2:20. Sunny, the kind of summer day he loved as a boy, plenty of afternoon left.

He eased the truck into traffic, headed south on Colony Street.

69

THE EXCITEMENT OF the day had peeled away, mostly, anyway. It was almost eleven at night and the former farmhouse was quiet. A light snore drifted from Rowdy, lying on foam at the end of the bed.

Jake's fingers traced down Hope's naked back. She was lying next to him on her tummy, sleek and beautiful, wearing only white cotton panties. They had finished making love a few minutes ago. Not intense, nothing aggressive like it so often was. Just enough to release the edge, slide into a restful sleep.

Jake's favorite time of day. Everybody down. Surrounded by solitude. And a new book. He moved onto his back, elevated his head on three pillows. A cone of light flared over his shoulder highlighting the pages of Rick Bragg's recent book about Speck, a half-blind stray dog that arrived, Rick stated, uninvited, half-dead, bony, and starved, on a ridgeline behind his house.

Two pages in, Jake knew he'd have this book in Hope's hands in the morning. Nobody wrote the South better than Bragg. He did the right thing, he took the dog in. Jake kept reading. Bragg wrote, "Speck is not a good boy. He is a terrible boy, a defiant, self-destructive, often malodorous boy, a grave robber, and screen-door moocher."

He chuckled when he read that, feeling his stomach muscles contract. He looked over at Hope, an athletic woman with a back and shoulders straight out of a DaVinci sketch. Chamomile and lavender reaching him from her night cream.

Gorgeous in her sleep.

Jake's dog Rowdy was a regimented animal. He lived life according to demands and rigid guidelines. Speck was another matter, a rascal full of devilment from snout to tail. Jake was through the third chapter by eleven-thirty, enjoying the tale of a free spirit while the strain of the day lost its grip. Ready to call it a night.

He jumped when his phone rang.

He twisted, grabbed it quickly off the nightstand, felt Hope move, heard a contented moan.

No ID on the caller. Local area code. He answered in a whisper. "Jake Montoya."

"Jake, I'm sorry, so, so sorry about this late call." *A woman's voice, older.* "But you gave me your card, said to call anytime day or night if something came up."

Jake squinted, trying to place the voice.

"Well, something has come up. Late this afternoon—"

"Whoa, I apologize. Who is this?"

"This is Elaine Starr, Billy's mother. Jake, I'm so sorry, I can get with you in the morning on this—"

"No, no. No problem. What came up? What'd you remember?"

"Well, okay. I fought the decision to call all evening, but just couldn't get to sleep."

"Mrs. Starr, I'm glad you called, I am. Fill me in." Jake sat up, sleepiness gone, energized.

"Okay. I don't know if you know anything about Kenmore."

"No. Who's Ken Moore? Where does he fit in?" Jake kept a pad by the bed to make notes for any idea that hit him in the night. He grabbed a pen, wrote down the name.

Elaine giggled. "No, not a person. One word. I'm talking about Kenmore appliances?"

Appliances? The enthusiasm drained away.

"Yes. I've heard of them."

"Good. Here's what you need to know. If you need an appliance, go with Kenmore. They run like beasts and live longer than an elephant."

Is this woman on Ambien?

"Yes, ma'am."

"Here's why I really called. It just tears me apart to bring this up ... that sweet Gage girl being your girlfriend and all. Always thought she had the dearest name, Sunshine."

This might be going somewhere. He gently slid out of bed, stood there naked, glanced back at Hope. Soft breathing, she hadn't budged. In the shadows from the reading lamp, he caught Rowdy raising his head.

"Yes, ma'am."

"Well, anyway, all the science with evidence and crime whatnot has gotten so advanced these days. Technical is what it is. I watch it on TV all the time. Bill, Billy's daddy, would be flabbergasted at what's out there."

"Yes, ma'am."

"But anyway. Were y'all able to get any information from that tissue sample?"

Adrenaline sizzled into his bloodstream. "What tissue sample?" His toes tensed against the oak floor.

"That sweet little Sunshine scraped the skin off that monster's body. But, Bill, my husband, had no DNA matches. You know, all I hear is this database and that database. I just wanted to know if anything popped out from additional information. They'd run that stuff immediately on *CSI: Miami.*"

"Mrs. Starr, I'm so glad you called. Super glad. Candidly, I haven't seen anything about the sample. Have you talked to your son about this?" Jake rubbed the back of his neck with his right hand.

The line was silent a few moments. "This is horrible for a mother to say. You probably can't tell, but Billy's not the sharpest tool in the shed. The answer is no, I haven't. And he's kind of a know-it-all, even when he's wrong."

I noticed.

"First thing in the morning, I'm going to look into this, Mrs. Starr. This could be critical. I can't tell you how important this could be."

"So glad to hear it, Jake. Well, I best be getting to bed. I'll sleep now."

"Yes, ma'am."

"Oh, wait a minute, I'm so crazy. I lost my train of thought. The real reason I called."

There's more? Jake paced the room, walking on air.

"Kenmore. The freezer. Bill bought one thirty years ago. Still running strong. I gave ours away today, cleaning out the garage. I live by myself. I don't need all that food storage. Anyways, Johnny Moore came by and picked it up today. He just lives three doors down. I'd been letting him store venison in it at my house forever. I finally told him to come get the freezer, take it to his place."

The heck she's talking about ... venison?

"Okay."

"Still running strong but Johnny's gonna put a new motor in it, rewire it."

"Yes, ma'am."

"But anyway. Bill stored a tissue sample from Sunshine in that freezer. Y'all probably have the sample but if you don't ..."

A feeling like two hits of speed blasted him.

"Elaine, what's your address? I'm headed your way."

70

TWENTY MINUTES PAST midnight, Jake arrived at Elaine Starr's house. She said she called Johnny, and he was expecting them.

A buckling sidewalk, easily fifty years old, was their path to reach the old freezer. The black August night showed only a sprinkling of stars, passing in and out between fast-moving clouds. An early morning chill in the air, leaves bristling. Rain on the way.

Jake knew this was likely futile. Even if the sample was there, it had probably been unthawed and refrozen many times, destroying the tissue integrity. "Mrs. Starr, this will be hard to answer, but how many times do you think the power has been off on the freezer?"

"You mean like the electricity off during storms, that kind of thing?"

"Yes, ma'am, exactly."

"That's an easy question. Never. Bill installed a natural-gas generator when we moved into the home. That freezer has never been turned off."

Jake felt a spring in his step as they reached Johnny Moore's front door.

"I plugged it in soon as we got in the garage," said Johnny. "Me and two boys loaded it on a flat warehouse cart." He pointed at a battle-scarred metal dolly, parked ten feet away. "Never got turned upside down or sideways or nothing. Couldn't have been unplugged no more than ten minutes."

Jake, Elaine, and Johnny were in his two-car garage, jammed in between a mid-'60s Jeep and a late-model Pathfinder. Gardening tools hung on the walls, the stink of gas and oil reeking off a dusty mower.

Driving from the Refuge of Hope, Jake dialed Tolleson in Washington. "Ross, I need you to wake up somebody at the lab who handles DNA testing. I mean right now. I need to speak to them."

"What?" Groggy voice. "The hell time is it?"

"Time for a break in the case, I hope. I think I'm about to get my hands on a tissue sample from the killer. Hang up and get on it. Have them call me directly. I'm waiting." Jake heard the acidity in his tone. Didn't care.

"Mr. Moore, I'm looking for some kind of container that could hold a bit of human skin tissue."

Moore's eyes squinted. He looked at Jake. Flashed them to Elaine Starr. She raised her palms. "Don't ask, Johnny."

"You know, I think I did see something in there at one time," said Johnny. "I've been storing my venison at Elaine's for years."

"A small container?"

"Something. Can't rightly remember." Johnny took a last swallow from his beer, set the can on a shelf. "Let's dig, pardner." He popped up the freezer top.

The men emptied the freezer of venison in two minutes, each pulling out packages two-fisted, like stealing money, placing them in the topless Jeep. Jake's gloom escalated the deeper they went.

"Agent, I don't see anything," said Johnny. He and Jake were looking into a big empty box. Only sound in the room was from the humming electric motor.

Jake's shoulders sagged. That evidence would likely have nailed the coffin shut on Eli Washington. "Well, damn."

Elaine looked at the floor, felt the disappointment.

Jake rubbed his chin, paced around the garage. Thinking. *So close.* That was the break …

Jake heard Johnny in the background, speaking in a whisper. "Good God, Elaine, I musta thrown it out. But I don't know why. I woulda asked you first."

"Not your fault, Johnny. For all I know, I threw it out years ago."

Jake's phone rang. He turned up the volume after speaking to Tolleson. Didn't want to miss the call. "Yes."

"Agent Montoya?"

"Yes."

"This is Dr. Chester Chan, director of the DNA Casework Unit at Quantico. Tolleson said to call you immediately. What's crackin'?"

Chan sounded wide awake, like a cheerful man after a good-night's sleep, a light breakfast, and two cups of coffee. Ready to launch an attack on the day.

Jake faced away from Johnny and Elaine but saw motion in his peripheral vision. They were carefully reloading the freezer with meat.

"Chester, deeply sorry to bother you at this time. False alarm. I thought I was going to have an old tissue sample for you to analyze. But I don't."

"Sorry to hear that. Tolleson said you've got your hooks into a serial case."

"Yeah, we're positive on that. Have a very strong suspect, too. I was hoping this sample might ID him as *the guy.*"

"Okay, save my number in your phone. Call anytime for anything. Let's get this mother."

"Will do. Thanks, Chester." Jake rang off. He imagined Chester as a trim Asian man, hair parted neatly on the side, wearing a white lab coat and glasses. Likely wore a sober facial expression. But he said "mother." Jake squeezed out a thin smile at that.

"I found it!" Elaine Starr hollered.

Jake turned in a flash, saw her holding a package of meat in her left hand and a plastic container in her right. It was only about an inch square. Clear plastic, black top.

"It was stuck to this package of meat."

"Well, damn, everybody. No better time for a beer." Johnny ran into the house.

Jake took the container, looked at it in the light, wiped off some frost, thought he could see a pale substance in frozen clear liquid. "Gotta be it." Stepped over and hugged Mrs. Starr. "I think you just solved this case."

"Nope, Bill did."

"He damn sure did."

Jake piled the last of the meat in the freezer, placed the plastic canister under a package of meat, closed the top. He felt the comforting vibration of the motor purring.

Johnny was back, handed each of them a Bud in a can. They popped the tops. "Cheers," said Jake. He and Elaine took a swallow. Johnny poured his refreshment down his throat like he was topping his truck off with gasoline.

Jake placed his can on the freezer. "Gotta make a call. Great work, you two." He stepped outside the garage into the night, redialed Chan.

"Chester Chan."

"Chester, it's Jake Montoya. We found it."

"Oh, hell, yeah, so what do you have?" A buzz in his tone.

Jake told him it was a tissue scraping from under a woman's fingernails, described the container, and told him it had been in a freezer for over twenty-five years.

"Frozen now?"

"Yes. Can you work with something that old?"

Jake heard Chan sucking in air.

"Hoh, boy. The answer is 'maybe.' Hopefully, the tissue was frozen quickly after extraction, but still, man," Jake heard a clucking sound. "We have to be lucky. Good chance there'll be artifact and that will gum up the results."

Jake told him they needed to find out, and fast. "Chester, I'm getting on a plane to DC this morning. American runs direct from Pensacola to Reagan. Just tell me how to pack it."

"Sure, it's simple, here's what you do ..."

TOLLESON SPOTTED MONTOYA at the curb outside of Terminal B at Reagan, a red Igloo cooler at his feet, messenger bag over his shoulder, and a Smashburger bag with drinks in his hand. Ross slowed the Ford to a stop. Jake slung open the back door, placed the cooler on the seat, hopped in the front, tore into his burger bag. "Hadn't eaten, been up all night."

The aroma of hot french fries sifted through the car. "Gotcha covered, Ross," Jake tapped the bag, "just get us on the highway."

They hopped off I-95 forty miles later. Took Fuller Road to the FBI lab at Quantico.

They parked outside a monstrous building, 460,000 square feet, the outside heavily clad in glass, surrounded by brick, with a stone foundation. A state-of-the-art fortress to crime-fighting technology.

Before the flight, Jake had looked up Chan on the Bureau website. Dr. Chester Chan immigrated to the Bay area from Hong Kong as a child. Grandfather initially supported the family with his beef jerky business. *Beef jerky?* Mother enrolled him in a small Christian school, where he excelled. Went on to acquire a master's in molecular biology and a doctorate in genetics from the University of California, Davis. *Nice.*

CHAN WAS REVIEWING a lab report in his office, nibbling on celery and ranch dressing, his foot keeping time with Robert Plant and Allison Krauss singing a duet in the background, when Montoya and Tolleson arrived. He looked up when his secretary announced their arrival, spotted a red cooler in Jake's hand.

Chan shot out of his chair in a flash, like Bruce Lee.

Jake saw an Asian man, maybe five-four, wearing scrubs, sporting a haircut that could have grabbed him an immediate role in a punk rock band. Close to shaved on the sides with one-inch gelled spikes on top. Practically a weapon itself.

Locking eyes with Jake, Chan unleashed a high-voltage smile, probably powered by the four cups from Starbucks resting on the desk.

"Agent Montoya, so good to see you. Agent Tolleson, so good to see you." Head nods, two-handed handshakes to both. He took the cooler from Jake's hand, held it up in the air, saying, "The Holy Grail?" Eyes closed, face scrunched, a raucous laugh shot from his mouth. Tapped his pointer finger on the cooler. "With this and my black magic, gonna burn that mother huggin' dirtbag." Laughed again.

Jake wondered about this dude. Comedian ... or esteemed scientist? But he spotted confidence in the man's eye, so okay, he liked this guy.

"Dr. Chan, I did my part, now pull out your voodoo."

"Absolutely. Start right now." No chitchat. Chan had his palms out, flopping them, indicating they were to leave now and let the scientific process begin.

Chan was closing his office door when Jake stopped it with his hand.

"I forgot what you said, Dr. Chan. What's your timetable?"

"Seventy-two hours."

"Doc, we've got women being tortured and murdered." Jake emphasized his need with a hard look.

"Twenty-four hours. Extra coffee. And I'll skip lunch." With both hands, he pushed the door closed against Jake's hand.

Last thing Jake saw was the smile of a caffeine-charged madman.

71

BLACK POINT, ALABAMA

JAKE AND ROWDY were lollygagging under a stand of live oaks at the animal sanctuary when his phone vibrated in his pocket. There was just enough breeze to cause the leaves to wiggle, which made the afternoon tolerable. He grabbed the phone, spotted a text from Chester Chan: **Call me.**

He dialed immediately, excited and worried at the same time. Chan answered mid-ring.

"Twenty-three hours, forty-eight minutes, Agent! New Chan record."

Jake pictured a smile like stadium lights and coffee cups littering a lab floor.

"I need good news, Chester."

"Great news, man, great news. I was able to extract DNA. The sample was viable."

"And?" Jake walked as he spoke, Rowdy next to him, eyes scanning the surroundings.

"Nothing on the Combined DNA Index System." Spoken with a subdued tone.

Jake exhaled. "Ahhh, man."

"No problem, though. All you need to do is get DNA from your suspect. I compare samples. Bang! We lock him up, case closed. Another one bites the dust." Shriek of laughter. "Love this stuff!"

"Yeah, yeah ... should be easy." While he was walking, Jake had been thinking about what Sheena Milroe said. *Eli was always a good kid. Everybody loved him ...* And Jake didn't disagree. "Chester, what if we have the wrong suspect?"

"Ha, Jake, already ahead of you. All is not lost. We're good, we have the DNA. The world is very different than twenty-seven years ago. I'm about to text you a name and a number. You talk to this woman, brother. One smart chickarita, this babe. Seriously."

Chan spoke briefly about forensic genetic genealogy, said that was the way to go. Told him the Bureau was behind the eight ball on this. The best work comes through the private sector.

The text popped: **Elise Grainger. One of the founders of Gene-US.** Phone number with an area code of 813. *Florida,* he thought.

Chan told him little, left him curious. He decided to do a web search on Grainger and her operation. Popped up the company website first. Impressive. If they didn't know what they were doing, you wouldn't know from the website. Spotted a tab for "Solved Cases." He saw quite a few recaps. No time for that now. Clicked on "About."

There she was, a professional portrait of Elise Grainger, CEO and Founder. She was photographed in a well-lit, pristine lab, a lean woman in a black dress with a dark pixie-style haircut highlighting a striking face. Shapely calves and glossy black heels. Smart-girl glasses and a stylish earring and necklace set completed her ensemble.

She was a woman maintained like a Ferrari. And substantially less plain than he expected from a woman of science.

He read a short paragraph about her. Born in Gulfport, Mississippi. Father worked at nearby Stennis Space Center. Biology and physics undergraduate at the University of Texas. Applied and accepted to medical school but rejected her acceptance. Ultimately followed her father's footsteps. Ph.D. in nuclear physics from Georgia Tech. She powered into entrepreneurship after working for the defense department, teaching herself genealogy.

Jake wondered if he had the intellect to even converse with her. He dialed her number.

"Leesie Grainger." Southern drift to her voice.

"This is Agent Jake Montoya of the FBI. Is this Elise Grainger of Gene-US?"

"It sure is. Chester said to expect your call. Jake, do you mind if I tell you a small-world story?"

Sounded friendly. Definitely some Mississippi backroads in her voice. "Well, sure, go ahead."

He *heard* her take a sip of a drink. "Hot down in Florida. A cold Corona helps with that. Anyway, fifteen years ago my husband and I lived in Alexandria for a few years while I was working at the Pentagon. We are both football fanatics and we had season tickets for the Redskins. Maybe you've heard of them." She giggled at her own joke. "And we both loved watching you play."

Ahhh, hell. He hoped he didn't have to go down the football trail. "Dr. Grainger, that's extremely kind of you to relay that, sure is. But another lifetime." He let out a friendly chuckle.

"Call me Leesie, please. Anyway, I can still hear my husband say, 'Montoya's such a badass, a super-fast badass.' Know what I said?"

Reluctant to ask. "Uh, no, what?"

"I said, 'Brad, don't sell him short, he's a *damn good-looking super-fast badass.*'" She sounded like a Tri Delt at Ole Miss—

sultry. "I only knew because you were in those Rolex commercials for that Washington jewelry store."

He laughed, hesitatingly. "Kind words, Leesie. Thank you." His brain replayed the day of the watch shoot. Filmed shirtless while wearing the Rolex Submariner on a retired America's Cup boat, off of Newport, Rhode Island. *And the models ... hoooh, man.*

He heard the crunch of a chip in the background followed by more crunches. Then the sound of a glass coming to rest on a table. "Sorry, Jake. I'm on my boat in Longboat Key at the moment. Just me, a nearly frozen beer, and chips and salsa. Wish you were here to go over this in detail. I can talk and tan my legs at the same time."

Bet you can.

"Okay, Jake. Chester says this is a big case. Maybe twenty victims over almost thirty years. And you have a solid suspect in your sights."

"That's right. And CODIS pulled up nothing on our DNA sample."

"First thing to know is that CODIS is only the tip of the iceberg. That's only for people convicted of crimes, or possibly arrested. But you know that. I will have access to millions of people's DNA."

"Sounds good." Glimpse of hope in his tone. Jake had meandered over to the shade of a live oak, leaned back on the craggy trunk, bent his right leg, placed his foot on the tree. "Exactly how does this work, Leesie?"

"We'll be looking at public genealogy databases."

"Whoa, hold it. I thought law enforcement was locked out of those sites."

"You're right, on 23andMe and Ancestry and a couple others. But we can hop on GEDmatch and FamilyTreeDNA. Participants on their sites can opt-in for law enforcement. The recent Golden State Killer case was solved through GEDmatch."

"Sounds good. So what's next?"

"First, we get a DNA sample from Chan. That profile is called an STR sample. Twenty Short Tandem Repeats. Our lab will convert that into SNPs, we call them snips. It's painstaking and expensive, but we make it happen. And here's what's cool. The SNPs, single nucleotide polymorphisms, are likely somewhere in more than 1 percent of the population. And if we have that 1 percent, we have a greater than 90 percent chance of identifying at least a single third cousin. All of this by running autosomal DNA, Y-DNA, and mitochondrial DNA."

"That's over my head, Leesie. Let's get back to something I understand, like a timetable. How long will this take?"

"Well," she chuckled, "it's not fast. Say we find a third cousin. There's extensive genealogical research to be done. It's common to run into brick walls on records and archive searches. Lots of man hours on my end. A lot of street work on your end. Law enforcement is not exactly full of cash to pay us for expedited service, as you can imagine."

Jake stood away from the tree, started pacing, thinking. "Okay, Leesie, tell me this. Say money was no object. How fast could it be done?"

"Hmmm, let me think. I could put eight staffers on it. I could probably dig up ten more freelancers if the price was right. Likely $200 per hour per person, including our fee. Depending on roadblocks, and with fifteen or so staffers, experienced genealogists, maybe three hours, or maybe two weeks."

"Leesie, be ready to move. I can tell you without reservation, money is no object."

"Jake, you say all this, so I'm assuming you've ruled out your suspect based on Chan's work."

"Nope. About to do that. But I want you to get started regardless. Send the contract and terms to me personally. I'll get it back to you with any retainer you require."

"Are you sure? It won't be cheap."

"I'm positive."

72

THE RAIN FIRST HIT in short bursts, warning shots, initially. Then, just after dark, it sounded like the house was being power washed. The leading edge of a tropical storm that came ashore in Galveston had reached Black Point. Then winds declined to occasional gusts of twenty-five miles per hour, not much to worry about.

Jake went upstairs to the bedroom, stretched out on the bed, tapped call on James Sloane's contact.

"Jim Sloane. Is this Agent Montoya?"

"It is, sir. I know it's approaching ten in Atlanta, but I had to call. I have some very promising news."

"I take calls all night, Jake. Give it to me."

Jake filled Sloane in on the DNA sample from the Gage murder. Working to match a strong suspect. Genealogy possibilities.

"Very pleased to hear that, can't tell you how much."

"Jim, I hope you're still good on your reward fund."

"Absolutely."

"Good." Jake told him about the call from Sheena Milroe. Told him about the lunch where her father had identified the Gage killer.

"So you're telling me this ninety-one-year-old Alzheimer's guy identified the killer and called him George?"

"Yep. But the suspect's name isn't George. But if that's the guy, I hope you'll pay the family the money. Their tip is breaking the case."

"Hold it. Who the hell *is* George?"

"Not sure yet. Might just be cobwebs in the old fella's head."

"Yeah, yeah. But without a doubt, I'll pay. Give 'em a new Toyota, too."

"Great, I'll be in touch."

Jake rang off, called John David Gage.

GAGE WAS ON HIS DOCK surrounded by citronella candles, reading Isaacson's *Leonardo Da Vici*. Wearing an LED headlamp to view the pages, he listened to the bay water splash the pilings. Five miles out, a large freighter sliced through the night heading into Mobile's port. Absolute tranquility. Gage looked at his phone, thought about it through a couple of rings.

"Yes, Jake. Almost didn't answer, trying to escape in a book about da Vinci. What's up?"

Jake told him the FBI DNA lab had a solid sample off the tissue from Sunshine's fingernails.

"Knew my girl wouldn't go down easy, knew it ..." John David went silent. That painful thought brought moisture to his eyes.

No time to lament.

"J.D., we need Eli's DNA. Fresh fingerprints, at least. Got to see if he's a match. If so, cased closed."

"Right. Anything I can do?"

"Yes. Invite him to your place for dinner. Tell him you want to discuss the investment possibility in a quieter spot, not the restaurant. Have Marin leave for a few hours. That way it will look focused on business. This is the important part. Serve red wine at room temperature in a glass that has no stem."

"Wine?"

"Yes. We need a dry glass and I only want you to touch the very bottom or the inside of the glass. Have the glass on the table and let Eli pour. Need his fingers on the body of the glass as well as the wine bottle."

"I can do that."

"And I want you to do one more thing. Thoroughly wipe down those photographs you showed me from the Cabo trip. Hand them to Eli, by the edges, then tell him to flip through them. Lay out the possibility that y'all could take a fishing trip down there, or something."

"Will do. I'll call him right now."

"One last thing ... about the dinner."

"Okay."

"Fix something garlicky or oniony, something to leave an aftertaste. Have some gum around. You take a stick, tell him you need to freshen your mouth, and offer him a stick."

"Slick, Jake." J.D. laughed.

"After a few minutes spit your gum in a baggy ... or whatever ... say something to him like, 'You're done, right?' Hold out the bag. The gum might be better for a DNA sample."

Gage harrumphed. "That might be a little weird. But I can make it happen."

73

JAKE ARRIVED AT Gage's bayside home just after eleven at night, three days after the conversation about the dinner. It was a five-minute drive from Hope's animal sanctuary. He killed the engine and stepped out into a symphony of crickets and katydids—a music too enchanting for the discussion of ugly business.

Gage directed Jake to the dining room table. "Haven's touched a thing. Glass right where Eli left it."

"Perfect."

"Gum is in the trash can. He pulled it out of his mouth, put it in a napkin, and tossed it."

"Not a problem." Jake pulled two freezer bags from his pocket. Placed his fingers inside the glass and slid it into one bag. Went to the trash can. "Did you put your gum in here?"

"Nope."

Jake opened the can, looked thoroughly, moved a balled-up paper towel and a box for microwavable mac and cheese. "Here it is." He placed the gum, still attached to the napkin, into the second bag.

"I'll get the wine bottle before I leave. Sit down for a second, J.D., I want to run over something with you."

Sitting at the table, Jake explained, "I've got something secondary in motion on the DNA thing." Jake summarized the forensic genetic genealogy play, describing his call with Leesie Grainger.

"The deal with Grainger is, this will be expensive. The FBI will be very slow to finance it. Bottom line, I told Grainger this is a go. I've got a contract from her back at Hope's place. I'm going to sign it and send the retainer fee."

"Whoa, whoa, whoa, man." Gage stood, ran his fingers through his silvery blond hair while a puzzled look covered his face. "You've got the guy! The son of a bitch was just sitting here ... right next to me. We were both standing right there when Tally Jenkins saw Eli and called him George. What am I missing here?" Gage's voice broke.

Jake stood, put his hand on Gage's shoulder, saw his moist eyes. "You're right, J.D. I just want to cover our bases. I hadn't even thought of it until a scientist at the Bureau suggested it. I don't want to lose any more time on this."

John nodded. "Okay, makes sense." No tears fell but Gage dabbed his eyes with the back of his hand. "But I will bear the costs on the genealogy. There will be zero discussion about that, you hear me?"

"Yes, sir, I do."

"I would spend my last dime to get this bastard."

74

ELIJAH WASHINGTON SAT outside, alone, at a black steel-mesh patio table in Black Point's downtown French Quarter. It was one-thirty in the afternoon, eighty-three degrees under the shade of a live oak. Water gurgling from the fountain next to him made him think he was cooler than he was.

He'd taken his last bite of a tuna panini when a big guy in chef's wear stepped up to the table. "Any good, Eli?"

"Pete, buddy, nobody does it better." They bumped fists. "Seriously good food, man."

"Good to hear."

Eli wiped his mouth once more with a napkin. "Pete, one more thing, and I'm not too shy to ask. Any chance you could get Fieri in one of my restaurants? Mention it on TV?"

Pete nodded vigorously. "Helluva good idea. I think he'd go nuts over the pork-chop biscuit. I'll put in the word." Pete Blohme, the owner of the restaurant facing the courtyard, stepped to another table to schmooze a customer.

Marcia Allen, displaying firm arms and muscular legs in a sleeveless cotton top and walking shorts, and Mark Benton, wearing an Auburn tee over cargo shorts, sat two tables away. Both were FBI agents out of the Mobile Field Office. While maintaining a meaningless chat, they ate their hamburger and fries slowly, keeping a tight watch on Eli out of their peripheral vision.

Forty feet down the narrow alley leading to De La Mare Street stood Stan Wills, a tall, well-built man in his forties. He held a smartphone in his hand with an earpiece cord attached to the phone, talking ... no one. He moved slightly as he spoke, stealing glances at Eli with a trained eye.

Just under two miles away, eighteen FBI SWAT agents sat in a conference room at the Holiday Inn Express. Wearing black fatigues, slivers of anxiety threaded through their confidence as they focused on what was about to happen. Pregame jitters. Means you're ready.

Three tactical trucks sat at the back of the parking lot, loaded with their gear. They could be in the trucks sixty seconds after receiving word.

Pike Tatum, Billy Starr, and Nia Cruz sat in the conference room of Black Point PD, electricity swizzling through their nerves. Too excited to eat lunch.

Montoya paced the floor. "What the hell is Chan doing up there? Said he was gonna call late morning, couple of damn hours ago." He tossed his hands in the air, kept pacing.

Eli Washington's pattern of life had been well established. On workdays he walked a block or two from his office on Magnolia Avenue to one of the downtown eateries, usually around one-fifteen. He tried to miss the crowds. Walked back to his office after lunch and worked until six.

Two days ago Tatum had picked up the office building plan from Black Point's building permit office for evaluation. Eli leased the whole third floor, a little over four thousand square feet.

Yesterday, Jake had Kimbo drop by unannounced, just to talk shop and scope out the layout.

Kimbo had explained that employee retention was killing

him at the grill plant. They bandied around a few ideas before Eli said, "Hey, I'd like to introduce my staff here. I want them to meet the genius behind the Big Jake Grill."

It was a quick meet-and-greet. One male, pale, early thirties, two women in their forties. Typical office rats, butts in the chairs too much of the day.

Kimbo informed Jake of the limited staff on the premises.

The plan was simple. SWAT-trained, Jake would armor-up. Nia Cruz would lock down the elevator. Two teams would ascend to the top floor from stairways at each end of the building. With a little luck, the three employees would be in their offices, out of the way. Black Point PD will cordon off the frontage street and building perimeter.

Jake looked at his watch. Two-fifty. About to jump out of his skin. "Dammit, Chan's three hours late. I gotta call."

"Yeah, call him," said Starr, eating Fritos from a small bag.

Jake was combing cell contacts when his phone rang. "It's him."

He stood, answered anxiously, glancing into space. "Give it to me, Chester." Facial muscles tight. A vein pulsed at his temple.

"Not the guy," said Dr. Chan.

Jake's chin dropped; his mouth opened slightly as he fought disbelief. Cruz, Tatum, and Starr saw the look. They glanced at each other, stunned ... and worried.

"How the hell, Chester? Gotta be the guy. It's him, I know it's him."

"Not the guy, man."

75

THINGS MOVED FAST. Chan overnighted a snippet of DNA from Quantico, Virginia, to Leesi Grainger's lab in Tampa. Her team quickly isolated single nucleotide polymorphisms from the sample. From there, fifteen genealogists went to work in the databases, working around the clock.

One full day plus eighteen hours later there were fist pumps and high fives.

It was 4:27 in the afternoon, with Florida's afternoon heat maxed out. GENE-US occupied a 5,200-square-foot space in an industrial sector of Tampa. Grainger was in her office, feet propped on a small filing cabinet, sipping on a Diet Coke, gazing absentmindedly out her window at the highways of pipe and steel across the street that were attached to the Yuengling Brewing Company.

Acoustic piano music soothed her soul as she gazed through, past, and over the beer plant, thinking about one thing. Public relations. If Montoya's guy had killed twenty-plus people over decades, GENE-US would make a splash in the headlines if they delivered the goods. Mighty nice for business.

She glanced at her watch, thought if she hustled, she could get in a cardio session at Orangetheory before the after-work crowd arrived.

Grainger clicked off the music, stood, placed her large purse on her shoulder, took a final sip of Diet Coke, and walked toward the office door. Her phone chimed as her hand touched the knob. She glanced at the text: ***Don't move a muscle. Be right there.***

Less than a minute later, a woman genealogist walked into Grainger's office without knocking. She pushed her black-framed glasses up on her nose as she smiled. She held a sheet of paper in the air with a family-tree template on it, wiggled it in her fingers. "Done."

"Done?"

"Done."

"Not even two days." Leesi's face creased into a look of satisfaction. "Incredible. Let's run through it."

SWEAT POURED DOWN Jake Montoya's face. He was shirtless and barefoot in shorts, hunkered into a shallow standing squat, a fighting stance, left hand up in front, right hand out beside his right hip, laser intensity in his eyes. The man in front of him held an eight-inch combat knife in his right hand, eyes threatening.

Ira Kravitz had formerly taught Krav Maga techniques in Tel Aviv to Israeli special forces. Now he was going to teach Montoya a lesson he wouldn't soon forget.

Kravitz was two inches shorter and ten pounds lighter than Montoya, but he was a physical specimen at thirty-three. It was his first session with Jake, set up by Jake's first martial arts instructor, Woo Chow.

Woo, seventy-five years old and gristly lean at 135 pounds, stood fifteen feet away, watching. His arms were folded across his chest, hands stuffed under his armpits, like a coach searching for deficits in his basketball team.

Jake had told Woo he needed to stay sharp on his defense against knife attacks. In the right hands, knives are rapidly deadly. Woo had an idea, suggested Kravitz, a guy who ran a chain of six Krav Maga academies between Gulfport and Panama City.

Today, they worked on defense of the straight-on stab. Jake moved cautiously in circles, light on the balls of his feet, like a jungle cat, slow, quiet, fast-twitch muscle fibers raging with electricity. He studied Ira's eyes.

Inside, Ira smiled at the assignment. Woo had told him he had an old student who needed to brush up on knife defense, but he was "a pretty tough dude." Ira had metaphorically rolled his eyes at that statement. He was twelve years younger than the man in front of him, and certain of his own "badness." Israeli special ops were far from a bunch of mama's boys.

As they slow-circled, Ira flashed the knife around in his right hand. Taunting him. Confusing his victim on the line of penetration. He noticed Jake locking his eyes on the knife. *Another dead guy on the street*, he mused.

Kravitz lunged in with the blade, fast as a blink.

Cobra speed. Jake sidestepped eight inches. He caught Ira's wrist with his right hand, pulling it to his torso. Kravitz moved to step back. Jake's left leg flashed in a brutish side strike, taking Ira's feet off the ground.

Jake's left hand locked on Ira's upper neck like a vise. He slammed the man's face into the mat while he jerked his right wrist up toward his neck, a point from which Jake could dislocate Ira's shoulder in an instant. Jake's knee crashed into the Israeli's mid-back. The man's air left him. The knife dropped. A left hand tapped the floor in surrender.

Woo Chow's eyelids squinted. His cocky smile lit the room, eyebrows raised. "Told ya, Ira, bad dude."

Jake's cell rang as he stood. He walked ten feet, picked it up off a towel, saw the caller. Leesi Grainger. He flipped off his bandanna, swiped his face with the towel.

"Leesi, hello." Breathing hard.

"Jake, are you huffing?"

"Yeah, I just got jumped on the street by a guy with a knife."

"What!"

"Just working out. You getting anywhere?"

"Better believe it, mister." Full of Southern-girl bluster.

Leesi Grainger described the process in detail. She told them that they put Eli Washington's DNA on hold before they went to work. "Jake, if I'm correct, Eli Washington has no idea he's been a suspect."

"That's right."

"So we put his DNA on the shelf, for now. He has never submitted his DNA through a commercial testing company, so he could not opt-in for law enforcement review. That keeps our research beyond reproach."

"Right. Good move." Montoya took a swig from a water bottle, walked the room in cool-down mode.

"So we ran the original DNA through the available databases after establishing the SNPs."

What came next was a blur of information. Jake squinched his eyes as she spoke. "We got a hit on a second cousin. As you know, a second cousin shares a great grandparent ..."

No, he didn't know that. Then came birth records, death records, newspaper obituaries, social media search, phone call inquiries, web-based people finder sites, criminal records search, and droning, on and on. He wiped the sweat off his chest as he listened, feeling Leesi's enthusiasm.

"Now, here's the good part, Jake. You were damn close on Eli Washington. He's in the bloodline, but as we know, his DNA is not a match."

"So whose does?"

"This is where detective work comes in. I'm going to send you a family tree that includes children from Eli's generation.

Midnight Man

But, of course, they were too young to have committed the first murder. So, I'd start with Eli's generation and work backward. Naturally, your number one parameter is to see who lived in the vicinity when the first crime occurred. I will email the family tree as soon as we hang up."

"Ahhh, man, that's awesome, Leesi. From what you know now, where do we start?"

"I'd go with Eli's father and uncles. They would have likely been in their forties when Sunshine Gage was murdered. Eli and his siblings and his first cousins were still teenagers. I mean, really? Teenagers?"

"Right, right." Jake's mind shot back, chasing his memory. He couldn't remember Eli's father. Eli and Zeke Washington were raised by their grandfather, the high school principal. *And there was no way Amos Washington was behind this.*

"Jake, I'm seeing Eli had seven uncles, three siblings, and eighteen first cousins. This is where you guys run these people, see where they were during any of these murders, and for the likely top suspects—"

"Get a sample of their DNA." He finished her sentence. "Leesi, you guys have done an amazing job."

"Thanks. I think you'll clean this up pretty quick. And could I ask you a favor?"

"Absolutely."

"When this is over, could you plug GENE-US for me?"

"Damn right, I will. Everywhere." Jake walked out of Woo's dojo into the sun, phone to his ear. He felt like he was walking on air.

"Oh, one other thing. Do you like to sail?"

"Haven't done it much, but, yes, I do."

"I keep a forty-eight-foot sailboat down in Exuma, in the Bahamas. Maybe you could fly down, and we could sail the islands for a week. De-stress after this big case."

Hmmm. Pulled up the memory of her website picture in the lab. Trim legs with heels, white smile, dark hair, dark eyes, not a bad thing. Thought about a fly in the ointment.

"Leesi, didn't you mention you had a husband? I assume he'd come also."

She giggled. It was soft and sexy, and so excitingly conspiratorial, he thought. "Well, yes, I guess I could bring him, I mean if you want to listen to an overweight alcoholic drone on about his stamp collection. Or you could focus your energy on a woman in a black bikini in the prime of her life that just happens to make the world's best margarita."

"B." He said it in an instant. "Option B." A smile draped across his face as he hung up.

... That sultry drawl ...

76

MARINA DEL REY, CALIFORNIA

JAKE ARRIVED EARLY, hopped out of a top-down Jeep, an airport rental. He glanced around, seeing nothing but the beautiful people. Tanned and fit, showing a lot of skin, wearing cool shades. He was at the In-N-Out Burger in Marina Del Rey. Seventy-three degrees, no humidity, beachy sunshine on a cloudless morning.

Southern California. Best weather in America.

A quick peek at his watch told him Ezekiel Washington should be there in twenty minutes.

THE DAY BEFORE yesterday, two hours after Jake spoke to Leesi Grainger, a meeting convened in the conference room of the Black Point Police Department. Montoya, Special Agent Nia Cruz, Chief Pike Tatum, and Detective Billy Starr. Jake's analyst, Ross Tolleson, Zoomed in from his home office in Alexandria. The fluorescents shone silver-white, casting a coldness in the room.

It was 7:20 p.m. in Black Point, 8:20 in Washington.

After handing out copies of the genealogy template, Jake reviewed what Leesi Grainger had shared.

Jake's pointer finger tapped the table over his copy of the

template. "Our killer is right here. He's on this sheet." A steely look crossed his face. "After twenty-seven years of hell, we're gonna get this son of a bitch."

A zap of energy riveted the room.

"I said it before, Jake, you're a damn genius, a pure T genius," said Billy Starr, sounding like he was auditioning for a hillbilly role in *Deliverance*.

"Jake, this is the first time the Black Point PD has been close to forensic genealogy. I appreciate you bringing it in, super cool stuff," said Chief Tatum, a cold Coke in his hand.

"The future is now, Chief. This technique is going to close a lot of cases on repetitive crimes," said Cruz.

"Okay, let's get moving, guys. Ross and Nia, I need you to get background on these people from Eli's generation back to his uncles. The children of Eli's generation are too young, and the fathers of the uncles are too old, or dead." Montoya's tone intense. *Need it NOW.*

"Sounds right," said Tolleson, fatigue on his face, speaking from a large flat-screen mounted on the wall.

"The first people we need to hit are the people closest to Black Point at the time of the Gage murder. And particularly anyone who may have been at the party. And we know Eli has been cleared. Thank God for that."

"Hold it, hold it, Jake," said Nia. "Cleared might be overstating it regarding Eli. From what you told us, that old fella with dementia looked him in the eyes and called him George, the killer. And not only that, but you've also placed Eli in almost all those cities where the other victims had been killed over the years."

Jake glanced at Billy Starr, then back to Nia. "Billy would know this. Elijah has a twin brother, Ezekiel. Their faces look alike. Besides that, Zeke was more ripped, Eli was heavier by at least twenty-five pounds, just looked a little softer, but, really, there wasn't anything soft about him."

Billy snapped his fingers. "That's right, Zeke. Yeah."

Jake stood, yawned, and stretched, the day's long hours catching up with him. "I couldn't remember Zeke at the birthday party. So before coming here I called Dr. Gage, as well as Kimbo. Kimbo couldn't remember. Dr. Gage said he distinctly remembers telling Zeke not to go 'OJ' in Los Angeles. Zeke signed and played for USC, just like OJ Simpson in the late 1960s. J.D. remembered Zeke said something like he had too many women already, didn't need to kill anybody."

"Jake," said Tatum, "you and Eli and Zeke were all the same year, right? Went into the pros at the same time?"

"Yep. Played college three years, then opted for the draft."

"Well, how the hell is Zeke going to be in those NFL cities for those murders? His ball club is playing somewhere else, unless it's the occasional game when Eli and Zeke are playing each other."

"I know, man, it's hard to fathom that." Jake looked up at Ross on the screen. "Ross, you have all the dates, and so does Steven Morelock. See if Steven can dig into any credit card transactions by Zeke in those cities. And see if your crew can find any flights, hotels, or rental cars utilized by Zeke."

"Could even be a simpler answer," said Starr. "Sunshine and the Sloane girl, and the woman in Destin, might be totally unrelated to the NFL cities."

Jake exhaled, leaned back, ran his hand through his hair. Thought a moment. "Could be. Yep, that could be." Ran his tongue under his lower lip, mulling that. "But they're so damn similar. The vaginal deal, the poison, nipples sliced off." Shook his head. "Just don't know. But if we could nail one guy for this ..."

All eyes were on Montoya. The energy in the room hummed

with expectation. The killer's name, at least Sunshine's killer, was on the paper in front of each of them.

"I'm flying to LA in the morning. I'm going to get the DNA of the one guy we know was at the Gage birthday party. A guy who looks just like George."

77

MARINA DEL REY

JAKE WAS SEATED at a window table in the burger joint, scrolling through boating ads on his phone. He was reading the details on an early-seventies Boston Whaler Montauk, listed in Traverse City, Michigan, when a bright orange blur outside caught the corner of his eye. The blur growled like a hungry lion.

The car's engine died. Out stepped a dark-complected Black man from a $250,000 McLaren. Shades covered his eyes. Arms with muscle like corded steel emerged from his tank top. Ezekiel Washington. He'd won the Heisman at USC, then survived ten battering years in the pros with Green Bay until his knees refused to run another foot.

Zeke was also the kid who had scored half the touchdowns that Jake Montoya had in a state high-school championship game.

Jake met Zeke at the door, gave him a bro hug. "Jake Montoya, lookachu, looking like a movie star, damn good to see you."

Jake grabbed Zeke's upper arm. "That's some serious steel, Zeke. What about you? Looking fitter than ever."

"Trying, man, trying. Let's get us some burgers. Tone my

physique with some grease and salt."

At the table, they briefly caught up on a couple of decades in twenty minutes. Zeke was a small-time film producer as well as a partner in a hip-hop label. Looking for a hit in both.

"But, man, FBI. I never could have imagined that. That's just wild. I wish we had some time for me to hear some stories." Zeke started singing the theme from *Cops*. "*Bad boys, bad boys, whatcha gonna do ...*"

Montoya smiled.

"Man, seriously, we should get together for a few days, stay with me at my place on the beach. Toss around some ideas for a cop property. Hell, you could star in it. Really, Jake, you've got a face for it, and you've always been LA cool."

Montoya blushed, a rarity. "Maybe so, Zeke. I might like going a little Hollywood." Coughed a laugh. Thought he might like trying to write an episode, though.

After the meeting the other night at Black Point PD, Jake had called Eli to get Zeke's number. Had no idea how different Zeke might be after living in the glow of California. As soon as he hung up with Eli, he dialed Zeke. Hoped, hoped, to get an answer. Got one. Told Zeke he was passing through LA, headed to Cabo, could they grab a quick lunch?

"Shitcheah," Zeke told him. "Got an In-N-Out near my place in Marina Del Rey. Close to LAX."

Jake stood from the table to leave, thinking this was playing out perfectly. He had a plan. "Oh, hey, wait a minute. You wanna talk cop shop, let me show you why I'm headed to Cabo."

Jake sat back down, opened his messenger bag. "Didn't want to leave the bag in the Jeep."

"Hear that, man, crooks everywhere. Oughta have three guys guarding my car." He glanced through the window at the McLaren, just to be safe.

Jake pulled a packet of five-by-seven pics from his bag, all glossy color photos. Opening the packet, he said, "Meeting two agents at the airport in a few minutes, headed to Cabo. We've got some video of a guy that was on the scene in the vicinity of both an Orange Beach and a Seaside, Florida, murder. We tracked his credit cards into Mexico."

He watched for any subtle changes in Zeke's face as he spoke.

Zeke took the pictures from Jake's hand, started thumbing through them.

"Two murders on the Gulf Coast in the last month." Jake watched Zeke's fingers flip through and study each picture, not worried in the least about leaving a smudge.

"Wha kinda sick muthafuckah does this shit?" Glanced up at Jake with his eyebrows raised, a disbelieving look. "Fool cut 'em, blowtorched their snatch ... shit, man, make love to that thang. I've been to Seaside, coupla times. Cool spot." He looked back down, kept flipping.

Jake had to go there. "This is exactly like what happened to Sunshine. I mean *exactly*, exactly. Desecration, everything."

Zeke's chin rose until his eyes locked on Jake. Montoya spotted sympathy, sadness.

"Ahhh, man. The birthday party. She sang. Mama there. Dr. G cooking some good burgers. Ahhh, hell." Zeke shook his head. Voice dropping off as he said, "That was a nice night, real nice ... couple weeks till graduation ... can't go there." Head shaking, his eyes dropped.

Jake felt beyond a doubt Zeke's gloom was real. He picked up the plastic bag, held it open. "Slide the pics in. I have to run back to the airport. Gotta take a leak first."

Both stood, latched together for a goodbye hug. Jake watching Zeke's eyes closely.

Zeke pointed to Jake's baggie. "That shit there, that's season one. It's ugly, it's brutal, but people eat that crime stuff up. Love that crap. I'm gonna make you a star, brother." Tapped his right pointer on Jake's chest.

Jake watched Zeke through the large plate-glass windows. The old running back squeezed his body down into the low-slung sports car that cost more than most houses. The sound of the big engine roared alive, reverberating into the restaurant. He slid on sunglasses, slowly backed out.

Montoya eased through the crash of voices of the dining room toward the men's room. A toilet flushed in a stall, one guy blow-drying hands under a wall-mounted jet engine, Jake unzipped at the urinal, starting to pee, staring straight at the wall. He knew one thing.

Ezekiel Washington wasn't the guy.

78

JAKE WALKED OUTSIDE the FedEx office on Del Rey, hopped in the Jeep, pulled up Dr. Chester Chan's phone contact, fired off a text: ***Photos with fingerprints from Ezekiel Washington arrive by 8 in morning. Run the DNA ASAP please!***

He slid the phone in his shirt pocket, clicked the seatbelt, put on his sunglasses, fired up the Jeep. Midland bouncing out of the speakers from an LA country station, singing about a drinking problem. He eased into a mad rush of Southern California traffic while his phone vibrated out a text.

Priority One, Jake! On It!

Good. Pictured Chan's smile at this moment, a flash of white like a nuclear detonation. He liked Chan, liked his happy camper demeanor. Trusted him.

Thoughts drifted back to eating lunch with Zeke a few minutes ago. *Interesting*, he thought. Don't see somebody for over twenty years, life racing past in a million different ways for each of you, living 2,500 miles apart. And it's like you saw them three days ago. *How is that possible?*

He pictured Zeke's face again. Not a hint of deception. Come in out of the blue, drop crime-scene photos down in front of a killer, all but the most habituated psychopaths will crap their pants.

Zeke had no fidgeting, no averted eye contact, no false

smiles. And there was a genuine sadness in his brown doe-eyes at the mention of Sunshine Gage.

List just got smaller. Progress.

79

LOS ANGELES INTERNATIONAL. Sky skidding into gray steel to the west, mid-afternoon.

The *LA Weekly* rag was opened in Jake's lap. He was reading the skinny about something in LA's dope world. It appeared that black market weed outsold the legal product two to one. Why? It cost less and you could get concierge delivery right to your home. Yes, happy consumers, your favorite hippie dude's still selling home-grown behind the bowling alley from his VW van. *Outrageous government taxes,* he thought. Bureaucratic morons cutting their own throat.

He closed the paper, thought about Agent Cruz, called her.

"Nia, I don't think Zeke's our guy. He didn't flinch when I showed him the photos. We'll know soon. His fingerprints will be at Quantico at eight in the morning. Chan's doing a priority run for us."

"Okay, good. Here's where we are. Eli had a twin, Zeke, who you just saw, and three sisters, all older. Putting them on the back burner. Eli and Zeke had eight uncles. Two are dead, one is in a nursing home. There's one in Jacksonville, one in Pensacola, two in New Orleans, one in Foley, Alabama, close by. Now, as you saw, there are eighteen first cousins. Three are in jail, ten are located in a straight line between New Orleans and

Jacksonville. Three that grew up in New Orleans are in Houston. One in Atlanta, one in Orlando."

"Okay, and step one is finding who was close by when Sunshine Gage was murdered."

"Absolutely. We're going to work the ones from New Orleans to Tallahassee. Tolleson will work the others. I've already got field agents on alert in these locales, ready to interview. Tomorrow morning we'll have some answers."

"Outstanding. I'm heading out of LA in just a few minutes. Talk tomorrow." Jake ended the call, stood to walk to the restroom. Phone rang immediately.

"Ross, hey, man, was just about to call you. Have to pee first."

"Don't pee yet, got something." Tolleson sounded out of breath. Jake had heard that tone before. *He's ripping the investigation's meat from the bones.*

He sat down, his urge to pee forgotten. "I'm listening." His right foot began to tap, adrenaline sluicing into his blood.

"Ezra Cain. Name mean anything to you?"

Jake was silent. His eyes looked through the plate glass. Sky darkening, but he didn't notice. Brain drowning out the sounds of rolling luggage, overhead announcements, and the booming thrust from jets on takeoff. Thinking.

"No, Ross, I don't think so. Who is it?"

"Try this. Babu Bankhole."

Jake coughed out a quick laugh. "Bob Butthole. That's what some of the kids called him. Let me think … He was a year or two behind me. Chubby boy. But we weren't buddies. Something happened somewhere … he moved or went to another school or something, after elementary school."

"Well, the old Bob Butthole is the new Ezra Cain. We tracked him back. He was in Sunshine's grade at Black Point Elementary. You were two years older. The last year you were in school with him, he was in fourth grade. Big-shot sixth graders don't hang with fourth-grade punks."

Jake hmmmphed a laugh but was listening, trying to unscramble the wires. "Go on."

"His father was born in Africa and came to America at age two. He was killed on a motorcycle when Babu was four months old. His mother, who is Eli's aunt, went on drugs, had a couple of arrests for selling herself, and overdosed when the kid was ten. After that, the kid spent time with his grandparents, Amos and Clara Washington in Black Point, but he was mostly in Mobile with his other grandmother."

"Interesting."

"He went to a Catholic school after elementary school in Black Point. He was smart, applied to the Alabama School of Math and Science, got in, excelled. He got a scholarship to Stanford."

"Stanford? Damn, he must be sharp." Jake's face scrunched, still trying to force his mind back to elementary school.

"I'll say. Guess what he majored in."

"Computer engineering."

"Nope. Medicine. He's board certified in internal medicine. He also has a Ph.D. in virology from Yale. Top schools. Now he's at the CDC as well as being an adjunct professor at Emory School of Medicine, in Atlanta."

Jake pictured the surgical removal of the victim's nipples as well as the precise excision of flesh on the back. "Wait a minute. So, who's Ezra Cain?"

"Bob Butthole, that's who. He legally changed his name his senior year at Stanford."

"Huh ... that's wild." Jake felt a buzz race down to his toes, like he was almost ready to fight somebody.

An announcement came from overhead. Delta Flight 869

was beginning to board.

"Great work, Ross. Look, keep digging in. Financials, rental cars, flights. See if you can track him to the NFL cities. I'll call tomorrow."

"Hold it, Jake. One more thing."

"Shoot."

"I've got recent headshot photos on my screen. Eli Washington from his pork-chop biscuit website and Ezra Cain from the Emory School of Medicine."

A flash of anticipation raked through Jake, he almost couldn't breathe.

"They are the exact same damn guy. Mirror images."

80

THE 767 WAS barely over the New Mexico line from Arizona when Montoya made the decision. He was staying in Atlanta during the changeover.

At Hartsfield-Jackson's soaring terminal, he called for a room at the Residence Inn on N. Decatur Road, slightly over two miles from the CDC and Emory. At Hertz he rented a bland, white Ford sedan.

Heading to the hotel, he pulled into a Target just off Moreland on Caroline. He bought enough clothes to skulk around in for a few days, casual stuff. Shorts, tennis shoes, T-shirts, socks, a boonie hat, and a UGA cap. Added a pack of razors, a toothbrush, floss, and toothpaste.

One thing kept pounding in his brain. *Had to be Cain.* It wasn't Eli. Very unlikely Zeke. Cain, Bankhole, was the closest cousin in the area ... *and he knew Sunshine.* Was in her class.

Is Cain George?

Driving to the hotel, he thought about it, staking out Cain, getting some early background on his routine. He wondered if Cain would remember him. If he'd killed Sunshine Gage, Jake felt he'd absolutely be recognized by Cain. In his mind he still looked very similar to his high school days, little in the way of aging. Weight within twelve pounds, same thick dark hair, plus, there was some notoriety from football and the grill commercials.

In the hotel room, Jake kicked off his shoes, slouched on the bed, pulled up the cloud site on his iPad. He wanted to read Tolleson's report.

But why? What had turned *this guy* into a serial killer? A man with all the promise in the world.

Two grades ahead, Jake hadn't spent time with Bankhole, just knew who he was because it was a small elementary school in a small Alabama town. His memory couldn't pull up more information than he'd been a chubby boy.

Bob Butthole. Amusing, but sad, really. Could that name-calling all the way through grade school turn a boy into a murderer? *Certainly not.* But Jake decided to get Ai Zhang's thoughts on that, at BAU.

Ten minutes later, he signed off, stripped, headed to the shower.

Made his first decision. *Don't shave, grow some scruff.*

MONTOYA LEFT THE hotel lobby in the last vestiges of darkness. It was twilight, 6:20 in the morning, sunrise in forty minutes. Wearing shorts, a Braves T-shirt, and a boonie hat, he crashed into the humid summer air and pushed on. He had the directions memorized.

Feet gliding on the concrete sidewalk of North Decatur Road, he was illuminated by the streetlights above, while headlights striped over him on the busy road. Atlanta was wide awake, traffic flowing like a river. After a quarter of a mile, feeling loose, he picked up the pace, enjoying the feel of the morning, and the promise of a major break.

Doctor. Old Tally kept saying, doctor.

Seventeen minutes later he was on the grounds of Emory University. The campus was rolling and verdant, thick with trees. The dark sky was shifting to gray in the east. Sweat began to ooze into his tee. Made his way to Clifton Road, turned north.

He had three locations to scout. He thought, *Big campus, lots of buildings.* He jogged the perimeter of Emory's hospital. Spotted a lot of medical scrubs and white coats heading to various entrances. New shift starting in minutes.

Hustled back onto Clifton. After jogging a quarter of a mile he reached the Emory School of Medicine. He studied the façade. *Impressive*, he thought. Three stories, clad in Georgia marble, red-clay roof. The stately stone cocooned some of the brightest medical minds in America. Jake walked around the structure, making mental notes of all the entrances.

Coming around to the front of the building, the sky was pewter above him with a red glow breaking to the east. Almost sunrise. Everything easily visible. Cars and buses spewed noise and exhaust on Clifton, delivering people to time clocks. He pushed further north on the sidewalk.

The Center for Disease Control was less than a mile away.

Montoya had no idea where Dr. Cain was at the moment, or his daily schedule. Coming up on the CDC headquarters, Jake stopped to admire a twelve-story, modern, curved-glass-and-steel structure. Building 21. Headquarters.

He slid on some shades as the first piercing ray of sunlight struck. It felt like an icepick hit his retinas. He eased into a slow jog onto the CDC campus, not realizing there would be so many large buildings. With the boonie hat and dark glasses, he was certain he could run right past Cain and not be unrecognized.

After eight minutes he stopped jogging. His eyes scanned across multiple government buildings. He felt the presence of the man. Ezra Cain was in an office or lab close by.

He'd felt anxious since his first step onto the government

campus. No longer anxious now, he felt his rage building. *Find his office, crush his skull.* End this twenty-seven-year nightmare. His fists tightened. *He's right here!* Ropey vessels popped on his forearms. *Deep breaths*, he told himself.

Do it right. We got him.

Jake backtracked to the hotel after running the CDC campus. This lab or that building, it was meaningless to him. He needed to download a map of the campus, find out *exactly* where Cain's offices were located.

Back at the hotel by 7:30, he'd put in six miles. He made his way to the fitness room, knocked out some arm, back, and chest exercises using dumbbells. Light weight and high reps. Tried to keep the strain off his joints. Finished it with 2,500 skips with a speed rope. Left the room wearing a full sweat, feeling alive. And hungry.

He took a quick shower, returned to the continental breakfast. He covered a plate with scrambled eggs, bacon, and two biscuits, grabbed a Diet Coke on ice and sat at a table with somebody's discarded *Wall Street Journal*. Glanced quickly at the headlines, then flipped to A.J. Baime's *My Ride* column. Some edgy gamer chick talking about her souped-up Ford Fiesta. *Ford Fiesta?* He smiled all the way through that nonsense.

Twenty minutes later, he pulled out of the parking lot in the white sedan. Headed to Cain's house in the Morningside area, three miles away.

JAKE PASSED THE DOCTOR'S home, moving slowly. The car windows were down, one hand on the wheel, WSB talk radio on low. He'd reined in his angst, was enjoying the feel of the Atlanta summer morning.

He was struck by the lack of pretentiousness of Cain's house. It was a single-story, brick-clad ranch with an open, one-car carport. Likely built sixty years ago. Neatly cut St. Augustine grass with a line of unimpressive boxwoods lining the foundation of the home. Nothing about this tidy place indicated it was the home of a prominent physician.

He thought back to a documentary he'd seen. John Wayne Gacy had twenty-six murder victims stashed in the crawl space under his home. And it was a small, brick-clad, unimpressive, neat ranch home.

Is this nonsense, chasing an Emory Medical School professor? A CDC doctor?

A block from the home, Jake slid the Ford to the curb, scrolled contacts on his phone, tapped call.

"Agent Montoya, good morning." Sheena Milroe must have saved Jake's number.

"Good morning, Sheena. I have a quick question."

"Fire away."

"Ezra Cain ... Dr. Ezra Cain. Does that name mean anything to you?"

"Nope." No hesitation. "Should it?"

"I'm not sure. How about Babu Bankole?"

Jake heard Sheena giggle. "Yes." She giggled again. "I shouldn't laugh. Hard to forget that name. The kids called him Bob Butthole. It was cruel. But, good Lord, that was years ago."

"Sheena, why would you remember him, besides the name?"

"Hmmm." She was quiet for a few beats. "Well, I have one specific memory, stored in the cobwebs, don't know why. One of my daughters came home from school one day saying Bob Butthole over and over and over. Probably second or third grade. I knew who she was talking about, the boy with the African father who was killed in an accident. I told her if I ever heard her say that again I'd tan her hide. But I haven't heard Babu's name since I can't remember when. So the name is the only reason I remember. What's the deal?"

"Not sure, yet. Think carefully about this question. Did Babu ever do anything with your dad involving the peanuts?"

Didn't miss a beat. "I have no clue, but I can ask my kids." Curiosity in her tone.

"Well, here's some news, Sheena. Babu is now Dr. Ezra Cain, a doctor in Atlanta. He changed his name when he was a senior in college. He went to Stanford, in California. But ask your kids if you could."

"I sure will. I'll let you know. My children know they better answer a call from their mama. And one other thing. I know Stanford is in California." She snickered, rang off.

Jake started the car, raised the back windows. Smiled at her response about Stanford. He enjoyed that lady.

His phone rang. Tolleson. Jake liked an active phone. Things hoppin'.

"Okay, got something for you, but not much. How's it going in Atlanta?"

"Just getting the lay of the land. I drove by the doctor's house a few minutes ago. It's a modest place, no indication an MD lives there from the road, by size it's more like a nurse's place. Earlier I jogged by the medical school and hospital at Emory, as well as the CDC, which is right down the street. I'm holed up in a hotel a couple of miles from there."

"Am I reading you right? You sound confident."

"Call it optimistic. What'd you dig up?"

"I tiptoed in trying to pull up a schedule on Cain. But I don't want to sound alarms that the FBI is on him."

"Good."

"On Wednesday mornings at 11:00, he teaches a virology class to medical residents. That's in a small conference room on the second floor of the medical school. The only other thing I could find was a music practice on Thursday nights at seven in a contemporary Christian church in Buckhead. He's a pianist of some renown in the praise band. Sings a little, too. And he plays for three services on Sunday."

"Good work, what else?"

Tolleson clucked his cheek. "Nothing that's tight. He's on call a lot for the Emory Hospital, I guess on viral diseases. But I think most of his time is spent in the CDC building. No clue of actual hours. The specific office locations are loaded into the cloud."

"Good work. Gotta run, Ross."

After hanging up, Jake sat in the car and thought. Through the windshield his eyes wandered over colorful, landscaped neighborhood yards, but he saw none of it. His mind raced through the immediate needs of the case. He'd already called Dr. Gage and Kimbo and asked about seeing Babu at Sunshine's party. Kimbo said he hadn't seen him since elementary school. Dr. Gage said he had no idea who Bankhole was.

There was not one solid reason to arrest him, swab for DNA, and question him. *Get some DNA surreptitiously?* Maybe, but how? Need some trash from the house. How to disguise the retrieval? *Borrow a termite truck, comb the property, open the trash can?* Maybe. Needed a team first.

Scanned contacts on his phone under *AGENTS*. Found it. *Dennis Hopkins Agent Atlanta.* Dialed. Voicemail after three rings. "This is Jake Montoya. I'm in Atlanta. Call me, Dennis."

Popped up his boss's number. Randy Garrison, in Washington. Dialed. Same thing, voicemail. "Randy, it's Jake, call me."

81

ZIPPING EAST ON N. Decatur Rd., banks, restaurants, dry cleaners, and Starbucks flashed by in Jake's peripheral vision. He cleared the light at Church Street, then cut left into a Whole Foods parking lot, an eighth of a mile from his hotel. He needed to pick up some snacks.

A smattering of cars in the lot, he parked on the perimeter. He listened to the last fifteen seconds of a Gordon Lightfoot classic, then raised the windows and killed the engine, hopped out. He hummed some of the song walking over the hot asphalt.

At mid-morning, the sun was starting to bake the city. Not a wisp of wind.

Two steps inside Whole Foods, his phone rang. "Montoya." Didn't bother to look at the screen. Expected Garrison or Hopkins. It was Sheena Milroe.

"Told you I'd get back to you." A smile in her voice. "Have news."

"That was fast."

"I spoke to Milton, my second-oldest boy. He's a building inspector in Gulf Shores. Busy as can be with all the construction at the beach."

"I'm sure. Fill me in."

"Milton was two years behind Babu in school, didn't really

Midnight Man

know him except for two things. Said he was fat and, supposedly, smart."

Jake listened intently, refreshed by the air conditioning.

"But here's what you want to know. Milton said he remembers Babu talking to Daddy about peanuts at one of the boiled-peanut stands. The little fellow was talking about how to grow more nuts from the same size piece of land. Milton thinks he was in the fourth grade then. Babu would've been in the sixth."

Jake processed the timing in his mind. *Just before Babu moved to Mobile.* "Sheena, that's very important news. I appreciate that."

"Oh, that ain't all, Jake. You're going to love this."

Jake stepped away from the store's entrance. "Already loving it."

"Well, after Babu left the peanut stand with Mr. Amos ... oh, you know, Amos Washington, the principal, was Babu's granddaddy. That was a good man, that Mr. Washington."

"He was. What happened after Babu left?"

"Oh, yeah. Milton said Daddy called Babu 'George,' being funny about it. That was after Babu was talking to Daddy about Dr. Carver."

Jake's heart rate jolted. "Well, I'll be damned. That's where *George* came from."

"Sure is. Milton never remembered any George until I asked him about Babu."

"Sheena, you're the best. Gotta run."

Jake didn't move from his spot. *What had Talmadge Jenkins seen?* Talmadge had told his family that George was Sunshine's killer. That was years after the crime, when dementia had begun to set in. Had he actually seen the murder take place? And ignored what he knew? What had scared him? Jake could only think of one thing: a very black boy and a very white girl.

That would have caused fireworks twenty-seven years ago.

His brain raced as he made his way to the produce section. He knew he needed apples. He picked up a large Honey Crisp, scanned it for bruises when he noticed a woman walking up directly across from him.

She wore a sleek, skintight yoga outfit, electric blue. He glanced back down, checked the skin on a few more apples. He thought about what he'd just seen. Dark hair to her shoulders, soft summer tan on her toned arms. Probably late thirties. He wanted to look again, and not be too obvious.

"Excuse me," she said. She'd noticed his broad shoulders and angular facial features.

Jake looked up, saw white, straight teeth and deep brown eyes. Probably five-seven, he thought. She was holding two avocados in her hand, small ones.

"Yes?"

"This might sound silly. You look like a fit guy, somebody who eats right. I was wondering if you had any quick ideas on a great pick-me-up salad for a lazy morning."

"Hmmm, let me think. I love salads."

"You've probably felt it, sometimes you get the pang to taste something new. Something exotic would be wonderful." Her eyes took a sleepy, sensual turn.

Jake noticed her hands on the avocados. *Caressing them.*

His mind processed faster than Einstein. He felt grimy from the run. Maybe she was, too. *What would a soapy, hot shower feel like with her?*

His face creased into an easy smile, his teeth every bit as white as hers. "I've got a few ideas for salads, but they're not for anonymous inquiries, it's kind of proprietary data." He cocked his head slightly.

"Oh, I'm so sorry." With excellent posture, she sauntered around the display stand, extended her right hand to his. "I'm

Midnight Man

Brooke."

Long feminine fingers, a firm grip. He enjoyed the feel. "Jake. I'm from Georgetown, just in Atlanta for a few days."

One of her eyebrows raised. "Have we met? It seems like I know you from somewhere?" He fought to ignore the large diamond on her hand, like something a bank president would buy his wife. But still, he felt a little dizzy at the prospects. Summer morning sex to ratchet back the stress.

He was about to answer her when his phone buzzed. He pulled it from his pocket. Agent Randy Garrison in Washington.

"Fill me in, Jake."

"One minute, Randy." He glanced at Brooke. "Brooke, sorry, business. Have to take a raincheck. Thanks so much for saying 'hi.' Oh, look up Perfect Summer Fruit Salad on allrecipes.com. One of my favorites." He tossed her a shy wave and walked away.

"Well, Randy," Jake took a deep breath, thinking about Brooke's figure. "Very good chance we've got our guy. I'm in Atlanta right now."

Jake quickly ramped Randy up to speed on Ezra Cain. He also told him he'd put in a call to Dennis Hopkins at the Atlanta office. Hadn't heard back.

"Man, that's great news. Okay, I'm about to light some fires. But one thing I'd like to know. Is Cain a football nut? Is he close to Eli? Do we know if he *was* in those NFL cities?"

"No clue, but at this point, I'm not asking Eli."

"No, hell no, not yet anyway. I'm about to jump Morelock's ass. We need financial info on Cain on those big city kills. Then Hopkins will hear my cheerful voice."

"Great. Oh, remind Morelock to get me financials on Zeke Washington. He's supposed to be on that, too."

"Will do."

"Thanks, Randy."

Walking to his rental, a big *what if* hit his mind. Could Ezra and Eli be acting in concert? Could that even be possible? Cousins, but how close were they?

It took three minutes to start the car and drive to the parking lot of the Residence Inn. He'd answered his own question, or at least thought he did. Babu had been two years behind Eli in school. Left the Black Point system at the end of the sixth grade, moved across the bay. Went to Stanford, not Auburn, like Eli. Almost no time to be together and bond. Would Babu call and say *Hey cuz, let's torture and kill some blond bitches?* Not likely. Could one cousin call another and say they like pro ball, could you grab a good ticket for some games? Very possible.

Walking into his hotel room with a brown paper sack from Whole Foods, Jake's phone rang. He put the groceries down, grabbed the phone from his pocket.

Agent Dennis Hopkins. Jake smiled.

He could imagine Garrison chewing his ass.

82

ATLANTA, GEORGIA

11:20 A.M. TUESDAY. Dr. Ezra Cain was in the middle of a sentence emphasizing the dangers of one of the TORCH viruses in a pregnant woman when he saw the eyes of several young doctors dart toward the door. They caught motion, a man glancing in the small, square window.

The reflex was natural, unavoidable. Cain turned to look. He saw a man with dark eyes and an unshaven face peering in. He wore a ball cap with a red bill. Couldn't read it, but the color made him think UGA Bulldogs. The man abruptly disappeared when he saw Cain looking at him.

Cain lost his thought, stopped talking. *Something about the guy.* What? Did he know him? Couldn't connect it. *But something.*

The doctor turned back to his audience of twenty-nine resident physicians, flicked his head toward the door. "Some guy that couldn't get a ticket to my sold-out performance on TORCH viruses."

A smattering of laughs. Cain continued speaking. "Let's continue with the threat from rubella ..."

Cain's mind was running on a dual pathway. Black eyes in the window. Something about that face shook him.

Thirty-two minutes later Cain's gut knotted. He knew. Montoya.

But how?

NINETEEN HOURS LATER. No hint of sun. Sky shades of granite with dark clouds racing by. Jake glanced at the weather on his phone. "The front's near the Alabama line, dropping heavy rain. Moving east at ten miles an hour."

"We should be long gone by the time it rolls into this neighborhood," said Agent Hopkins.

By 11:30 yesterday morning, Randy Garrison had made things perfectly clear to Hopkins after laying out the scenario. "I need eyes on Dr. Ezra Cain today. Got that? *Today!* Find out where he is, the CDC, Emory, Starbucks, wherever the hell, and get on him. You'll be reporting to Montoya. As soon as we hang up, I want you to call him. This is big. Cain's looking like a major player. Media is going to eat this alive, Dennis. *A killer doctor."*

Montoya and Hopkins were sitting in a shiny white Chevy van wrapped with the DirectTV logo. The truck was used by the Atlanta field office for surveillance. Two ladders were mounted on a roof rack. Jake was in the driver's seat and Hopkins, the front passenger. A smattering of never-used tools and electronics cluttered the rear of the van. They were parallel parked on the curb of a tidy side street with a straight-on view of Cain's house. One by one, cars and SUVs were leaving homes for work or school.

Hopkins had a gym-rat look about him, six feet, maybe 200 pounds, strands of gray slipping in on a smart Harvard clip up top, buzzed tight on the sides. Could have been a fit lawyer, except for the clothes.

Both men wore navy pants, a DISH logo cap, and a white polo shirt. Hopkins clean-shaven. Montoya with a dark scruff.

"Cain's backing out," said Hopkins. Montoya glanced at him, ready to roll.

"Give 'em the call," said Jake.

There were agents in three vehicles within a fifteen-minute drive. One perched at the CDC entrance. One at employee parking. One at Emory Medical School faculty parking. Hopkins hit call. One ring. Answered.

"Cain's left his home in a black BMW SUV, presumably coming your way. Alert Weil and Laughlin. Call immediately when he arrives."

"Copy."

Hopkins rang off. A few minutes to kill. "Jake, you have any thoughts on the SEC this year? Kirby Smart's really coming on at Georgia. Could be his year."

"Who's Kirby Smart?"

Hopkins glanced at Jake with a puzzled look on his face. Jake's face was down, glancing at his phone, digging into the day's weather in Georgetown. "Didn't you play at Bama?"

"Barely made the team. Seems like a hundred years ago. Dennis, we should have some financial data on Cain from the last twenty-five years, soon, hopefully by lunch."

Hopkin's eyes didn't leave him, mystified at that response.

Seventeen minutes later a text hit Hopkins' phone: **Cain out of his car, walking into the CDC building. Do your thing.**

The DirectTV van fired to life, eased to the stop sign, turned right, drove forty yards, parked on the street in front of Dr. Ezra Cain's house.

The FBI was on the property.

83

THE TEXT HIT Cain's phone at 9:55 a.m. He was in his office at the CDC, lights down low, a classical violin playlist streaming from a small, wireless speaker. Related to his role on the editorial board at the *Journal of Virology,* he was peer reviewing an article for several European researchers on the effectiveness of the interferon Lambda treatment regimen to control lethal Middle East Respiratory Syndrome-CoV.

But he couldn't focus.

He fought swirling paranoia after seeing the face in the window yesterday during his lecture in the auditorium. *Ridiculous,* he thought, *couldn't be Montoya.* Just some guy in the hall looking in. Probably maintenance.

A text came in: ***Ezra, call me when you get a minute. Big question.***

It was Pete Keeting, the eighty-two-year-old Georgia Power retiree who lived two doors down. He spent a good part of his day on his front porch, reminiscing to no one and keeping his eyes on the neighborhood. He told anybody who'd listen that America was circling the drain. He wore a red MAGA cap.

Cain dialed him.

"Thanks, Ezra, for calling so quickly. Need advice." Voice sounded like a man running out of gas.

Cain chuckled. He liked Pete. "On what?"

"I want to know what plan I should get on a satellite TV system. Cable's wearing me out. Always on the fritz and damn expensive. When I grew up down in Perry, Georgia, we had rabbit ears and picked up stations from Macon and Columbus. Ted Turner ruined the planet with that Channel 17 Superstation and then all-damn-day lefty news."

Cain coughed a quick laugh. "You got me there, Pete. I don't have a satellite plan."

"Well, you might now. I just watched two guys unload some equipment from a DirectTV truck at your house. One carried a large box into your backyard. I thought that might be a dish. You know, the Georgia state flower." The old man coughed a raspy laugh. "They were there for an hour or so."

For a cold moment Cain was speechless, jaw clamped tight, eyes focused across the room in a blank stare. His mind raced to process Pete's news.

Thought he felt sweat breaking out on his forehead when he spoke. "Know what, Pete? Somebody did speak to me a couple weeks ago about a free trial. They must be out there making sure there are no obstructions. Look, thanks for the call. I'll get back to you on any plan I decide on."

Cain stood, walked to his office window, twisted open the window shades.

Blinding sunshine washed over the concern on his face.

84

LEAVING CAIN'S, Hopkins piloted the van through the leafy residential neighborhood into densely packed commercial corridors to reach the Northeast Expressway, I-85. Once on the freeway, he gunned the truck up to almost 90, stayed in the left lane. Mid-morning traffic was light leaving the city, moving fast.

Jake turned down the radio, punched Chester Chan's number into his phone, all the while scanning the highway. Like most men, he got edgy at speed when he wasn't driving.

An answer after three rings. "Agent Chan."

"Chester, it's Montoya. I think I might have good news."

"I'm all ears." Jake could practically feel Chester's excess energy.

"Sending you a package today and I hope you'll be able to pull off some DNA."

"Well, whose is it?" A cat-and-mouse tone.

"I'd bet my life it's the killer. Our guy."

"That sounds good, Jake. I can get on it in about a week. Heading to a family reunion in California this afternoon."

"What the hell? No way, Chester. You gotta skip the trip."

Jake heard a howl like hyenas fighting but it was Chester laughing. "Screwing with you, man. I'll be in my office when the package arrives tomorrow."

"Okay, yeah, you got me." Jake returned the laugh, relieved.

"Send it FedEx First Overnight. Guaranteed by eight, but our guy usually hits us before that."

FIFTEEN MINUTES LATER, Jake was changing out of his DirectTV uniform in a restroom of the FBI's Atlanta headquarters. He'd met Hopkins back in his office. The space was airy, with a large window providing a magnificent view of the building's dumpsters. Sunlight suffused the room. A bookcase held family photos, a smattering of FBI manuals, a UGA football helmet, and a small bowl of dried petals and spices. For a man's office, it had a surprisingly homey scent.

Hopkins had a cold bottled water waiting for Montoya. "Thanks, Dennis." Jake grabbed the bottle, downed two big slugs, sat in a lightly padded, utilitarian armchair that reminded Jake of a doctor's waiting room.

Jake fought the current flowing through his body. He wanted to stand, throw the chair through the glass, stick his head out and scream, "We got this son of a bitch! Got him!"

Moments away from putting Sunshine's killer in prison for life. That's all he really wanted, Sunshine's murderer. That's where the DNA came from. Anyone else was gravy.

Jake finished the water quickly, screwed the cap on, stood, and tossed the bottle in the trash. "Let's do it. Get some evidence bags, then let's get in a conference room." He picked up the half-filled kitchen trash bag and followed Dennis out of his office.

They emptied the bag of its contents onto a conference table. The items were few. They hadn't wanted to take all the trash from Cain's outside container. At the doctor's house, they'd opened the big rectangle Herby Curby, pulled out several large bags, opened them, spread the contents on a patio table, and sifted through. Then reloaded the bags back into the can.

With two fingers, Hopkins held a smushed Chick-Fil-A bag with used napkins inside, plus a Styrofoam cup that still held a straw. "I like this," he said, pointing at the straw. "We'll get something off it."

"Think you're right. How about this little grocery bag?" Jake untied it, looked inside. "This had to come from a bathroom trashcan. Plenty of tissues and several strings of floss."

"We've got DNA. Definitely," said Hopkins.

"Yep. Let's bag it all, get it to FedEx."

Jake bit his lower lip, thinking about FedEx. Looked at his watch. Eight past ten a.m. "I need to make a call." He pulled a chair away from the conference table, twisted it sideways, sat, and crossed his leg over a knee. Found a contact on his phone, tapped call. Five rings, no answer. Next came Sarah's southern accent. "It's Sarah, leave a message."

"Ms. Sarah, it's Jake. Please call me as soon as you can."

Hopkins sat with one-half of his rear on the conference room table, watched Jake with curiosity in his eyes. "Who is ..."

Jake placed a palm in the air. He went to the message mode on Sarah's contact. The phone rang before he could finish. "Ms. Sarah, hello, thanks for getting back."

"Just giving Galileo a bath. I think that booger rolls in the mud *just so* he can get in the tub. Total stinker."

Jake laughed to sound interested. Galileo was a rescued mutt and a fine one. "I've got a big ask, Ms. Sarah. Is the jet available?"

"It is. Why?"

"I think we're about to get the guy. The serial killer we're chasing. I need to get some evidence to Quantico to check some DNA."

"Oh, my. Is this the guy you think that killed—" Her tone was solemn.

Jake stopped her before she could utter "Sunshine." "Yes, it is. I need to lease the jet from you to fly to Atlanta, pick up the evidence, and fly it to Quantico. Naturally, I'll cover all fuel and pilot expenses. Do you know if Steve is close?"

"Hold it, son, hold it right there. I'm in my eighties, okay? Do you have any clue how hard it is to get rid of hundreds of millions of dollars?"

Jake laughed. "No, ma'am, I don't. Doesn't sound hard." Chuckled again.

"Jake, you ain't paying me one dirt-red cent, you hear? You can't fathom how much you've meant to me and the admiral, God rest that dear man's soul. Now you've got Steve's number. Call him, tell him to get out of that dang golf cart and get to the plane."

"Will do. I love you, Ms. Sarah. I'll be back in Georgetown soon."

Jake had lived rent-free in a carriage house on Sarah's estate since his first year with the Redskins. He rang off and a thought spritzed through his mind and not for the first time. The karma of the universe. He'd never done anything to deserve his amazing adoptive mother, Bonnie, or the incredible Ms. Sarah. Not a single thing.

"Dennis, what's the closest airport for a private jet?"

"Peachtree-DeKalb." He pointed his finger in a westerly direction. "Close by. Fifteen minutes, tops."

Jake nodded, scrolled contacts. Found STEVE WANTLAND-PILOT, tapped call.

Answered after two rings. "The legendary Jake Montoya. What's up, man?"

"An emergency, that's what. What are you doing?"

"I'm on the sixth hole at Old Hickory in Woodbridge. Playing eighteen with an old navy buddy."

"I just spoke to Sarah and she said to call you. I'm in a

crisis. I've got critical evidence to get to Quantico. It needs to be picked up in Atlanta. I need you *NOW.*"

"Okay, sure. Weather's good. The plane's in Manassas, about forty-five minutes away. Already fueled. I can be in the air in an hour and a half. Be there in another ninety minutes or so."

"Great. See you at Peachtree-DeKalb."

"Sure, been there many times. Jake, I'll need you to clear us for landing at Marine Corps Air Facility at Quantico."

"Done. I'll be waiting at Peachtree. Call me once on the tarmac." Rang off.

Jake glanced at Hopkins with steely eyes, help up a finger. Pulled up Chester Chan's number. Chan answered after two rings.

"Change of plans, Chester. The evidence is arriving by private jet at Quantico tonight. My estimate is ..." Looked at his watch. 10:35. "Let me think." Assumed three hours from now to make Atlanta. Throw in three hours for a ricochet. "I think you can have it by five this afternoon. Now, how long to evaluate it? Need a hard answer."

"Normally, twenty-four to seventy-two hours. But I'll do this myself with two assistants. We'll use the integrated microfluidic system."

"Cut the science malarkey, Chester. It's imperative to this case. How damn long?" Nails in the words.

"Four hours and five minutes, with my top two assistants."

"That-a boy. I'll call you when the plane is wheels-up from Atlanta."

Jake rang off, looked at Hopkins.

Dennis Hopkins' smile covered his face. "Very, very, impressive. So that's how an NFL Hall of Famer gets it done."

Jake snorted out a laugh, his eyes burning with intensity. "Dennis, I need contacts for HRT and SWAT commanders.

This'll move fast."

Leaving the FBI office, Jake walked into a hot breeze carrying a wall of Atlanta humidity. The sky was darkening, the front closing in from the west. Deep in the background, he heard the whirr of traffic on the expressway, three-quarters of a mile away. He loved summer, including the squalls. And it felt the same everywhere, Atlanta, Black Point, Washington, DC.

Bring the heat.

His shirt was damp when he reached his rental in the parking lot. He popped the lock, hopped in, fired up the engine, lowered all the windows, twisted the AC to high. The driver's door was open, his left leg sticking out.

He dialed a number in Mobile, Alabama. Special Agent Nia Cruz answered on the second ring. "About to think you dumped me."

"Not a chance. Here's the deal." Nia was informed about scouting Dr. Cain's work locations, plus his DNA heading to the FBI lab later today. "So, where are you with anything on the Gulf Coast cousins?"

"Nothing promising. Waiting on one interview report. It's a guy who lives in Panama City, has worked at the Bay Point resort golf course as superintendent for sixteen years, married, wife's a schoolteacher. Sleepy life. Don't expect anything there."

"Okay, well, here's the rest of the deal. Want you up here, fast. You've been in this from the start, I want you to grab some glory."

"Yeah, buddy. Ass kickin' time. I'll get on the road this afternoon." Jake felt the exhilaration in her voice, the cop's inbred passion for the take down.

Nia knew this would be no ordinary grab. Not if the media jumped on the story.

"You're not driving, Nia. Get a plane out of Pensacola or

Mobile. I'll pick you up at Hartsfield."

"Will do. Oh, hey, with DNA confirmation, just me and you making an arrest, right? Smile for the cameras." She grinned at the question.

"I'd prefer that ... without the cameras." Jake hung up, dialed Hopkins.

He answered, "Yeah, Jake."

"Driving back to my hotel. Need a local spot to eat. Any suggestions?"

"Sure do. The Colonnade on Cheshire Bridge Road. An Atlanta landmark."

85

JAKE SCANNED THE menu as he spoke. "Let's try the grilled rainbow trout, squash, and mashed potatoes, no gravy. And sweet tea." He raised his eyes to look at the waitress next to him. Her nametag said, *Mary. 37 years.* Easily in her seventies, she had teased honey-blond hair, and wore rimless spectacles over a face covered with wrinkled smoker's skin.

She nodded. "Good choice. The fish arrived from the mountains an hour ago."

Watching her walk away, he thought about thirty-seven years doing one job. Couldn't imagine it. He pulled up the contact for the Hostage Rescue Team commander, tapped call. A guy named Fitch answered, told Jake he was involved in a water training exercise on Lake Lanier. In thirty seconds Jake gave him the overview.

"Agent Fitch, I need you guys back in Atlanta. Hope to have word on a DNA match by 11:00 p.m. Hopefully, we're going for an arrest tonight."

"We'll get packing," said Fitch, anticipation in his voice. Jake rang off, dialed another number.

He was on the line with Agent Sam Reynolds, a SWAT leader, when his food arrived. He'd given a quick lay of the land, finished with, "Sam, you're on notice. We'll likely be on a takedown tonight. Waiting on DNA confirmation. Fitch is getting his HRT team ready this afternoon. We've got agents on the suspect 24/7. Talk soon."

SKY PEWTER GRAY. Rain stopped thirty-five minutes ago. Jake spotted Ms. Sarah's Embraer Phenom coming to a stop on the tarmac, the twin Pratt and Whitney engines whining.

He hustled over damp concrete toward the plane. Steve spotted him from the cockpit, popped a chin nod, dropped the airstair. Jake hustled up into the plane without coming to a stop.

"This is Bud Ogletree, Jake, an old navy pal." They shook hands.

"Great to meet you, Bud."

"Whatcha got there?" said Steve.

Jake held two bags. He lifted his left hand. "Evidence. Don't take your eyes off it." He lifted his right hand. "Ran by a sandwich shop and picked up some cold subs, chips, and drinks, in case you get hungry in the air."

"Excellent, we're starving. Now get off the plane, Jake, we're on a mission."

"Steve, you're cleared for Quantico. An agent named Dr. Chester Chan will pick up the bag. Thanks, guys."

86

ATLANTA'S SOUTHBOUND DOWNTOWN traffic sat at a standstill. Five lanes of cars jammed tight as a Manhattan parking lot. It was almost evening rush hour, a moderate rain had begun to fall out of a dark sky, killing the speed. Georgia Tech was on his right and the Varsity on his left. Jake didn't notice—he was late.

He dictated a text to Agent Cruz: **Nia, jammed up downtown on the freeway, headed your way in a white four-door Chevy sedan. Hang tight.**

A return text hit two minutes later: **Got it. I'm at Pickup Zone N2. I'm the tall, gorgeous Black woman with a red duffel at my feet.**

Twenty-three minutes later, Jake swirled through the chaos of traffic at the airport. Eyes darting, watching cars, scanning signs. *Where are you, N2?* Fighting to negotiate between the cabs, vans, and black-car vehicles, to get to the pickup lane.

Phone rang. *Bad time.* Answered anyway. "Montoya."

"This is Agent Weil. Cain just got in his car at the CDC. We have chase cars and five agents. We're on his tail."

"Thanks. What's your first name?"

"Brian."

"Okay, Brian. He's probably headed home. Don't lose him." Eyes fixed on the crowd as he spoke.

There she was. Jake eased to the curb. Nia opened the rear door, tossed in the duffel, hopped in the front passenger seat. "Hit it."

Jake looked in the rearview then over his left shoulder. Waited on a Toyota Highlander with a packed roof rack. Then kicked it. Tires screeched.

"Speed up, bro." Nia chuckled through a happy smile.

JAKE BLITZED NORTH on the interstate, the former Olympic Stadium on his right. Traffic was thick, he kept pace doing seventy-five. His phone rang. Quick answer. "Montoya."

"Jake, Chan here, I've got it. I'm leaving the airfield now." Chan was wired, sounded like he was talking through a thirty-two-tooth smile.

"Great, we've got a lot of folks waiting to hear what you have to say, Chester." Jake rang off, shot a thumbs-up to Nia, slowed as he curved onto I-20 East. "Evidence made it to Quantico."

Nia nodded, anticipation in her eyes. "Good."

87

DR. EZRA CAIN zipped out of the CDC building in a rush, laptop case in his right hand, a gray, wide-brimmed rain hat on his head. He hustled through a light drizzle to reach the parking deck. Inside his BMW he brushed off some rain with a towel. He fired up the car, light jazz playing on SiriusXM. He killed the music, eased out to Clifton Road, turned right, focused on the wet street.

He never spotted three teams of FBI agents eyeing him.

Cain's day had been a waste. His mind felt blurry with racing thoughts. Mostly, *be cautious.*

He passed Druid Hills Golf Club and Fernbank Museum just before the Ponce de Leon Avenue intersection. He cut west onto Ponce, heading into midtown Atlanta.

The four-lane took him through Druid Hills, a magnificent neighborhood of old Atlanta mansions, trees, and gardens.

Streets were wet, afternoon traffic heavy. Two FBI agents zipped past him in the left lane, spray jetting from the wheel wells. Cain paid no attention.

Anxiety had caused him to skip lunch. Now his appetite was back, he was thinking more clearly at the moment, a plan coming together. He glanced in the rearview mirror for a moment, tried to memorize some vehicles.

Afternoon drivetime. Traffic was bunched, moving even

slower on the slippery asphalt.

Passing Moreland Avenue, Ponce turned commercial. He spotted a massive beverage store on the left. Chipotle was on his right. He made a quick turn into the restaurant, parked.

He placed the transmission in park, waited, watched, with the AC running. Rain almost at a stop.

Two minutes later a Honda SUV pulled in and parked. A young mommy hopped out with two little girls wearing colorful rain boots. A ragged Silverado pulled in a moment later. Sign on the door said Nero's Block and Concrete. Marietta phone number. An aging Black man exited wearing khakis and unlaced boots covered with dried red clay.

Four minutes later, feeling safe, Cain stepped out into steam rising off hot asphalt. He entered the restaurant, laptop case in his hand, took a seat on a stool fronting a bar table. He was positioned to look through the plate glass to the street. He scanned the businesses across the road.

Nothing unusual.

AGENT WEIL DIALED Montoya. Jake saw the caller ID. "What do you have, Brian?"

"Cain didn't drive home. Right now he's at a Chipotle on Ponce de Leon. Pull it up on maps."

"Will do. Don't lose this guy. He's canny."

"Roger."

CAIN REVIEWED THE narrative in his mind, then found the contact. He punched call to reach old man Keeting's phone, his retired neighbor.

"Hello, Doctor. Find anything on the satellite plan?" Voice rusty with age, speck of hope in the tone.

"That's what I wanted to talk to you about. I have something to share with you. It's important." Cain lowered his voice into a conspiratorial tone. "Need you to sit down, Pete."

"I am sitting, Doc. Sitting on my front porch, eating cheese straws and drinking sweet tea. Now this sounds serious. What's going on?"

"Pete, it is serious. Can I absolutely trust you to keep this only between us?"

"Sure, Doc, if you say so. I'm a river-baptized Nazarene. My word's my bond."

Cain rolled his eyes, knew that tea was packed with rum and honey.

"You're the one guy I know I can trust, Pete. So listen, over at the CDC, I'm the point man on a collaboration between the United States government and a large pharmaceutical concern that I can't name out of privacy concerns."

"Huh." Cain heard Pete take a long sip of tea.

"We've got a competing vaccine in progress to Jynneos, the only approved monkeypox vaccine. The Chinese are trying to steal our IP."

"Eye what?"

"IP, intellectual property. Our research and vaccine formulation, that kind of thing. Extraordinarily valuable data. I'm almost certain they're trying to get into my house. I'm positive that was them this morning in the satellite truck."

"Dang, Doc. Spy movie right under my nose." Another sip of tea.

"Right. I need you to check out the neighborhood first, right now, then keep your eyes on my house, into the evening. Call me with anything suspicious."

"Doc, I'm just an old telephone-pole lineman, not a secret agent."

"Pete, here's what you do. Snap a leash on Pickle, take a slow walk through the neighborhood. Call me back with anything unusual."

"Sure, Doc, let me knock back the rest of this tea. I'll call you back in thirty minutes, after these old bones take a quick look-see."

Cain folded his laptop under his arm, went through the line to order. He returned to the same spot with a burrito bowl and a large lemonade. He popped open his computer, logged on to the *New York Times.*

A middle-aged couple had come into the restaurant since he arrived. Both crisply dressed. They'd ordered and were eating when he walked by with his food. Cain watched them in his peripheral vision. They didn't appear to notice him.

Could be agents, he thought, *the woman's too attractive for the man.* Or they could be two hungry people off work from one of the midtown business towers.

Cain scanned the horizon over the top of his computer, briefly glancing at the *Times* as he ate.

Nine minutes later, the couple left. She got in a red M3 ragtop. He got in a crew-cab pickup. *Unlikely feds,* he thought. The dark-haired woman with kids shuffled out next.

He thought he caught a side-eye from her.

He spotted the time on his laptop. Twelve minutes since he spoke to Pete Keeting. He dove back into the *Times,* clicked on the science section, jumped into a long article on the ten-year anniversary of Doudna and Charpentier's groundbreaking work on CRISPR, a tool that allows scientists to easily alter DNA sequences and modify gene function. He sat back, distracted himself by thinking about that, but the words were a jumble in his mind.

He jolted when his phone rang. *Focus, dammit.*

"Doc, it's Pete."

"Yeah, Pete." Felt a twinge in his gut over what he might hear.

"I think we've got spies. They want that monkey vaccine,

guarantee you that."

"What'd you see?"

"About seven houses down, near Ferguson's two-story, a couple guys were sitting in a van. Said Shorty's Electric on the sides. Staring down your way. And I did you one better. I popped it into Google. Ain't no Shorty's Electric in Atlanta."

Cain's eyes squinted at this news, a quiver of concern vibrating through his body.

"And down the other way, near the subdivision entrance, a woman and a man, late thirties or forties were sitting in a car. Just sitting there. I've never seen them, and I've never seen the car. And I've been here fifty-two years. But here's the thing, Doc. Nobody looked Chinese."

Cain found some inner calm. "Pete, good work. I knew I could count on you. And that's how the Chinese work. They hire American private detectives through shell companies. They don't even know they're working for the Chinese. But it doesn't matter, there's nothing useful in my house anyway. I appreciate the help."

"Sure thing. I think I need another tea after that walk. A touch humid out here."

Cain shut down the laptop, loaded it in the case. Steepled his hands under his chin, sat there a few moments. *They're out there.* He didn't see them but knew they were. He smiled without showing any teeth, positive of one thing. They didn't have his intellect.

He grabbed the laptop, strolled out of the restaurant with a jaunt in his step.

Let 'em see a man without a care in the world.

88

TEN MINUTES UNTIL 7:00 p.m. Rain had left the city covered with humidity like a steam bath. Cain drove west on Ponce under dark gray skies, wipers on intermittent, mostly scraping road spray off the windshield.

Weather reports said showers off and on until 1:00 a.m. A strong low-pressure system circling Atlanta. Moving easterly, slowly. *Good.*

He turned left on Juniper, quickly reached the light at North Avenue. It was red. He stopped, then turned right, west, watched in his rearview. Four cars behind him. Crossed over Peachtree Street, spotted the Coca-Cola headquarters tower a half-mile away, dead ahead.

Coming off the bridge over the ten-lane interstate, he landed onto the Georgia Tech campus, pushed west another mile to the western edge of the Tech property, cut down a side street that had a smattering of privately owned commercial buildings and a mixture of vintage early-twentieth-century industrial structures mixed in with the sleek glass and steel buildings.

Cain pulled into the parking lot of a three-story, aged masonry building, found a parking spot close to the main entrance, as most of the workers had finished their day. A sign on the building said Bio-South and also included a phone number for those interested in leasing space. The building was a historic former bottle-manufacturing site, having been built in 1898 of oversize brown brick with rough mortar seams. The developers had renovated it into a 95,000-square-foot center dedicated to the biotech industry.

Rain fell like bullets riding a westerly wind that racked Cain as he eased out of his car. He snugged his hat down, held tight to his laptop, and hustled toward the front door under high-intensity LED outdoor lighting. The sky above was now charcoal black. Darkness had rolled in forty-five minutes early.

Inside, the doctor took the steps two at a time to reach the second floor. His small lab was at the north end of the hall. The was no sign on the door. The lessee of the space was Data Compilation Services, LLC, incorporated in the state of Wyoming. Dr. Ezra Cain's name was listed nowhere. A Wyoming lawyer paid the lease in six-month increments.

Cain punched a six-digit code into an electronic lock, saw the green light, entered the space. The lights were off, and he left them that way. The unit was 2,600 square feet, mostly lab, with a small office fronting the parking lot and street.

He stepped into the office. The blinds were closed. With two fingers he tweaked open a couple slats and gazed across the parking lot. He'd studied the cars when he arrived. Almost sure there was nothing new in the parking lot.

A flicker of light caught his eye, inside the windshield of a truck parked on the street, fifty yards down.

Somebody on a cell phone.

89

MONTOYA ANSWERED AFTER one ring. "What's happening, Brian?" Jake was sitting on a couch in the lobby of the Residence Inn in Decatur, a low-power voltage spooling through his nerves. Dark chinos, black polo shirt, .45 auto on his left hip, grip forward. Nia Cruz was twenty feet away, checking into a room.

"We're sitting in the rain just off the Georgia Tech campus. Cain just walked into a building called Bio-South. The web says they rent space for biological research. There's no tenant list online. Don't know if he's just visiting somebody or leases space."

"Huh, right." Jake became quiet. Thinking.

"Agent Callie Davis is parked at a building close by. She's in a Honda minivan. We're gonna have her run in, look at a tenant board. She doesn't look like an agent, more like a thirty-two-year-old sorority chick."

"Okay. Get back with me. Oh, hey, text me your address." Cruz was putting her ID away as Jake stepped to the counter. "Let's stow the duffel. We're heading over to a commercial lab science space near Georgia Tech. Cain is in an office there."

CAIN WATCHED THE light go off on the cell phone. The truck remained dark, its occupant inside.

A minivan passed the truck, headlights carving through the falling rain drops, water sluicing off the tires. The vehicle cut into the Bio-South lot, lit up under the bright lights.

Cain knew he was looking at a white Honda Odyssey. He'd seen one just like it at Chipotle. *Couldn't be the same one.* The one at the restaurant had dumped out two small kids in rain boots and a young woman in a red parka with dark hair clipped at her shoulders.

He watched the van park, not in the closest space, but in a nest of three vehicles farther from the building entrance. He found that suspicious.

The driver's door opened. An umbrella extended out, popped open. Someone stepped out of the vehicle, closed the door, cocooned under the umbrella, and walked briskly toward the entrance.

It was a woman with dark hair clipped at the shoulders wearing a red parka.

Cain's eyelids hooded.

90

MONTOYA AND CRUZ moved fast to get out of the hotel. Cruz wore a dark hooded parka over a ballistic vest, black polo, and black twill slacks. She carried a .40 caliber Sig in a shoulder rig. Eight-inch tactical boots on her feet.

At six feet, Black and fit, she was an intimidating woman.

"Slow down, man. They've got him covered," said Cruz. Jake pushed the sedan hard on the slippery surface streets, causing dizzying moments of hydroplaning at times. His brain was locked tight on one thought: Dr. Ezra Cain killed his girlfriend twenty-seven years ago. And if he had his way, Cain wouldn't live till sunrise.

Montoya followed the same streets that Cain had taken. Turning onto Ponce, rain beginning to flood down in sheets. Crosswinds buffeted the sedan. Jake slowed, clicked the wipers on high, flicked on the high beams.

"Damn, thank you, for slowing down. I'm sweating." Nia shot a harsh stare at Jake through the glow of the dashboard.

EZRA CAIN STEPPED into the lab, closed the door, flicked on the overhead fixtures. It was a gleaming facility, 6,000 lumens of crisp light falling on precision stainless-steel instrumentation.

The landlords had created a state-of-the-art, ready-to-move-into laboratory. Fume hood overhead with dual HEPA filtration systems. Ultra-centrifuges. GeneAmp PCR machines. Microscopes. Stainless-steel storage. Glass-front refrigerators.

A locked freezer registered -130 degrees Celsius. Ultra-cold. A biohazard sticker was glued to the door.

But what had sold Dr. Cain on the space was the German-made bioreactor for amplifying virus growth and the cryopreservation system. The virologist had everything he needed to manufacture evil in large quantities. Billions of lethal viral particles. And a nice, chilly dormitory to store them.

The space was a magnificent Biosafety Level 2 space, but with far below the security of the BSL-4.

His concern? The lab held what was arguably the deadliest virus on the planet.

Red X-81.

That monster should never exist in a lab with the defense of a screen door.

NEVER.

91

AGENT CALLIE DAVIS closed her umbrella at the double front doors of Bio-South and leaned it against the brick. Stepping inside, she was confronted by a stunning mahogany-wood enclosed receptionist station. Two short couches with a single chair at each end faced each other in front of the station. A magnificent Persian rug was placed between them on polished concrete that had been stained riverbank tan. *Classy setup*, she thought.

Not a person in sight. Quiet. The only sound was the hum of airflow in the overhead AC duct.

Oversized elevators were located on each side of the receptionist's area. A building directory was wall-mounted next to each elevator. She stepped back, snapped a photo of the reception area and elevators.

She went to the directory, snapped two shots, walked thirty feet to the other directory, snapped off two more photos. She studied the pics. Perfect light. In focus. *Got it.*

The hallway ran parallel to the length of the building. She walked to one end, intentionally holding her breath, intently listening for footsteps, eyes alert. There was a ten-foot-wide stairway climbing to the second floor. Snapped a photo. She walked past the receptionist station far enough in the other direction to see an identical set of stairs. Snapped a pic. Had what she needed.

She walked out the main entrance, opened her umbrella, walked with a casual gait to her minivan. She forwarded the pics to Agents Weil and Hopkins, then dialed Weil.

"Get 'em?"

"Yeah, got 'em."

"Okay, I'm headed home. It's only a mile and a half from Chipotle. Two little girls need a bath."

"Hey, great work today. You can tell your kids they did their first surveillance when they were five, eyes on a suspect eating a burrito."

Agent Hopkins was in a black Tahoe seventy yards from the building. He texted the directory board to Jake.

Jake texted back: **Got it. Thirty seconds out.**

Jake pulled the sedan up behind Weil. Called him. "Brian, that's me behind you. I'm sending the directory to my analyst in Washington. We need to know where this guy is in the building."

"Copy." Rang off.

Jake forwarded the photos to Agent Ross Tolleson. Ross was finishing a plate of homemade lasagna with *Jeopardy* on in the background. Read: **Dial me.** His forehead wrinkled. *Dammit, Jake.*

Jake's phone rang in twelve seconds. Quick answer.

"Need to jump on it, Ross, who are these companies are in the directory? We've got Dr. Ezra Cain inside some science building here in Atlanta. Raining like hell outside. Don't know what he's doing or exactly where he is."

Tolleson studied the directory photos while he listened to Jake. "I count eighteen tenants on the directory. Every name sounds scientific."

"Well, that observation should get you a promotion." Jake heard Ross laugh. "Need your team on it. *RIGHT NOW!* Where is he? What do all these companies do? We've got evidence running at Quantico right now. Hope to have a DNA match by eleven o'clock tonight."

"Okay. I have six guys on call. We can work this remotely. I'm going to conference call them right now." Tolleson's tone now reflected the gravity of the ask. "I'll give three companies to each, let them dig in. I've got the landlord's name and number in the photo. Looks like a Dallas number. It's after hours, but they'll have somebody on call. I'll work them."

Jake nodded. He knew Tolleson could see around corners. See things nobody else did. "Sounds good."

Jake dialed Weil. "Brian, we have this building buttoned up, right? Covering all entrances?"

"Oh yeah. Hopkins has the south side. I've got the front. Two guys covering the north entrances."

"Who's got the rear?"

"It backs up to train tracks. Hopkins says it's fenced off, both to the sides of the building and the tracks. He won't be leaving that way."

Jake didn't like that answer. "Let's be smart, Brian. I've got Agent Nia Cruz with me. She's the SAC in Mobile. We'll take a look at it. Call me with anything."

"What?" said Nia.

"Open perimeter, the rear of the building. It's fenced off, abuts railroad tracks. We can't leave it open. Need eyes back there."

"I've got it."

"Okay, thanks. I've got to get back to our assault teams, get them lined up."

Nia Cruz ran her fingers over the Sig in her holster, zipped her parka, checked her pocket for her Maglite, pulled her hoodie over her head. She looked toward Jake, extended her left hand to the roof light, clicking it to *OFF*. They faced each other in the dark. Nia said, "We've got him. Tonight, man, we've got him."

Cruz popped out of the sedan, closed the door gently. Rain slapped her face as she disappeared into the shadows, dodging puddles reflected off ambient lighting.

Deep in the background, easily two miles out, heavy steel clattered. The rain competing to smother a throbbing diesel-electric engine.

92

CAIN EYED THE FREEZER. Unless you were a complete fool, there was always paranoia around a hot zone. Cain was no fool, he'd seen what Red X-81 could do from five feet away.

The demon was double-boxed in bio-sealed Lexan. Even if dropped, it wouldn't spill open ... in theory.

The doctor grabbed a twenty-quart hard cooler from the stainless shelving, placed it on the floor beside the freezer, opened the top. A spool of duct tape was placed next to the cooler.

He pulled a full-body Tyvek suit from its box. It was XXXL, allowing his large body to slip into it with clothes on. He kicked off his shoes, stepped into the suit's booties, pulled it on.

He could feel his heart start to boom, thoughts of Lea Lea Sloane sloshing blood all over the Airstream in Black Point. Dying in agony.

He slipped a Racal hood over his head, sealed it at the suit junction, flicked on the battery-powered air unit. He triple-gloved his hands.

The transfer would take less than sixty seconds.

Suddenly the interior of the hood felt terrifyingly lonely as circulating air hissed through his ears. A hint of claustrophobia crowding in. Cain squelched the panic.

His face was flat and focused as he leaned down to the digital freezer lock. Chills like pinpricks raced into his hands, stabbing his nerves. Slowly, accurately, he punched in seven digits. The freezer unlocked with a click. His memory kept dancing back to Lea Lea Sloane ... blood draining from her eyes.

He opened the door and removed the only container in the freezer. It held a hundred small vials, each packing untold millions of virus copies. The Lexan unit was placed in the cooler, gently. Cain covered the plastic with dry ice he kept on hand. The cooler top was closed, two latches snapped. His final step was to encircle the cooler with duct tape.

Cain unseated the protective hood, stepped out of the suit, left everything littered on the floor. He bent and tied on his shoes.

Now that the virus was packed, he felt free to rush. No clue how many agents were out there waiting. Likely to start banging on the office doors any moment. But so what?

They've got nothing on me. Nothing.

He heard rain lashing against his office window. The boom of thunder rustled through the building. A half smile creased his lips. Loving the weather.

One final exercise.

His large hand slid open a drawer on a stainless-steel cabinet. He pulled out two large vials of medicine. Ketamine and midazolam. Next, four syringes preloaded with eighteen-gauge needles, thick jobs. He pulled up two heavy doses of each med into the syringes, capped them, slid them into his pockets.

Two ponchos hung on a coat rack. One safety yellow, one black. He slid the dark one over his head, picked up the cooler, walked to the office's rear door.

Dr. Ezra Cain was twelve short feet from an outside fire escape. He silently chuckled as he crossed the distance. He was leaving through the back of the building, ready to cross the train tracks.

He opened the door two inches, silently, glanced out. Movements furtive.

He stepped onto the fire escape, nothing more than a night shadow.

Cain descended like a panther.

93

CRUZ FROZE DURING lightning strikes, hoping to stay unseen. She crept swiftly, using ambient light, her pupils dilated. With both hands on the ground for balance, she slid down a five-foot grassy embankment to reach the back of the building.

She swiped rain from her face using the back of her hand. Nothing stopped the water from draining down her front collar, soaking her ballistic vest, filtering down her polo shirt into her bra. A cold shiver ran through her.

Reaching the fence, she glanced up, gauged the height. Ten feet. Three strips of barbed wire were on top, running parallel. She tugged on the fence, wondering if anyone had sliced an opening. The homeless, a hobo, a thief, anybody. Nothing. It was snug.

She hopped down onto the train track. There were three separate tracks. Clanging steel getting louder in the distance. A diesel-electric engine pumping up-tempo. With her foot on a rail, she felt a tremor in the steel. A train headed her way, moving very slowly through the big city.

No LED lights out back, only three metal-caged vapor-tight fixtures mounted to the building, holding incandescent bulbs. They were dimmed by the rain.

Cruz cautiously walked the middle of a track toward the other end of the building. She stopped twice to study the brick structure. Several offices showed traces of light behind blinds. It was evident where the old freight-door openings had been bricked over.

Two heavy steel fire escapes zigzagged down the wall from each end of the building.

It was an eerie black night, no movement anywhere except falling rain. Downtown Atlanta was lit up to the south. In midtown, to the east, the old IBM Tower glowed in the night.

Nerves shimmered through her. Subconsciously, she rubbed her right hand over her Sig as she moved forward. She stopped when she came to a gate that opened onto the tracks. A lightning flash illuminated a padlock. She fingered the lock, jiggled it. It was latched tight. She moved on.

Reaching the south end of the building, she climbed up from the tracks, walked the fence, pushing the chain links for laxity. Tight. Tight. Tight.

Then it wasn't.

She found it. Eight feet from the building, the fence had been sliced in a neat line along one of the poles. A slight tug and the chain link peeled back. Cruz turned sideways and slid through onto the building's old railroad loading dock. She was standing on decades-old, pock-marked concrete.

EZRA CAIN EYED the moving figure. Wondered at first if it could be one of the homeless in the area. He quickly discounted that. They fought to stay dry, not wander around in the rain.

A cop. Had to be.

The figure moved away from him. He studied the fire escape. With the rain, it was practically invisible. But the lightning. *Dammit.* Like getting photographed with a flash bulb.

He decided he was going down to ground level. As slowly as possible, he edged forward, one baby step at a time. An occasional creak in the steel. It blended into the noise of the evening.

Just as the shadow reached the far end of the building, Cain reached the old loading dock. Two quick steps landed him into a shadowed seam in the brick, an indentation in the wall. The old warehouse doors, long gone, had formerly latched two feet inside the exterior wall.

Cain had a tiny, two-foot-deep cubby. He turned sideways, pasted his back against the brick, took a breath, waited a few moments, leaned to his side, placed the cooler on the ground.

He teased his head forward three inches. With one eye, he glanced down the loading dock.

He saw a silhouette walking his way.

THE OVERHEAD SKY was inky black, fully closed in. No moon. Not a single star. Agent Cruz crept as covertly as she could. But still, she was unconcealed.

She moved toward the building and leaned on the old brick wall, back first. The roof, three stories above was flat and had no overhang to blunt the rain. She pulled out her cell, held it close to her body, minimizing the screen's glow.

Texted Jake: **On loading dock. All clear. Maintaining surveillance.**

Quick reply: **Great. Thanks! SWAT enroute here and Cain's home.**

The rain. The storm. A serial killer close by. A feeling like she was in a Hitchcock movie.

Then a spigot opened, sending an adrenaline rush through her, a reaction to her fear.

Cruz stepped three feet off the wall, continued her surreptitious walk down the length of the building, agile, traveling light on the balls of her feet.

Ten feet down the dock, a sheet of rain raked her back. Almost like someone tickled their fingers over her. She jumped. A buzz of nerves. Tension becoming untenable.

Enough, her brain screamed. She unzipped her parka slightly to pop the snap on her shoulder holster. The black .40 slid free of the leather, firmly held in her right hand, finger on the trigger.

She snugged up the zipper, feeling the calm only a weapon can bring.

DR. EZRA CAIN had one eye on Cruz as she backed against the wall. Spotted a light falling on her face. Text or call, he wasn't sure. It concerned him. He continued to watch, saw her push off the wall, and begin moving his way. *Good.*

A flash of lightning strafed the sky, bolts jagged like fractured glass, thunder on its tail.

The storm was on top of them.

Cain inched back into the shadows.

Waiting.

CRUZ CONTINUED HER slow amble. Like in her basketball days, nimble, slight flexion in the muscles, ready to launch.

She was approaching the fourth, and last, of the former openings for the freight doors. Inching forward, forty feet from the second fire escape and the end of the building.

EZRA CAIN WAS as still as the brick he leaned against. His whole being was immersed in the black night. A shadow emerged beside him, no more than four feet away. Rain smacked their parka.

He sized the guy up. Big. Close to his height, but not quite. Looked bulky in the jacket.

He fingered the syringes through his poncho.

Cain stepped directly behind the man, silent, invisible. His muscles drew tight. A red rage began to boil inside him. *Hard and fast,* he thought. *No fear, none.*

Nia Cruz stopped dead in her tracks.

AGENT CRUZ FELT a rush. It wasn't water. It was a wave of fear flooding her brain. She stopped, became stone still. Breaths coming quick and deep. *Somebody there?*

The train was approaching. The clang of steel and diesel rumble almost caused phonic vertigo. She turned completely around. Slowly.

Her eyes locked onto a nightmare, a mountain of blackness standing before her. Heartbeats hammered her chest. Blood pounded her eardrums. She screamed, but it was muffled by the storm.

It was barely a moment. Cruz's gun hand raced upward.

And her head exploded.

Bolts of white and red electricity flashed through her skull. Her vision went black. Cruz's six-foot body fell hard to the ground.

Cain headbutted her with a skull as hard as a bowling ball.

He dropped to his knees, placed a hand on Cruz's throat, slammed his heavy-boned fist into her face. It struck like a brick. He did it one more time.

Agent Nia Cruz was down.

Cain fumbled under his poncho and pulled out a syringe of ketamine. Slammed the fat needle through her pants into her thigh, dumped the anesthetic into her with a hard push.

He looked into the guy's face. Not Montoya. Cain tugged Cruz's hood back. *I knew it,* he thought. *A woman. Men don't scream like that.*

He vibrated at the thought. *Another power bitch.* This one tall, sturdy.

A tremor of anticipation thrummed through his nerves.

The train previously had been white noise. But not now. Cain watched a powerful light beam fire down the length of tracks, the train attached to the ass end of the light. Right next to him, the screech and squeal of steel grating against itself reached its peak.

Cain laid flat and still on the wet concrete, next to Cruz. Waiting for the river of steel to pass.

Time to think. *A cop.*

It was only a moment, a decision dawning with clarity.

I'm taking the bitch.

94

"**HOW DO YOU** want to handle it?" Agent Sam Reynolds, the SWAT commander, had just arrived on the scene. He was sitting in the back seat of Weil's Suburban, water dripping off his body, Montoya and Weil in the front seat.

Jake shook the man's hand with an introduction. He twisted around to speak, talking over his left shoulder. "How many did you bring?"

"Fifteen here, ten at Cain's house. Five of the guys outside are HRT. Fitch is at the house."

"Sounds good. Here's the deal. A DNA match is being processed at Quantico this very minute." Jake blipped his phone, saw 9:55.

"If we're lucky we'll have a report in an hour. Then it's time to rip the building apart. Sam, I don't know what you know, but we're almost certain this guy has viciously killed over twenty people in the last thirty years. He's an intelligent, critical thinker who blends anonymously into society. An honest-to-God nightmare next door."

A low whistle from Reynold's lips. "We'll take him."

"But we don't know what the hell he's doing in this building," said Jake. "This guy's an associate professor at Emory's med school and on staff at the CDC. My analyst in DC has his team running every tenant in the building, trying to determine any connection to Ezra Cain."

Reynolds nodded, absorbing it, thinking. "How's your perimeter coverage?"

"Covered, but light. Let's get six of your guys and plant two at the front and each side. The back is completely fenced in, and dumps onto some railroad tracks. We have an agent covering it."

"Roger." Reynolds went clicked his radio, selected six agents, passed on instructions.

The train was leaving the area, noise weakening, becoming thready. Lightening flashed deep in the eastern sky, far enough away to not generate any thunder noise, rain now gentle and warm.

EZRA CAIN'S EYES never left the train. Boxcars, covered hoppers, auto racks, and flat cars chugged past. Eight minutes and the clatter had passed.

He popped up off the concrete, slipped a key from his pocket, sprang over to the rear gate, inserted the key in the padlock, popped it open, pushed the gate free. Three months ago, he'd cut off the original lock with bolt cutters, installed his own.

Cain had always been a meticulous planner, had been since he was eleven, when he overdosed his mother. He took great pride in intricacy, the more calculated, the better.

He was prepared for this current predicament.

Back in a squat next to Cruz, he knew he had about twenty-five minutes left on his ketamine clock.

He grabbed her wrists, dragged her to the gate. He jumped down to the tracks. Wearing a ballistic vest and wet parka, she was easily over 200 pounds. He thought about removing them, but no. He wanted her gone *in toto*. He pulled her closer, ran his hands through her pockets. Small wallet, likely holding a driver's license. Left it. Fingered a phone. That's what he wanted. He pulled it out and threw it like a baseball down the tracks.

Kill any digital tracking.

Gun? Where was it? Dug around. Nothing. Hopped back onto the loading dock, ran quickly to the takedown spot. He picked up the Sig, placed it in his poncho pocket.

He jogged back to Cruz, hopped down to track level. The loading dock was even with his waist. He took a rough, long breath, bent down, scraped Cruz up onto his shoulder like a sack of potatoes, turned to flee the scene.

Heavier than he thought. He knew most men could not carry this kind of bulky heft.

No close-by lightning to hit him like a spotlight. *Good*, he thought.

He stepped gingerly, crossing three rows of train tracks. *Careful, careful, move slow,* he kept telling himself. Easy to twist a knee, sprain an ankle.

It took fifteen minutes to reach his destination, but it felt like two hours. Cain laid Cruz on the ground next to a dark gray Mercedes Sprinter camper, which looked like an oversized van with an expansive roof rack. It was supported by large, tough tires. A rig for rugged travel. It was parked in the far reaches of a parking lot near a Georgia Tech printing facility, sitting in deep shadow.

The truck, registered under the name Transglobal Geological through a Delaware corporation, was topped off with fuel and food. Cain moved the truck's location every three days, leaving it in spaces with sparse lighting and devoid of cameras.

Cain caught his breath, but only for a moment. He unlocked the side door, slung it open, and leaned down to Cruz.

She moved before he could touch her. Mumbled something.

No time for this. Cain pulled a syringe of sedative from his pocket. Didn't know which one. Didn't matter. Pulled off the needle cap with his teeth, spit it out, jammed the syringe in a muscle, pulled out, tossed the open needle over his shoulder.

Two minutes, and Cruz was quiet. With a deep grunt, Cain strained getting her off the asphalt. He juggled her into the van onto a small bed and silently closed the door. It was a struggle removing her parka and Kevlar. He knew if he had to shoot her, he didn't want a vest in the way of a bullet.

He cinched her wrists and ankles with heavy nylon zip-tie cuffs, secured her to the bed with braided paracord.

He fired up the truck, turned on the lights, slipped it in drive, eased out of the parking lot. Driving east on North Avenue, college buildings passed by in a blur. Streets strangely empty for a big city.

Cain edged the van onto the freeway, I-75/85, at the northern edge of downtown Atlanta. No rain falling, but road spray misting his windshield. Downtown buildings shot into the sky, blazing with light. Bank of America Plaza, 191 Peachtree, Georgia-Pacific, the iconic circular Western Peachtree Plaza.

Reaching Grady Hospital, located at the edge of the freeway, his foot dove in deeper on the accelerator, mind fizzing with the fun he'd have.

Cain headed south. Six hours' worth.

95

JAKE'S PHONE VIBRATED at 10:37. He boiled with impatience, waiting on Tolleson and Chan to call. His eyes were locked on the Bio-South building. It was Tolleson, calling from his home office. Quick answer. "I need something, Ross."

"Nothing solid, but we do have a suspicious tenant."

"How so?"

"First thing, I was lucky to get somebody in Dallas to give up a list of tenant contact numbers. There's one tenant that's not listed in the photos you sent. Data Compilation Services. Every company in the building is listed and each has a website, some have a Facebook page, too. There's nothing out there on Data Compilation."

"Huh." Jake sat up straighter in the car seat, focusing.

"The guy in Dallas gave us a number for Data Compilation. We called it. A young woman answered with the company name. She didn't know a thing, said we'd called an answering service in Laramie, Wyoming."

"Wyoming? What the hell is that about? But that's him, gotta be."

"Odd, for sure, so she checked something, came back and said her company had been paid a year in advance by a lawyer named Sam Hatcher, based in Sheridan, Wyoming. We tracked down one of Hatcher's paralegals. Hatcher is at his ritzy golf-course house on some island in Savannah, Georgia. Guy's a golf nut, she said."

"Need to speak to him."

"Two agents from the Savannah office are en route to his house."

Before Montoya could respond, another call came in. Chan on the ID. "Gotta run, it's Chan." Jake felt his gut knot as he clicked over to Chan.

"Got him, Jake, got him. It's the guy, man!" Chester Chan sounded like he was running 100-meter sprints. Oxygen deprived.

Jake slammed his hand on the dashboard, phone still to his ear. "We got him!" He twisted and high-fived Weil and Reynolds. "You're sure, Chester, absolutely sure?"

"One-hundred-ten percent. That guy's DNA was under Sunshine Gage's fingernails."

"GOING IN." Agent Sam Reynolds radioed his team. "Gather at front door, now." It was 10:50 p.m. Rain stopped. Air steamy. A city glow of light pollution reflected off the clouds.

"How about this, Jake? You come in with the team, we'll let Weil and Hopkins and their guys cover the perimeter."

"Sounds good." Hopkins and Weil also agreed. The cab of the Suburban vibrated with nerves, excitement … and fear.

Jake found Nia Cruz's contact, dictated a message: **We have confirmation! Cain's DNA matches! Cover the back. We're going in for the takedown.**

DR. EZRA CAIN locked his speed at sixty-five, stayed hard in the right lane. Now on I-85 South, he'd just passed Hartsfield-Jackson International, and crossed to the outside of I-285, Atlanta's perimeter highway.

Cain was in the wind.

96

TWO SWAT AGENTS stood sentry inside the front doors of the Bio-South building. After searching the first-floor restrooms, seven men ascended one set of stairs to the second floor, led by Reynolds. Six men climbed the stairs at the other end of the hall, headed to the third floor. Montoya, vested, with a Glock .45 riding easy in his right hand, tailed them.

Every man, ominous creatures in black, moved in a combat crouch, quickly but silently. Military precision.

First order of business, search the restrooms. Then locate the office of Data Compilation Services. The teams were efficient. In less than two minutes, the restrooms were cleared ... and they had a problem.

The leader of the third-floor squad stood in an empty restroom, spoke into his mic with a furtive whisper. "Third floor. No office identified. Repeat, no office identified."

Reynold's responded. "Have Montoya come to the second floor."

Jake, wearing rubber-soled hiking shoes, speed-stepped as silently as a cat down the stairs. He spotted Reynolds. The SWAT commander gave a hand signal. They entered the men's restroom, eased the door closed without a sound.

"Any unidentified doors on three?" Reynolds spoke in a low tone.

"None. Even the janitorial door has a nameplate."

"We've got two on this floor, doors with no ID. One in the center of the hall, one, the last door on the north end."

Jake held up a pointer finger. He pulled out his cell, dialed Tolleson. Jake told him he needed the name and number of the landlord rep in Texas.

The contact arrived immediately in a text. Jake dialed it. Mike Hall answered after three rings, sounding wrung out from the day.

"Mike, this is Agent Jake Montoya of the FBI. We've got a problem in your Bio-South building. Tolleson is my analyst. I hope you can help me with some critical info."

"I'll certainly try." Hall stifled a yawn as he spoke.

"What office is Data Compilation Services? There's no sign."

"Hang on."

Jake's heart thumped with anxiety. *Cain's right here! Right... here!*

"Agent, I just pulled up a schematic on my laptop ... hold on ... okay, the office is on the second floor, Room 211. It's a fully outfitted BioLevel-2 lab space with an office attached. A little over 2,400 square feet."

"Is that in the middle of the building or on the end?"

"Last office on the end. Walking into the building, that would be the left side. The north end, it looks like."

"That's what I need. Thanks, Mike." Jake rang off and a sudden thought. Cruz. Looked at the text he'd sent her. No response. He frowned, worry seeping in. Typed another text: **Nia, we're in the building. His office is last one on north end of building. We're going in. Respond!**

"Office at the end, Sam."

Reynolds radioed his team. Keep two guys on the third floor. Sentries maintain the front door. Every other man meets at the north end of the second floor.

Stepping out of the restroom with Reynolds, something raked Jake's mind like a cat scratch. Nia Cruz. *Where's her response?* It should be immediate. Checked his phone again.

Nothing.

AN IMPOSING MAN, six-four, easily two-forty, wearing all black including a ballistic vest, a helmet, and safety goggles, stood at the door to Room 211. He held a forty-pound battering ram by two circular handles. It was round, like a cannon barrel. He leaned toward the door with his head twisted back, eyes locked on Reynold's face.

Reynold's nod was subtle. All it took.

The big boy took a long heave backward, exhaled as he crashed the heavy steel though the lock, splintering the door.

Eight men burst into the office, most carrying HP-5 submachine guns, and others, the cut-down M4 carbine.

Reynolds and Montoya stood at the door.

"Clear. Clear. Clear. Clear."

In five seconds they determined Dr. Ezra Cain was not in the lab. Jake holstered his Glock, entered. Scanned the small quarters. Spartan. No computers, no landline phone. He ransacked a desk. No papers, nothing.

"Where the hell is he?" It came out as a shout.

He exited the lab, men following him out, looked down the hall, thoughts firing. Looked to his left. A sign. FIRE EXIT.

"Six of you go to the other end, take the escape to the ground." Jake burst through the door nearest him. Seven men followed.

Only seconds to hustle down one floor to hit the pitted concrete. He looked both ways down the damp loading dock. The four incandescent fixtures provided enough barely light.

Nobody.

He scanned the chain-link fence, from one end of the building to the other. Spotted a gate in the middle. Open.

Montoya ran to the gate. A padlock on the ground.

He grabbed his phone, dialed Nia Cruz's number. He stood dead still, huffing, hoping.

Out of the corner of his eye, he spotted a match-size flicker of light. About eighty feet away, in the middle of the tracks. Nia Cruz's phone lit up. On silent.

She's gone.

97

"HE'S GOT HER, Sam." Agent Reynolds jogged over to Jake at the gate, all the while scanning 180 degrees, studying the dark railroad tracks, eyes finally locking on a 40-story building just to the east of him. The red-lit script at the top said *Coca-Cola*.

Jake hopped to the tracks, hustled to near where he'd seen the phone. He dialed Cruz's number again, spotted the light ten feet away. Reynolds was right with him. In a tone of anger and dejection, Jake admitted with an exhale, "Cain's got Agent Cruz."

"What? How the hell could this happen?" His tone quickly turned from angry to grim. He slid a phone out of his pocket. "Gotta alert DC."

"Call Fitch first, tell him I'm heading to Cain's house. We're going in."

"Got it."

"Get your team, set up a grid and run a search of the area. Call in every agent possible. Call in Atlanta PD. This is a scary dude, Sam. And Cruz is a big, tough, woman. This guy has to be a serious hoss to get her out of here."

Montoya, Weil, and Hopkins walked across the parking lot to Cain's BMW. Jake approached the driver's side door. Like a flash of lightning, his right foot shattered the glass with a side kick. There was enough parking-lot light for the agents to see each other. It was well known in the Bureau that Montoya sparred with MMA fighters, and he'd just proved it.

Jake popped the locks and trunk. They rifled through the glove box. Weil pulled the spare tire out of the trunk. Found nothing other than a vehicle registration and a stethoscope on the passenger seat.

TWENTY-TWO MINUTES. That's how long it took Jake to rip over the traffic-free, damp streets of midtown Atlanta to reach Fitch and his crew at Cain's home. It was late in the evening, only nineteen minutes until the next day.

The team was ten men and three women, the majority on the Hostage Rescue Team, the Bureau's elite commando squad.

The squad maintained their position in four dark SUVs parked at vantage points covering inlets to Cain's neighborhood. Fitch's spot was in the heart of a broad shadow of a large live oak whose roots were digging up the sidewalk. Jake killed the lights entering the neighborhood, eased his sedan right behind Fitch, hopped out, and approached the driver's window.

They had an unobstructed view of Cain's front door and driveway. Fitch had his .45 in his right hand, finger on the trigger, eyes in the side mirror, as Montoya approached. HRT guys are cautious.

The car window was down. Jake could see the night heat was causing Fitch to sweat in his heavy gear. "Agent Fitch, I'm Jake Montoya."

Fitch loosened his grip on the pistol, stuck his right hand out the window for a shake. "Garland Fitch. People call me Bunk."

Jake leaned on the car's sill with both hands. In dim ambient light, he was looking at a man with a graying crewcut wearing black plastic-framed glasses that were perfect if you were trying to emulate a respectable, block-headed nerd.

"Here's the deal, Bunk. We're neck-deep in shit. One of our agents is a hostage—or may be dead." Jake rapid-fired the story. The odd deal of Data Compilation Services, the corroborating DNA, Nia's phone found on the tracks.

Hearing the story and the anxiety in Jake's voice, Bunk nodded. "We've got the neighborhood buttoned up. Nobody's gone into Cain's house."

"Well, we're going, right damn now."

98

FOUR BLACK SUBURBANS, lights off, came to a hard stop in front of Cain's house. The team spilled out, throwing silent shadows carrying automatic weapons. Interior lights off in the trucks, doors closing silently.

Two agents hustled around each side of the house, meeting at the back door. The others went to the front stoop, one man unscrewing a lit bulb from a fixture by the front door. A small yard sign as well as a sticker on the door advertised: ***24 Hour Protection by Peachtree South.*** Fitch called the 800 number, identified himself as FBI and said they were going in. He provided an identifying law-enforcement code to grease the skids.

They listened a moment, scanned the street and adjacent homes. Mostly dark at this hour, a work night, a neighborhood asleep. Intermittent sounds of light traffic on Piedmont Avenue in the distance, several hundred yards away.

"On my count," said Fitch into his mic. "Three-two-one—" No battering rams, front and back doors kicked open by tactical boots. "Clear. Clear. Clear. Clear."

The home was lit with low light. Lamps on in the kitchen and master bedroom. Dim beam on over the stove in the kitchen.

HRT operated with extreme efficiency. Flashlight lit weapons swinging left-right, up-down, men moving briskly.

Nobody home.

MONTOYA AND FITCH trailed the men into the house after the all-clear was called.

"Tear it apart. We're looking for any address that could be a location for Cain. And, of course, anything that looks like evidence of murder," said Montoya.

Jake walked through the house. Again, he noted, surprisingly modest for a successful physician. Good location for work, though. There was no TV, but there were multiple shelves of books. Not surprising for a man of intellect. The floors were polished oak, likely from the origin of the home. Oriental rugs were frequent, even one in the kitchen.

The living room held a dark leather couch and two matching armchairs. High quality, Mission-style cherry end tables abutted the couch. Jake bent to one knee, looked up under the tables, had guessed right, Stickley furniture. The couch and chairs were arranged to focus on a gleaming black Bosendorfer grand piano. His eyes scanned the walls, studied the art. The pieces were Afro-centric, mostly colorful landscapes of savannas, river basins, and mountains, certainly originals. While the room gave the vibe of a decorator's touch, Jake's intuition said that the fastidious Cain had done it all himself.

One thing tickled the back of Jake's mind as he viewed the house. No photographs. Not a single one.

"Bunk, let's hit his study." Fitch, a five-eight dump truck of a man, led Montoya into a small bedroom converted to an office. Serene, light gray paint covered the walls, glossy white on the trim. Two large gallery-framed black-and-white photographs on the wall. Jake stepped closer to study one. It was nothing more than a squiggly line with a hook like a shepherd's crook. Abstract art?

In the lower right corner, written in pencil on the white

matte, was *Electron microscopy, Ebola Zaire, 1979.*

The room held no computer or phone. One large bookshelf covered an entire wall. It was filled with hardcover medical and science textbooks, as well as journals arranged by year in magazine-file boxes. Jake wasn't surprised to spot seven textbooks on chemistry, Cain's undergraduate major at Stanford.

A group of paperback novels was stacked on top of each other, spine facing out. *Congo, Sphere, Next, The Andromeda Strain, Jurassic Park.* Jake knew the books—he'd read them all, loved them. All written by Michael Crichton, a Harvard-trained physician and a hardcore science nerd ... but not a serial killer.

They found nothing of note in the room and not a single tome on poisons.

Leaving the study, Jake stopped, took a second look back at the squiggly shape in the black-and-white photo. *Was it a picture of a virus?* he thought. *Was it Ebola?*

He turned to leave and bumped into an HRT agent. "Sir, follow me, please."

Four steps led them to a large bedroom with a walk-in closet. The wall of a third bedroom had been taken down to create a spacious closet and master bath. Contents from the dresser drawers were scattered on the floor. All the clothes and shoes from the walk-in were strewn on the king-size bed. Feds were on a search.

The agent indicated with a finger waggle for Jake to follow him into the closet. The space was empty. Jake felt a light drift of wind. He looked up into the blades of a ceiling fan spinning on low. A fan in the closet? *Strange,* he thought.

"Whatcha got?"

The HRT man tapped on the rear wall. The hollow sound of a larger space reverberated. "Something's back here."

Jake stiffened but kept an impassive face. He stepped to the wall, tapped it with a fist in six different spots. It produced an eerie sound, like a tomb. He felt around for anything that could spring a door. Nothing.

"Let's bust in." Jake squatted as he said it, hands running along the baseboard. He was about to stand when his phone vibrated. Tolleson, in DC.

He stood, answered. "Whatcha got, Ross?"

"We woke the guy up in Savannah, the Wyoming lawyer, Hatcher."

"Hold on a minute, we're searching Cain's house. About to rip into a wall. I've got to step outside."

Jake turned, bumped into two black-clad guys holding excavation tools, a baby sledge, a crowbar, and a curved nail-puller. As he was leaving the closet, he caught the face of one of the agents. Dark eyes, long lashes, clear skin. A woman. She held the gaze long enough for Jake to detect a sparkle.

Jake hear the noisy slam of the first sledgehammer blow as he stepped out the front door. Cool air, compliments of the rain, hit his face. It felt good but was still heavy with humidity.

He put the phone back to his ear. "Okay, Ross, shoot."

Ross chuckled. "So old Sam Hatcher, reportedly wearing a robe at the front door, was pissed we woke him. Something about an early tee time or whatever. Anyway, we asked him about Data Compilation Services. He said, number one, that's confidential. Number two, he has no recollection of Data Compilation. He said he was a registered agent for 9,000 companies, and he didn't have time for late-night FBI harassment. 'Get a subpoena.' He tried to push the door shut on our guys."

"Awww, hell." Jake snorted a chuckle.

"Oh, yeah, and listen to this. So this chick walks in the room, a young woman, I guess. Early thirties, hot looking babe, they said. One of the agents said something like, 'Good evening, Mrs. Hatcher, we just need to borrow your husband.' Now picture this, Hatcher's edging up on seventy-two, right?" Tolleson started laughing. Jake was affected. He started laughing.

"And, Jake, she says to Hatcher, 'You fucker, you said you weren't married.' She grabbed a vase and threw it at him. And then one of the agents said, 'Mr. Hatcher, we just talked to your wife in Wyoming. She gave us this address.'"

"Then what?"

"The woman dog-cussed the hair off his head. She grabbed her phone, took a picture of Hatcher in a robe, took some shots of the bedroom, ripped off her nighty, and took selfies. *Nude.*"

"Holy—"

"Then she started screaming, 'Hatcher, you're about to pay this bitch!'"

"Our boys cut it short, told him to put his pants on, they were taking him in, this was a serial murder case. Then he got religion, he accepted Jesus into his heart on the spot."

Jake snorted, again. Tolleson continued, "He opened up his computer, looked up Data Compilation Services, and gave the agents the name Wayne Jackson. Also a mailing address at a UPS mail shop at a Buford Highway address in Atlanta."

"Good work, Ross." *Wayne Jackson has to be Cain.*

99

ONE LAYER OF sheetrock. The agents quickly realized they didn't need a sledgehammer. One guy shone his Maglite through a six-inch hole. "Got a glass case back here, guys. It's holding some jars. Let's be gentle, no hammers."

The woman went to her kneepads, used the curved nail-puller to rip the sheetrock, increasing the access into the hidden chamber. The first man used a crowbar to do the same. In three minutes, they'd removed the gypsum back to the studs, leaving white dust sprinkled on the floor.

Two agents were on their knees, another, bent, looked over their shoulders. They were eyeing a cabinet situated a couple feet into an open space. It had sliding glass doors, the kind with indentions in the glass for opening and closing. The cabinet was four feet tall, with three shelves. The bottom of the cabinet served as a fourth shelf.

Denny counted to himself. "Twenty-seven jars." Each jar held fluid and tissue. They were labeled with a month and year written with numbers and slashes. They also had a physical location. All printed using a thick, black Sharpie.

"Holy crap. 'Silence of the Lambs' shit," said the woman. A lone bottle sat on the top shelf. She focused her flashlight on it, read out loud, "Ain't no Sunshine when she's gone. Point Clear, Alabama. 05/1995." She picked it up, turned it over.

The back of the bottle said: **Sunshine Gage.**

The agents were focused on the jars, oblivious to a wire that snaked down a stud, crossed the floor under a strip of duct tape, and connected to an electrical switch on the side of the cabinet.

Bunk Fitch entered the closet, edged into the cleared opening, pushing two others out of the way. Switched on his flashlight, rolled the beam over the glass-front cabinet. "What the— holy mother of God. We've got this demented sumbitch. Got him!"

Fitch said, "Look out, let me grab a bottle by the top, show it to Montoya. He's gonna crap his pants he sees this."

Three agents stood back, standing crowded between closet shelves, bunched into each other's personal space. They watched Fitch reach in and slide one of the glass doors to the side.

Immediately, a loud hiss sizzled through the closet space when the glass shifted, like an old hobby rocket launching off the ground. Four seconds of high-pressured air. Then nothing, The agents, blindsided, jumped. Heartbeats pounded. Muscles tensed.

"Hell was that?" said Fitch. Their eyes shot upward. The fan.

The closet, ten feet by twelve feet, was filled in a micronized mist, appearing like a fog from the fan motor. The swirling blades sent the gas into their eyes, and each breath drew the odorless pathogen into their respiratory tracts, lodging deeply in their lungs. An invisible, tasteless layer settled over their lips.

They stood there, gobsmacked, like stupid ten-year-olds staring point-blank into the business end of a mosquito fog truck.

Dr. Cain had created this monster in his Bio-South lab.

He'd followed simple guidelines listed for all to see in the Merck Index, a bible of chemical preparations. The ingredients were ordered online from a chemical supply house, paid for with a prepaid credit card. His talents in organic chemistry had allowed him to pull this off.

Four FBI agents had just been doused with heavy inhalational and ophthalmic doses of a toxic nerve agent eighty-one times more lethal than cyanide.

Sarin gas.

LISTENING TO TOLLESON, the name Wayne Jackson struck a memory in Jake's mind. He zoned out for a moment. He hooked it as Ross said, "Anything else?"

"No, no, don't think so." The words came out in a distant, distracted tone.

Bits and pieces coalesced in Jake's mind. Wayne Jackson was a boy who had died when he was in elementary school. Leukemia. He was in Sunshine's grade, which meant he was in Ezra Cain's grade. Jake had a remote memory of jumping on Wayne's trampoline ... Sunshine was there, too. A cute, skinny tomboy getting just as grimy as the boys. Montoya was lost in the sweet thought when somebody hollered.

"Get in here, Montoya! We've been poisoned."

100

JAKE SPRINTED INTO the house. *Poisoned?* He stopped at the threshold, hand on the jamb. "OUT! EVERYBODY OUT!"

An agent reported a loud hissing noise, "And it may be a gas, from inside the closet."

Jake hit 911 on his phone. Sounds of coughing and retching reached him as he began to tell the operator he was an FBI agent and needed multiple ambulances and a HAZMAT team at Cain's address.

All but four agents rushed out of the house. Back door, front door, didn't matter.

Jake froze. He watched four agents stumble into the living room, then crash onto the hardwood, obviously in distress.

They needed help, but Jake didn't know what. *Poison gas.* What could he do? *What?*

WITHIN TWENTY SECONDS, the agents began experiencing tight chests and watering eyes.

At fifty seconds, their pupils had shrunken to pinpoints, and they were blinded. Clear drainage dripped from their nostrils. Dry coughing escalated quickly into deep, harsh hacks.

"My head's killing me," said the woman, voice high with surprise. She ripped off her helmet, wrapped her arms around her head, bent forward.

The others followed suit. It felt like their skulls were being crushed.

At one minute, fifty seconds, Bunk's gravelly, deep cough was interrupted by a sudden splash of projectile vomiting. He wanted to say something, but couldn't, unable to catch his breath.

Through a wheeze, another agent huffed, "Outside." He pointed with a weak arm.

Something was wrong with their muscles. Twitches turned to jerks. Then came painful spasms, like fibers being hand-cranked on a reel. Stumbling over each other, they made it to the living room, just ten feet from the front door.

And dropped dead.

Pausing at the door, looking with horror at the still bodies, gripped with helplessness, Jake heard the first wail of ambulances in the distance.

No longer a soft summer night in Atlanta.

101

SEVEN MINUTES AFTER 2:00 a.m. Agents Hopkins, Weil, and Montoya were standing by a car on the street at Cain's house.

"Headed to the hotel. I've got to digest this mess." Low on sleep, Jake's voice trailed off. His shoulders sagged.

HAZMAT had sealed the house and placed the dead agents in body bags. The other agents had been taken by ambulance to Grady Memorial, a Level 1 trauma center in downtown Atlanta.

Harsh coughs could be heard as the ambulance doors closed.

Jake's mind was filled with concern for Nia Cruz. No sign of her near the Bio-South building.

Cain is going to kill her. But where?

He eased into the driver's seat, started to twist the key, thinking hard. He removed his fingers from the ignition, pulled up Pike Tatum's number on his phone, tapped call.

It was picked up after two rings. "It's late, this can't be good." Tatum had sandpaper in his voice.

"Well, you're right about that." Jake passed on the quick version of recent events. Positive DNA to Sunshine Gage. Dead FBI agents.

Tatum sounded wide awake as he said, "Poison gas? What the hell! How can we help?"

"Not sure yet. There's a nationwide BOLO for Cain and Cruz. But we have no idea how he's traveling or where he's heading. We've got his car, and he only has one registered in his name. Let's do this—Get some extra patrols on the road. If he's driving that way, it'll be five-and-a-half to six hours before he arrives. Focus hard on vans, he used that Ford for the Sloane girl. Watch for Georgia plates. And remember, this guy is extremely dangerous."

"I'll say. We've got his photo. I'll get on it."

Jake rang off, looked at his watch. Screw the hour. There was some good news here. Jake then made three successive short phone calls. Dr. John David Gage. Kimbo Gage. And Jim Sloane, Lea Lea's father. The message was the same: DNA match. All-points bulletin out nationwide. "We've got the son of a bitch."

After the last call, Jake rang off, stared down the tidy residential street. Streetlights glowing. Empty sidewalks. No flashing red-and-blue lights. Quiet again. He had passed on good news to three people who needed it. But he knew he'd lied. They *didn't* have the son of a bitch.

Montoya was certain he'd never hunted a wilier suspect. Cain was dangerous in a whole different stratosphere. He wasn't some dumbass, clown criminal. Jake figured the man had contingency plan after contingency plan. Then he thought the worst.

We may never grab this guy.

One more call. Eli Washington. Before now, Jake had been careful to never mention the FBI trail that had led to Eli. It rang four times and switched to voicemail. "Eli, it's Jake Montoya. It's very important. Call me." He hung up and sent the same message in a text.

Jake didn't start the car, not yet. Still thinking. He needed a direction. The weight of the long night was crushing him. Deciding if he needed to eat or sleep. He didn't like to react, he liked to force the action.

There was only one place he could think of: Black Point. Where it had all started with Sunshine. And only weeks ago, Lea Lea Sloane.

The realization hit hard. He twisted the key with a plan. Destination, Hartfield-Jackson International. First flight out to Pensacola. Grab a rental car, drive fifty miles to Black Point.

Then his phone rang.

Jake saw the caller, answered first ring. "Thanks for calling, Eli." He killed the engine. "This can't be good, Jake, at this hour."

"No, it's not good. Really not good. You in Black Point?"

"Naw. In Dallas. Touring some restaurants for about a week. Why?"

"Need you to sit down. I've got some news. But first I need a hard, straight answer to a question."

"Okay."

"When's the last time you saw Ezra Cain?"

No quick answer. Only silence. Jake wondered. *Was he about to lie?* He waited as long as his nerves allowed. "You there?"

"Yeah. Trying to remember. Exactly remember." Eli snorted. Not quite a laugh, but close. "Jake, I still call him Bob, like when we were kids. You know what kids called him. The little pricks. I was one of them, too. Nobody called him Babu Bankhole. But today it's unnatural for me to call him Ezra."

"What's the answer to my question, Eli?" Tone filled with impatience.

"Actually, within the last six weeks. It was in Orange Beach when we opened that new Sweet E's restaurant. Bob has 10 percent of ownership, so he came down. He stayed a few days,

I think, enjoying the beach."

Jake's thoughts jumped to Lea Lea Sloane. "Eli, I need you to look at your notes. When *exactly* was he there?"

"Yeah, I'll do that. But look, man, you're starting to scare me. You need to tell me what the hell's going on. Cut this jig crap out."

"Alright. We've got irrefutable evidence that Babu killed Sunshine Gage after her birthday party. You were at the party."

"Bullshit!"

"Was he there, Eli? Was Bob there?"

"Long time ago ... not sure, he might have been. But I don't know why he would've been. He was going to the math and science school in Mobile."

"I'm sorry, but here's the deal. We have DNA evidence from under Sunshine's fingernails. After all these years we've been able to match it with new technology. One-hundred-percent match to Bob."

"*Sunshine?* That's ridiculous, Jake." Eli's voice went weak.

"Another question, Eli. Did Bob ever travel to any of your NFL games? There were women murdered in a number of cities around the time you had a game."

Another long silence. Jake gave him time. When Eli spoke, Jake heard his whisper through silent tears. "Yes ... he loved to get out of town. He never played but he loved the game. I provided tickets, hotel, travel, food. I paid for it all. Felt sorry for him. He was always such an outcast. Just a super smart, friendless nerd."

Jake hit on it immediately. That's why they couldn't pick up the trail in those NFL cities. Eli had covered the costs.

"Jake, he's a doctor. How can this be? Are you sure? I mean absolutely?"

"I'm sorry, Eli. There is zero doubt about Sunshine. Now listen, I need you to focus on this. Bob has kidnapped a female

FBI agent in Atlanta within the last hour. It's almost a guarantee he's going to put her through a horrible death, if he hasn't killed her already. He's not at his home or the CDC. I'm focused on Black Point. Or close. Where would he go?"

"Hell, why would he go to Black Point? I wouldn't go to Black Point."

"Where, dammit? Focus, Eli."

"Only one thought, but he's way too smart to go there. When Amos and Clara died, our grandparents, they left their land to me, Zeke, and Bob. They gave the girl cousins money. About a year ago, Bob wanted to know if Zeke and I would sell our shares to him. Said he wanted a connection to where he was born."

"Did you? Sell it?"

"Not yet. Some kind of deal is in the works, though. You know that Zeke and I, just like you, made out like bandits with NFL money and some decent investments."

"Right."

"Bob's a doctor and makes a handsome income. But he's nowhere near our financial level. Zeke and I talked, and we decided to give him our shares. Bob balked over that, but we told him if he wanted the property, that was the only way he was getting it."

"Did he go for it?"

"Yes. But he said he'd make it up to us, somehow. But, you know, we'd never take anything from him."

"Is he using the house?"

"No. Not that I'm aware of. Yard needs cutting, place is getting grungy. Last he told me, he was going to take two weeks off around Christmas, and he wanted to come down and interview some contractors about remodeling the place."

"Huh."

"I drove by the homestead a couple weeks ago for old time's

sake. Nothing going on but childhood memories going to tatters."

"Okay, thanks for the update. This whole thing is bad. You need to get in touch with Zeke, let him know what's happening. If he knows something, have him call me. By mid-morning, Eli, every major media outlet will be spraying this shitstorm across the globe. You'll be getting calls and media showing up at your house. You'll be stalked. Your reply is 'No comment.'"

"Got it."

"Gotta run, Eli. And, sorry, this is some hard news. Let's keep each other posted."

"Will do."

Weakest voice Jake had heard in recent memory.

102

CICADAS SANG THROUGH Jake's open window as he pulled up Expedia flights on his phone. Atlanta to Pensacola. Then replaced Pensacola with Mobile, Alabama. He exhaled deeply, surprised. Nothing that would get him to Black Point before 11:30 this morning.

Time on his phone said 2:25 a.m. EST. He reached up, pinched his lips with fingers on his right hand, thinking hard. Dead tired. Needed a couple tabs of speed to keep the circuits firing. He had some amphetamines at the hotel. Cop coffee for overnights.

Leave the hotel by three, be in Black Point at nine. He'd drive it.

He turned the key, fired up the engine, gunned it down the street, eyes on high alert for those street-sleeping night cats. Braked hard at the stop sign. He dialed Chief Tatum, got him on the second ring.

He pulled out of the stop onto a dry, empty surface street, and filled in Tatum with the homestead story. "Stake out the place, Pike. Carefully. Stay well hidden. Get your guys in some personal vehicles, or maybe some pickup trucks."

"We'll do it. Think he's got Nia?"

"Man, I hope so, hoping she's alive. I'm driving down. I'll be there three hours before I could with a commercial flight. Let's keep in touch." Rang off.

AT THE HOTEL, Jake popped ibuprofen and an amphetamine into his mouth, leaned down and took a sip of water from the sink. He striped his toothbrush with a layer of paste, brushed briskly, finished by splashing cold water on his face, toweled off, took a leak, and washed his hands.

Leaving the room with his duffel, he grabbed two Coca-Colas from the minifridge, two packs of cheese crackers, and two Snickers bars.

Twenty minutes later, he was cutting south off I-20 onto I-75/85 South, lightest traffic of the day. The buzz from the speed and caffeine started to flush through his blood. He turned on the radio, heard a searing guitar riff starting a song his mother used to play years ago. He sang out loud with Clapton's universal question.

"What'll you do when you get lonely?"

A fleeting memory zipped through mind. *How can a song do that? Transport you immediately to another place and time.* He'd caught his mother dancing to "Layla" in the living room, alone, lights low. He watched her, knew she was happy. She spotted him, pulled him to her, said, "Let's dance, son." The thought warmed him. He was fourteen years old.

The memory filtered into the mist.

It was a long, dark night on the highway. Alone.

The number one best place to think.

103

AN HOUR OUT of Atlanta, Jake had the Chevy running eighty, night bugs squishing on the windshield, windows down. A flash of light beside him. Call coming in. Pike Tatum.

"Yeah, Pike."

"Just an update. Everything is dead at the house. We skulked around, everything dark, didn't see a hint of anybody. But we're hiding in the weeds on Colony Street. We'll spot him if he shows up."

"Good work. Thanks."

Three miles later Jake spotted a billboard for a Love's Travel Stop. He exited the interstate five minutes later, feeling the effects of too much caffeine. The truck stop was right at the exit, lit up like a meteor shower.

Standing at a urinal, Jake's third best place to think, it hit him. They weren't just staking out a ranch house. That place had heavy acreage.

Back in his car he pulled up Bay County, Alabama, real estate records, found the plat for the house. Not quite 200 acres. Checked the time. 4:10 a.m. He closed his eyes, made a quick calculation. It was around 9:00 p.m. in Alice Springs, Australia.

He needed a technical job done fast. Extremely fast. And, mostly, on the down-low.

The Ghost could handle it.

He scrolled contacts to get to Mercedes Repair, a number disguised in his phone. The Ghost was paranoid about people obtaining her contact number. He fired up the car, raised the windows, jumped on I-85 South, pushed it ten miles-per-hour over the speed limit. Tapped call.

Three rings. Jake held his breath. "Well. Isn't this a surprise on a cold Australian night?" The feminine voice was deep, confident, and arousing. The kind you'd like to hear on a late-evening radio talk show explaining what women really want in bed.

It was Bella Antoine. Jake had met her eighteen years ago at Sarah Bradley's estate in Georgetown. She was visiting with Sarah's husband, Buck Bradley, the former admiral who was running the CIA.

The memory was vivid. He had stuck his hand out as he admired her athletic figure. "I'm Jake Montoya."

She took it with a firm grip, held it a beat too long, with a glint in her eye. "I'm the Ghost in the wires."

She was three years in service with the CIA after leaving Naval Intelligence. Today, she was with the NSA in Alice Springs, Australia. The facility was Pine Gap, code-named Rainfall. The Ghost and her colleagues monitored conversations around the world from satellites located 20,000 miles above the earth.

"Good evening, Bella." Jake felt a twitch of nerves in his belly. The Ghost did that to him, in bed ... and elsewhere.

"Wondered if you'd died after our trip to Lake Como. I thought it was quite nice."

"It was nice, extremely nice. Let's do it again ... soon."

"Just say the word. Now, Jakey, what's the ask?"

He grimaced at her bluntness. "I need satellite imagery of a piece of property. It's somewhere just under 200 acres. But here's the deal, I need it fast ... in hours." He ducked his head when he said it, hopeful.

A deep, soft giggle came through the phone. Erotic, like a playful laugh during sex.

"Might I suggest you take your federal budgetary allotment and buy a drone at Best Buy and fly the property?"

"It's delicate. I can't be seen in the area."

"Hmmm ... Okay. Twenty-five."

"Twenty-five what?"

"Twenty-five thousand dollars. Same account in Tripoli. And, oh. A week in the Maldives. You, me, and a thatch-roofed bungalow."

Jake wondered what she was wearing right this moment.

"That could work."

104

BLACK POINT, ALABAMA

GRAY-BLUE TWILIGHT, blackness fading, the sun thirty-five minutes from breaking the eastern horizon. Coolest air of the summer day.

Dr. Ezra Cain's plan for ingress to the back of the property was generated from childhood knowledge. Arriving from Atlanta, he approached the middle of the county on a road twelve miles east of Black Point, avoiding the town. He drove south of the farm, turned west, drove twelve miles, and cut north. Driving with lights out, Cain snaked the husky Mercedes through tired, empty farm passageways to reach the deep rear of the farm.

Easing off a rutted, red-clay dirt track, he shifted the truck into park, stepped out, and unlocked the thick chain blocking the weed-filled pathway. He pulled the camper van through, relocked the chain.

Branches from young swamp tupelos and sugarberry bushes edged in to hide the old logging trail. Limbs eerily screeched against the van as it made the hundred-yard-long journey to the two Airstream trailers.

Cain killed the engine. The windows were down. A peaceful melody of cooling engine clicks and morning birdsong was all to be heard. The musky smell of damp earth. The scent of decaying leaves and humus saturated the air like an organic mountain candle.

Cain had been up twenty-four hours and was feeling recklessly tired and hungry. He stepped into the back of the van. Nia Cruz's eyes were open ... hard and angry. An odor of urine sifted through the air.

Cain winked at her. "Almost done, baby. Get some rest. I want you wide awake for the festivities."

With a ginger ale from the refrigerator and a box of Pop-Tarts, he made his way to the smaller Airstream for a rest. He found a news talk station on a battery-operated radio, turned it on low, then downed two pastries and half the drink. Curious about any news out of Atlanta.

Cain stretched out on a blow-up air mattress, closed his eyes. A grim smile crossed his lips as he thought about the closet at his home in Atlanta.

Surprise!

105

THE ODOR OF grease, bacon, and coffee sifted through the small restaurant. Chris Stapleton growled out a tune through the speakers. Chief Tatum and Jake Montoya sat in a booth at the Waffle House on US 98 in Black Point. "You know, Pike, one of God's great blessings, Waffle House," said Jake, as he held a forkful of hash browns to his mouth.

"Ain't that right," said Tatum, never looking up as he bathed a waffle with syrup. He sliced a piece, stabbed it into his mouth, talked while he chewed, pointing his fork at Jake. "Might be wrong about Cain, coming back to Black Point. Should have been here by now."

Jake returned a silent, pensive nod. Crunched a small bite of crispy bacon. "You're probably right. He knows we know who he is. And he's a doctor, a thinker, not a dumbass criminal." He let out a fatigued sigh. Ashy, half-moon circles were starting to show under his eyes. "He'd be a fool to come back to Black Point."

Jake ate fast, pushed his plate to the side, took a long pull of sweet tea, ran a napkin across his lips.

"Don't know where else to look. Gotta hope somebody somewhere sees the guy, calls the cops. His picture's flashing everywhere." Jake looked outside through the plate glass. Feeling exhausted. Parking lot a third full, thick clouds racing on the wind. "Hell of a mess, man. Four agents dead. Three guys on respirators in the ICU." He shook his head, stood. "I'm headed back out there, Cain's place, look for a little hidey-hole."

"We've got four patrolmen in civilian vehicles watching the house. Plus, Billy Starr's lurking around town in his Silverado, thinking he's General Patton."

Jake laughed, followed it with a yawn. "Talk soon."

He fought doing what he desperately wanted to do. Call the Ghost, ask what's up. But she had a short fuse when pushed.

DR. EZRA CAIN SPARKED to life after five hours of restless sleep. Never felt he truly went down. Couldn't help it. He felt his body vibrating, nerves swizzling like radio static. His next victim was mere feet away in the van. A full-on, FBI power bitch.

A razor-sharp smile creased his lips.

Time to feed.

He slid the Lexan container out of his bag, carried it from the Bambi into the Land Yacht Airstream, and placed it on a stainless-steel medical stand. From a cabinet, he removed a vial of midazolam and ketamine, drew up a heavy dose of each. He guessed Nia's weight at 190 to 210. Solid.

He stalked like a lumbering monster toward the van, wondering for the thousandth time how he'd never been caught all these years.

Piss and body odor smacked him in the face as he slung open the van door. "Whew. Good gracious, missy. You need a good shower, but there's no time."

Cain stepped up into the van. Went straight for Nia, carrying the syringes. Her eyes flashed to his hand. Nia began to shake, fighting her restraints. Her groans ricocheted around the truck.

She had no chance of breaking free. Cain uncapped a needle. Bang. Needle in the left thigh. Uncapped the other. Bang. Needle in the right thigh. He leaned down to her face, cocked his head.

"Just a little sleepy juice, nothing to it."

CAIN EMERGED FROM the smaller Airstream unrecognizable, a hooded monster in safety yellow. The biohazard space suit had him looking like he was six-eight and 300 pounds.

It was late afternoon, sun shadows slicing through the woods. Pines straw-dry from the heat of the day.

Cain walked across the twelve-foot bridge, opened the door to the Land Yacht, and peered in. Through the plexiglass covering his face, his eyes locked onto Nia Cruz. She was strapped onto a stainless-steel exam table with the back raised forty-five degrees.

Stepping inside, he closed the door, activated the bio-seal. He turned on the ventilation fan in his suit. It was over ninety degrees in the trailer. The air was refreshing.

Cruz saw his cold eyes. Pure evil in a yellow space suit. Her gut knotted. Fear pounded her in waves. She felt every hammering heartbeat in her ears. Muscles tightened. Breaths came fast and shallow.

Adrenaline activated the fight reflex. She kicked and fought, rocking the table on the floor. Cruz's head rocked left to right. It looked like seizure activity. It wasn't.

It was untempered desperation.

And the leather straps held like anchor chains.

"You motherfucker!" Cruz screamed the words. Then more and more words. Cain saw her lips move but couldn't make out what she was saying over the fan.

His eyelids lifted in a smile. He got the gist.

Earlier, Cain had used heavy emergency-room shears to cut

off Cruz's clothes after placing her sedated body on the table. He studied her physique as he strapped her down. An African goddess of a woman. Powerful. Large breasts. *So much fun to carve on.*

Breaking the mold from his usual blond fare.

He gathered supplies from a surgical cabinet. Bleach, hydrochloric acid, two scalpels, and two specimen containers containing Formalin. He placed them on a stainless-steel table.

He stooped to a dorm-size refrigerator, removed a small Lexan container, opened it, and removed a vacutainer blood collection tube. It looked like a test tube with a rubber stopper on the end. Inside was a dark, viscous liquid.

Blood from a rhesus macaques lab monkey.

It was infused with Red X-81. Hundreds of thousands of copies of lethal virus.

It took five, maybe six, copies to kill a human.

Cain thought about it for a moment. He picked up a syringe with an 18-gauge needle. *Do I want to risk it?* One of the deadliest agents on the planet was in his hands. His thoughts drifted to Lea Lea Sloane just weeks ago in this Airstream. Hemorrhagic virus. Bleeding out. Blood everywhere.

EVERYWHERE!

Only a fool would be in the same county as Red X-81.

Hell yeah, I want to do it. Wanna watch that movie again.

Triple-gloved, he gingerly slid the needle through the rubber stopper into the tube, sucked up some liquid evil. Very slowly, he removed the needle, watching for any blood leakage. The syringe held two milliliters of agonizing death.

He placed the syringe on the silver table.

Leaning into Cruz's face, he locked a maniacal gaze on her.

She was wild-eyed and shivering, electrified with fear.

Heat waves washed through Cain. Unrestrained ecstasy. He hollered at her through the hood.

"Let's have some fun, shall we?"

MONTOYA WAS STARTLED awake. His cell phone was ringing. It was 3:35 in the afternoon. He'd left his position near Cain's house a little over an hour ago. Now at his mother's house, he was stretched out on the same bed where he'd slept as a boy.

The cottage was dead silent, nobody home. Fatigue had washed him into a deep sleep as soon as his face hit the pillow.

His phone was near his hand, on the bed. He grabbed it, rolled to his back. Answered through a yawn. "Montoya."

"It's me. Sorry for the delay. I've been really, really busy. Don't quote me, but there's some crap stirring with a couple of terrorist cells tucked away in the Dearborn, Michigan, area. Large Muslim population, that's all I can say."

Me was the Ghost. Calling from her NSA spy hub in backwoods Australia.

"Bella, thanks for calling. Anything?"

"Yes. Well, maybe. I put together a dynamic satellite review of the property stretching back a year. The house itself has had no activity. No vehicles, no human traffic."

Jake exhaled. "Ahhh, man, I'll call that a strikeout."

"Hold on, buddy. Oh, one question. Besides black, what other bikini colors would you like to see me in?"

"Bella, not now. We're racing the clock. I've got an abducted FBI agent." His voice trailed to a whisper. "Probably dead already."

"Okay. There's something interesting for you to check out on the property. It's at the far rear, southwest portion, deep into a heavy overgrowth of vegetation. Trees, bushes, that kind of thing. Can't imagine it's visible from the road or the house."

"What is it?"

"It's a trailer, an RV. Our camera picked up the Airstream

logo on the rear with a red number above it. I checked. It's a registration with something called the Caravan Club. But, anyway, archived imagery indicates it was hauled in six months ago. A month later, another Airstream was pulled in and parked next to it. Slightly smaller. A metal walkway connects them. I measure it as twelve feet. I've sent ten images to your email, the one at the grill company."

Jake swung his legs to the floor, sat on the side of the bed, ramrod straight, wide awake. The news had lit a fire.

"Trailers? What else? Tell me fast. I've got to move."

"Several weeks back, there was a white van on the property. Our satellite hit it arriving. It was sometime around one in the morning."

It's him!

"What about today? Anything?"

"Last sweep was three days ago. No activity. The NSA doesn't feel a high threat-factor from the woods of south Alabama."

"This is awesome, Bella, I gotta run." Jake stood, naked except for his underwear. "Great job, girl, that's our guy. I'll be in touch." About to hang up when it hit him.

"Blue, Bella. Electric blue. The bikini color."

Jake rang off, tapped another contact. Chief Tatum answered after two rings. "Got anything, Jake?"

Montoya filled him in quickly, never mentioning the information came from an NSA spook. "Pull in everybody that you can. Get armored up. Let's all meet over at the city works site on Colony Street."

"I can have six, seven guys there in twenty minutes. Plus me and Starr."

"Do it. I'll be waiting. Oh, I need a vest and a pump shotgun ... or an M-4 if you have it."

"We've got it. See you in twenty."

Jake dialed Agent Mark Benton as he shuffled into the kitchen.

"Mark, it's Jake Montoya. Got something." The phone call was over in sixty seconds. Benton would be rolling toward Black Point with five SWAT-trained agents.

He pulled a Diet Coke from the fridge, grabbed cookies from the counter, and went into his bathroom. He tapped out a ten-milligram tablet of amphetamine from a translucent orange bottle. At the table, he opened his laptop. He pulled up his grill company email. He never used FBI email in business dealings with the Ghost.

There they were. Twelve spectacular images. One with a white van. It had the same muddy license plate that had been revealed with the beach cam. He studied the images while he ate his snack and popped the tablet of speed, focusing on the best ingress to the area. Using a search engine, he dug up a city map. Next, he opened a county map for a little more detail.

Closing the laptop, he remembered something. He owed the Ghost $25,000. And she wouldn't forget.

Jake knew that 25K was only a rounding error in his financial profile.

106

TWENTY MINUTES UNTIL 5:00 p.m. The summer heat was thick and damp. Montoya slipped through the woods like an Indian scout, quiet, slow, and fast. He wore black chinos, a ballistic vest, and hiking shoes. A pistol-grip 12-gauge pump shotgun was in his right hand. Forty-five caliber auto in a cross-draw holster on left hip. He wore a tactical radio earpiece for comms.

Time factor critical.

Jake spotted the bright silver, aluminum trailer sixty yards out. He zigzagged tree to tree until he was twenty-five yards away. Standing in briars, he peeked around a white oak, studied the scene. He felt his heart hammering against the Kevlar. His damp T-shirt clung to his chest under the Kevlar. Sweat trickled down his forehead. He swiped it clean with his forearm.

The woods were silent. No birdcall. No dancing squirrels. Tension thick in the air, smothering Jake like night fog.

"Pike. I'm twenty-five yards from the trailers." Speaking in a whisper.

"Copy."

"No vehicle at the site. Approach quickly. Radio when close."

"Roger."

Eight men rushed from the macadam road to the east and

a two-track farm road to the south. Jake heard movement in the foliage. Then he saw them. Black fatigues, black helmets, M-4 rifles. They dropped to a knee.

"In position, Jake."

"Everybody listen closely. We're going in. Move very slowly. Assume there are booby traps. Watch the ground for trip wires. Scan the trees for infrared devices. This guy's smart and deadly."

Jake followed his own order. Moved slowly. His right pointer on the trigger of the shotgun, left hand on the sliding forestock, eyes sweeping the site.

He approached the gangway between the trailers. His eyes landed on a jumbled pile of safety-yellow plastic material. Tatum and Starr approached from the other side, two other men flanking them. More cops encircled the trailers.

"The hell's that?" said Starr.

Jake eyed the plastic, stepped forward. With the barrel end of the shotgun, he pushed the plastic around. "Looks like a HAZMAT suit. Has plexiglass for a faceplate." He looked up at the chief. "Pike, call in a HAZMAT team. I think we've got a hot site."

"Hot with what?" Starr again, eyes filled with concern.

"Don't know. But bet your ass it's deadly."

Jake tried to focus. Fatigue was threatening to overcome him, the hour-long nap helpful but just not enough, waiting for the speed to kick.

Is Nia in one of these Airstreams?

He knew she was.

Had to get in. Wondered if he'd get killed trying. Rigged doors? Gas, like Atlanta? Explosives?

His eyes cut over to the decontamination showerhead just outside the larger RV. *The big trailer has to be the hot zone.*

He stepped onto the bridge between the Airstreams, looked

out toward the chief. "Pike, y'all back off. I'm going to open a door." He stepped over to the smaller trailer, placed his hand on the door handle, took a breath. His nerves buzzed. Muscle fibers tightened. He was ready to take a quick leap backward.

He popped the door handle, waited ten heartbeats, opened the door no more than an inch. He leaned forward, peering through the narrow opening, spotted three boxes stacked on each other. A thick foam mat on the floor. A red mechanics cart pushed against the wall.

Jackpot. A large brown corrugated box sat on top of the cart. A Dupont product. BSL-4 safety related. A lab-grade biohazard suit. Jake scanned the door for wires and infrared monitoring devices. Nothing. He eased the door open with the barrel of the shotgun, counted to ten, stepped in, and went straight to the box.

"Pike. Get in here."

It took seven minutes for Jake to suit up. Pike helped. Neither knew what they were doing.

When the hood went on, Jake fought a sudden rush of claustrophobia. Small breaths helped him compensate. He walked across the bridge to the Land Yacht. Pointed for Pike and his officers to get back. Cracked the door an inch. Scanned the opening. Clear. He opened the door enough to step into the trailer.

One step and he was standing in a slaughterhouse. Blood soaked the floors and walls in the tight space. He froze, stood stone-still outside of the blood splatters. The RV was infused with a stench of vomit, feces, and urine. The suit protected him from the odor.

Agent Nia Cruz lay in front of him strapped to a stainless table. Drying red slime covered half her face. Lips and chin bloody from nasal and oral bleeding. The whites of her eyes were fire-engine red. Dried blood at the tear ducts. A pool of viscous black liquid covered the table at Cruz's vagina and rectum.

Red X-81 had maxed out its destruction inside her. The viral fiend had forced her body to bleed like an open faucet.

Jake studied the scene without moving.

Her skin color hid the hundreds of small petechial hemorrhages. Tissue around Cruz's groin had been boiled off. An empty container of hydrochloric acid was laying on the floor. Three-inch-diameter open wounds bled on her breasts where her areolas should be.

Could she be alive?

He locked his gaze on her eyes. Her pupils were dilated, looking into nothing.

The death stare.

He waved his arms. Hollered her name. Nothing. No movement.

Beyond doubt. Dead.

The presence of Cain's space suits told Jake this was a biological attack. But he had no clue what. Nerve gas? Bacterial? Viral?

Red X-81 was rapidly dying inside of Nia Cruz. The virus craved another host to invade. Its nature was to replicate, to amplify.

In two more hours, there would be no trace of the sub-microscopic demon inside her.

Jake's face flushed. He bent forward, hands on his knees, and bellowed into his hood like a dying cow. He retched, only once. Didn't vomit.

He raced out of the Airstream, trembling with anger.

And fear.

107

JAKE FOLLOWED AGENT Benton, driving north from Black Point. It was 7:15, dusk closing in around the edges. Benton drove a black Bureau Suburban with three agents as passengers. Jake was in his rental.

Highway 181 cut through pastures and farms fifteen years ago. Today it was massive housing subdivisions as far as the eye could see. Homes gave way to a thriving commercial district in Spanish Fort. Shopping, restaurants, car dealerships, medical offices. They crossed I-10, spotted a chicken-finger joint and an Olive Garden on the right, then turned left into the entrance to Timber Creek, a 900-home golf course community.

For the twelve-mile journey, Jake felt like he couldn't breathe. He searched for the proper words. The right look for his face. Anything he could do to make this less painful.

At the murder scene, Agent Benton told Jake he'd handle it. Montoya shook his head. "This is my fuck-up. Should have never let Nia go behind that building alone. Never."

After several turns inside the subdivision, Benton reached the destination, parked on the street. Jake pulled into the driveway. The home was single-story brick with dark shutters and a side-load garage. The grass was recently cut, and the shrubs had a neat trim.

Suburban tranquility. *There will never be happiness in this home again.*

Montoya and Benton stepped out of their vehicles and slowly walked toward the front door. Their faces were gray with fatigue and sadness, their shoulders slumped.

Approaching the entrance, they walked between two planters stuffed with dazzling summer flowers.

"Nice flowers," said Jake.

"Yeah," Benton uttered, a break in his voice.

Jake reached the front door, stood tall, inhaled deeply, composed himself. Still fighting to choose the right words. Hoped they came out naturally. He rang the doorbell once. In only moments he sensed footfalls from inside. He puffed his cheeks, then exhaled.

Mary Weathers, Nia Cruz's wife, opened the door. She was a five-five, cute blond in her late thirties, wearing shorts, a tank top, and a kitchen apron.

Without an introduction, she knew she was looking at Jake Montoya. She read his eyes, his face. The moment she never wanted to face.

The cheerful glint left her eye, terror kicked in her gut. She sagged. "Noooooooooooo." Mary's knees buckled.

Jake stepped forward, wrapped his arms tightly around her, pulled her close, left hand behind her head, absorbed her sobs.

There were no words to say.

108

PULLING OUT OF Timber Creek onto the four-lane, Jake felt bloodless, like all life had abandoned him. He was tired and hungry and weak. His thoughts were in disarray, not knowing his next move. Never saw this coming. Never. Jake and Benton had stayed with Mary until her sister arrived from Daphne. They offered more condolences and moved on.

Night had fallen, the day losing its steam. A McDonalds was on his right, a quarter of a mile down from the subdivision entrance. An oasis in a sea of commercial lights. He pulled in, circled through the drive-thru, left with a Big Mac, drink, and fries.

Pulling out, he drove south on 181, crossed over I-10, saw quiet lightning deep in the western sky. He hit green on two lights, caught the red in front of Lowes. He'd plowed through most of the food by the time he pulled away from the light.

Cleared from the heavy commercial area, the four-lane turned dark, traffic light at this time on a weeknight. Radio off, windows down with the smell of freshly mown grass sifting in. The caffeine and calories recharged his mind. Feeling as good as he could, he guessed, after telling someone the love of their life was murdered.

He placed his left elbow on the door sill, listening to the whine of rubber on asphalt, rolling with the night. Not really sure where he was headed.

Driving a slow forty-five for eight miles, he decided to run by and speak to Dr. John David Gage. The doctor processed life deeply, critically thinking through every step. Jake wanted a layman's take on events.

And Gage was a night owl.

County 44 took Jake past Black Point High School and dead-ended at old Scenic 98 in Battles Wharf, on the bay. He turned south, passed the Magnolia Hotel a half-mile later, steered left then right through the S-curve. A few drops of rain speckled his windshield, not enough for wipers.

A dark gray Mercedes Sprinter van with heavy tires and a roof rack was nudged in between an Accord and a pickup in the poorly lit employees' parking lot, across from the hotel.

Montoya never saw it.

Jake slowed approaching the hotel, bright lights on, illuminating the knee-high sign at the end of a driveway. GAGE. He swung in, heard the tires crunch on the long shell drive.

Headlights striped the house as the truck twisted to a stop. He killed the engine and was swallowed into blackness.

The home's front floods were off. Didn't normally see that. He was still a moment, pondering. The rain picking up. He twisted his head toward the bay. Dock lit up per usual. He squinted. Didn't see anyone. Sometimes John David liked to sit on the dock at night and read, listening to the slap of water on the pilings.

I should have called, or texted J.D. Jake thought about doing it right then, but didn't.

Apprehension flooded from his primordial brain. An unsettling feeling.

He reached up, disengaged the overhead light. Pulled the keys from the ignition, dropped them on the floor mat.

Jake stepped from the car, stood, listening, looking.

Raindrops tapped around him. A buttery three-quarters moon sat high in the eastern sky, clouds rushing past it, riding a western wind. Fronds rustled on several tall sabals.

The song of the cicadas stopped with the breeze. Live oak limbs shivered. Fallen magnolia leaves swirled at his feet.

There was something in the air. More than weather.

Jake reached around to his left hip with his right hand. Slowly, a coal-black .45 caliber automatic emerged in his right hand, pointer finger massaging the trigger.

IN THE MASTER bedroom, Marin Gage was tied to the king-size bed with green paracord. Ezra Cain knelt at her side, heavy ER shears in his hand, snipping the leg of her thirty-year-old bell-bottom jeans.

Cain had duct-taped her blubbering mouth so he could hear the music. He hummed along to Ravel's "Bolero" as the vinyl spun on a Cambridge Audio turntable. The cellos mesmerized him, focused his mind, plied him with desire.

For decades, he'd rambled across America as anonymous as a star in the sky. Cain was an unbridled lightning bolt ready to strike. Always signing off his works of art by carving an MN in the flesh.

MidNight.

His large hand slid up Marin's right leg, from her ankle to the edge of her panties. Her smoothness stimulated him.

"So smooth, so, so, smooth. Just like Sunshine." Cain looked her dead in the eye. "Always wanted a mother-daughter duo. So glad it's you, Mrs. Gage." His lips creased into a smile as sharp as a sickle blade.

Marin couldn't control her trembling. Her cheeks were damp with tears.

A flash of light hit the room. Over in an instant. He thought he blinked funny. Hopped off the bed, turned down the music, looked out the window. Saw clouds racing past the moon in a black sky. Not a single star. He knew rain was expected tonight; in fact, he was counting on it.

Lightning outside. Storm's coming. Good, he thought.

But the light was courtesy of Jake's Land Cruiser.

STILL WEARING A black tee and chinos, Jake was invisible in a night that smelled of algae and ozone. He moved gingerly around to the rear of the home, a slight bend in his knees, holding the pistol in front of him with two hands, combat style. More light on the bay side of the property, mostly falling through the row of French doors in the great room. He slid into the shadows, avoiding the ambient light.

Reaching a live oak, he was thirty feet from the back porch. A small lamp flickered on a porch table. Through the French doors, he spotted two more lamps on in the great room. A large flat-screen TV played a Braves game.

Nobody watching baseball.

In a crouch, he bolted to another live oak. He peered around the coarse-barked tree. This time he could see the kitchen, open to the great room.

Nobody there.

His respirations increased. Heart rate clicked up a gear.

Rain began rolling in off the bay, hitting harder with fat drops, slamming the tin roof on the home. In the eastern sky, the moon disappeared, smothered by the clouds.

He made a dash to the far corner of the house. In darkness again. He walked quickly, silently down the side of the house, hugging the wall until he reached a lit window. It was a half-bathroom, he knew. Quick turn of his head and back again. Eased over for a longer look. A night light plugged into a wall socket.

Nobody.

He moved forward toward the front side of the home, passing three windows. All unlit. Turned the corner. Saw light from a double window. Master bedroom. His shoulder tickled the siding like a feather as he strode in a weightless glide toward the glow.

He reached the edge of the window, stopped. Adrenaline blew his pupils wide open, muscles tensed. Rain dripped down his back, causing a shiver.

Slowly, slowly, slowly, he moved his head toward the window. Just enough to peek with one eye. The blinds were closed halfway.

He had a clear view of the room.

IT'S HIM! IT'S CAIN!

He nudged to the center of the window, focused.

Cain was kneeling over Marin, a large pair of scissors in his hand, snipping straight up the center of her tank tap. Both legs were exposed. Still wearing panties.

Where's John David? Where? Dead?

Rage boiled through him.

He stepped backward from the glass. Rain flowed down his face. Raised the pistol with two hands, arms loose, steady. Blinked water out of his eyes. He aimed center mass on Cain's chest.

A flash of lightning exposed Jake like a spotlight.

Cain's head came up, his eyes glaring through the blinds.

Jake exhaled, felt preternaturally calm. He squeezed the trigger. *Follow through.* Squeezed again. *Follow through.* And again.

Window glass exploded.

Forty-five caliber hollow points blasted Cain backward off the bed.

CAIN MELTED INTO ecstasy. He felt the power between his

legs. He'd let her see, sure would. Just like he'd shown her daughter. Marin Gage's tank top had been sliced up the middle like a zipper, cotton pulled to the sides.

"Pretty little bra, just like Sunshine wore." It was white, sheer enough to reveal dark areolas. "Let me guess. B-cup, right?" His eyebrows flew upward with the question.

Her wrists bled from the struggle with the paracord. Tough nylon. Her panties were damp with urine.

"Oh, no. You tee-teed. I've got some heavy-duty cleaner for that, miss lady, so don't you worry.

"Now let's check these mature titties out." Cain slid one blade of the open scissors under the center of her bra. "One little snip should do it."

Lightning sliced the air outside the bedroom, brighter than stadium lights. Cain jumped. His eyes darted to the half-open blinds.

A silhouette in black, sliced horizontally by the blinds. *A MAN!* White face. Holding something.

Dark again in a nanosecond.

Cain's circuits overheated. *Jump.*

He spotted three flashes of inferno heat.

Three cannonballs knocked him off the bed.

HE'S DOWN. Montoya raced to the rear of the house. Turning the corner, gusty rain splattered his face. The storm front pounded the pier, pushing hard and fast toward the east.

Jake sprinted through the screen doors onto the porch. Three strides later he was at the French doors. Tried the knob. Locked. Stepped back, launched a front kick near the doorknob. Wood splintered. Doors open.

A blinding strike of lightning.

Everything went black. Coal black. TV dead. Lamps off.

A second flash of lightning lit the room for a moment. Jake

looked toward the bay. The dock was dark.

Electricity out.

Inky black. Rain pounding the roof. Eerie. The room sizzled with an undercurrent of danger.

Jake pulled out his cell, activated the flashlight. He raced toward the master bedroom, stopped at the threshold, hit the room with the flashlight.

Marin looked his way. Eyes bloodshot, filled with fear, still fighting the rope.

He scanned the floor with the light, pistol tight in his right hand. Nothing. Dropped to the floor, looked under the bed. Nobody. He stepped to Marin, ripped the tape off her mouth.

"Where'd he go!" Jake huffed out the words, breathing fast. "I shot him."

He pulled the phone to his face, scanned, tapped call. Tatum answered on the second ring. "Cain's at John David Gage's house. *Get out here now!* Bring everybody. Need ambulances. I hit him three times with the .45 but he's moving." Jake's jaw drew tight, eyes stony, focused.

"Copy." Tatum rang off.

"Out the door," said Marin. "Get him, gettt himmm." Jake pulled a knife, flicked it open with a wrist snap, sliced the rope at Marin's wrists and ankles.

"Where's John?"

"He was beaten ... dragged to Kimbo's old room." Marin hopped off the bed, wearing only bra and panties, went to the dresser, grabbed a gown.

"Stay here. Get in the closet. Don't say a word."

"Swear to God, I'll kill him." Marin's tone spit bile, lips trembling.

CAIN HAD A fractured sternum. Another rib was broken, displaced. The hollow points had mushroomed when they hit his

Midnight Man

ballistic vest and delivered an intense but nonpenetrating blow.

Midnight could barely breathe without screaming.

He was standing just inside the door of a half-bath, the lights out, when he saw Montoya crash through the screen doors. He backed further in.

He'd watched Montoya kick through the French doors.

The house had gone dark.

Cain didn't move.

MONTOYA SLINKED INTO Kimbo's old bedroom, silent as a panther. Placed his left hand on the doorknob, paused to listen, hoped to hear at least a moan from John David.

Heard something else. Footsteps. Other side of the house, near the kitchen. Not John David.

Check John David or chase Cain? Had no supplies and an ambulance was coming. Cain.

Jake flashed the room quickly with his light, then killed it. Nobody.

Heart jackhammering.

Flashlight in his left hand, .45 in his right. Jake ran in a crouch toward the noise, rubber soles silent on the hardwood.

CAIN HEARD MONTOYA talking to Marin. Heard his call to the police.

No time! Gotta run!

He moved swiftly from the half-bath toward the kitchen, hand on the outside of his vest, applying compression. Pain in his ribs screamed as he moved. He fought the urge to moan.

Over his shoulder, he spotted a beam of light. Montoya moving down the hall.

Cain moved faster, into the kitchen. He'd left Cruz's gun in the van. *Need a weapon.* Didn't open a drawer. Ran his hand along a dark counter. Felt a butcher block. A cache of knives. His fingers slipped around a knife handle, grabbed it, and he kept on moving.

He held a five-inch prep knife. Razor sharp.

Cain made a noise as he moved. The flashlight glow died at the sound. Montoya had heard him.

Had to process, fast. *Can never outrun Montoya. Montoya could shoot him in the leg ... or the head. Hand to hand, my only chance. Get the knife in him.*

Cain felt his way to a walk-in pantry, sucking up the pain in his ribs.

Waiting.

JAKE CHANCED another flash of light. Like lightning. Bang and gone. Nobody. He worried Cain had a gun. *Why wouldn't he?*

There was a door into the garage at the edge of the kitchen. Likely that had been the noise, Cain exiting the house.

Jake slid that way, dropping deeper into a crouch. Muscles rippling. Fear and anticipation in his gut.

Out of nowhere, Jake remembered the words of a wise Chinese man. Jake had been twelve when Woo Chow first uttered them.

Empty your mind, become formless, shapeless. Be like water. Drown your adversary.

Baby-stepping past the pantry. Eyes focused forward, toward the garage door.

Shadow movement to his side. It was quick. Heard a grunt. Fire ripped into Jake's upper back.

Stabbed!

He spun to shoot. Two powerful arms wrapped around him at chest level. Jake's elbows were compressed to his sides, pistol pointed down.

Montoya's head suddenly exploded in pain, red and white lights scrambling his vision. Headbutted by Midnight.

Squeezing tight, the monster drove Jake backward as fast as he could.

Jake's back slammed against the door. The knife blade sank to the handle.

Blood gushed into his right lung.

CAIN'S RIBS SCREAMED as he jumped at Montoya. He stabbed hard with the knife, felt the flesh rip when he drove it into Jake's back.

Got you!

He felt Jake fight it, try to twist. *Have to get this right.* Cain reached around Jake, squeezed him into a bear hug. Midnight had thirty pounds on him. Arms, chest, and back bulky with muscle. He ratcheted down.

Cain felt the blood pulse in his temples as he crushed Jake. Breath blew from Montoya's mouth. Midnight slammed his forehead into Jake's face again, heard nasal bones crack.

Blood from Jake's nose splattered Cain's face.

Midnight pumped his thick legs like a locomotive, driving Montoya back into the door. The wood buckled, cracked.

"How 'bout that, Montoya!" The words sounded maniacal. An unhinged madman. "I'm outta here."

Midnight heard an explosion. Then two more.

NO AIR. BLOOD IN HIS EYES. Jake fought to grab a mouthful of air. His lungs were on fire. Stunned at Cain's strength.

Don't pass out. Don't pass out. Don't pass out.

He knew he had a concussion. Fireworks sparked in his head. He felt Cain's Kevlar vest against his chest. *That's why he's not down.*

Heard Cain scream his name.

Somehow, Jake still had his gun. He squeezed the trigger. A .45 round shattered Cain's femur from seven inches away. Another squeeze. A fat hollow point fragmented Cain's knee.

Cain bellowed, let go, dropped backward. A third hollow point whizzed past his head, missing in the dark.

The room suddenly lit up.

Electricity was back.

Cain was flat on his back, both hands on his left leg, twisting, rolling with agony, moaning.

Jake attacked, enraged. He slammed his right foot into Midnight's groin.

Just as Woo Chow had taught. *Jake ... On the street, fight street. No rules!*

Jake dropped a right knee in a free fall, slamming it into Cain's chest, aiming to crush the ribcage. He carried his motion forward, landing a vicious elbow strike to Cain's face.

He grabbed Cain's throat with his left hand, squeezed the monster's windpipe like a vise. Pulled his right fist back, ready to launch a blow.

Thick, black steel nudged under Cain's chin. A gun barrel.

"MOVE, JAKE!"

Midnight's head detonated.

Blood, bone, and brain splattered across the floor.

Jake launched off Cain, stunned by the explosion.

Marin Gage stood with an icy glare and a gun stock at her shoulder, staring down evil.

A children's book author had blown Dr. Ezra Cain's head off his shoulders with a 12-gauge turkey gun.

"He killed my baby girl."

ABOUT THE AUTHOR

Sam Cade lives on the Gulf coast in Fairhope, Alabama with his wife and their golden retriever, Rowdy. He works full time in medicine, plays tennis three or four times a week, and squeezes in time to daydream and write.

Share any thoughts, ideas or questions via email at samcadebooks@gmail.com

WEBSITE: samcade.net

If you have a sec, please leave a review on Amazon! Thanks!

Made in United States
Orlando, FL
05 February 2024

43334248R00251